Haven Brook Series

'Til Death Do Us Part

The Cradle Will Fall

The Ties That Bind

A Very Haven Christmas

Three Strikes, You're Gone

'Til Death Do Us Part

Samantha Baca

Cover Design: Oh So Novel

<u>One</u>
Mia

The night sky was consumed by darkness as I continued to run, the loose gravel crunching beneath my bare feet. My lungs felt like they were on fire as I struggled to catch my breath, knowing that I didn't have time to stop. I paused for a second and looked over my shoulder to see if he was near. A car approached a few miles behind me, so I quickly darted behind a bush by the side of the road, hoping it was dark enough to camouflage me. My legs ached from running and had started to shake as I tried to hold my semi-crouched position behind the bush and catch my breath. I strained to listen for any signs of movement, hoping he hadn't caught up to me yet. I watched anxiously as the car passed by and waited for the perfect moment to cross the two-lane highway.

"If you walk out that door, it'll be the last thing you'll do. I'll find you and make you live to regret it!" His voice boomed inches above my head. The smell of whiskey was still fresh on his breath. I tried to move, but the weight of his body on top of me, combined with the numbness from the last few blows, had made it feel impossible.

I shook my head, trying to get rid of the image. Now was not the time to think about it, I reminded myself. I had to keep moving. I took a few deep breaths, filled my lungs with as much air as they could hold, and forced myself to push through the physical pain to stand up. Anxiety coursed through my veins as I checked my surroundings, one last time. Far off in the distance I saw the light on upstairs in the place that used to be my home. That reality was gone now. I can't go home. A single tear trickled down my cheek as I used the back of my hand to brush it away. The immediate sting from the touch reminded me of why I left, why I ran, and why I would never be able to stop running.

The highway was deserted this time of night with very few cars passing by. I took one final deep breath as I quickly ran across the highway and into the tall grass on the other side. The wild grass was waist high and thick, which provided coverage as I moved through it. Exhaustion threatened to take over my body, but I kept pushing, the need to get further away my biggest priority. In the distance I saw the neon light of the gas station glowing against the pitch-black sky, and took comfort knowing that refuge was within reach.

Feeling lifeless, I laid on the floor and allowed the numbness to take over. I looked to the side and saw a pool of blood forming on the tile next to me from the open cut on my forehead. I closed my eyes, wishing the floor would open and take me away. Away from the pain. Away from the danger. Away from Damian. Away from this hell.

One last kick to my ribs, then I heard his footsteps fading down the hall as he went to his study. The door slammed shut and I let out a sigh of relief, praying that it was over. I struggled to roll onto my side as I tried to get up, but my body was in massive amounts of widespread pain. I knew he could come back at any minute, so I forced myself to my feet, taking a moment to catch my balance.

I don't remember where my shoes ended up, they went flying across the room at some point during the attack. I had scanned the kitchen quickly, looking for them when I noticed my purse thrown on the kitchen table next to my cell phone. Without thinking, I grabbed both and opened the back door. I winced as I heard the chirp of the alarm confirming the door was opened, aware that Damian had heard it as well. I ignored the shakiness I felt as I pulled the strap of my purse over my head, across my shoulder, and took off running as fast as I could. I heard footsteps behind me, which forced me to run faster, making it to the wooded area next to the house before he could reach me. If I had any chance of surviving this, I had to run.

I quickened my pace as I approached the gas station, relieved that I was almost there. Off to my left I heard a vehicle headed toward me on the highway. I had almost made it to the end of the grassy area that merged into a paved sidewalk when I noticed a car slowing down as it pulled into the gas station. Not just any car. I squinted to try to get a better look at the vehicle and felt my heart stop when I saw that it was a black BMW with LAWMAN1 on the custom license plate. I pulled back into the grassy area immediately, taking a few more steps until my back was up against a tree.

Standing still, I hid in the shadows as I watched Damian park his car and get out. The gas station was quiet, only the store attendant and a few customers who were pumping gas. Damian walked over to the man at the closest pump and began talking to him as he pointed to something on his cell phone. The older man leaned in and looked at the phone before shaking his head no and turned his attention back to pumping his gas as Damian continued talking. I saw him glance in the direction where I was hiding and slide further back into the shadows of the trees. I peered around to try to get another glimpse of what was happening when I found the older man pointing in my direction and shrugging his shoulders. Damian looked to where the man had pointed, then back at the man who gave him another shrug which appeared to annoy Damian. For a moment I felt relieved that I was in such a dense wooded area which would make it hard for Damian to use his tracking app to find my cell phone. I debated whether to ditch it in the wooded area so he wouldn't be able to track me or keep it in case I needed to call for help.

Damian walked off and approached a group of guys who were busy loading a few cases of beer into the back of their lifted truck. He showed them his phone and I watched as they all shook their heads no as well. I continued to follow his every movement as he went inside the gas station and talked to the attendant while the group of guys finished loading the beer into the truck and took off. Damian's jaw was clenched as he passed the older man who entered the store while he walked out. The car door slammed shut as he fired up the engine and launched out of the parking lot, heading in the opposite direction. Either he had given up looking for me and planned to go home, or he went back to search the wooded area that I would have come from to find me. I didn't have time to wait and see. Damian's car passed by a few seconds later, the sound fading in the distance. With time so crucial, I pushed my way out of the grassy area and ran at full speed towards the store.

I was almost to the door when I saw the older man walk out, recognition on his face when he saw me. Fear flooded me as I tried to find a way out that didn't involve making a scene. I felt my body start to tremble as we stared at each other, concern etched on his face. My eyes stayed focused on his every move as he slowly opened the door, shielding me from the attendant's view, which wasn't hard given that he was consumed by something on his cell phone and wasn't looking up. I eyed the man cautiously as I backed away from the door, allowing him to open it.

"I saw you coming out of that wooded area, before the black car pulled up. At first, I thought maybe it was a bear or coyote, but then I noticed it was a person," he said as he nodded toward where I had been hiding. "When I saw you run back and hide, I knew something was wrong."

I stayed silent, unsure of what to say.

"He showed me a picture, asked if I had seen his wife. Said she's been missing, and he's worried about her." He paused for my reaction, which was met with continued silence as I took in what he was saying.

"I confirmed that I had seen something running along the side of the road. Might have been a person, it was too dark to see."

My heart sank. My only chance for help. My last lifeline. All were gone.

"Told him that whatever it was, was headed that direction, towards the motel at the other exit." He offered a warm smile as he pointed in the direction that Damian went when he left.

"Then my wife and I decided that we needed some water and snacks." He looked down and patted a brown paper bag that was resting against his hip.

"We're heading to Manchester, New Hampshire. It's about an hour and a half drive from here. You're welcome to come with us, though I reckon we better get a move on it if you don't want your husband coming back to find you." Another smile crossed his face and he nodded towards a white Camry with lightly tinted windows.

"Thank you, anywhere away from here is perfect," I said with a smile as I walked with him to the car. I waited for him to open his door before I opened the door and got in. I pulled the seatbelt and glided it across my sore body, fastening it as I looked out the window for any sign of Damian.

An older woman with rosy cheeks and gray hair turned around to look at me, her soft features instantly calmed me. I imagined these were two of the nicest people I had ever met.

"Not to worry dear, we'll get you out of here," the woman said softly as she passed the paper bag over the middle console that separated us, waiting for me to take it. I hesitated before reaching for the bag. The movement itself required me to lean forward which was painful. I forced a smile to hide the pain and try to show my gratitude as I pulled the bag into the back seat with me and opened the bottle of water that was inside. I took a long, slow drink, and allowed my body to take the break it needed. It occurred to me that I didn't know where I was going and I had no idea how I was going to get there, but for now, I was free.

Two
Mia

The drive from Winchester to Manchester took almost two hours due to some traffic delays, however Mr. Bennett was pretty accurate with the original time frame he had given me before I got into the car. I had learned that he was retired law enforcement, and his wife Arlene, had recently retired from teaching for 35 years. Arlene bragged about Joe as much as he did about her. They were obviously a couple in love as they were headed to the airport for a 6:00 am flight to Ireland to celebrate their 50th wedding anniversary. As they continued to share stories with me, I learned that they lived in Colorado but had recently come to Boston to visit her mother who was starting hospice care. Part of me wanted to share personal stories of my own with them, like how I was also from Colorado, but I knew better. The less they knew, the better.

I listened as they told stories about how they met and fell desperately in love, despite their parents trying to separate them early on in their relationship. They had always wanted to have children and start a family; the cards were just never dealt that way for them. The trip to Ireland was the first of many to come, I was assured, as they saved their whole lives to spend their retirement years traveling the world.

My phone vibrated in my hand as a slew of text messages came through after we had reached an area with better cell service. The battery had dwindled down as my phone had been consistently searching for service. I touched the message button and stared at the screen of unread messages from Damian.

Damian: Your biggest mistake was leaving.

Damian: Did you really think I wouldn't come after you?

Damian: Like I said Mia- 'til death do us part.

Damian: It appears you have chosen to part. You know what comes next.

Damian: I will find you, and you will pay for this.

Damian: You can't just up and leave me.

Damian: Did you forget that I can track your cell phone?

Damian: How about a game of hide and seek? You TRY to hide, and I'll let you wait in fear before I come to find you.

I stared at my phone in terror. I knew that Damian was already tracking me and knew where I was. I discreetly shifted my position in the back seat to try to get a better view of the vehicles around us. While I had seen too many over the top movies where the crazy man comes flying up next to them on the side of the road and tries to force them off the road, I didn't necessarily put anything past Damian at this point.

A silence fell over the car when Arlene turned in her chair and looked back at me as she waited for a response. I felt bad, I had been so caught up in the text messages from Damian that I hadn't heard what she had asked. Her face had immediately turned beet red as she realized what she had asked might have offended me, given my silence in response to her question. Her eyes lowered in embarrassment and I watched her look at the scratches and cuts that covered my bare legs, covered in dirt and debris from trekking through the wooded terrain. I didn't want to be rude and ask her to repeat herself, especially when she already appeared to be beating herself up for asking whatever she had asked. Given where she was looking, I knew the question had to be about Damian. Self-consciously, I pulled at the bottom of my cutoff denim shorts, hoping they could shield her eyes from what had happened.

"You don't have to talk about your husband, unless you would like to, Robyn." Joe assured me as he caught my eye in the rearview mirror.

I had no intention of lying to the Bennett's. When asked my name, I froze, and Robyn was the first name that came into my mind, so I went with it. Instincts told me that I shouldn't give them my real name. It wasn't just for my own protection, but for theirs as well. They would never be able to say that they saw or spoke to Mia Stone if they never knew her name.

I watched as Joe reached across the console and took Arlene's hand in his, patting it in comfort as she turned her head to the window, avoiding eye contact.

"I was married for five years. We met my senior year in high school when I went to Boston for my senior trip. He was living there at the time while finishing law school and worked as a bell boy at the hotel that my class stayed at. We stayed in contact after I graduated and, on a whim, I decided to move to Boston. After I moved there, we started dating and eventually moved in together, getting married shortly after." I tried to be as personal as I could be, given that they were so open with me, but in the end, I kept it vague.

"What ended up happening after that, dear," Arlene asked with hope in her voice.

"He died."

Another awkward silence filled the car the last stretch of the drive and continued on as Joe went inside to check in. I knew that he had to be wondering why I would say that my husband had died when he had just talked to him at the gas station. As far as I was concerned, my husband died the day he first laid a hand on me. Someone else took over his body and my husband had never been back since then. A few minutes later, Joe came back with two key cards in his hand and I got out of the car, ready to say my goodbyes.

"This is your room key. Unfortunately, they only had two rooms left this late at night and they are on different sides of the parking lot, so we won't be close by. But we'll be in room 149 if you need anything." Joe extended his hand out to me as he waited for me to take the key card.

"Thank you. How much was the room? I have some cash." I had discreetly gone through my purse and the contents of my wallet while Joe was inside. To my surprise I found a stack of bills tucked inside of one of the inside pockets of my purse. On top of the bills was a torn off piece of napkin with a series of numbers written on it. I assumed this was Jade's doing, we met for lunch yesterday, which was disastrous to say the least.

"No need to pay for the room, it's the least we can do," Joe replied as he rocked back on his heels. I had a feeling that warm and fuzzy wasn't really his thing.

"Well, thank you, again." I clutched the key to my chest and felt relieved that I had a place to stay for the night. Deep inside I still felt anxious that Damian would pop up at any minute which made it impossible to relax or let my guard down.

"Get some rest. Oh, and we're leaving for the airport around 4:00 am tomorrow morning. We'd be happy to give you a ride as well."

"I appreciate the offer, Joe. I'll see you guys in the morning." I smiled and headed toward room 113, the key held tightly in my hand.

As I opened the door, I felt around for the light switch and immediately turned on the lights. I stepped inside, finding nothing to be suspicious, and closed the door behind me. I turned and locked the door, then secured the deadbolt. Anxiety continued to flow through me, so I moved the armchair that was next to the bed and forced it in underneath the doorknob.

There were two full sized beds in the room separated by a nightstand in the middle. I sat my purse down on the bed closest to the bathroom and pulled my phone out. The battery was down to 20% and there were another 7 missed calls and 8 text messages, all from Damian. His texts had turned from angry to sinister, taunting me in each message. There was one voicemail, my fingers trembling as I pressed the button to play the message.

Sleep well, Mia. Be sure to get some rest. You're going to need it. And don't forget to check under your bed, you never know where the boogeyman might show up.

I turned my phone off and put it down on the bed next to my purse. I laid back on the bed and closed my eyes as tight as I could, granted the swelling under my left eye made it painful, and tried to picture a happier time. The last two weeks had been a nightmare. From all of the scary movies I had ever seen, I knew it only really stopped once the bad guy was dead. So that must be my fate, I thought.

A knocking sound on the door interrupted my thoughts and I sprung up off the bed, ready to hide. I knew that he knew where I was, yet I was shocked that he was at my door. Panic filled me as I searched for a way out or a place to hide that he wouldn’t find me. My hands began sweating while my mind continued to race.

“Robyn?” Arlene called through the door before knocking a second time.

My heart was beating a mile a minute. I walked to the door and pushed the chair out of the way so I could open it. With caution, I looked through the peephole to make sure she was by herself and that Damian wasn’t standing outside with her.

“Yes?” I answered through the door without opening it.

“I’m sorry to disturb you honey. I thought you might need a change of clothes, and possibly some shoes?” She called through the closed door as she leaned closer to the door so I could hear her.

I looked down at my dirty bare feet and remembered that I didn’t have shoes. I looked through the peephole once again before I stepped back and opened the door.

“I know it may be ‘old lady’ clothes but I thought it might come in handy since you don’t have anything else with you,” Arlene said as she handed me a pile of neatly folded clothes and a pair of tennis shoes piled on top.

“Not at all, this is very sweet and generous of you. Thank you, Arlene.” I took the pile from her and smiled warmly at her, satisfaction on her face when I accepted her offer. My eyes darted around the parking lot, looking for a sign of Damian or his car.

“Well, good night.” She waved as she walked off. Across the parking lot I noticed Joe standing in the open doorway of their room as he watched Arlene.

I closed the door and locked all of the locks once more, then pushed the chair back to its original spot. The pile of clothes looked to be more than one outfit, so I sat on the bed and unfolded each item Arlene had given me. There was a pair of denim jeans, a pair of black cotton elastic waist shorts, a pink tank top, a white button-down cardigan, and two pair of white ankle socks. The tennis shoes were solid white and appeared to be brand new. Sadness filled me when I thought about Arlene giving me clothes and shoes that she would need for her trip. I had already accepted the gift, it would be rude to turn around and give it back.

I left the clothes on the bed as I made my way to the bathroom and saw travel sized bottles of shampoo, conditioner, and body wash. I stripped off my dirty clothes in record time as I turned the hot water on in the shower. I didn't want to be in a vulnerable position in case Damian found his way in, but I needed a shower to wash away the life I had left behind. I covered myself with a towel as I walked the small distance of the room and made sure each lock was still secure.

The shower was quick and the water was hot enough to be soothing to my sore muscles, yet too hot for the open cuts and scratches that covered the majority of my body from running through the thick brush and trees. I finished my shower and had turned off the water when I heard a knocking sound. I stood still and waited, unsure of where it was coming from. The beating of my heart rang so loud in my ears it made it nearly impossible to hear anything else. My mind had to be playing tricks on me, I thought to myself as I heard another knock. This time it sounded closer. With a towel wrapped around my hair and another around my body, I slowly stepped out of the bathroom and into the open space of the room.

Nothing was out of the ordinary and looked exactly as I had left it. I tip toed to the door and leaned over the chair to look through the peephole. A knocking sound almost sent me flying before I could look through the peephole. I tried to steady myself and pushed forward again, this time making it to the peephole. I looked out the tiny hole and found no one by the door or close enough to knock on my door.

A few doors down I noticed a couple of girls walking out of their room, allowing the door to slam shut behind them. They were giggling and stumbling, apparently already intoxicated. A few seconds later, three guys walked out behind them. Two of them went to catch up with the girls while the other went to the next room and pounded loudly on the door. I immediately recognized the sound and took relief knowing that was what I had been hearing. I sighed and pushed off of the chair as I pulled the towel tighter around me.

I grabbed the black shorts and tank top from the bed and slid them on, thankful for clean clothes. I picked up my dirty clothes from the bathroom floor and hung the wet towels on the bar over the toilet. I made sure things were tidy and dirty clothes weren't left on the floor; old habits die hard. Here I was, fighting to survive my husband, and the one thing that I'm focused on is whether the dirty laundry is tidy. At that point, I wanted to kick my own ass.

One last check of the locks and I made my way over to the bed furthest away from the window and laid down. My dirty clothes were added to the clean clothes Arlene had given me, and all were crammed tightly into a small reusable tote. I always had a plan when I would go to the store for our weekly necessities, and it never failed that Damian would need something in addition while I was there. Our store no longer offered plastic bags, so I kept an extra tote bag in my purse for the times I needed it. And tonight, I had needed it more than ever.

The clock on the nightstand showed that it was almost one o'clock in the morning. My body was exhausted, but I felt uneasy about going to sleep, something just didn't feel right. I picked up my phone and remembered that I had turned it off shortly after I got here. It didn't matter at this point anyways, Damian confirmed he already knew where I was. Now it was a game of him fucking with my mind while he tormented me from the shadows.

I needed to rest if I was going to keep running. I forced myself to relax as I closed my eyes and tried to silence my mind. The room stayed bright with every light turned on and I was alerted by every little sound, so resting proved to be quite a challenge.

My mind was restless while images of the night haunted my sleep. I felt trapped as I struggled to get away from Damian. He was stronger than me and held me in a position that I couldn't get out of. Fight! I yelled at myself. Fight! He's going to kill you! His hands wrapped around my throat, my airway crushed as he closed them tighter.

I gasped for air and shot up off the bed. I stumbled in the dark, unsure of how the lights got turned off. I felt around the wall behind me as I tried to make contact with the light switch. Finally, I found it and flicked it up, fluorescent light filled the small room. I gasped when I looked at the open door, the chair moved out of the way. On the bed by the door sat Damian with his hands folded calmly in his lap.

“Found you.”

Three
Mia

I've never had a nightmare that felt as real as the one I had last night of Damian in my room. In my dream I could physically feel him as he strangled the life out of my limp body. I felt the heat of his body as it overpowered mine. I smelt the whiskey that was always on his breath these days. I realized that at some point, my life itself had become a nightmare.

A few minutes after I had been jolted awake by the nightmare, Joe and Arlene had come by my room on their way to the airport and without thinking twice, I took them up on their offer for a ride. I had no idea where to go. The wildest thing I had done in my life was move from Haven Brook to Boston, and while that was scary, it was also thrilling and exhilarating to do something new with my life. Back then, I had a bevy of opportunities and was ready to embark upon my next adventure.

Now I was forced to make quick decisions, to constantly be one step ahead of Damian. I didn't have time to think about where to go or what to do, I had to keep moving. I was reluctant to purchase a plane ticket in case Damian found a way to track me with my credit card, but I also didn't want to spend all the cash that I had on a ticket either. Being the consistent hero that he was, Joe stepped in and purchased the ticket for me using his credit card, winking as he gave me an early birthday present.

I had never met anyone as sweet and genuine as the Bennett's. My heart was sad that they were never given the child that they so clearly wanted. Joe's eyes had saddened when he had asked about my father and I had told him that according to my mom, he never wanted to be in the picture and had left her before I was born. I imagined they would have been wonderful parents. Arlene asked if there would be a way to contact me after their trip, so she could make sure that I was okay. With a sad shake of my head, I declined the offer as I didn't want to risk them having any connection to something linked to Damian. The less they knew, the better off they would be in the long run.

It was bad enough that Joe now knew my real name, when I had to give my information to purchase the ticket. He seemed completely shocked when I gave my real name to the flight attendant, the color drained from his face as he looked at me in disbelief. I had felt bad for giving them a fake name, but I hadn't expected this reaction from Joe. It was as if I had personally insulted him. We said an uncomfortable goodbye with him embracing me in the tightest hug before pulling back as a tear slid down his cheek. Arlene looked as confused as I felt. I watched as they walked off towards their gate, Joe urgently whispering something in Arlene's ear before she turned around and looked at me with the same shocked face as Joe had.

I made my way to the waiting area by my gate and sat down. My purse and tote bag were light enough to continue to carry, however I felt like I might relax more if I took them off and sat them next to me. It was only a few minutes until they started boarding my flight, so I decided to turn on my phone and check if there were any new messages from Damian. I had hoped on the drive to the airport that he wouldn't be able to track my phone if it was turned off, which might give me some additional time to stay ahead of him. At the end of the day, I had no clue how the tracking app actually worked, but I did know that he would be able to find my exact location on it. He had done so many times before.

Damian: MHT is a busy airport this early in the morning, isn't it?

Bile rose in my throat as I tried to choke it down, along with the fear that threatened to take over again. I stared at the phone in my hand for what felt like minutes, before I was interrupted by the sound of the intercom, confirming they were boarding class B for my flight. I looked around, searching for a sign of him. Deep down I hoped he was bluffing, that he wasn't really at the airport, watching me. Maybe, if

I was lucky, he was sitting at home in his stupid recliner, tracking my phone and sending me text messages to make me think he was here. As subtly as I could, I sat my phone down on the arm of the chair and leaned over to grab my purse and tote bag. Without looking back, I walked away to board my flight, leaving my phone behind.

The early morning flight was almost sold out, with each seat filled and luggage bins overfilled. I had searched the passengers already onboard as I made my way to the back of the plane, taking a window seat in the very last row. I continued to watch the remaining passengers board, relieved when Damian wasn't one of them. A few hours later the pilot made an announcement over the intercom, letting the passengers know that we were about to land at Charlotte Douglas International Airport. The airport had been surprisingly busy at 8:30 in the morning on a Sunday with people whipping past me to get to their next gate. I pulled out my boarding pass, confirmed the gate that I needed, and found a place to sit for the hour layover before I boarded the next plane.

I had no phone and no idea where Damian was. For the first time, I was 100% on my own. My stomach grumbled as I smelt the breakfast sandwich a few rows behind me and I was reminded that I had yet to eat an actual meal since before the fight with Damian. There were a few food kiosks around me which allowed me to grab something without having to go far. Ten minutes later I had inhaled a bacon breakfast sandwich and finished the creamy caramel latte. My body hummed in approval as I allowed the food to settle in my stomach.

Time passed quickly as I waited to board the flight to Denver, thankful once we were in the air. I had made the decision to go back home when I couldn't think of anywhere else to go, which meant that I needed to make it to Denver first. Calling Haven Brook "home" felt odd as home should be filled with family members and warm childhood memories. But I didn't have an actual home to go back to, and the family that I did have, weren't really family.

I closed my eyes and tried to picture my childhood growing up as warm memories, unfortunately, there were very few. Images of Chase and Noah popped into my head, a smile brought along with them as I remembered our junior high and high school days together. They were the only good things that I remembered from my childhood. Two rough and rowdy boys who loved each other like brothers and treated me like their little sister. I had no siblings of my own, so I had clung to them as the only family that I did have.

A few moments later their faces were replaced with my mom's. She had a lit cigarette in one hand, and bottle of vodka in the other, as she sat on some guy's lap and laughed at me. I remembered this was one of the first times that I realized just how terrible of a person my mother was.

I was 11 years old and had been trying to get situated in middle school, but a few eighth-grade girls were bullying me. I had gone to my mom, crying, and explained what had happened. They had dumped my lunch tray in my lap in front of the entire cafeteria, then pointed and laughed as everyone else joined in. I was mortified. My mom had thrown her unruly, curly blonde hair up in a messy bun that bounced each time she threw her head back as she laughed at me. She was wearing a red silk robe that was loosely tied around her waist, pulled open to show off the black bra that barely contained her breasts.

I had wanted motherly compassion, for her to pull me into a hug and promise that it would be alright. Instead she had pointed at the stain on the front of my pants and said that it looked like I had peed myself. The harder she laughed, the more her body bounced, which forced her boobs into the creep's face that she was still sitting on.

Mortified again, I fought back the tears that threatened to spill over. My body trembled as it threatened to break down in front of my mom. I squared my shoulders and glared at her, not knowing what to say without risking her hitting me for talking back. It had been her newest thing, ever since the last guy had started trying it on her.

"Oh, you're such a God damn baby," she snarled when she noticed that I was upset. "Get over it and move on, Mia. Life isn't fair and it's time you learned that most people won't like you anyways."

My mouth hung open as I stared in disbelief at the words that my mother had spoken. Maybe it was all for show in front of her guy friend, but my mom had never spoken to me in such a degrading way before. Sure, she had been mean to me plenty of times and I couldn't remember ever hearing her say that she loved me, but this had been different. This had been intentional to create low self-esteem and to disregard how I had felt. She had it in her mind that she needed to control those around her so she could get what she wanted.
"In a few years, your boobs will finally come in and the guys won't have to question whether you're a boy a girl. I recommend you start padding that training bra now and take advantage of finding yourself

a guy to take care of you while you still have something to offer. It's not like they are going to want your *winning personality*." Bonnie continued, making air quotes as she shook her boobs in the guy's face. I watched on in horror as the guy wiggled his eyebrows at me before he leaned forward and nipped at my mom's boobs.

When Damian and I had first met, he wanted to know about my life and where I came from. I kept the details as vague as possible- I grew up in Colorado but didn't confirm which city; I was the only child of a single mother; I didn't have any connections to Colorado and therefore there was no reason to invite any one to our wedding. He pried, and I continued to keep everything locked inside.

Damian's mom had been curious about why my parents would not be attending the wedding, all the way up to the day of the wedding. I had been sad that I didn't have a father to walk me down the aisle or a loving mother who would weep from the front row as her baby got married. But I couldn't make something out of nothing, so I had asked everyone to let it go and we moved forward with the wedding. Damian's uncle, Ronnie, had walked me down the aisle which had made me feel special given the close relationship he had with him. Damian's father had died when he turned 13, and his uncle had stepped in to help raise him. The day had been a day to remember. Hundreds of people had filled the ballroom that overflowed with hundreds of white roses and white sheer fabric adorned across the ceilings, complimenting the crystal chandeliers. We stood under a beautiful handcrafted wooden arch that was covered in beautiful flowers of every color as we looked into each other's eyes and said our vows.

"Mia, I promise to love you always, through the good times and the bad. I promise to always protect you and to provide you a safe place to build our lives together. I'll always be your rock; someone you can lean on and who will stand up tall to defend you. I will weather any storms we encounter and help you to find dry land. I promise to give you the fairy tale ending, the happily ever after, that you've always dreamt of. 'Til death do us part." Damian beamed with pride as he held my hands and promised me a lifetime that I had always longed for.
Startled by violent shaking, I whipped my head up to see what was going on.

"Just a little turbulence." A flight attendant in the open space behind me assured me with a smile, calm and collected.

I let out a breath and focused my attention in front of me. As I had attempted to clear my mind before we landed in Denver, I had inadvertently done the opposite. According to the pilot, we had begun our descent and would be landing shortly. Whether I felt I was ready to go back home or not, I was more than half ways there. I had been so focused on getting away from Damian that I didn't think about what it meant to go home and have to face the life I had left behind.

Four
Damian - 2 Days Ago

"Doris! Is my coffee going to grow legs and walk itself into my office?" I growled at my secretary over the intercom.

I sighed and picked up the stack of paperwork that had been sitting on my desk all morning, apparently needing my attention. It would have been great if there was a note indicating what they needed instead of just being piled up on my desk, waiting for me to be some miraculous fucking mind reader.

The office door started to crack open and I glanced up without raising my head, seeing the meek frame of my worthless secretary approach my desk with my coffee in her unsteady, shaky hands. Doris had been my secretary for the past few weeks while my actual secretary was out of the country on her honeymoon. Why the fuck did I ever approve a 3-week vacation, I'll never know. Lisa promised me that I wouldn't notice a difference with the temp she picked from the agency we work with, but apparently Lisa was also delusional.

Doris quietly approached my desk with the coffee, watching me with terror on her face the closer she came. You'd think this girl had a job of feeding wild lions. Irritation quickly built and I shot her a look that told her to put the mug down already.

She quickly reached over and sat the mug on the coaster on my desk then popped back up and held her hands up like she had just been robbed. For fuck's sake. I let out a breath and tossed the pile of papers back onto my desk and turned to look directly at her while she waited for me to address her.

"Is there something I can do for you, Doris?" I asked sternly.

She reached up and pushed her glasses back up onto her nose and pulled at the hem of her shirt that was three sizes too big and hung over the loose skirt that flowed to the floor. I wasn't sure what fashion statement she was trying to make, but I would guess it was a cross between Amish and a nun. Hopefully for her sake, the outfit would soon swallow her up and be rid of the waste of space.

"Yes, Mr. Stone. Um, there's um a pile of papers that Mr. Ronnie Stone, your uncle, um left for you. They um, need your, um signature. Sir." She continued to pull at the bottom of her shirt as I contemplated humane ways to put this poor creature out of its misery.

"And where are these papers?" I asked sarcastically. "It would be helpful if you actually left notes on what you need, Doris." I felt the need to continue to address her by name. Not to be polite and show that I knew it, but because I liked to watch her squirm like a child who was being disciplined.

"There was, um, a note sir. It's right there." She pointed to a post it note that was sitting on top of the file beside the paperwork she was referring to that I just had in my hands.

I picked up the note and read it out loud.

"Mr. Stone, please sign the attached documents regarding the Heape case. Smiley face." I looked up at her with my eyebrows arched in disapproval of the handwritten smiley face.

"I'll sign these and take them to Ronnie when I'm done. Is there anything else?" I asked pointedly so she got the hint to leave.

"Yes, sir. Um, your wife called to let you know, that um, she was finished with her yoga class, and um, was meeting a friend for lunch."

I wondered why Mia didn't call or text me herself to tell me that she was done. That was our usual routine, she checked in with me everywhere she went, including lunch dates with so called friends. Mia didn't really have any friends and she never meets anyone for lunch.

"Who's the friend?"

"I'm sorry, who's who?" Doris asked confused, sliding her glasses up her nose. Again.

"You said that Mia said she was having lunch with a FRIEND. Who. Is. The. Friend?" I spelled it out for her, knowing that I was being a dick, but she had been irritating me long enough already.

"Oh, yeah, sorry. Um, I think she said Jake?" Doris replied, her eyebrows pulled together in an attempt to help her remember. "Yeah, it was definitely Jake."

Who the fuck was Jake? Mia better not be having lunch with that asshole waiter. My nostrils flared as I remembered his smug face from a few weeks ago and I pictured myself beating his ass into the pavement.

"Anything else?" Doris asked as she rolled forward to balance on the balls of her feet, desperate to leave.

"That's it," I said dismissively as she turned and walked out of my office, closing the door behind her.

I grabbed my cell phone and found 2 missed calls and 5 text messages. Three of the text messages were from Mia and two were from Claire. I opened Mia's first.

Mia: I'm at my Yoga class. I'll text when I'm done.

Mia: Yoga is over, we're going to grab lunch at the cafe next door if that's okay?

Mia: Haven't heard from you, called your cell twice. I left a message with Doris that I'll be at lunch. Call if you need me.

Maybe I was overreacting, but Mia never said in her texts who she was having lunch with. Was she really having lunch with some guy and acted so nonchalant about it?

I reached into my bottom desk drawer, pulled out the bottle of whiskey and added some to my coffee, to where it almost overflowed. I screwed the lid back on and put the bottle back in my drawer.

It was almost empty, again, which meant I needed to stop by the store on my way home.

I took a sip of my coffee to keep it from overflowing and gently stuck my pen in the cup to mix the whiskey in. As I waited for it to cool down, I opened the text messages from Claire.

Claire: Saturday night was fun, too bad we kept getting interrupted.

Claire: Maybe we should look into a conference or seminar out of town so we can get away together for the weekend. I can't wait to finish what we started.

A smile crossed my face as I read her text. She had been with the company as a new paralegal for a few months now and every day she wore tight skirts that hugged her ass and made me want to rip them off her. She was super curvy with big, plump tits that looked like they would bounce nicely in my face as she rode me. I had never been into redheads until she walked into my office to introduce herself and now, I've been walking around with a hard on ever since.

Damian: Sounds like you had something specific you were wanting to do Saturday night. Why don't you tell me about it.

I sat back in my high back leather chair and watched the dots bounce on the screen as she typed her response. I grabbed my cup of coffee and brought it to my lips to take a drink, spewing coffee across my desk as I choked when I read her response.

Claire: After sucking you dry, I'd let you fuck me from behind, letting you watch my sweet ass that you can't get enough of.

I had not been expecting that from her. We had only recently begun flirting and I was still trying to figure out what she was wanting from all of this. No need to wonder anymore.

Claire was so different than Mia. She was aggressive and powerful and took charge. Mia was passive and always let me walk all over her. Claire could walk into any room and men took notice of her. Mia could stumble into a room and few people would notice her. I used to find Mia attractive when we first started dating but she's changed over the last 5 years that I no longer felt like my needs were fulfilled by her.

Sure, she was the perfect wife. She cooked and cleaned constantly. She ran all of the errands. She attended all the bullshit events that I was expected to attend. She was the perfect fit for that life. But she was nothing more than that; hadn't been for a while and wouldn't ever be.

I never intended to start something with Claire, it just happened. There was this chemistry and I liked it. I liked the way she looked at me under her eyelashes as she showed me something in a report that I was reading. Or the way she leaned in close and allowed me to look down her shirt at her tits that were barely contained in her bra.

I debated on whether to text Claire back right away as I took another drink of coffee. Once it had completely cooled down, I finished what was in the mug in one big drink and wiped my mouth with the back of my hand. A few minutes later a loud burp that smelled like whiskey escaped and I was thankful that no one else was in the office with me. If any of the partners knew that I was day drinking, I would be terminated immediately.

I glanced up and saw Doris walk past my office and suddenly remembered that Mia was having lunch with someone and I needed to find out who. I opened the tracking app that I have on her phone and confirmed she was still at the cafe by the yoga studio. I grabbed my cell phone and car keys from the desk and walked out of the office, the door slammed shut behind me. Doris jumped at the sound as fear filled her face.

"Clear my schedule for the remainder of the day," I said as I walked out of the building.

The sun was brighter than I imagined it would be, so I quickened my pace to the car. My fingers felt around as they tried to get the key into the ignition, shaking in the process. Finally, I got the car started and began backing out of the parking spot when I heard a loud honking sound. I glanced in my rear-view mirror and saw a car passing by that I almost backed into. The driver gave me the bird while I impatiently waited for them to move so I could continue pulling out.

The drive was quick and didn't take long to get there when you ran red lights and didn't follow speed limits. I put the car in park and stumbled out, tripping on the curb in the process. I let out a slew of curse words under my breath and adjusted my tie as I tried to play it off to anyone who might have seen it.

I looked around the mini strip mall at the business names and spotted the yoga studio which was a few doors down from Jasmine's Cafe. Bingo. I walked over as I noticed a few tables outside on the patio with a few people sitting at them. I peered around the corner, into the cafe, and saw more people inside than out, and started searching for Mia. I saw her before she saw me. I watched as she threw her head back, laughing at whatever the person in front of her said. I tilted my head to the side, trying to make out who she was with, nothing to help me other than short black hair that was shaved in the back, like a guy's.

My nostrils flared as my blood pressure started to rise with my anger. I stormed over to where Mia was, surprise then fear crossed her face as I got closer to the table. In an instant, I reached out and grabbed her by the back of her head, lacing my fingers into her hair to maintain a better grip. If she thought she could have lunch with another man, she was seriously mistaken. People at the other tables jumped up in response and I heard the gasps as they took in what was happening. The guy across from Mia jumped up and backed away. Probably the smart thing to do, little coward. I watched out of the corner of my eye as he watched me. Part of me hoped that he would try to be the hero and step up to me so I could pound his ass into the ground where he belonged.

"Damian, stop! Let go of me!" Mia cried out as her hands tried to pry my hand out of her hair.

I ignored her as I tried to keep pulling her toward the door, her strength surprising me as she tried to fight back.

"Enough, Damian! What has gotten into you?!" She demanded as she finally got her elbow loose and jabbed me in the side, forcing me to let go of her. Everyone watched us with horror on their faces as I put a hand to my rib where she jabbed me.

"You think you can come have lunch with another man?!" I yelled accusingly at her.

"What man?!" She yelled back, throwing her hands up in the air in confusion, bewilderment on her face.

"Doris said that you called to say you were having lunch with Jake and here I find you with this asshole," I said as I jerked my head and pointed to the guy standing against the window, looking at us. Except it wasn't a guy. It was a very attractive female with short black hair that framed her face in the front, and apparently was shaved in the back. Someone who I would normally try to fuck. From the few times I had ever seen her, I now recognized that it was Jade.

"I told Doris that I was having lunch with Jade. Very clearly, I said Jade. I don't even know a Jake, Damian!"

I saw the anger and frustration on her face and knew that I'd embarrassed her. Instantly I wished that I would have added a little more whiskey to my coffee before coming here. It probably would have helped.

"I'm sorry," I mumbled as I looked back and forth between Mia and Jade.

"What did you say?" Mia asked with her arms crossed over her chest, still pissed.

"You heard me," I said with an assertive tone. While I didn't apologize to her often, it didn't mean that I wouldn't when I was in the wrong, but I also expected her to know her place. Women who thought they had power in a relationship was a dangerous thing.

Mia stayed quiet while she looked at Jade, then back to me. I let out a deep sigh and raked my hand through my hair. It was time to go and quit making a scene.

"I'm leaving, I'm assuming you'll be home shortly as well?" I asked even though we both know it wasn't a question.

"Yes. I will finish my lunch then go to the grocery store before I come home," Mia replied curtly with an edge to her tone.

"While at the store, pick up another bottle of-"

"Whiskey." Mia offered a smug smile as she finished my sentence.

I glared at her one last time before I looked at Jade and walked away. The room began to fill with quiet chatter as I left the cafe, everyone continued to stare as I made it to my car. I drove home in silence as I contemplated the ways that Mia would pay for her actions today when she got home. Disobedient wives needed to remember that even the best of husbands had breaking points, and I had reached mine.

<u>Five</u>
Mia

The speed limit dropped from 75 to 35 mph over the last 10 miles which confirmed I had made it to Haven Brook. I looked around and immediately recognized the small town that I had once called home. Off in the distance there was construction where they were building new homes. The car slowed to 30 mph as I made my way onto Main Street, careful to stay under the speed limit. I didn't want to draw attention to myself by getting a speeding ticket within the first five minutes of being back. Lord knew I needed more time to get settled in without anyone seeing me.

I pulled into the parking lot and found a spot close to the front of the store, which was helpful as it had started raining and I didn't want to get soaked. It had been a while since I'd been inside of a General Bob's store. Memories of my youth flooded my mind as I remembered coming here with my mom as we shopped the clearance racks when I would run out of clothes that fit me. That was the only time I ever got new clothes and was usually tied to a birthday or Christmas gift so she didn't have to get me anything later.

The store was still set up the same as I had remembered which allowed me to move through it quickly and get the things that I needed. The majority of my time was spent on the toiletries aisle, picking out shampoo, conditioner, and soap. I focused on finding the best deals to make what cash I had left go as far as it could. As I added a toothbrush and toothpaste to my cart I caught a glimpse of myself in the security mirror and decided I needed a few more things and went back to grab some hair color and make up.

A hundred and fifty dollars later I walked out of the store with bags loaded on my arms, filled with toiletries, some clothes, and basic food that I could store in the car like granola bars and meal replacement shakes. I pressed the button to unlock the rental car and popped the trunk open as I loaded it with the bags. My stomach growled and I contemplated whether to drink a meal replacement shake or sit down and have an actual meal while I figured out my next step. I didn't have anywhere to go which made the decision an easy one.

I glanced up and saw the sign for SlowMo's across the street from where I was parked and decided to treat myself to a home cooked meal. SlowMo's had been around as long as I could remember. The owner, Moby, was an older man from the south who ended up in Colorado when the love of his life moved back to care for her parents. His love of cooking comfort food led him to open SlowMo's which became an instant success in Haven Brook.

The restaurant was quiet with only a few patrons inside which was reassuring that I might be able to avoid running into anyone that I knew. When I left Haven Brook the town was steadily growing and had a population close to 50,000 people. I was curious to know what the current population was as I didn't recognize a single face, luckily, which meant they didn't recognize me either. I waited for the hostess, hoping I would be given a table in the back. Within a few minutes I had a table off to the side, away from everyone else, and had been looking over the menu when I heard a familiar voice in front of me.

"Well, well, well. Look at what the cat dragged in," Noah said as he slid into the opposite side of the booth across from me.

My stomach sank. While I had missed Noah, I wasn't ready to see him yet. I had hoped that I would have time to get myself together and not look like the trainwreck who came running back home, only for him to say- I told you so. Noah and Chase had tried to warn me not to run off to be with some man I barely knew, but I was so desperate to escape my mother and the town that I felt trapped in, that I didn't listen.

I let out a shaky breath as I forced myself to lift my head and look at him. The hint of a smile that had been on his face when I first looked up quickly disappeared when he saw the bruises on my face. He no longer looked happy to run into a friend he hadn't seen in a while, he now looked worried and concerned. My eyes dropped to my menu and I tried to focus on the words that blurred across the laminated page as tears stung my eyes. It seemed it would have been a better decision to skip lunch and find a motel to hide in until my face cleared up.

I had been gone for almost seven years and had no idea if people would think that I had changed much while I was gone. But seeing Noah after seven years, I could see that he had changed for the better. Butterflies danced in my stomach as I wondered what Chase looked like after all of these years. Then dread filled me as I wondered if he was here with Noah, knowing that they had rarely gone anywhere without each other.

As much as I thought I wanted to see Chase, I wanted to give it some time so I wouldn't feel his judgement for not listening, though I was sure it was inevitable. Our last few years of high school brought the three of us closer together, and I inadvertently ended up with the biggest crush on Chase. Which of course meant that his opinion of what I did with my life mattered more to me than Noah's did.

Chase always had this easy-going charisma that made him easy to be around, which meant that he was also one of the most popular guys that I knew. Every girl wanted him. He was incredibly good looking with dark brown eyes that bordered on black, depending on his mood. Back in the day his jet-black hair was short enough to keep it from being too wild, but always slightly disheveled as the girls couldn't keep their fingers out of it.

"Mia," Noah called, breaking my focus on the menu and unnecessary thoughts about a crush I should be over after seven years. Butterflies still filled my belly as I thought about running into him. I let out a sigh when I realized how off course my life had gotten and reminded myself that I needed to live in the present and forget about the past.

"What's going on, Mia?" Noah asked in the brotherly tone he used to use when we were younger.

"Nothing. It's good to see you," I replied with a fake smile as I gave up and finally looked at him.

"Bullshit. Did that guy in Boston do this to you?" He pointed at the bruises on my face.

"Let it go, Noah." I didn't feel like getting into it with Noah nor did I want to pick up where we had left off seven years ago.
"You know Mia, I let things go seven years ago. And that was the biggest mistake of my life. I'm not about to keep making the same mistakes. So, either tell me what happened, or I'll get Chase involved and we'll find a way to figure out what happened," Noah said sternly as he leaned back and folded his arms across his chest. I had made the mistake of confessing my feelings for Chase to Noah one night after too many beers. One of the reasons I hardly ever drank since then.

"You're really going to go there? Really?" I asked with an eyebrow arched as I leaned forward in the booth to look at him. "I thought we were friends Noah." I laid the sarcasm on heavy with the last sentence, which he knew was a jab, not a question.

"Okay, fine. It was a low blow with the Chase comment. I'm sorry. One of us had to mention him." He let out a sigh and winked.

"But really Mia, you can't come back to Haven Brook, covered in bruises, and not tell me what's going on. People are going to ask because they are nosey. I'm asking because you're family, and I care. Let me help you, Mia."

"I don't need help." I lowered my eyes so he couldn't see the lie I tried desperately to hide as I bit my bottom lip to keep from crying.

"Really?" He said studying me, not buying a word I said.

"So, where are you staying? Are you going back to Bonnie's?" I felt his eyes on me as he watched for my reaction.

My head flew up, anger evident on my face. He knew my relationship with my mom had never been good and that I vowed to never see her again when I left for Boston.

"Okay, so that's a no. Then where are you staying? That Mazda you pulled up in?" He nodded outside to where I had parked.

"How do you know what I'm driving? What are you, some sort of secret spy since I left?" I taunted as I tried to loosen up. I adjusted my back against the worn-out leather of the booth and tried to make myself look more relaxed. If I was going to be back for a little bit, I would need at least a friend or two. It didn't do any good to burn every bridge along the way.

"I was finishing a phone call in my car when you came in. Nearly shit myself when I thought I saw the ghost of Mia Johnson walking into the same place I was about to have lunch." He smiled and I was thankful to see the playful side of Noah come back. He gave me a hard time like a big brother would, but at the end of the day, he was always Noah. The most kindhearted, genuine person I had ever known.

The waitress walked toward our table, confusion on her face when she saw Noah sitting opposite of me. I smiled at her as Noah turned to look at who I had been smiling at.

"Two today?" she asked when she reached our table.

"Yes, just the two of us." I felt a blush creep up my neck, assuming she must think we were here on a date.

"What can I get you to drink?" She looked back and forth between Noah and I, her pen hovered above her notepad, waiting to for our answer.

"Water is fine for me, please." I pushed my menu to the side of me. I had been here a million times and knew the menu better than their own staff probably did. In the few minutes that I had been back, I had already found that very few things changed around here.

"Same for me," Noah said as he reached into his front pocket and pulled out his cell phone. I watched as he swiped his phone a few times, silencing the vibration.
"Do you all need a few minutes to look over the menu?" She pointed her pen toward the menu laying in front of me.

"I think I'm ready, if the lady is." Noah winked at her before they both turned their attention to me. He was always such a womanizer, even when he wasn't trying to be. I hated being the center of attention, even in situations like this.

"I'll have the biscuits and gravy, with an extra sausage patty, please." I smiled before looking away and breaking eye contact, making sure she knew that I was done.

"I'll have the same."

"You got it. Be right back with those waters." She pushed the pen into the messy bun on top of her head and grabbed the menu off the table before heading towards the kitchen to put in our order.
I felt Noah looking at me and desperately wished I could get out from under his intense gaze. He was studying me, and I knew he was going to keep pushing until I talked about what had happened and why I was back. I didn't know if I was ready to talk about it yet. Every few minutes I was still searching around me, looking for a sign that Damian was there.

I had made it to Denver without any problems and knew that if he dug deep enough, Damian would be able to find my name when I rented a car. I went with one of the bigger car rental companies, hoping they were harder to hack and relying on them to maintain customer confidentiality. Granted it was usually fake in the movies, I still entertained the thought of him finding a connection to someone who could access their system and tell him what I was driving.

I had picked up a prepaid cell phone while in Denver in case I broke down somewhere or needed help. The cash that Jade had left me was dwindling quickly between the rental car, the cell phone, gas, and my visit to General Bob's. While Noah knew that I needed help, I don't think anyone, including myself, knew just how much help I needed. I had $250 left to my name to pay for this meal and hopefully find a cheap motel to stay in unless I wanted to live in the car for a few days. If I was going to stay in Haven Brook for a while then I needed to find a job ASAP.

We sat in silence for a few minutes, my thoughts scattered everywhere. Noah caught my eye and for a moment I remembered being a teenager and fearing my mother. Noah would always reassure me that he would protect me as he walked me to his house to stay for the night. Comfort embraced me and for a moment I wanted to sink into that feeling and allow Noah to help me again. To have that feeling of comfort again, knowing I was safe, but I knew better. If I told him what happened, I wouldn't be able to protect him if Damian ended up finding me.

"I remember when we were in junior high. You were constantly fighting with your mom and she kept threatening to kick you out of the house. One afternoon you had gone home after school and there was a torn-up suitcase on the front step with all of your stuff inside. You tried to get in, but she had changed all of the locks. When you knocked on the door, she looked out the window and laughed at you." Noah took a deep breath while he continued to look at me. "I found you a few blocks away, hiding in between the dumpsters, crying."

"I remember that day."

"You looked so defeated, Mia. The girl that I once knew, she was gone. I searched your eyes and I couldn't find her. But then you agreed to go home with me and my parents refused to let you leave. You fought us on trying to help you, but in the end, you stayed with us that summer and you were a tremendous help to my mother. After a few days of being with us, you felt safe again, and I saw the light come back to your eyes." His voice grew softer.

I wasn't sure why he was bringing this story up, but it brought a tear to my eye. I was so young and naive; I didn't know what to do when my mom kicked me out. Left to fend for myself, I was scared and had no idea where to go for help. I had decided that I would figure it out on my own. I would be strong. I would become a survivor. Noah's parents sat me down and told me that at 12 years old, I shouldn't have to survive my childhood. They explained to me what a parent should and shouldn't do as their eyes welled up with tears. I listened as they discussed their expectations for me and outlined the rules of their house. My mind was blown when things like going to school every day, doing my homework every night, and no drinking were on their list of requirements. These were things that I did on my own because I wanted to do well in school. It felt odd to feel like these adults cared about me, that they included me as part of their family.

"The light in your eye is gone again, Mia. Let me help you," Noah coaxed. "It's okay to trust me, I would never hurt you or let anyone else hurt you."

His words broke my heart and before I could stop myself the tears flowed down my cheeks as my body shook with every breath I tried to take. I had been holding everything inside since our first fight a few weeks ago and I knew that it would eventually consume me. It would eat away at the person that I had once been until there was nothing left. I desperately wanted to find the carefree, happy girl that I had been for a short period of time, before my life crumbled before me.

Noah quickly slid out of his side of the booth and into mine as he wrapped his arms around me and held me as I cried. I prayed that for just a moment, I could allow myself to have the comfort that he offered without having to fear Damian. I closed my eyes and allowed my breakdown to continue. A tear fell for every time Damian had called me a name or insulted me. Another tear for every time he hit me. More tears fell as I accepted that I had reached a point in my life where I once again needed help. I needed someone to save me because for so long I had been allowing myself to drown. For once, I wanted to live. I wanted to fight and I wanted to figure out my path in life. Footsteps approached and my eyes flew open, relieved when it was just the waitress bringing our glasses of water, and not Damian. She looked at me with concern and I struggled to smile, my face still buried in Noah's shoulder. I watched as she sat the glasses down on the table and pulled two straws out of her apron, setting them beside the glasses before she walked away.

I pulled away from Noah and reached behind me for a napkin to dry my face. My breathing was staggered as my body tried to recover from the breakdown. I tried to take a few slow, deep breathes as I blew my nose and wiped my eyes again before looking at Noah. I set the used napkins off to the side by the wall and slowly turned to look at Noah as I saw the waitress coming back with our food. Noah smiled up at her as he waited for her to set our plates down before getting up to take his seat on the other side of the booth.

"You all need anything else?" she asked while studying my face. My instincts told me that she was likely a mother with the way she eyed me with concern and stared Noah down for possibly making me cry. I shook my head no as I unwrapped the silverware from the napkin and set it to the side of my plate.

She walked away, throwing one more accusatory glance at Noah. I tried to hide my laughter, but I had already reached the point of hysteria and it found its way out. I tried to cover my face behind my napkin as I laughed harder than I had in years. The thought of this woman giving Noah dirty looks and judging him for making me cry sent me into a frenzy. I felt Noah pull my napkin down and laughed even harder when he had a full-blown smile across his face.

"Thanks for turning me into Ike Turner with the waitress," he joked as he tossed his wadded-up straw wrapper at me.

I tried to stop laughing but it was impossible and turned into a snort laugh that sent me into even more hysterics. My sides hurt from laughing which reminded me of the recent trauma my ribs had suffered and put a damper on my fun. My laughing tapered off and I watched as Noah noticed the change as well.

"It was nice to see you laugh," he commented softly.

"It was nice to have something to laugh at. It's been a while."

"I can see that." Sadness laced his voice and I knew that he still wanted to know what had happened.

"I left Damian." I blurted out. Whether I wanted to talk about it or not, I knew I needed to.

Noah stayed silent as he ate, waiting for me to continue.

"I left last night after we had a fight. We have been having a lot of fights lately, but each one feels like it gets worse than the one before. I didn't plan to leave last night," I chuckled as I remembered the events of the night and how chaotic everything had been since then. "But when he tried to kill me, I knew that I didn't have a choice. He was no longer content with just hitting me a few times and yelling at me. He actually seemed to enjoy watching me in pain, and the more violent he became, the more I was afraid of him." I shuddered at the thought as memories made their way through my mind, reminding me of the violence I had endured.

I watched Noah struggle as I continued to talk to him about what had happened with Damian. I told him about the charity event that we went to a few weeks ago, that we were kicked out of, when he got drunk and loudly accused me of flirting with the waiter. That had been the first time he had hit me. I mentioned the hidden cameras around the house I had found that he was using to watch me on, including the one in the bathroom. There was the fight we had while I was out to lunch with Jade a few days ago, and his secretary had mistakenly told him that I was having lunch with another man. The fight we had last night after his company summer BBQ that we were forced to attend to appease his uncle. Damian was working hard to make partner, which meant we had a lot of social appearances we were expected to make. That got harder to do when my body was constantly wearing the evidence of what he had been doing to me.

"Last night he claimed that I was yet again, flirting with one of the partners at the BBQ. On the way home he had reprimanded me and lectured me on my behavior. Reminded me that I was his and that no one else would ever have me- *'til death do us part*. It was really creepy the way he said it," I shrugged as I felt as hopeless as I had felt last night when I left. What were you supposed to do when someone wanted you dead?

"We got home a little after nine and the second that we walked in the door, I felt him push me from behind. I tried to catch my balance but the force was too much and I fell forward and hit my head on the island." I absentmindedly touched the cut on my forehead as it replayed in my mind.

"He kept screaming at me, slurred words about me cheating on him. I couldn't focus on what he was saying. There was this ringing in my head that made it impossible and at that point I was just trying to stay conscious. I knew that he was drunk, but not drunk enough to really slow him down." I took the breath I needed and forced myself to continue moving on with the story. "I knew his habits and knew that within a few minutes he would go get another drink, and that would be my break from him. Once he made it to his study, he would pour his drink and down it. It didn't take him long, it wasn't like him to sit and enjoy it. He would down it and come find me. I knew that if I was going to leave, I had to go while he was in his study. So, without thinking twice, I grabbed what I could and I took off. I haven't stopped running from him since."

I took a deep breath, allowing my lungs to replace the oxygen I had expelled with the verbal vomit I had just unloaded on Noah. It felt good to have someone to talk to and to be able to tell someone what had happened. I had been living such an isolated life for so long that I missed having a friend to confide in.

Noah stayed quiet for a few minutes, his jaw clenched as he looked out the window. Anxiety started mounting as I waited for the lecture I was sure was coming. I didn't blame him for being disappointed in me. I wasn't able to get away from my abusive mother as a child, what made me think I could escape my abusive husband?

"Mia, that's a lot," he said as he took a deep breath and leaned forward. "Have you told anyone else what happened? Have you gone to the police?"

"No. No one knows but you. Jade was suspicious that he was hitting me when I missed the yoga class, but I didn't tell her what happened. She had tried asking about things at lunch, but it got interrupted." I gave a half shrug as we both knew what had happened after that.

"Did she know that you were going to leave?" he asked as he took a bit of his food and nodded to me to eat mine as well. I felt bad that both of our meals were now cold.

"I didn't tell her that I was going to. After I had left, I found some cash in my purse with a torn off piece of napkin with numbers on it. I think Jade stuffed it in my purse when I went to the bathroom at lunch. She was really shaken up about what had happened with Damian during lunch and begged me to leave. And I know she had cash on her, she had talked about making a down payment on a new car she was buying herself since hers was on its last leg. I feel horrible because I know how long she had been saving up for a car."

"Do you think that he knows that you're here?"

"I have no idea. I constantly pray that he doesn't, but at this point, anything is possible."
"I know that you don't want help, and I get it Mia. Really, I do. But you have no idea how helpless I am going to feel if you don't let me help you." His eyes met mine as he silently pleaded with me.

"I do need a job. Do you know anyone in town that's hiring? And maybe needs someone *on the side*?" I asked with hope in my voice that he might know someone that would let me do some side work for cash until I could get on my feet. I don't want anything tied to Mia

Stone and make it easier for Damian to find me.

"Actually, I have a position open that is yours if you want it. You can start tomorrow." His smile stretched across his perfectly handsome face as he beamed with pride that I was going to allow him to help.

"Really? That's great, thank you!" Excitement quickly replaced the helpless feeling that had been eating away at me. One step at a time, that's all I had to get through.

"Don't you want to know what it is?" He laughed, knowing that I didn't care.

"Do I have to be employed as Mia Stone?" I questioned, hopeful that the answer would be no.

"No. But it does mean that Amelia Johnson would officially be back in Haven Brook." He grinned a wicked grin.

I groaned as he said my birth name out loud. I had gone by Mia since I was a little girl and very few people knew me as Amelia. But it was a compromise that I didn't mind making, especially since Damian never knew that my birth name was Amelia. I had legally changed my name to Mia as a teenager and manipulated my drunk mother to sign off on it when I threatened to tell the school about her drinking and recreational drug use. This had allowed me to sign our marriage certificate as Mia Johnson.

"Ugh. Alright. Fine. Amelia Johnson will start tomorrow. Just tell me what time and where to go." I sighed as dramatically as I could before picking up my fork to finish my food.

"Deal." Noah wrote the information down on the back of the receipt that the waitress had brought back sometime during my long rant. I hadn't even noticed that he had discreetly paid for my lunch until I saw him writing on his copy of the receipt.

"Thank you for lunch, you didn't have to pay." I smiled as he slid the receipt my way and put the pen down at the end of the table with the signed copy.

“You’re welcome,” he said with a wink. I could tell something was up with the way he was acting. He had this smirk he would get whenever he did something he wasn’t supposed to, which had me worried about what he was up to now.

We finished our lunch and walked together to the parking lot, relieved that the rain had stopped. I gave Noah a hug, thanked him for lunch, and went to pull away when I felt him pull me back towards him.

“There is one other thing, Mia,” he said with a crooked smile.

“What’s that?” I narrowed my eyes at him, suspicious of what he was planning as I saw the wheels in his head turning.

“When we were younger, you stayed with me and my parents, so we could help you with your mom.”

“Yeah. And?” I was confused at what he was trying to get at.

“You’re going to stay with me again, at least until you get on your feet.”

“Noah, no, I can’t do that. I appreciate you offering me the job, that’s more than helpful.” I stammered through my sentences as I tried to process what he was offering. It would help me tremendously to stay with him and not have to pay for a hotel or live in a car, but I couldn’t take advantage of him.

“It’s not negotiable, Mia. So get in your car so you can follow me to my house and we can get you situated.” He smiled as I started to speak and put his finger up to my mouth to cut me off. I knew I wasn’t going to win this one. It felt nice being with Noah again, the family that I’ve always had and never let me down.

<u>Six</u>
Chase

"Alright, Liam, pull your shoulders back a tad, like this," I coaxed as I helped adjust his posture into the correct position. "Now, take a deep breath, and keep your eye on the ball."

I slowly took a few steps to the left, allowing him the space he needed to hit the ball as it came flying toward him. He had a stern look on his face as he focused on the ball, swung at the perfect moment, forcing the ball over the fence. He tossed the bat to the ground and made his way around the bases, a huge smile on his face as he ran toward me.

"I did it! I did it! I got a home run, Uncle Chase!" He launched himself into my open arms as I kneeled down to catch him. I hugged him tightly, thankful that he hadn't reached the age where he would be embarrassed to let me hug him. I dreaded when that day would come.

"You did amazing! I'm so proud of you, Liam! One day, you'll be even better than your daddy." I winked as I heard heavy footsteps behind us, knowing they would hear me. I watched as his smile grew wider at the idea and lit up his face.

"Oh really?" A deep voice boomed behind me as Liam squirmed out of my arms and went running to his dad.

"Uncle Chase said that if I stayed focused, like really, really focused, that I could hit the ball. And guess what dad?! I did, I hit it really hard! And it went way far up over that fence!" Liam pointed excitedly in the direction the ball had landed. He was 7 years old and had recently decided to give sports another try.

"Way to go! I'm so proud of you, son!" They gave each other a high five followed by a secret handshake they had recently created and had been working on perfecting. "Sounds like you did a really good job. What do you say we celebrate by getting some ice cream on the way home?" Grant smiled at Liam and wiggled his eyebrows which got another giggle out of his son. "Just don't tell nana."

Liam got even more tickled with the thought of having ice cream before dinner, knowing that nana would have a hay day if she found out about it. But we all knew she would find out about it. She knew everything.

Grant was my younger brother, who was now a single parent to Liam after Liam's mom recently lost her battle to cancer. Grant and Renee were high school sweethearts, nothing could tear them apart. Well, technically ovarian cancer did. Our lives were forever changed the day Renee passed. It was a loss felt by everyone who had the pleasure of knowing her.

It took a few weeks of everyone working to convince Grant to accept help. He was always such a proud man, and being the middle child, felt he had something to prove. I had helped my mom raise him after my dad passed away unexpectedly my senior year of high school. Grant was a year behind me, and Wyatt was starting his freshman year when we lost my dad. It was a hard position to be in because neither of them was old enough to be on their own and both of them resented me for trying to keep them in line.
My mom, also known as Nana to Liam, convinced Grant to move in with her six months ago, so she could help with Liam. Grant worked 50+ hours a week and nana couldn't stand the thought of Liam being in daycare when she was all by herself in that big empty house. Those were her words, but they worked, and Grant moved them in without any more fuss about it.

"You wanna come with us to get ice cream?" Liam asked as he pulled at my shirt. I looked into his innocent brown eyes and knew that I would spend my life trying to give this kid anything he wanted. I knew what it felt like to lose a parent and I hated that he had to know that feeling at such a young age. He would never know what it was like to have his mom teach him how to dance or pick out a tuxedo for prom. There were so many memories that I had with my mom growing up, that I wished I could give to Liam. The aching in my heart accelerated when I thought of all of the things in life he had been robbed of.

"I wish I could, champ, but I have to get going. Maybe next time?" I felt horrible for saying no but I knew that Grant needed some bonding time with his son and I didn't want to get in the way. Grant had worked overtime this week and it showed on his face. He was an exceptional dad and would spend every waking minute with his son, even if it meant he didn't get any sleep or time for himself. I wasn't going to stand in the way of the time they needed.

"Are you going to come to our house for dinner? Nana said that she's making fried chicken with mashed potatoes and peach cobbler." He looked up as if he was trying to remember his lines from a script. I waited for the line I that I knew was coming.

"Oh, and that you haven't been by to see your mama in almost two weeks so she expects to see your behind at dinner." I chuckled as he wagged his finger at me, apparently fulfilling his duty to guilt me into dinner by my mom. Grant laughed as he watched his son lecture me.

"Is that so?" I asked as I tussled his wavy brown hair before he could dart away. His friend, Luke, laughed and pointed at his messed-up hair. I smiled and watched the two boys, happy that I was able to take Liam every Sunday afternoon to get him out of the house. Luke had joined us today for some practice now that Liam wanted to try little league again.

"Well, you tell nana that I have some errands to run real quick but I'll be there for dinner. You go enjoy your secret ice cream with your dad, and there better be some fried chicken left by the time I get there." I pointed my finger back at him, mimicking him.

"Okay! See you in a little bit, uncle!" Liam took off running with Luke to the car as Grant and I walked behind them.

"So, what errands do you have to run?" His eyebrows arched as he waited out my response.

"Or is that the name you use for your sexcapades now? Don't even bother to learn the girl's name these days?" Grant joked and bumped my shoulder as we made it to his car. He was barely a few inches taller than me and always tried to use it to his advantage.

"Let's see, that would be…… none of your business," I shot back with a smirk as I climbed up into my lifted Tacoma and started the engine. I waved at the boys and Grant as I made my way over the 5 speed bumps that lead the way to the main road.

I hadn't planned on doing dinner with my family tonight but my mom was right, I hadn't been there in almost two weeks. After Renee died 8 months ago, I vowed to spend more time with family and to be the best uncle that I could be for Liam. It was time that I made my family a bigger priority.

My cell phone buzzed repeatedly in my pocket as the console on my dashboard alerted me of a phone call. I glanced at the screen and saw Nadia's name. We had been talking for a few weeks after we bumped into each other, very literally, at the gym. Tonight I was supposed to take her out to dinner, and if things went right, drinks at my place after.

"Hey Nadia." I pushed the button to accept the call.

"Hey, handsome." Her voice played through the cabin of the truck laced with a flirty tone. I hated to cancel our date tonight which left me focused on trying to figure out what to say so she didn't think I wasn't interested.

"I can't wait to see you tonight. I've been thinking about you all day."

"There might be a slight change of plans, I'm sorry." I wracked my brain, desperate to figure out a way to do dinner and still see Nadia.

"Does that mean that you're cancelling on me?" If I had her on a video call, I would be willing to put money on her pouty face that I was positive she had on right now.

"I need to do dinner with my family, but I shouldn't be too long. I might be able to finish up around 9. Are you free then?"

"I have a 5:30 flight to New York in the morning. It will be an early night for me."

"When do you get back?"

"Next Sunday. I'm gone a full week."

Fuck. I had really wanted to see her tonight. There was so much flirting when we were at the gym, followed by explicit texts and some nude photos on her part, that my body was demanding that I see her. The constant teasing had me aching for a release. I blew out a breath as I fidgeted in my seat.

"But maybe we can do a few video calls while I'm gone? You know, late nights at the hotel can get so lonely," she purred into the phone.

"They sure do." I glanced at the screen as a new call alert came through and distracted me. Noah had the worst timing sometimes. I debated whether to answer the call or let it go to voicemail when I heard her sigh heavily.

"Well, you seem busy or distracted so I'll let you go and maybe we'll talk this week. That hotel room might not be so lonely after all." Nadia hung up, silence replaced the flirty tone from a few minutes before. I looked at the screen again and found a voicemail and missed call alert from Noah. "He can wait." I grumbled to no one as I turned onto the road that led to my mom's house. I guess I had it coming, but in all fairness, phone sex and continuing on with the teasing games weren't really my thing. I had more than my share of women and there was always a new prospect lining themselves up for me so I didn't really care too much if Nadia was pissed at me. While my body disagreed with that statement, I knew I only had to make a few phone calls after dinner tonight and I could have that problem taken care of.

<u>Seven</u>
Mia

It was a little after 10 when I heard the door open and saw Noah walk in with a petite blonde wrapped around his neck. He glanced at me sitting on the couch and pulled the girl's hands off of him as she grunted in protest. My guess was that she was barely legal and way past intoxicated. My eyes shot up in question as he shrugged his shoulders with a coy smile.

Growing up with Noah and Chase, I watched as they made their way through the pool of girls that were always throwing themselves at them. They were two of the hottest guys in school and every girl wanted to be the flavor of the week. Neither of them ever had an actual girlfriend that I could remember, and it didn't look like any of that had changed since I had been gone.

I knew that Noah had a date tonight, I should have assumed that he would bring her home. I had planned on hanging out in the spare bedroom so I could stay out of his hair, but my anxiety was already high from everything that had happened over the past few days that I decided to sit on the couch and veg out for a while. A warm blanket consumed me as I sank into the soft couch, reruns of Seinfeld on for distraction.

"I like the new hair," Noah commented as he tilted his head to the side, checking out what I had done while he was gone. I reached a hand up to my hair, my cheeks flushed at the compliment.
My hair was no longer long and blonde, a lifetime of the same look, gone. I had cut a little more than six inches off, leaving it to barely touch my shoulders. The color was a dark brown, and depending on the lighting in the bathroom, had looked almost black. Why I never colored my hair before, who knows. I immediately loved the new color and how it made my baby blue eyes stand out even more.

"Well, I'm off to bed." I folded the blanket and laid it on the back of the couch where I had found it. I didn't want to make it anymore awkward with Noah bringing a girl home so I made my way to the guest room and closed the door behind me.

The room was painted white with a few pictures hanging on the walls. There was a full-sized bed in the corner with a nightstand next to it and a dresser on the opposite wall. It was simple and yet felt cozy. I had taken the time earlier to take the tags off of the new clothes I had purchased, and with Noah's instructions before he left, had done a load of laundry while he was gone. The clothes were hung in the closet with a few things in the dresser.

I had rearranged my purse and was able to store the makeup that I had purchased in the cosmetic bag without it overflowing. While Noah knew that I would be with him for a few weeks until I could get on my feet again, I didn't want it to look like I had fully moved in or that I was invading his space.

There was a small tv sitting on top of the dresser with an antenna behind it. I curled up on the bed and turned it on, looking for something to watch. My mind was still busy, wondering where Damian was and trying to figure out my next steps. I flicked through the channels, not paying attention to what was on them, as I heard a thump against the wall.

Startled, I jumped off of the bed, my hand to my chest, as I tried to figure out where the sound was coming from.

Thump.

I quietly walked slowly around the room, tilting my head as I strained to listen.

Thump. Thump. Thump.

It was getting quicker and more rhythmic.

Thump. Thump. Thump. Thump. Thump.

"Ohhhh, Noah!" A muffled moan made its way through the wall into my room.

I palm smacked my forehead when I recognized the distinct sound. I should have known. The thumping continued as I turned the sound on the tv up some to drown it out, making sure it wasn't loud enough for Noah to hear.

I sat down on the bed, happy to know that I wasn't under attack, it was just Noah having sex. Granted, I didn't necessarily need to know about that either. Bored, I grabbed my cell phone from the nightstand and unlocked it. The home screen was bare, a generic stock photo as the background image. How depressing. I hadn't taken the time to play with the phone since I got it yesterday, not that there was much that I needed to do. People always bragged about their new phones and how they customized their settings to make their lives easier, I never bothered.

Damian had always controlled my phone and set it up for me, that way he could control what I had access to, and what he wanted to have on it to monitor me. I opened the settings menu and scrolled through the options available.

Loneliness consumed me as I thought about the few people that I needed to add to my contacts. I didn't really have anyone, except for Jade, but I had no way of getting in touch with her unless I tried to find her on Facebook. Damian had the passwords to my social media accounts, as well as my email, so I didn't want it to alert him that I had logged into them from another device and him be able to track where that device was located.

It was better to start fresh if I was going to have any social media accounts. I found my way to the App Store and my finger hovered over the button to install the apps, uncertain of whether I should. I gave in and downloaded the Facebook and Instagram apps as I convinced myself that I didn't have to do anything with them.

I desperately wanted to talk to Jade to let her know that I was okay and to make sure that she was okay. Damian was crazy so I wouldn't put it past him to go after Jade, thinking that she had information about where I went. The look of concern on her face during lunch on Friday flashed through my mind as I remembered our last conversation.

"Mia, please, you have to leave him. Run, and don't ever come back," Jade pleaded as she reached across the table and held my hand. Tears filled her eyes as she continued to plead. "It won't stop, Mia. I know firsthand that it won't. I lost my sister because I was too late. I don't want to lose you too."

I blinked my eyes to force the tears away. Jade had looked so desperate when we said goodbye, it was like she held on a little bit longer, knowing it was our final goodbye. I thought back to the cash that she hid in my purse, knowing how selfless she had been to make sure that I had money if I decided to leave.

It wasn't like she could say anything about it, we both knew that Damian probably had a way of listening to us without being there, so we always talked as if he was there. When we said goodbye, she had whispered in my ear, *you'll be okay, just remember I'm always a call away.*

I hated that I didn't have my old cell phone, even though I was thankful that Damian could no longer track me on it. If I had it then I could call Jade and talk to her. Why would Jade say she would always be a call away if she knew that Damian was monitoring my phone? Why encourage me to leave then suggest that I call her when it could be tracked?

Clarity hit me and I sprung off the bed, grabbing my purse from the top of the dresser, and sat it down on the bed next to me. I quickly opened the pocket where I had found the cash and felt around until I found the piece of napkin with numbers on it. I had completely disregarded it when I first found it, unsure of what it was. It looked like a code or a password and I had assumed that she had accidentally left it with the cash.

I stared at the numbers 16175551782, waiting for something to make sense. It was too long to be a phone number. Or was it? I rolled my eyes when I separated each number and was able to make out a phone number. Jade had added in the 1 to make it less apparent. 1-617-555-1782.

A feeling of giddiness washed over me as I stared at the phone number. I wanted to immediately call her but fear took hold and I wondered if Damian was there and was waiting for me to call her. My fingers hovered over the keypad, unwilling to make a commitment.

I decided to avoid a phone call and test the waters with a text.

Mia: Hey

I sat the phone down and stared at it, waiting for something to happen. Apparently, I had turned an ordinary cell phone into some sort of magical device, expectations high that it would be Jade and that I would be free to talk to her. I watched as the new message alert showed on my screen.

My fingers trembled as they fumbled with unlocking the screen. I hoped it was Jade and that I hadn't text someone else thinking that it was supposed to be her phone number.

Then a terrifying thought occurred to me- what if the money was never from Jade? What if Damian was trying to test me, to see if I would leave? If he thought that there was a possibility that I would leave, then what if he was the one to put the money in my purse? He was the one who had been pissed at me for wanting to leave him, when I had never said that I wanted to leave. He put the idea out there, not me. What if he left the money, along with the phone number, so he could trick me into telling him where I was, knowing that I would think it was Jade.

The unread message stared at me as I struggled with whether to read it or not. If it was Damian, I just gave away my safety net of him not knowing where I was by being able to track my new phone number. I knew it didn't have the tracking app on it like my other phone, but I also knew that he had other resources and would find a way. I silently prayed that it was Jade and that there was no connection to Damian.

I realized there was nothing to lose by opening the message since I had already sent the first one. I pressed the button and read the message as a shiver ran through me.

Unknown: Where are you?

<u>Eight</u>
Mia

Those three words made me freeze as I stared at my phone. Had I been right? Was it all a test from Damian to see if I would actually leave him? Had I fallen for the ultimate trick?

The phone began vibrating in my hand, the number I had just sent a text message was displayed as the caller. I watched as it rang, unsure of what to do. I still held out a sliver of hope that it was Jade but my gut told me to stop the wishful thinking. The vibration stopped and a missed call alert replaced the image on the screen.

I took a deep breath as I tried to calm myself. There was no way of knowing who I had actually reached. Maybe it was Jade. Maybe it was Damian. Maybe it was some random person. The unknown was eating away at me.

A few seconds later a voicemail notification showed up on the screen. I hesitated as I pushed the button to play the message.

Hey Mia, it's me. Jade. Or at least I hope this is Mia and that you found the money and the number in your purse.

There was a pause and I could hear faint movement in the background before she came back to the phone.

If this is Mia, please call me back. I really need to know that you're okay. I've been worried sick about you after I called and texted you and you haven't responded. Then I got a call from Damian. So yeah, I'm worried about you. Call me?

Her voice sounded worried as I played the message again. I had no idea what I was trying to find in the voicemail but I kept searching for anything that would tell me that she was also okay and that Damian wasn't there, forcing her to play a role in his psychotic game. My breathing had started to return to normal as I tried to relax. I tried to think through all of the possible scenarios when I felt my phone vibrate again. Another call from Jade. Reluctantly, I answered the phone.

"Hi," I whispered into the phone.

"You have no idea how happy I am to hear your voice. Are you okay?"

"Yeah, I'm okay."

"Are you safe? What happened? Where are you?" Her questions came out in rapid fire, one after another.

"I'm fine." I kept my response vague, I still had no way of knowing whether Damian was with her. It could all still be a ruse.

"Mia, you don't sound fine." Her voice grew softer.

"Things are just, in the air right now." I didn't technically lie. While I had planned to stay in Haven Brook for a little while, I was more than prepared to run if this call took a turn for the worse. I had a feeling my life from here on out would constantly be up in the air.

"Are you sure you're okay? Is he there with you?" Jade lowered her voice and I could hear her cover the phone with her hand as she spoke again. "Use the word yoga if you're not okay and I'll find a way to get help to you."

I almost laughed as I realized that while I thought Damian was there with her, she thought that Damian was here with me. She was smart and I loved her quick thinking with a code word that was unique to us. Yoga wouldn't be anything out of the ordinary for me and Jade to talk about since Damian knew that we went to a weekly yoga class together in Boston. What he didn't know was that we rarely actually went to the class. While Jade was flexible and could easily do any pose, I could barely master corpse pose without injuring myself.

"I'm okay, really." I loosened up a bit as I felt more confident that she wasn't being coerced on the other side.

"You know, I would really just feel much better if I could see you. What kind of phone do you have? We can video chat."

I felt uneasy about doing video chat with her in case he was there but realized that he had better luck tracking the cell phone than finding where I was based on the bare white walls of Noah's guest room. After a few prompts from Jade I found the settings and answered as she called in again.

I answered the new call and watched the screen as it loaded, happy to see Jade's smile as she came onto the screen. She looked happy and didn't show any signs of being beaten by anyone recently so I assumed she had been safe from Damian.

"There you are," she said with a warmth in her voice, like a mother playing peekaboo with a baby. I watched as she took in my new look.

"Hi. It's nice to see you too."

As much as I was happy to see her, there was this unspoken tension as we looked at each other. It was like we were reading each other's minds, waiting for the other to say the obvious.

"He's not here with me," Jade said as she offered a sympathetic smile. "Watch." She took her cell phone and kept herself on the screen as she quickly walked around her apartment, opening doors and showing me behind the shower curtain. I smiled at the effort and was thankful that I didn't have to physically voice my concern.

"Your turn." She nodded to me and waited for me to show her that

Damian wasn't with me either. I showed her the small guest room, opened the closet door, and walked back over to the bed.

"What about the rest of the house?"

"Noah brought a date home and I don't want to be intrusive by walking through his house, taking some girl he doesn't know on a virtual tour of it."

Jade's eyebrows went up as she acknowledged that I said a man's name. I wanted to smack myself for what I had done. She needed to know that I was safe, not exactly where I was. I remembered a conversation I had with her when we first met, shortly after I had moved to Boston, when we were waiting tables together. We had a large party that night of drunken college guys, out for a bachelor party. The tips were scarce and the compliments unflattering. Jade had complained that there were no real men left in this world and that she was destined to either die alone or end up a crazy cat lady. I assured her there were still a few left, and that she would have to move to Colorado to find them. I warned her that Noah was one of the most desired men in Haven Brook and that she would have her work cut out for her if she wanted to try to tame him. Apparently she remembered the name.

"Are you back where you told me about early on in our friendship?" She looked at me with wide eyes as she made sure I got the hint she was trying to give. I appreciated that she respected me enough not to say the name. She knew how crazy Damian was and even though it appeared he would have no way to hear our conversation, we played it safe.

"Yes." A simple answer. That was all that was needed as I watched her sigh with relief and sink back into her chair. We had talked about my childhood before Damian and I had moved in together, and while I had kept it vague, I had eluded to my mom being abusive and that I had been lucky to have Chase and Noah to constantly protect me. At the time I had gone on and on about finding a man in Boston that would also protect me, little had I known.

"I'm really happy to hear that."

I smiled and for a moment we took in the silence as there wasn't anything more that needed to be said. I wished that I could bring Jade here, to have a friend in the place that I had decided to make my home again, but I couldn't ask that of her. I couldn't ask her to uproot her life and come join me as I constantly watched over my shoulder.

Involuntarily I yawned, the lack of sleep from the past few days had caught up to me.

"It's late and I'm sure you've barely slept. I should let you go."

"It's okay, I like talking to you." I blinked my eyes as they started to feel heavy. I was exhausted but I didn't know when I would get to talk to Jade again.

"Mia, get some sleep. You need it. We'll find a way to talk again soon, okay?" Her voice reassured me that we would find a way. We said goodbye and I heard the front door close as I sat my phone on the nightstand and plugged it into the charger.

A light tap at my door then it slowly opened as Noah peeked his head inside.

"I saw your light on and thought I heard talking, just thought I would make sure you were alright."

"I'm good, thanks." Another yawn. "That was my friend, Jade."

"Is she single? Is she cute?" He opened the door with his shoulder and watched me with a grin on his face as he waited for my answer. "She lives in Boston. You're unlikely to ever meet her because I'm unlikely to ever see her again." I fought back another yawn. "But yes, she is single, and very cute." I winked just to torment him with the thought of there being a woman that he couldn't have. A frown formed on his face and I laughed.

"You're tired, you should get some rest." He nodded toward the bed that I was already sitting on.

"So I've been told."

“I’ll likely be gone by the time you get up in the morning so I left a key for you on the kitchen counter by the coffee pot. It’s programmed to come on at 8:30 before I leave, but I set it to stay warm until 10. You can come in around 11, when we open, if that gives you enough time to get up and ready?”

“I can go in whenever you go in if you need me to, I don’t mind.” Another big yawn. I was getting irritated and wished they would stop.

“Mia, you’re exhausted and I would rather that you sleep in some and rest. There’s food in the fridge, be sure to eat breakfast and pack a lunch before you go in.”

“Yes, sir.” I mockingly saluted him.

“Cute.” He rolled his eyes.

“I try.” I batted my eyes and tilted my head to play up the part.

“Alright, I’m off to bed. My room is next door, just come get me or bang on the wall if you need anything. The walls are pretty thin so I’ll be able to hear you.”

“Yeah, I know how thin they are.” I gave him a knowing look and watched as the blush crept up his neck.

“My bad.” He chuckled and smiled as he walked out and closed the door behind him.

I scooted over and pulled the blankets down as I slid under them, feeling cozy with the heaviness of the comforter. My head turned as it found the right position on the pillow, and before I knew it, I was fast asleep.

Nine
Damian

"Why the fuck do you call yourself an assistant if you don't actually assist anyone?" I yelled into the phone as I slammed it down and hung up. I had been in the office for 3 hours, yet the only work I had done focused on finding Mia.

I had turned the whiteboard in my office into an information database on what I had collected so far. Unfortunately there was very little on it at this point. I knew that she had made it to Manchester based on the tracking app I had installed on her cell phone, but by the time I had sobered up enough to make the drive, bought a random plane ticket and made it through security, she had just boarded the plane and I missed her. I had grabbed her cell phone from the abandoned armrest and tucked it in my pocket as I caught a glimpse of her as she faded out of sight. The flight information on the board showed she had one layover and was set to arrive in Denver around 11 am, their time. Mia had mentioned when we first met that she was from Colorado but I never bothered to listen when she told me where. Instincts told me that Denver was just another stopping point or a distraction in case I was able to track her that far. She was smart, I had to give her that.

With Mia leaving her cell phone behind, I had no way of physically tracking her anymore. I went home and went through her call logs and texts. I looked for anything that I might have missed when I had been checking on her after she first left. Given that she went back to Colorado, I focused on looking for recent contact with any of her old friends since she didn't have any family. It had surprised me when she left, I never thought she had it in her. On some level, I had hoped that she didn't have it in her. I wasn't looking forward to what would have to come next. If only she would have listened.

I spent the morning calling car rental companies in Denver, checking to see if anyone had rented a car to Mia Stone. There was one who was rather loose with their information but the kid was too stoned to know whether he should give me the information or not. By the end of the conversation he was convinced that I was trying to rent a car and that I go by the name Mia. He thought the secret was that he wasn't supposed to tell anyone that I was a man posing as a woman, dumb ass.

There were two rental car companies left that I hadn't called yet, though I had little hope that they would give me the information that I needed since I had hit so many dead ends. I picked up the phone and started to dial the number when I saw Doris's head bob outside my door before she cracked it open and peeked inside. I couldn't wait until my actual assistant was back from her fuck-fest, aka her honeymoon.

"Mr. Stone?" she asked meekly, her mousy voice made me want to put her head through the wall.

"What?" I snarled, annoyed as I put the phone down and glared at her.

"Mr. Ronnie Stone would like to, um confirm your reservation, um this weekend for the conference in D.C. Will you be bringing your wife?" she asked as she remained hidden behind my door. If I still had my dart board, I could use her head as target practice.

I was so focused on how much she annoyed me that I hadn't heard what she had asked. Or maybe it was the remainder of the bottle of whiskey that made its way into my coffee that kept me distracted. Either way I had no idea what this broad wanted but I was ready for her to go away.

"What?" I asked with annoyance, forcing her to come into the office and closer to my desk. Lovely.

"The conference in D.C. Will you, um, be attending with, um, your wife? Um. Sir?"

Shit! I had forgotten about the fucking conference. Ronnie had just talked about it this morning at the staff meeting and had rambled on for twenty minutes about how it was mandatory as he looked at me when he said it. I didn't have time to go out of town this weekend, nor did I have time to be stuck in D.C for an entire week. I needed to find Mia before I ran out of time and she was gone for good.

"Tell him neither of us will be attending." I shot her a look that told her not to question me about it and she turned and walked out of my office.

I took a few sips of coffee, using my pen to stir it. One big gulp and I felt ready to make the remaining calls. The phone was in my hand as I started to dial the phone number when my office door flung open. Startled, I jumped in my chair, dropping the phone on my desk. Ronnie stood in the doorway glaring at me as his eyes strained not to bulge out of his head. I had seen my uncle angry on numerous occasions, but I rarely saw him like this. He stared me down as he reached behind him and slammed my door shut. Fuck. "What is this that I hear that you're not going to the MANDATORY conference next week in D.C?" he asked as he approached my desk, leaning forward to slam his hands on the end of it.

"I have other things going on that need my attention," I replied as calmly as I could. Ronnie raised me after my dad died and had the unpleasant experience of getting me through my teenage years. He'd always been able to call me on my bullshit and the look on his face said he was about to do so now.

"What do you have going on that needs your attention? You haven't worked an actual case in weeks," he taunted, knowing that I hadn't taken a new case in almost a month. I glanced at the files sitting on my desk and grabbed the file on top of the pile.

"I'm working this case and it's going to need more attention. There's a tight deadline or it will be out of the statute of limitations," I replied as I tossed the file towards him for dramatic effect. I had no fucking clue whose file it was. For all I knew I could be claiming to represent a six-year-old who was suing her brother for ripping her Barbie's head off. I kept my poker face and watched to see what he would do.

He picked up the file and sat in the chair across from me. He leaned back and opened the file, reading the summary of the case. Damn it. My hands started sweating as I reached for my coffee. I was mid reach when he peered up and watched me, guilt forcing me to pull my hand back. It felt sac religious to drink coffee filled with booze while my uncle sat in front of me. Talk about a slap in the face to him after I had sworn to his face 2 years ago that I would stop drinking.

"So you can't go because you're working a case for a crooked cop that was caught red handed helping his wife embezzle from her place of business? An incident that happened 2 months ago. That they have on video," he questioned as he stared at me over the top of the open file. "Seems to me that this is well within the statute of limitations, and quite frankly, an easy case to work given they have proof. Therefore, you're going to the conference. We already paid your way. I just needed to know if Mia was coming so we could make her arrangements as well."

"She won't be attending," I said curtly as I shifted in my seat and adjusted my tie. Suddenly it felt like the room was void of oxygen, the weight of his stare suffocated me.

"Why not?" He leaned forward and sat the file back where I had originally pulled it from.

"She's been under the weather." I lied.

"Well, surely she will be better by this weekend and can attend." He pushed.

"I think she also had plans this weekend. Some gardening show in Boston that she wanted to go to with her friend, Jade." The room grew hotter by the minute as I struggled to stay one step ahead of my uncle. He was purposely pushing for information about Mia and I was determined not to give more than I had to. How would I explain that my battered wife had vanished and that I was trying to find her so I could further silence her?

"What's going on? You're lying to me. What happened with Mia?" He raised his voice and leaned forward to invade more of my space.

"We're having marital problems. I wanted to try to go to counseling and spend next week with her, trying to reconnect. She blames the distance between us on my job and the late hours I've been working." I laid it on as thick as I could, knowing that my uncle would be relieved to hear that I was trying to make my marriage work after he watched my parent's marriage crumble as I was growing up.

He eyed me cautiously as he took in the information.

"Okay. Well, if that's the case." He stood up and pulled at his pant leg, forcing the material back down. He was a short, round man and suits didn't tend to agree with him. "Bring Mia by for lunch on Friday. After I talk with her, if your story pans out, then I'll let you off the hook for the conference. If she's not there for lunch on Friday then be prepared to pack your bags for D.C." He glanced down at my coffee mug and paused to look inside. He shook his head as he walked out of my office and closed the door behind him.

I let out a sigh and sunk back into my chair, relieved that he was gone. How the fuck was I supposed to bring Mia to lunch on Friday when I didn't even know where the fuck she was. I slammed my hand down on my desk in frustration, the pens in the pen holder rattled in response. It looked like I was taking an unwanted and incredibly inconvenient trip to D.C. next week.

<u>Ten</u>
Mia

The sun filtered in through the mini blinds as I rolled over and picked up my phone to check the time. 9:30. I couldn't remember the last time I had slept this late but I was sure it had to have been when I used to live here. Back to old routines I thought as I sat up and stretched. My body was still sore from the other night, though I finally felt more rested. Thankfully sleep came easy to me last night, with Noah in the next room and no sign of Damian knowing where I was.

I stood under the hot water of the shower and allowed it to run over my body as I closed my eyes. For a moment I felt relaxed, and for once, at peace. I thought about my new life and tried hard to focus on making things the best I could this time around. If I stayed focused and cleared my mind, I could purposefully create the life that I wanted.

A shiver ran through me as I felt the water temperature change, a sign I had been in there long enough. I turned the handle to off and slid the glass shower door open to grab a towel. Now that I didn't have the expectation of getting ready and looking a certain way for Damian, I was actually excited to get ready for my first day at my new job.

I decided to wear one of the new outfits I had picked up yesterday, hoping that a new outfit and new hair would continue to make me feel like a new woman. My jean shorts were a dark denim and fit loosely on my hips. I paired them with a white tank top that had a lace overlay on the front, hoping to keep it casual, while still dressing it up a bit. I didn't want to look like a slob or be unprofessional. Noah had mentioned a casual dress code but didn't elaborate any more than that.

My makeup was light, aside from the heaping amount of concealer used to hide the bruises. I tried to keep it from looking caked on and tried to highlight my eyes and lips to take the focus off of the purple bruise on my cheek. Maybe I would get lucky and Noah would have me working in the back where I wouldn't have to see or interact anyone. I'd hate to drive off business for him by scaring them with my beat-up face.

It was 10:30 and I had checked that there was a bus coming at 10:45 that would have me to The Vine by 11:00. I had given Noah the keys to the rental car yesterday before he left for his date. He had friends that were going up to Denver for the week and agreed to take the car back for me so I didn't have to figure out how to get it back. I shoved my phone in my front pocket and tossed the lipstick in my purse as I grabbed the spare key I had found next to the coffee pot this morning, as promised. I locked the door and made my way to the bus stop. It was a warm day, which made me want to sit outside and soak up the sun. Once I got to the bus stop, I closed my eyes and took a deep breath as I enjoyed the warm sun beating down on me while I waited for the bus.

My eyes opened and my head turned to the left as I heard the bus approaching. It screeched to a stop, the old thing grumbled in the process. If I had to bet, it was the same bus I used to ride as a teenager. I waited for the doors to open then boarded the bus as I paid my fare. There were a few seats open toward the back, so I made my way down the aisle and took a seat. I was surprised how many people were on the bus at 10:45 on a Monday morning so I turned to look out the window, avoiding eye contact and any opportunity to make small talk.

The bus inched down the road, stopping every few miles for passengers. There were two stops before the one I needed. I kept my eyes on the road, waiting for the stop before mine so I could stand and be ready to get off at the one I needed. As I stood, the elderly woman seated across the aisle from me looked up and fear flashed across her face. She subtly nodded toward a guy a few feet ahead of us who was standing against the pole with his back turned to his. He had a dark hoodie on with his head covered, which seemed odd given that it was already almost 80 degrees out.

She kept making eye contact with me as she tried to get me to acknowledge that I had seen the man she tried to warn me about. I felt scared as I watched the guy from behind. I had no idea who he was, but I prayed that it wasn't Damian. The bus slowed as it approached my stop and I clutched my purse tighter against my body as I held onto the bar above my head for balance. My body jerked forward from the impact of the stop and as I stepped forward, the man in the hoodie turned around and faced me.

I gasped as my hand went to my mouth, my eyes wide in shock.

"After you." He nodded with his head as his hands stayed in the pockets of his oversized hoodie. It made me wonder what he had in his pocket as I noticed the outline of something other than his hand. I stepped forward and got off the bus as I glanced over my shoulder to see where he had gone. Out of the corner of my eye I saw the dark figure run off into an alley and I let out the breath I had been holding. I was thankful that it wasn't Damian but he scared me nonetheless.

The guy appeared to be in his mid-twenties and had a deep scar across his right cheek. Underneath the hoodie I could make out a tattoo of a snake that wrapped its way around his neck. He had a black eye that was fading and a cut above his eyebrow. While I had been relieved that it wasn't Damian, I was still bothered by the guy and couldn't figure out why. My heartbeat continued to race as I looked for the building I needed.

I looked around at the businesses around me, some familiar from when I lived here, and some that were brand new. There was a vintage looking sign mounted on the outside of a newer looking building that was set back from the street. I squinted against the sun, my hand held up to block some of the glare and read: The Vine. I went in through the wrought iron gate and through a small courtyard that lead to the front entrance. Double doors greeted me as I pulled one open, surprised by how heavy it was. A bell chimed as I walked in and looked around the brewery. The atmosphere was warm and welcoming with a bar counter along the back wall offset by some high-top tables along the opposite wall. In the middle of the room there were long picnic tables with bench seats that filled the majority of the space, and double glass doors to the right that lead out to a beautiful, fully enclosed, outdoor patio. It felt calm and relaxing with cream colored paint on the walls and very strategically placed décor. I immediately knew that Noah's mom was the person responsible for decorating and creating the ambiance, especially after seeing how decorated Noah's guest room was.

A door off to the left of me opened and startled me as Noah walked out. I hadn't paid attention to the door as it blended in with the wall, so it surprised me when he came out of it. There was nothing else on that wall, which made sense given that the room then opened up into the brewery. It was an L shaped room with bathrooms on the opposite wall, close to the entrance.

"Do you need a hand?" I asked as I saw Noah balance a crate with glasses on his hip as he made his way past the door.

"Nah, I'm good. Thanks though." He sat the crate at the end of the bar as I made my way over.

"This place is beautiful, Noah." I continued to look around as I admired the place I was going to be working at. When he first told me that it was a brewery, I had immediately pictured a dark, dingy bar environment.

"Thanks. It feels like home to me, I really enjoy spending my time here. Which is probably a good thing, given how much time I actually end up spending here." He laughed and started unpacking the crate of glasses on the counter behind the bar.

"If you want to go ahead and put your stuff down in the break room, it's the open area at the end of the hall. And there's new hire paperwork that you'll need to complete. Chase should be in his office, it's the second door on the right."

"Chase?" I struggled to pick up my jaw that I was sure had dropped to the floor.
"Yeah...."

I could tell that he knew that he was caught by the way he avoided looking at me and how his sentence dropped off. There it was. The other shoe finally fell. I was nervous and excited at the same time to see Chase, the combination of feelings made me a bit nauseous.

"Noah?" I arched an eyebrow at him as he tried to dodge my glance.

"Did I forget to mention that we are business partners? We bought this place together. Chase handles the operations, including new hire paperwork, and I handle the fun stuff."

"Like flirting with drunk girls every Saturday night?"

"Sometimes they come in on Friday nights too." He winked and my mood lightened some.

I shook my head at him as I pulled my purse over my shoulder and walked to the door that led to the back offices. I didn't hear anything coming from the office as I made my way back to the break room. My plan was to sit my stuff down, get myself together, then go do my paperwork. I was so distracted that I didn't hear someone coming out of the office. Immediately our bodies collided, and I was embraced by strong arms and a broad chest. I didn't have to look up to know whose arms I had just landed in. I would have recognized the smell of his cologne and the feel of his embrace anywhere.

I pulled back and looked up into his dark brown eyes, feeling a flash back of my youth. For a moment it felt as if nothing had changed as he looked at me with concern, which was quickly replaced with a smile as he helped steady me.

"You always knew how to make an entrance," he joked as he stepped back to allow me some space while maintaining a grip on my elbow so I didn't fall. His smile stretched across his face and lit up the room.

"Well, you know me. Always the graceful one," I joked back, making light of how clumsy I was. It was one of those traits that just never left, no matter how hard I tried.

"Welcome back, Mia. It's nice to see you again." He leaned back against the wall, his T-shirt pulled tight as his muscles flexed when he crossed his arms over his chest. His eyes were soft, genuine sincerity in his tone.

"Thanks."

"I have your paperwork ready to go over, whenever you're ready. You can put your stuff in any of the cabinets along the back wall, and feel free to put your lunch in the fridge." He pointed to the cabinets that lined the back wall as he walked into the open space with me. I had anticipated a regular break room with a table, fridge, and microwave but this was an actual kitchen with a full pantry, stove, microwave, fridge, and cabinets. There was a 6-foot table with 8 folding chairs scattered around it and off to the side was a single person restroom. Mounted to the wall across from the table was a decent size tv. To the left of the tv was a door that had a sign above it that said kitchen. I looked at it, confused, since we were technically already in a kitchen.

"We have a small food menu." He nodded toward the kitchen. "Pablo and Maria run the food side, and on occasion, their daughter Isabell fills in for them. They moved here a few years ago and ran a food truck that everyone loved. When we decided to open the brewery, we talked to them about going in together and they jumped on board right away."

"Wow, I had no idea. I thought it was just drinks." I shrugged, not having many details of what the job would actually entail until now.

"They handle all of the food stuff. You'll take the orders and put them into the system, then they'll prepare it and deliver to the tables. So you'll only have to worry about putting the order into the system and handling the drinks. It's pretty easy, I'm sure you'll get the hang of it right away."

"I'm going to head up front to talk to Noah about a few things, but it shouldn't take long. Go ahead and get yourself situated and I'll meet you in my office in a few." He paused to look back over his shoulder. "It's the one you tried to tackle me in front of a few minutes ago." He chuckled and walked down the hallway as I tried to blend in with the walls, hopeful that they would swallow me so he wouldn't see the blush that had turned my entire body a new shade of crimson.

Ten minutes had passed as I sat in Chase's office, admiring the rich colors he had chosen for his office furniture. A mahogany u-shaped desk took the main focus with a high back leather chair situated behind it. There were a few framed landscape photos hung on the wall behind him, enclosed in by floor to ceiling bookcases.

"Sorry, you know Noah, he likes to talk." Chase came around the desk and took his seat on the other side. I found myself fidgeting, nervous about his presence, and folded my hands in my lap.
Chase has always had this effect on me. Regardless of what we were doing or what had been said, I constantly felt so nervous and clumsy around him. It's like when you try to make the best impression you can but instead you make a total ass of yourself. That's me.

We finished the paperwork fairly quickly and Chase didn't ask any questions about the name I was using or the fact that I was using Noah's address, which meant that they had already talked. It made sense, it was business related and they both owned the business. I had no idea how many of the personal details they had discussed as friends. Chase wasn't asking any personal questions so I decided to just assume that he knew everything.

I spent the next few hours working with Noah, learning the computer system and how to enter the food items. The day seemed to go by in the blink of an eye and before I knew it, it was already almost seven. Noah was hustling behind the bar, trying to wait tables, and clean up behind the early dinner crowd that had come in. I jumped in where I could and took over waiting on the new tables as customers came in. Noah seemed pleased and we worked seamlessly until closing time at 9.

"That- was a freaking long day." He sighed as he locked the front double doors and turned the sign in the window to closed.

"Is it always this busy on Mondays?" I finished wiping down the last table and threw the washcloth over the side of the bin I had collected dirty dishes in.
"Yes and no. Right now we're busy with the start of summer break, all of the college kids are celebrating the semester being over before they head out of town for the summer. It'll die down in a few weeks then pick up again a month before the next semester starts. Some kids will stay here the entire summer, which means the weekends will stay busy."

"I'm sorry you ended up staying late, I had planned to get you out around 7," he said apologetically.

"I don't mind. It was nice to feel useful and help out." I pulled a hair tie out of my pocket and pulled my hair up into a ponytail to get it out of my face. "Besides, it looked like you needed the help."

I laughed as I recalled Noah trying to take an order while balancing a pile of plates in the other hand. Every attempt he made to jot down their order on his notepad, the plates would sway and threatened to fall. He had always been stubborn and reluctant to ask for help. Apparently, even with his own employees. I had seen the struggle and grabbed the plates from him on my way to clear another table.

"Well, thank you, I do appreciate the help." He smiled back at me as he worked on closing out the day in the computer system and emptied the cash drawer. I watched as he wrote a few things down on a slip of paper and tucked it in a bank deposit bag along with the cash that was bundled together with a rubber band.

"What else do we need to do?" I looked around, waiting for him to give me more duties.

"That's it, we're pretty much done. We'll grab our stuff from the back, then I'll take you with me to drop off the deposit." He zipped the bag shut as he made his way around the bar and we walked down the hall to the back offices. I grabbed my purse from the cabinet and met Noah in the hallway outside of his office.

We were at the front door and had already turned all of the inside lights off when Noah realized he forgot his cell phone on his desk and had to go back to his office to get it. He handed me the deposit and I heard him walk down the hallway as his steps faded. It was eerily dark outside, with very little light by the front door. I peered up and noticed that one of the lamps by the door had a broken light bulb, which explained the darkness. The other lamp was further away which shed some light, but still left the entrance to the door hidden in shadows.

Out of the corner of my eye I saw a quick movement in the shadows as my heart jumped into my throat. I looked over my shoulder for Noah when I heard a fist bang on the heavy glass of the door and found a man in a hoodie staring at me. His face was covered by the darkness which made it hard to see him.

"Open the door." He pulled his hand out of the pocket of his hoodie and pointed a gun at me.

"Now."

Terror flooded through me as I stared at the gun, unable to react to what had happened. My fingers trembled as they gripped the deposit bag tighter, his eyes watched my every movement. I waited for him to lift his head, even half an inch, so I could see if it was Damian. It had to be Damian, who else would be here, pointing a gun at me and demanding that I let them in? I knew he would find me.

My breaths came hurriedly as my ears echoed the sound of my racing heartbeat. His eyes flickered to look at something behind me, something that caught his attention. I was too afraid to move, paralyzed where I was. I waited for him to pull the trigger and for it to be over. I closed my eyes and waited. Any minute now and my life would be over. He would make sure of it.

I felt footsteps behind me and in a swift movement I was pushed out of the way and shoved behind a large plant in a ceramic pot by the doors.

"What the fuck are you doing here, Jimmy?" Noah continued to block me from seeing what was happening. Who was Jimmy? I slowly tilted my head to the side to try to see what was happening. Did Noah mistake Damian for someone else? I had to warn him, he had no idea what he was up against. I started to push forward when I felt Noah reach back and push me further back against the wall.

"Just give me the bag."

Bag? What bag? What was happening? I arched my back as I leaned back as far as I could and peeked through the plant leaves. They were big and thick, which provided good coverage to keep me hidden, but also made it hard for me to see anything.

"You know damn well that you're not getting the bag. You're not getting a damn thing other than a bullet in your ass if you ever come back here again." Noah reached behind him and I saw him pull a black handgun from the back of his jeans. He hid his hands down by his side as I watched him mess with the gun, all while keeping his eyes on the man. I glanced down at the bank deposit bag in my hand. I had completely forgotten about it until now.

"I ain't playin man. Just give me the fucking bag. You don't want that girl to get hurt- do you? Cause that's all on you man. You know ima take it from her the second her skinny ass steps out this door, yo." The guy started bouncing around and wiped at his nose with his free hand. The hoodie had shifted back off of his face and I gasped when I saw the scar on his cheek and the snake tattoo on his neck. It was the guy from the bus this morning.

"Look Jimmy, I'm getting real tired of your punk ass. I'm gonna give you 10 seconds to get your high as fuck loser ass off of my property." Noah turned to whisper to me while he kept Jimmy in his sight.

"Go call 911 and ask them to send Lieutenant Dickson. Let them know his kid is out and causing trouble here. Just tell them it's The Vine, they know where it's at." He nodded toward the office and I slowly crept along the side of the wall, staying out of sight, as I made my way to the phone.

I hated leaving Noah by himself with a crazy person who was high on drugs and had a gun. Noah seemed to know the guy and apparently kept a gun on himself, so I did as I was told. My heart was still racing as I sat in Noah's chair, unsure of what else to do. I couldn't go back up there and risk the guy seeing me and going crazy. That wouldn't be smart.

Ten minutes later I heard voices upfront and made my way up to the front.

"Sorry about the hassle, Noah. I wasn't told he had been released. He's predictable so my guess is that he wasn't out for long."

"No problem, Lieutenant. Just happy that no one got hurt."

I slowly walked up to where Noah was talking to a tall, muscular man, wearing sweats. My guess was that it was the Lieutenant. I felt his eyes take me in, unsure of who I was and why I was stalking around. He appeared to be in his fifties or sixties, though his physical appearance looked like that of a twenty-year-old.

"Hey." Noah stepped to the side as I stood beside him. "Lieutenant Dickson, this is Amelia. Amelia, this is Lieutenant Dickson."

I reached out and shook his hand as I offered Noah the deposit bag back. I felt uncomfortable holding onto it when I had just barely started that day, and it had already been the source of drama with the Lieutenant's son.

"How about I give you two an escort over to the bank for the deposit?" He nodded at the bag as Noah took it.

"Nah, it's okay. We will be fine taking it. I'm showing Mia the ropes tonight but she won't be doing any of the night deposits. I'll still be the only one who handles them."

"It's the least I can do for what happened."
Noah smiled in acceptance as we followed the Lieutenant out and Noah locked the doors. The bank was literally across the parking lot so the escort consisted of him walking the short distance with us as he kept watch while Noah showed me how to slide the deposit bag into the night drop box on the outside of the bank. A loud thud echoed as we heard the bag land in the bottom of the box. I pulled the handle to open it one more time and looked inside, just to make sure it had really made it in. Noah chuckled as we walked back through the parking lot, said goodbye to the Lieutenant, and got into Noah's 4Runner.

The first day had plenty of ups and downs and I felt exhausted. We stopped and grabbed dinner through a drive thru on our way home, both of us too tired to go sit down somewhere. Once we got home, I felt more relaxed as we ate our food and talked about old times growing up. He gave me the back story on Jimmy who had been in and out of the system since he was sixteen. Given that his dad was the Lieutenant, you would think that it would make Jimmy stop getting into trouble, but it seemed to only make it worse. Jimmy wasn't afraid of the law, he was however afraid of his father. Noah continued to explain that Buck was also a body builder and had won numerous competitions, which explained his physique. Everyone in town knew Jimmy's past and when they saw him pop up around town, they didn't bother calling the police anymore. A call to Buck, and Jimmy was dealt with. Noah assured me that he would be locked up again, given that he was a felon in possession of a firearm. He wasn't the smartest and made no efforts to stay out of the system.

It felt normal getting back into the swing of small-town living where everyone ended up knowing your business, whether you wanted them to or not. While I desperately wanted to keep my business hidden, I didn't anticipate too many people would actually ask about it. There would be general questions about what life was like in Boston, and why I had decided to come back, other than that, no one would care about the other details. If I could lay low for a little while longer, that was all I would need to get my new life started on the right foot.

Eleven
Mia

I tilted my head back as Chase kissed his way down my neck, slowly moved over my shoulder, and down towards my breast. A shiver ran through me as I ran my hand through his hair and took in the scent of his aftershave. Our bodies were desperate to find each other, hands reaching for whatever they could find. I lifted my head and looked into his eyes, wishing he would fill the emptiness I've felt inside for so long now.

Our lips touched, a gentle kiss as he held his muscular body on top of mine. I watched as he slid his boxers off, his gaze steady on mine as he waited for a sign that I might change my mind. I smiled and licked my lips, confirming this was what I wanted. His smile spread across his face almost as quickly as he made his way back up on the bed and positioned himself next to me. This was it, this was the moment I had been fantasizing about since I was a teenager.

I jolted up in bed, a noise outside startled me awake. Noah's door opened and his footsteps faded quickly past my room as I heard him go to the front door. I got out of bed and opened my door, peeking into the hallway to try to hear what had happened. Noah came back down the hallway a few minutes later, his cell phone in one hand and his gun in the other. I would have thought that it would bother me with Noah always having his gun on him, but it actually made me feel safer.

"The neighbors next door are out of town and they forgot to put their trashcan in the garage before they left. Looks like it got knocked over. Probably a bear looking for food."

"Scared the hell out of me. I was sound asleep and that was a hostile awakening." I remembered the dream I was having about Chase and felt my cheeks flush. Noah quirked an eyebrow in response. He missed nothing.

"Good dreams?" The smirk on his face made me blush even more. It was impossible for him to know what they were about, and I hated that he could read me so well to know that I was embarrassed. His eyes quickly darted down to my chest and I looked down to find that in my time of need, my nipples had very pointedly betrayed me. I crossed my arms over my chest in an attempt to hide them. It wasn't cold so I couldn't blame it on that.

"Assuming that we are safe from hungry bears, I'm going back to bed." I tried to play it cool as I turned on my heel and walked toward the bed.

"Yeah, I'm sure you're eager to get back to that dream. Don't worry, I won't tell Chase that you were calling his name while you were sleeping. Wouldn't want his ego to get any bigger." He winked and tapped the wall a few times with his knuckles before walking to his room, closing his door behind him.

I walked over and closed my door, mortified that not only had I said Chase's name out loud while I was asleep, but Noah had heard it! The dream was random and I had no idea where it came from, but I definitely wasn't ready to analyze it with someone else knowing that it had happened. It made it even harder to forget now that Noah knew. I sat on the bed and brought my knees up to my chin as I hung my head in embarrassment.

The dream was good, I would admit that. It was damn good. A part of me wondered what it would really be like to be with Chase. Would he be as smooth as I had dreamt he was? Would he say the right things and do the things that would send me over the edge? For years I had wondered what it would be like to be with him, but then I met Damian and I put those thoughts out of my mind.

There was an unknown tension that I felt coursing through my body as I thought more about the dream. While part of it was physical from the dream being so arousing, there was a part of it that was mental and I couldn't figure out how I really felt about everything. I hadn't thought of another man since before I met Damian, and regardless of what he thought, I hadn't been flirting with anyone. I barely even noticed that they existed. While I didn't get much attention or affection from Damian, I also wasn't seeking it out.

It had been such a long time since I had a man show me any attention, I couldn't remember what it felt like. Maybe that was why the dream had made such an impression on me. A longing that I've had for years to be seen, and even more so, to be wanted. Something that no one had tried to fulfill. I felt guilty for wanting that from another man when I was a married woman. But on the flip side, I was married to a man who was trying to kill me, so I guess it wasn't the worst thing in the world to want to find someone who at least liked me.

Now that my mind had allowed these thoughts of Chase to enter it, I couldn't get rid of them. I wanted to see him. I wanted to flirt with him. A part of me wanted to be a free woman and not be tied to Damian anymore. A huge part of me wanted to explore what kind of woman I really was. I had been living a lie for so long, always focused on being who Damian wanted me to be, that I never allowed myself to discover who I really was.

I laid down and rolled onto my side, the clock on my cell phone showed it was 3 in the morning. My mind was overwhelmed with thoughts of Chase as I slowly drifted back to sleep.

****

It was after 8:00 Saturday night and it had started to pick up a little as the college crowd made their way in. There was a group of guys that had come in and took over 3 of the high-top tables in the back. They were laughing and joking, all putting on a show for the table of girls that were at one of the long tables across from them. Shortly after, four girls in short dresses and stilettos joined the guys and their attention was redirected as the other girls finished up and left. I vaguely remembered those days and part of me regretted that I settled down with Damian so quickly and never got to fully embrace that part of growing up.

I wiped down the bar for what felt like the millionth time. Not because it needed it but because I was constantly running out of things to do. Noah had taken the tables on the patio and I was given the tables inside, but so far there was only the one group and they already had their drinks so I was stuck killing time until more tables were occupied. As I worked my way from one end of the bar to the other, I looked up to see Chase walk in. He was off tonight so I wondered if he was here to talk to Noah, or if he ended up coming in to work. It was my first Saturday working and I hadn't figured the dynamics out in the time I had been there. I was just thankful that this Saturday was a lot better than last Saturday. It felt like more time had passed, things had happened so quickly. Part of me wondered where Damian was and if he was still looking for me. It felt unsettling that I hadn't heard anything from him and for a moment, I prayed that I had been better at hiding than I originally gave myself credit for.

One of the guys pulled out a barstool and slid it in Chase's direction. I watched as his eyes met mine as he pulled one leg up and over the stool in a fluid motion. The movement reminded me of the movements he had done in my dream and I felt my cheeks flushing again. I lowered my eyes and tried to escape the feel of his eyes on me. Noah came in from outside and made his way around the bar to work on closing out a tab. I smiled as he walked past me to the computer in the corner, his head quickly glancing in Chase's direction where my attention was still focused.

One of the girls at the table kept trying to get his attention and finally gave up when he refused to look her way when she called his name, over and over and over. Quite frankly, it annoyed me as well so I didn't blame him for ignoring her. I watched as she stood up, ran her hands down her leopard print dress that was painted to her body, and flung her red curly hair over her shoulder as she walked around the tables to where he was sitting. His eyes shifted to look my way before he looked at her. I knew Chase well enough to know the look on his face. But that also didn't make me any less jealous of this woman who was being so forward and aggressive with getting his attention.

Little miss provocative tramp, in her 5-inch heels, leaned in and whispered something in his ear. I watched as she brushed her lips against his ear and saw the way she pushed her breasts so they touched his arm. I rubbed the cleaning towel on the counter in circles as I worked to clean a water ring that had formed. It was far from dirty, but the ring had been driving me crazy.

Chase allowed her to continue whispering in his ear as his arm reached up and touched her elbow. She adjusted her body and angled it toward his, allowing him to lower his hand and grab her ass. I watched intently as I waited to see what Chase would do. What could she possibly be telling him that is taking so long?

Probably telling him all of the slutty things she wants to do for him. I rolled my eyes. I don't know if I was still annoyed with the other woman or annoyed with myself for how jealous I was acting. It wasn't like Chase had ever expressed any interest in me. If anything, I was mad because I felt he was cheating on me, when the only time we ever had a moment was in a freaking dream. I needed to stop watching and just focus my attention elsewhere but I found it impossible to stop watching.

 I watched as the girl slid her hand up Chase's arm as he leaned in to talk to her. The way he's reacting to her made me wonder if they were an item or if they had ever dated. Chase seemed really comfortable with her now, a smile on his face with something she said. Why wouldn't he be dating someone? Chase was a sexy man, with a wonderful personality. I didn't have to stay in Haven Brook to know that all of the women were still lined up for their chance to be with him. I chewed on the inside of my lip as I continued to wipe the same spot on the counter as I watched him.

"You know, if that doesn't get that spot clean, let me know and I'll just get a new countertop." Noah shoulder bumped me as he nodded at where my hand was still rubbing the towel in circles. I watched as he walked past me to go say hi to the group at the table. Chase smiled when Noah approached and gently pushed the girl away from his ear. The look on her face confirmed she wasn't pleased about being interrupted. She looked Noah up and down and continued to glare at him as she made her way back to her chair at the other end of the table. She sat down and began talking to the other girls as Noah said something to Chase that made him look in my direction.

Embarrassed for getting caught and frustrated for being so easily attracted to Chase I decided to take a much-needed break and walked to the back. I needed to clear my head and get away from the thoughts of Chase from last night. It was just a dream, so why wouldn't it just go away already?

I decided to clean the bathrooms which meant that I needed to get the supplies from the top shelf in the break room. I pulled one of the chairs over and used it to help me reach everything except the glass cleaner that was sitting too far back and out of my reach.

"Need a hand?" Chase offered. I jumped at the sound of his voice, I hadn't heard him come down the hall and didn't know anyone else was in the room with me.

"Nope, I've got it." Reluctant to accept any help, I reached as far forward as I could and grunted as I grabbed the bottle of glass cleaner. The amount of force it took to reach the glass cleaner was enough to rock the chair beneath me. My eyes went wide as I watched the chair wobble beneath me.

In an instant Chase was by my side as he grabbed the chair to hold it steady. He had one hand holding the chair down and his arm wrapped around my waist. I looked down at him, a gasp escaping my throat due to the sudden physical contact. Something changed inside of him as well as I felt his hand twitch and his eyes shift.

"Need help down?" he offered as he continued to wrap his arm around me.

"I think I'm good but thank you." I attempted to turn around to step off of the chair, not much room to work with. His arm moved down slightly and was almost to where it was wrapped around my ass instead of my waist as he looked at me for me to change my mind and accept his help. I realized that if I continued to turn around and tried to get down, it would force his hand to be on my ass now instead of my waist. Apparently, Chase realized the same thing as he lowered his hand even further, watching for my reaction.

"You're impossible." I decided to avoid the opportunity for any kind of contact with Chase and swatted his hand away as I squatted and got off of the chair.

"And why is that?"

"Any opportunity for you to grab some ass. Trying to act like you're being a good guy and do a nice thing but yet all you're really thinking about is your ulterior motives."

"Hey, I was just trying to help a friend so she didn't fall on her ass." He raised his hands up in self-defense.

"Please, I've known you long enough to know that look in your eye. Always the ladies' man. I'm sure that girl up front is still waiting to jump your bones." I knew the second that I said it, I would regret it. Any jealousy or insecurities I had, I just laid them out in front of him. Put everything out there for him to start asking questions about why I would even care.

I turned around with the cleaning supplies in my hands to see Chase leaned back against the counter, arms folded across his chest, with one foot crossed over the other. Damn him for making everything look sexy.

"I really get to you, don't I?"

"What would make you say that?" I turned away from him, hoping that my face had returned to its pale color instead of the scarlet hue I was sure was still lingering around.

"In all of the years that I've known you, I've never known you to be so feisty with me. It's like you've got all of this extra tension built up and you're needing a release." He waited for me to look at him. I was going to kill Noah if he had told Chase about last night. It was embarrassing enough already, I didn't need Noah telling Chase about it. And Chase had to know, why else would he be acting this way with me right now? This wasn't like him.

 "I could help with that you know?"

"I hate to break it to you, Sparky, but you couldn't be more wrong. And even if I was in need of a *release*, you're the last person I would be coming to." I tried to muster as much sarcasm as I could. It was hard to convince someone else when you know that you're lying. Even more so when you know that the other person knows that you're lying.

"You can call it what you want to Mia, but there's a chemistry between us. I feel it and I know that you feel it. Sooner or later you'll give in. And trust me, not only will you be coming to me for the release, you'll be coming for me."

"I can't believe Noah. When did he tell you about the dream?"

"What dream?" His interest piqued as he pushed off from the counter and walked toward me.

Shoot.

"It was nothing." I chewed my bottom lip as I forced myself to rearrange the supplies that I had been messing with on the table while trying to avoid looking at him.

"What dream?"

I blew out a long breath and looked up at him. He had a coy grin on his face as he waited for me to tell him about the dream. Over my dead body. There was no way that I was going to tell him that I had a sex dream about him. No thank you, I didn't need that kind of embarrassment, followed by immediate rejection.

"I'm waiting."

"I had a dream last night. And you were in it. End of story." I squared my shoulders as I said it, an attempt to make myself feel stronger towards him and not give in and tell him.

"What was I doing in the dream?"

"Will you just let it go? It was just a dream."

"Sounds like it was a good dream if it's got you this wound up."

"Are you doing that thing, where Noah tells you something- then you pretend that he didn't tell you so you can try to make me tell you myself?" I folded my arms over my chest, matching his stance.

He stayed silent as his eyes remained focused on me. He was purposely trying to make me squirm and to get information out of me. There was no way that Noah hadn't told him something about my feelings for him. Either as a teenager, or now. That had to be what this was about.

"Noah hasn't told me anything, Mia."

"Then why are you being so---- whatever this is?" I was reluctant to say flirty, what if I was reading too much into this? What if I was trying to force this to be something that I wanted, instead of something that it was?

"Interested? Flirting? Forward? Which word do you want me to use?"

"Whichever one is the truth." I licked my lips, a nervous habit I've had since I was a little girl.

"All of them are the truth. Noah didn't tell me anything. You did."

I thought back to when I might have accidentally said something to him that would elude to me being interested in him. Nothing came to mind. He wasn't at the house when Noah heard me through the wall.

Unless Noah told him, which he kept saying that he didn’t, I didn’t know how Chase knew.

“What are you talking about?”

“I have a gift, Mia. I always have. It’s the natural ability to know when a woman is interested in me. And your body language has been doing a lot of talking.” He stepped closer, the air around us changed.

“You watched me tonight when you thought I wasn’t looking. You were engaged in what you saw, jealous of another woman who was talking to me. You didn’t pull away when I touched you earlier. You blush constantly around me. And your nervous habits go into full force when I get close to you.” He ran a finger over my lip as I chewed the bottom of it, freeing it.

“I know that you have barely been back almost a week and that you are going through something really difficult and traumatic. I’m not going to be a dick and try to make the moves on you until you’re ready. I respect you, Mia, and I know that when you’re ready- and you will be ready- we can try and see where things go. For now, I’m here for you as a friend, as family, as whatever you need me to be. But don’t allow yourself to be embarrassed about what you’re feeling. It’s okay to allow yourself to be attracted to me. It’s okay to want to explore how you feel about things. I know that you’re still technically married, but you owe it to yourself to decide what you want and make that your priority moving forward.”

The conversation took a completely different turn than what I could have ever imagined. Chase knew me better than anyone did when we were growing up. He always knew my nervous habits and knew when I was lying. I felt blindsided by hearing him admit that there could be something between us. How long had he been interested? Was he only interested because he thought I was? There were so many thoughts floating around in my head, I tried to make sense of them when I saw him grinning at me.

“You better get back up front or Noah is going to think we’re back here having sex on his desk.”

“Why would he think that?” I looked up at him with confusion. If they hadn’t been talking about what Noah knew, then why would he say that?

“Because I threatened to fuck you on his desk after he sprung it on me that he had hired you." Chase walked past me and went back up front while I was left in the breakroom with his words floating around me.

Twelve
Chase

I sat at an empty table on the patio while Noah cleared the glasses from the tables that had just left. It was almost closing time and I wasn't ready to leave just yet. I spun the bottle cap from my beer on the table and watched it spin in circles as I glanced over my shoulder to check on Mia. She spent the rest of the night avoiding me as she took care of the tables inside. In an effort to escape Nadia, I came outside to hang out with Noah as he worked.

"Man, that girl really has a thing for you." Noah sat the last glass down in the bin and lifted it off of the table as he wiped it down.

"Who?"

"The red head that was all up on you when I walked in earlier."

"Nadia." I let out a sigh as I peeked around the wall and saw her still sitting at the table I left her at earlier. The majority of the group had left and she stayed behind with a few of the guys. Either she was trying to make me jealous of the other guys, or she was hanging around to see if I would take her home with me. I didn't care either way, my mind was still on Mia.

"Wow, how many girls were all up on you tonight?" Noah joked as he looked up at me with a knowing look on his face.

"None, just her." I dodged his stare.
"Oh, so that's why you had to ask which one?"

"And why did you disappear to the back after Mia went on her break?" I heard the judgmental tone in his voice, asking what he already knew.

I looked at him but stayed silent. He met my silence with his own as he gave me a judgmental look.

"Look, like I said before- just stay off of my desk." He shifted the bin as he added another dirty glass and looked at me. I tried to keep the smile off my face but it was relentless.

"So, Mia said you knew about the dream she had?" I figured now was as good of a time as any to probe and see what I could find out.

"Did she tell you about the dream?" He arched an eyebrow.

"She said that you would tell me."

"Oh really? I find that hard to believe."

"Why's that?" I leaned forward in my chair, hoping that he would give me some insight into what the dream was about. It was killing me to know that she had a dream about me and no one would tell me what it was about. And by the way she reacted to me knowing about it, I knew it had to be dirty.

"Because Mia nearly died of embarrassment when she found out that I knew what kind of dream it was. She didn't give me the details, and quite frankly, I didn't want to know." Noah rotated the bin to his other hip and walked toward the doors that led inside.

"I have plenty of sex to keep me entertained, I don't need to hear about either of your fantasies. If I were you, I wouldn't bug her about telling you about the dream."

"Why not?" I stood up to follow him inside.

"Because I would hate for her illusion of how great you were in her dream be tarnished by how cocky and egotistical you are in real life. She's not like the other girls that are always chasing you, you need to remember that." He opened the door and I followed him inside as I let that information sink in.

Noah was right, Mia was not like the other girls. She was in a class all on her own and that's what made her so alluring. I was tired of the girls that were always chasing after me. It might have been flattering when I was in high school but not anymore. Sure, I could have almost any girl, any time I wanted her, but that didn't mean anything to me.

I wanted someone who was a challenge for me. Someone who kept me on my toes. Someone who would make me work harder for things. Someone who would push me past my limits. Someone who would force me out of my comfort zone. Someone like Mia. Maybe it was the fact that I couldn't have her that made me want her, but deep down I felt like it was more than that. I had a crush on Mia as we were growing up, but that was adolescent teenage hormones mixed in with a hot teenage girl always around.

Noah locked the front doors while Mia was busy closing out the register and prepared the deposit for Monday. I watched as she worked, fascinated with everything she did. She kept her head down as she looked over the reports she had printed and pulled a pen from the messy bun she had put her hair into after the last customer left. A small strand of hair curled behind her ear as it laid on her neck.

She stood at the register, the report in one hand and the pen in the other. Frustration showed on her face as she absentmindedly tapped the pen on the counter. She shifted her weight and I took notice of how small but curvy her body was. Her jean shorts were loose to where they hung low on her hips but not too baggy where she looked sloppy. Just baggy enough that I could easily slide them off without any effort. She had a white tank top underneath a short-sleeved button-down plaid top that was left open. It was a sexy mix of country paired with city girl.

"Noah, I can't get the totals to match. Are all of the sales in the system?" she called out to Noah as he made his way over to the register.

He took the report from her and looked over the last few pages as she watched over his shoulder.

"Sorry, it looks like I forgot to close out the last tab. Let me do that real quick and then I'll reprint the report. We should be fine after that." He entered a few things in the computer as I watched Mia walk down the hall to grab the new report that he had printed.

"You know you don't have to stay, Chase," he called over his shoulder to me. I had sat at one of the high-top tables and purposely avoided leaving right away as I saw Nadia's car still in the parking lot.

"I'm killing some time."

"Is she still outside?"

"Who's outside?" Mia asked as she made her way back to the counter and handed Noah the report. She looked at me as she waited for an answer.

"Some girl he's trying to avoid. She doesn't want to take no for an answer." Noah emptied the cash drawer into the deposit bag and added the reports to the others Mia had originally printed.

"Oh, poor Chase, can't escape the women throwing themselves at him. It must be so hard having every woman wanting you." I was surprised to hear the cattiness in her voice but I liked that she was still jealous of Nadia.

"Not every woman." I looked up at her and met her eyes. She looked surprised and taken aback by my remark.

"Yeah, the elderly ones don't care too much for him." Noah tried to cut the tension as he walked past us and went to put the deposit in the safe.

Mia and I were alone for a few minutes and I desperately wanted to take advantage of the time I had with her. I got up from the table and walked towards her. Her eyes grew bigger as she watched me invade her personal space. I wanted to take things slow and not overwhelm her. I needed her to trust me, to know that I wasn't going after her because I was bored with my options. I wanted her to know that I was genuine and sincere.

"Mia, I'm sorry if I was too forward with you earlier. I never meant to make you uncomfortable." I stood in front of her and made sure she looked at me so she could see the truth in my eyes.

"Thank you." She shifted her weight as she folded her arms across her chest then immediately unfolded them. She was fidgeting and I found it interesting that she was so nervous around me. She could deny that she wasn't feeling anything for me but her body language told a completely different story.

"You guys ready to go?" Noah turned the lights above us off as he waited by the front door.

I walked behind Mia as we walked into the parking lot and saw Nadia's car waiting for me. I sighed as I ran a hand through my hair, I had no energy to deal with her tonight. I had purposely ignored her texts and calls while she was gone after she hung up on me last weekend. I wasn't one to play games, I didn't care how good the sex might be.

Noah and Mia looked at the car and then over at me. I rolled my shoulders a few times as I looked at the car. I felt Mia's hand take mine as she walked with me to my truck. I had no idea what she was doing but decided to just go with it.

"See you tomorrow, Noah." she called as he walked to his SUV, looking just as confused as I was. She walked to the passenger side of the truck, which faces Nadia's car, and leaned in close to me.

"Open the door and help me in. Be sure to run your hand over my ass as you help me in," she instructed as she waited for the door to open.

The truck was lifted so she needed help getting in either way, however I was more than pleased to follow her command as I helped her in and glided my hand over her ass. The feel of her skin felt hot against mine as I tried to etch this memory before it could fade.

Out of the corner of my eye I saw Nadia's car still parked and knew she was watching us. Her lights flipped on and cast a light around us. I looked back to Mia who was looking past me at Nadia. I was about to close her door when she turned her body toward me and grabbed my shirt to pull me closer to her.

She opened her legs to allow my body to be close to hers as she reached up and wrapped her arms around my neck. I held onto her thighs as I watched her eyes, trying to figure out what she was doing. Her hands gently pushed my head down as our lips met in a soft kiss. I felt her body tense the moment we made contact and tried to pull away. Her hold around my neck got tighter as she opened her mouth further.

I heard an engine start and knew that Nadia had left as she revved it as she passed us. If she was mad before, she was even more pissed now. I slowly moved my hands up Mia's thighs and let them gently wrap around her waist. I could feel her pulling away from the kiss as she released her hands from my neck.
I stepped back and allowed her some space as I looked at her to try to get a feel for how she was feeling. I had no idea what had just happened, but I wasn't about to complain. That kiss was completely unexpected and took me by surprise.

"You looked like you needed a little help getting rid of her." Her voice was quiet and shaky. I knew she was trying to process what had just happened.

"Thanks, I do appreciate the help." I had no idea what to say. I didn't want to be an ass and make it seem like I didn't welcome the kiss, but I also didn't want to take advantage of her and keep going if she wasn't interested.

I never really thought about what it would feel like to kiss Mia. I'm sure whatever I would have imagined it would have been like, would be a disappointment compared to what it was actually like. Her lips were soft and she tasted sweet.

"Um, so Noah just left and the buses don't run this late, do you mind giving me a ride home?" She looked up at me and I wished I could kiss her again. "I mean, you do kind of owe me." There was a teasing tone to her voice which made me relieved that she wasn't overthinking what had just happened.

"You saved me from having to deal with a crazy chick tonight, I owe you more than just a ride home." I waited for her to pull her legs in before I closed her door and made my way around to the driver's side. I smiled as I got in, my night just got a whole hell of a lot better.

Thirteen
Mia

I climbed the second flight of stairs and walked down the hallway until I found apartment 825. The apartment complex was larger than I had expected and was relatively new. I got lucky when an apartment opened at last minute and I was able to secure it with the money I had saved from my first paycheck. I was even luckier that it was fully furnished so I didn't have to worry about buying furniture.

I turned the key in the lock and opened the door to my new home. It was bright and airy inside with white walls and an open floor plan. As I stepped inside I found an island to my left with cabinets along the wall. There wasn't much in the kitchen and it was rather small, but I was thankful that it had a full-size fridge, stove, and dishwasher. I didn't need much counter or cabinet space. Off to my right was a linen closet. I opened it to look inside, feeling silly that I still checked behind closed doors.

The kitchen flowed into the living room which had a tv mounted to the wall directly across from the door. There was a plush couch and an armchair by the wooden coffee table that sat in the middle of the room. Just past the end of the couch was a sliding glass door that led out to a balcony. I could picture myself enjoying a few dinners sitting out on the balcony, watching the sunset.

I shifted the bags on my arms as I made my way down the hallway that led back to the master bedroom, guest bedroom, and bathrooms. It was a short hall with the master bedroom on the left, the guest bedroom on the right, and an extra bathroom at the end. I walked into the master bedroom and sat my bags down on the bed. There wasn't much in them, just the items that I had collected and brought with me from Noah's. He had offered to help me move and I laughed as I held up the bags that I had and assured him it was really just a one-person type of job.

I looked around, taking in the bedroom that I would be sleeping in. To the left was a king-sized bed with a cushioned headboard and a white down comforter that looked like it belonged in a plush hotel suite. There were two nightstands, one on each side of the bed, and a long dresser that stood against the wall across from the bed and was big enough to store all of my belongings.

I walked through the room and opened the closet that was partially hidden behind the bedroom door. It was a small walk-in closet but big enough to hold the clothes I had when I lived in Boston. I walked past the bed and made my way into the master bathroom. There was a shower tub combo in the corner, a toilet right next to it, and a vanity with a large mirror and sink that took up the majority of the space, but still gave me plenty of space for me to get ready in the morning.

It was still early in the day so I took a look around at what had been provided, and what I needed to get. I had the basic toiletries from living with Noah, but I wanted to get my own towels and sheets to make it feel more comfortable. By noon everything was unpacked and I had my list of things I needed to get. I grabbed my keys and tucked my cell phone in my pocket as I made my way down the stairs and into the parking lot.

Part of what attracted me to these apartments was that it was a new development so everything was modern and not likely to break. My apartment had a small washer and dryer added in the guest bathroom which meant I didn't have to constantly take my laundry anywhere, and it was walking distance to both The Vine and General Bob's.

The store was busier than I expected for a Saturday at noon. I made my way through the store, collecting the items on my list. I was almost giddy when I found an entire aisle of clearance home goods and grabbed some other items that I wanted. The towels that I picked were a charcoal color and on sale, the sheets were buy 1 get 1 half off. I had completely forgotten the bargain deals I used to love coming here for when I was growing up.

I added a small coffee maker, coffee, and some creamer, in addition to a handful of groceries to get me through the week. I had been tracking the cost of everything as I went, making sure I wasn't going over what I actually had to spend. I glanced down at the calculator on my phone and added on what I guessed would be the tax. I should still have $60 extra from what I budgeted, thanks to all of the clearance items. I was almost to the line to check out when I saw a display with different wines and decided to stop. I browsed each of the bottles, admiring the artwork on each one as I ran my hand over the label. I was about to put the bottle back when I heard a voice behind me.

"Didn't peg you for a merlot kind of girl. Figured you would prefer the sweeter wines."

I turned around to find Chase standing behind me, a handheld cart balanced across his forearm. His smile beamed across his face as he waited for my response. "I was just admiring the artwork." I put the wine back on the shelf and turned back to my cart. I had been trying to avoid Chase for a full week after we kissed in the parking lot. Okay, so maybe WE didn't kiss. I kissed him. And told him to grab my ass. Now I was wishing I could just open the wine right there and stick a straw in it.

"It's a good wine. You would probably like the Moscato, it has a nice flavor and is pretty sweet."

"Okay, I didn't peg you for a sweet wine kind of guy." I rested my arms on the handle of the cart, unsure of what to do with myself. I hated that he made me so nervous. It was like going through puberty all over again.

"I drink it on occasion, depends on whose company I'm in." He smiled and I knew that he meant it depended on what girl he was with. As much as I didn't want to be, I was jealous again.

Not knowing what else to say I started pushing my cart around the display.

"Well, guess I'll see you around." I started walking past him when I heard his footsteps beside me.

"Noah said you got settled in your apartment today." He said it more as a statement than a question.

"Yeah, just getting the few things I need and I should be all set." I nodded toward the basket of my cart that was filled with more than what I actually needed.
"How about a housewarming dinner?" he offered as he kept pace with me as I made my way to the check out and got in line.

I didn't know what to say to his invite. I wanted to spend time with him but I didn't know if could trust myself not to make an ass out of myself again. There was this weird tension between us and I didn't think it would be a good idea for us to be alone together until it was gone. I was sure he was only interested because I had led him on last weekend. I sighed heavily as I remembered the details and the softness of his lips.

"Why don't you take some time to think about it and after you're all settled in, you can let me know when and we'll do dinner. I can even cook. Just let me know, no rush." I could see him backing off as he said it, a look of rejection on his face. I hated that I had caused that look.

"Okay, sounds good. Thanks." I smiled as I moved forward in the line and Chase walked off as he waved goodbye. Relief flooded me that I didn't have to worry about messing things up with him but I also felt disappointed that I didn't get to spend time with him. I paid for my stuff and made my way back to the apartment with bags lined up both arms. Note to self- only buy what you're able to easily carry back to your apartment. Times like this I missed having the rental car but was also relieved when Noah had one of his friends take it back to Denver to return it for me so I didn't have to keep paying for it.

It was almost one thirty and I had an hour before I had to leave for work. I threw in a quick load of laundry to wash the new linens and made myself lunch as I sat on the balcony and watched traffic go by. It was so peaceful and relaxing that I almost lost track of time. I glanced at my phone and checked the time. As I was getting up to take my plate inside I saw a text message pop up from Jade.

Jade: yoga?

I smiled at her text message and our new code word for Damian.

Mia: No yoga. You?

I waited as I watched the three dots bounce across the screen.

Jade: No yoga for me either. Talk later?

Mia: I get off at 10, talk then?

Jade: 10 it is.

I slid my phone in my pocket as I cleaned up my mess and went to work.

Fourteen
Damian

"It's been almost three weeks. THREE. FUCKING. WEEKS! Why haven't you found her yet?" I slammed my hands down on my desk as I stared at the pathetic client in front of me.

"Damian, I've told you that it's not that easy. For one- I'm not active on the force. Remember, that little thing about me being fired for embezzlement? That means no one wants to talk to or help a dirty cop. I have a few contacts that I can ask for help, but it's going to take time." Hank leaned back in his chair and stared at me. He was lucky that I agreed to take his case, not because I wanted to, but because I had stuck my foot in my mouth with Ronnie and said I was working on it.

Truth was the guy had no case. All I would be able to do for him was possibly pull some strings and get him a lesser sentence. I knew if I could get him and his wife to rat on the other manager that was also involved, I could get them a deal since it would take down the entire structure. But I wasn't going to tell him that until I got what I wanted.

Mia had been gone almost three weeks and it was infuriating me that I had no idea where she was. Hank confirmed her flight had gone to Denver, which was pretty useless information given that I knew that when I looked up her flight information at the airport. I needed him to find out more before people started asking about where Mia was. I had been able to keep Ronnie at bay while I was in D.C. last week but he had already started asking how Mia was feeling and I was running out of bullshit to tell him. I needed this to be over already.

"If you have connections then use them. Now isn't the time to play around with me, Hank. I'm not someone you want to mess with."

"Are you threatening *me*? You *really* want to threaten a cop?" He leaned forward in his chair, invading my space and trying to show force.

"*Former* cop. Remember your place." I shot him a look that forced him back in his chair again.

"Find where she went. She's a dumb housewife, it shouldn't be this hard to find her, damnit!" I pushed the stack of papers next to his file off to the side in frustration.

"I'll keep trying but it's not like I have a ton of options. There are a lot of cities and towns around Denver- she could be in any one of them. She might not even be in Colorado anymore. Without more information, it's hard to know where she went. She's not using any of her credit cards, and nothing has popped up under Mia Stone."

"Look under Mia Johnson."

"Johnson?" Hank raised an eyebrow in question.

"Johnson is her maiden name. She might be using that instead."

I watched as Hank pulled out a pen and jotted the information down on a scrap piece of paper.

"I'll see what I can find and let you know." Hank stood up to leave and walked toward the door when I stopped him.

"You have a week. Find her within the next week or you and your wife lose any plea deal options."

"You're kidding me." The look on Hank's face said he knew that I wasn't.

"How am I supposed to find her in a week? I need more time than that."

"You've had a week to figure that out." I looked up at him as he lingered in my doorway. "Thought cops were supposed to be good at finding people?"

He glared at me as he opened the door and stormed out, slamming it behind him. I rubbed my temples as the headache I had been fighting the past few days started to build again. It was nine in the morning and I had a long day ahead of me so I needed something to get rid of it. I opened my bottom desk drawer and looked at the bottle of aspirin sitting next to the almost empty bottle of whiskey. I debated my options before reaching for the whiskey and added it to my coffee.

I stirred the whiskey in with a pen as my door opened and Claire walked in wearing a tight black skirt with a white button-down blouse that showcased her perfect tits. I looked her up and down as I took in the show she was putting on as she stalked toward me, one stiletto in front of the other.

"Mr. Stone, I have the Lewis file that you asked for." She laid it on my desk, reaching across me so her tits were in my face.

"What are you working on?" she purred in my ear as she leaned down and let her breath hover over my ear. I reached down and ran a hand up her bare leg, caressing my way up her thigh. I waited as she took a step to the side and allowed me to slide my hand up further.

She looked down at me, a smirk on her face. I scooted my chair back as she pulled away from my touch and hiked her skirt up, her bare pussy greeting me. She leaned forward and worked quickly on undoing my pants before she straddled me and slid my thick dick inside of her.

I watched as she let her head fall back as she bounced up and down, her tits almost popping out of her shirt. I reached forward and pulled her blouse open, unhooking the clasp on the front of her bra. Within seconds her tits were free and she watched as I leaned forward and pulled a nipple into my mouth. She rode me even harder as my teeth nipped at her other nipple, pushing both of us close to climax. I felt the buildup and knew I was close to coming.

Why the fuck hadn't I put on a condom before we started? I looked around frantically, knowing it was too late. She caught my eye and held my gaze as she drove herself down deeper on my dick, taking every inch of me inside of her. I tried to push her off as I was about to come but she grabbed onto my shoulders and held on even tighter as I came undone inside of her. She smiled a wicked smile as she watched, knowing that I came inside of her. Once I was done, she climbed off, fixed her clothes, and smiled as she walked out of my office, shutting the door behind her. It was the first time we had sex but something told me it wasn't going to be the last.

Fifteen
Mia

Saturday was so busy that Jade and I never got the chance to talk that night after I got home from work. I really wanted to talk to her and catch up but I was exhausted and she ended up with a last-minute date. We had tried to set aside time for a call on Tuesday but that fell through. So did Wednesday. It was Thursday morning and I sat on the couch, watching my cell phone as I waited for it to ring.

My phone vibrated in my hand as I saw Jade's name on the screen. Excitement filled me as I slid the button to answer the call.

"Hey, I'm glad we are finally able to sit and talk for a few." My tone was cheery until I saw the bruise on Jade's face and a mark on her throat. My stomach dropped. Her eyes were reluctant to meet mine and I started to panic that he was there with her. We hadn't text in advance so I had no way of knowing whether she was okay before I answered the call.

"Jade, did you go to yoga?" I asked as calmly as I could and angled myself to where the plain white wall was behind me. I didn't want anything to give away where I was or make it easier to find me. Although if he was there with her, I knew he would find a way to trace the phone number that she had called so it didn't really matter.

"No yoga. Not today." She met my eyes and there was sadness behind them.

I challenged her with my stare, still unsure of whether she was alone.

"I'm by myself," she assured me as she stood up and walked around her apartment like we usually do. "All clear."

"What happened?" Concern took over as I worried that Damian had done this to her. It was possible that it was also the guy she had gone out with Saturday night. Her eyes looked down at the floor, refusing to meet mine.

"Jade. Talk to me." I needed to know what had happened to her.

"Do you need me to show you yoga on my side?" Maybe she was concerned that he was there with me, though it seemed unlikely given how I was talking to her. I was desperate to do whatever it took to get her to talk to me.

"No, I know he's not there with you. I know because he just left my apartment." She looked up at me and I knew that he had done that to her.

"Oh my God, I'm so sorry." I fought back the tears that wanted to flow and forced myself to keep it together. "What happened? Tell me everything."

"He followed me home Saturday night from work. He had come into the bar while I was working and recognized me from lunch. He started getting angry and caused a scene so management kicked him out. By the time I left for the night, I didn't see him around so I went home. It was already late and I didn't want to panic you so I lied about having a date." She took a deep breath and I watched her bring her hand up to her neck.

"I wasn't expecting anyone this morning so when I heard someone knocking on the door, I just answered it. I didn't think anything about it. He pushed his way inside my apartment and pinned me to the wall by my throat. He kept demanding that I tell him where you are. I told him that I didn't know and that you hadn't contacted me so I didn't know where you went. He hit me a few times after he pinned me down and tried to strangle me, then he left. He said he'll be back soon to see if my story has changed."

I stayed staring at her for what felt like hours. My heart was broken knowing that I had put my only friend in danger. It was my fault that he had attacked her. It was my fault that he was coming back for her. I tried to think of what to do next when she started to speak again and interrupted my thoughts.

"Mia, I didn't tell him where you are. I didn't tell him anything, I swear. But he's looking for you. He knows that you went to Denver, he tracked your flight."

There was panic in her voice and I felt it in my blood. He would find a way to find me, no matter how hard I tried to hide.

"You have to leave Jade. Today. You have to go before he can come back for you. He won't leave you alone until he gets to me."

"Mia, I can't do that. I don't have anywhere to go. I don't have family. I don't have friends. Where am I supposed to go?"

"Come here." I blurted it out before I even thought about it. It was insane to ask her to come here and risk that Damian could follow her here. If he did that then I would have inadvertently lead him directly to me. But I didn't want Jade to have to be on her own. Honestly, I didn't want to be on my own either. They say there's safety in numbers so if I could get her here without Damian knowing, we could keep each other safe.

"Mia, that's crazy. You know there's a risk."

"I know. But it's the only thing we can do at this point. You're not safe there."

"How are we going to do this?" I could hear that she was reluctant to go through with this, I felt the same way. It was going to be tricky but we could do it.

"I'm going to work in thirty minutes, I'll call you at the cafe we used to hang out at when I first met you. Neither of the landlines will be on anyone's radar so we can avoid using cell phones. Can you be there in thirty minutes?" My voice was filled with hope and I prayed that we would be able to pull this off.

"Yeah, I can get there in thirty minutes."

"Take time to look around." I hinted so she would know to watch for him. "And take only what you need."

"I'll talk to you in thirty."

We hung up and adrenaline coursed through me as I got dressed and made my way to The Vine. It wasn't open for business yet but I knew that Chase would already be there. I walked as quickly as I could, making sure I got there a few minutes early. My mind was racing as I tried to think through the rest of the plans. I used my key to open the front door and immediately regretted that I didn't give Chase a heads up that I was coming in. I heard his footsteps coming down the hall as I locked the door behind me.

"Hey, everything alright?" He looked past me to make sure no one else was behind me.

"Yeah, can I use the phone?" My nerves were still on high alert which made me look twitchy and caused Chase to take notice.

"Of course. What's going on, Mia? Are you okay?" He led the way back to his office and stepped to the side with his hand extended so I could enter.

I made my way behind his desk and checked the clock. I still had five minutes before I was supposed to call. I rubbed my hands together, my body felt cold despite the summer heat.

"Mia- tell me what's going on. You're really freaking me out." Chase came around the back side of the desk and sat on the edge of it, facing me as I sat in his chair.

"I need to help my friend Jade. Damian attacked her this morning, trying to find information about where I went. She needs to leave but we couldn't talk about it on our cell phones in case he tries to trace the call."

“How would he trace the call?” Chase frowned as he tried to process what I had just told him.

“He’s a lawyer and has connections. He had a tracking app installed on my phone so he’s pretty good at navigating that kind of stuff. We don’t want to risk him having a connection that can trace the call. It would lead him right to me.” I glanced at the clock and waited. Three more minutes.

I unlocked my cell phone and opened Google. I had started to type the name of the cafe when Chase’s hand reached out to stop me.

“Mia, there’s an actual computer in front of you. Use that one.” He nodded to his computer and I took the mouse to navigate to the page with their phone number.

I picked up the phone and called the phone number on the screen, praying that this would work. After the seventh ring I started to feel uneasy that my plan would backfire.

“Giovanni’s Cafe,” a woman huffed into the phone.

“Hi, I’m looking for a customer- her name is Jade. She’s expecting the phone call.”

“Ma’am this is a place of business, not a place for customers to receive personal phone calls.”

I listened as she started to move the phone away and knew she was going to hang up.

“PLEASE! She’s in trouble. Please don’t hang up.” I begged as loud as I could, praying she would hear me. There was a faint sigh on the other end and I knew she had heard me.

“Let me call out and see if she’s here.”

“No! Please don’t do that. There’s a chance that a man followed her there.”

“Okay, what do you want me to do?”

"Um, can you tell me if there are any men there?"

"There's a handful."

"Any that are sitting by themselves or with a girl?"

"A few that are with a girl, none that are by themselves."

"Okay, do you see a woman with short black hair and a bruise on her cheek?"

"Let me take a look around. I'll be right back." I heard her sit the phone down and waited anxiously for her to come back.

"Nope. No women that match that description."

I let out a deep breath as I closed my eyes and pinched the bridge of my nose to keep from crying. I felt Chase's hand rub my back lightly.

"Hold on a minute." My head perked up as I waited for her to come back.

"You get the hell away from her. Right now!" She was screaming at someone and I could hear a man's voice faint in the distance. "You come one more step towards her and I'll whack you with this frying pan. Don't you mess with me, asshole."

There was commotion in the background and I struggled to hear what it was. I looked up at Chase who looked as confused as I was even though he couldn't hear what was happening on the other end. I looked around on his phone until I found the button for the speaker phone and pressed it. I put the phone on the receiver as we listened to the commotion that was still happening on the other line. I heard footsteps getting louder and waited.

"Alright, I found her. Here she is." The woman sat the phone down again and a few seconds later I heard someone pick it up.

"Yoga is cancelled today." Jade said with a sigh.

"Are you okay? What happened?"

"Some guy tried to steal this woman's purse as I was walking in and she went off on him. She's a feisty one." Jade laughed and I felt relieved to know that she wasn't the one who had been in trouble.

"Did you make it there okay? Any sign of him following you?"

"None that I saw. I took several side streets and checked behind me several times. I even cut in through a few stores and popped out the back exits. I think it's clear."

"Perfect. I'm glad to hear that." My breathing had started to return to normal as I knew she was okay.

"So what's our plan? I brought the things I needed and left the rest. If he goes by my apartment at any point, it will look like I still live there."

"That's good. I'm sorry, I know that it sucks to up and leave everything. I never wanted this to happen to you."

"It's okay, Mia. It's not your fault." She tried to reassure me but I knew 100% that it was my fault she had to uproot everything and start over.

"There's a couple ways to get here but I worry about you buying a plane or bus ticket, he might be able to track your purchases."

"I could rent a car and drive. It would take a while but I could do it."

"That might be the only way. But it would still be linked to your name." Frustration was building quickly as we tried to figure out a plan without much luck.

"I can try to get a different ID."

"There's no time for that and do you even know anyone who does that anymore?" I asked with uncertainty in my voice.

"No, but desperate times call for desperate measures."

"I can help, ladies." I heard Chase next to me and for a moment I had forgotten that he was sitting next to me, listening to the call.

"Who's that?" Jade sounded alarmed and I immediately felt bad for not telling her that she was on speakerphone and he was in the room.

"Sorry, that's Chase. I'm in his office."

"Oh, that scared me." I heard her let out a sigh.

"Let me make a phone call real quick and see what I can do." He got up and walked into the hallway while Jade and I stayed on the phone.

There was a lot of background noise which made me relieved that she was surrounded by people while we talked. For the moment I didn't have to worry about her. A few minutes later Chase came back into the office with his cell phone pressed to his ear.

"Perfect, thanks Marty, I owe you one." He hung up the phone and put it back in his pocket.

"Jade, do you have a way to make it to the Budget rental car lot on Frost avenue?" He spoke loudly to make sure she could hear him.

"Yeah, it's only a few blocks from here. I can walk."

"Great. Head over there and ask for Marty. She has a car ready for you and it will be under Wendy Ryder." He smiled as he said the name and I could tell he was proud of the name he had made up.

"How did you do that? Aren't they going to need my ID?"

"It's one of my mom's close friends, she's like family and she owed me a favor. Just check in with her when you get there and she'll get you on your way. No paperwork or ID required."

"That's really nice of you Chase, thank you." Jade sounded relieved which made me relieved.

"Oh and Jade?" He waited to make sure she hadn't hung up.

"Yeah?"

"Everything is paid for already. I've taken care of the rental fees so you won't need to pay for that. Be sure to check the glove box when you get in, Marty said she will leave you a care package as well."

"That's amazing, thank you. I can't wait to meet you and personally thank you. Now I see why Mia loves you so much." I blushed at the words as Chase looked down at me and smiled. It was now apparent that I had been talking about him to Jade.

"Be careful, Jade. Make sure to always check your surroundings and please try to check in when you can from a pay phone. I'll see you as soon as you get here." I listened as she said goodbye, both of us knowing that we wouldn't hear much from each other until she got here. Sadness filled me as I worried about her making it out here safely. I still felt an enormous amount of guilt over her leaving.

I looked up at Chase as I slouched back in his chair. He never ceased to surprise me with how kind and generous he was.

"That was really nice, what you did for Jade. Thank you."

"I'm glad I could help." He smiled down at me as he sat on the edge of his desk.

"It was really nice of your mom's friend to do that for Jade. What's in the care package?" I asked curiously.

"I'm not sure to be honest. I gave her a quick summary of what was happening and she took care of the rest." He let out a breath before continuing. "She was a victim of abuse as well. Boston was where she went to escape and after her husband was locked up in prison, she vowed to always help others to pay it forward as a thank you to those who had helped her."

"Is she covering the cost of the rental car?"

"Nope, that I'm taking care of. I gave her my credit card information, she'll run everything on that. The only thing she will have to pay for is gas, but Marty said she was giving her the most efficient vehicle she had so it shouldn't be too much."

"Wow. This is just— it's all too much. Thank you for helping. I really appreciate it." I patted his thigh without thinking about it. I felt his hand reach down and grab hold of mine as he gently squeezed it.

My hand lingered on his thigh and as much as I knew I needed to move it, I couldn't find it in me to actually do it. My eyes reached his, a heaviness hung over them as he licked his lips. I swallowed hard as I continued to meet his gaze. My pulse quickened as I waited for him to make a move, too afraid to do it myself. His hand ran up my bare arm, sending goosebumps in its path. He kept his eyes locked on mine as I felt the heat from his touch spread within me.

He adjusted his position and stood in front of me, pulling me up to a standing position as well. We were face to face, close enough that our breath could be felt on the other's skin. His fingers found mine, a slow touch as he caressed my hands. He stepped closer, invading more of my space. My breaths became harder and came quicker as my body reacted to being in such close proximity with his. I felt him lean forward and closed my eyes as he came close enough to kiss me.

"Morning." Noah called as he walked down the hallway and stood outside of Chase's door.

Chase let out a frustrated sigh as I took a step back, embarrassed. He ran a hand over his face and looked back at Noah. The look on Noah's face was half surprised to find us there together and half amused that he had walked in on us.

"My bad." He chuckled as he walked past the office and went into his.

"I should get going." I said as I stepped to the side of him, grabbing my cell phone from his desk and sliding it in my pocket. He kept his head down as he nodded in response and stepped back so I could get past.

"Bye, Noah." I called as I made my way out of the building as quickly as possible and went back to my apartment.

Sixteen
Chase

Fridays were by far my favorite day of the week. It was the end of the work week, the start of the weekend, and today, I got to see Mia the majority of the day since she was working the day shift.

We didn't see each other much yesterday after Noah interrupted our almost kiss. By the time she came in for her shift, I was leaving for the day. While I wanted to stick around and try to get any time with her that I could, I decided it was best to leave and allow her some space.

Yesterday I felt the chemistry between us. I felt her body respond to my touch. The way she leaned in to meet me for a kiss. I could tell that she wanted it as much as I did. I was glad that she had let me be part of what she was going through with Jade, it felt like she trusted me. That was the most important thing for me, to make sure that she knew she could trust me and that she felt safe with me. We were making progress on both ends.

I sat in my office, trying to focus on the report I was supposed to be working on, distracted as I waited for her to come in. I knew that she was coming in at nine to work on projects before we opened at eleven. It was 8:50 and it felt like time was passing by slower than ever.

There was a noise up front as I heard the door open and close, followed by light footsteps approaching down the hallway. I looked up and smiled when I saw her walk by on her way to the break room. She looked sexy in a short denim skirt with a black lace tank top and sandals. Fridays were a good day for tips and she was wearing the perfect outfit to take home a full paycheck worth.

I stood up from my desk and smoothed down the blue polo I was wearing, more out of habit than actually needing to. She was turned away from me as she put her purse in the cabinet when I walked in. I leaned against the wall as I admired her from behind.

Her hair was pulled up into a high ponytail which left her neck and shoulders exposed. I longed to walk up behind her and kiss the bare skin. Her skirt sat low on her hips and covered her legs mid-thigh. The skirt was longer than what I saw most girls wear these days and I loved that it was still sexy without being slutty. It left plenty to the imagination.

I had been staring at her so intently that I hadn't paid attention to the fact that she didn't know I was in the room and accidentally startled her when she turned around.

"Oh my God!" Her hand flew to her chest as she braced herself against the counter.

"You scared the shit out of me. How long were you standing there?"

"Sorry, I didn't mean to scare you. Not long, I was just coming to see how you were doing today. Have you heard from Jade at all?" I stood up straight and shoved my hands in my jeans, hoping she would buy my bullshit about checking on her instead of the truth that I was checking her out.

"I haven't heard from her yet. I hope she's okay. It's just hard not knowing where she's at and what's going on. It sucks, it's all my fault that she's in this position." She walked to the table and held onto the back of a chair.

"I'm sure she'll be okay. She sounds like a really smart girl." I smiled genuinely to try to put her mind at ease.

There was a silence between us as we looked at each other. I knew she was thinking about what had almost happened yesterday, just like I was. I waited to see if she would bring it up as we continued our silent standoff.

"Well, I better get started on unpacking the new glasses before we open." She pushed away from the chair and walked to the boxes in the back of the room that held the new glasses I had ordered. Her back was turned to me so I took that as my sign to leave her alone.

"Sounds good, I'll be in my office if you need any help."

"Thanks," she said as she looked over her shoulder to smile as I walked back to my office.

I wanted to spend more time with her. Just being in close proximity to her made me feel excited. I hadn't felt this way about a girl- ever. It was new and exciting and I felt like a teenage boy learning about girls for the first time. It was embarrassing what she could do to me. She could ask for a unicorn riding an abominable snowman and I would figure out a way to get it for her.

Two hours had gone by and I still hadn't gotten any work done. I sighed in frustration as I leaned back in my chair and tossed my pen on the desk. I needed to clear my head and get work done but I couldn't focus for the life of me. I heard my phone vibrate on the desk and picked it up.

"Hey mom, what's up?" I hadn't called my mom in a week so I expected that she would be calling to check in on me.

"He's gone, Chase! I can't find him anywhere!" Panic filled her voice and I leaned forward in my chair as I pressed the phone closer to try to hear what she was saying.

"Who's gone? What's going on?"

"Liam. He got into a fight with Grant and I thought he was upstairs in his room. I called him down for lunch and he didn't come so I went to look for him and I can't find him. Chase, he's gone!"

"Okay, mom, try to calm down. I'm leaving now, I'll start looking for him. Have you told Grant?"

"No, I haven't told him yet. I didn't know if I should or not. What if he finds Liam and he runs again? The fight was pretty bad."

"What was the fight about?" I picked up my car keys and walked out of my office, poking my head into Noah's office. I covered the mouthpiece of the phone as Noah looked at me, knowing something was wrong by the look on my face.

"Liam took off, I need to go find him." I whispered to Noah. He nodded his head and waved me off as I walked out of the door and got in the truck.

"Liam was talking about Renee and felt like Grant wasn't listening to him, which he wasn't because he was still working from his phone. Liam accused him of forgetting about Renee and Grant lost his temper." My mom summarized their fight as quickly as she could and I knew right away where to go find Liam. I hung up with my mom as I drove towards the pond and parked my truck.

I jumped out and jogged over to the willow tree that Liam used to sit under with his mom. She used to bring him here for picnics when he was growing up and they would sit under the tree and watch the ducks swim in the pond. I saw him before he saw me so I slowed my pace as I quietly approached him. He looked up and saw me but made no effort to get up. His face was red and splotchy, dried tears on his cheeks.

I sent a quick text to my mom to let her know that I found him as I walked over and sat down in the grass next to him. I looked out at the pond and waited for him to talk first.

"How did you know I was here?" He sniffled and wiped his face with his T-shirt.

"I know how important this place is to you. It's where you go when you want to be close to your mom." I kept my eyes ahead of me as we talked and picked at the cool grass under my legs.

“Why doesn’t my dad miss her?” He looked up at me with tears in his eyes. I wrapped him in my arms as he sobbed into my shoulder. I held him as tight as I could, wishing I could take this pain away. I waited for him to calm down so I knew I had his full attention before speaking.

“Liam, your dad misses your mom more than any of us could ever know. He would have done anything in the world to make her better if he could. Hell, any of us would have. He fought so hard for her, to try to save her, and now, he fights so hard for you. To keep you happy. To keep you safe. To keep you from knowing how much he misses her.” I watched as he looked up at me, listening to the words I spoke.

“Why doesn’t he want me to know that he misses her?” Innocent eyes looked up at me and my heart felt like it might crumble.

“Because his heart is broken, champ. When your mom died, a part of your dad went with her. I think he’s still trying to figure out just how big that part was.” I let out a jagged breath as I fought back my own feelings. Liam stayed silent and looked back toward the pond as I continued to talk.

“Your daddy may not talk about her much, but it’s not because he doesn’t want to. It’s because it makes him sad that she’s not here. And he doesn’t want you to see that he’s sad. He wants to be strong for you, and to him, that means that he has to be brave.”

“Brave for what?”

“Brave for you. So that you know how to be strong as well.” I looked at the pond and tried to think of the right things to say to make him really understand.

“Your daddy loved your mom more than anything, then they had you, and they found that they could love someone even more. You became their entire world. So believe me when I say that your dad loved your mom, and he struggles with how much he misses her every single day. He sees her when he looks at you. We all do. And we’re so blessed because in a way, we still get to have a piece of her here with us because we have you.” I smiled and watched him smile back at me.

"Your dad is a wonderful man, Liam, and he will go to his grave constantly trying to prove to you how much he loves you. He works hard to try to provide the very best he can, to give you the life him and your mom always dreamed of giving you. Try to be patient with him, he's still trying to figure out how to do this on his own." I hugged him again and hated that this even had to be a conversation. Liam deserved to have his mom as much as my brother deserved to have his wife. It was a real shitty hand that they were dealt.

"Thanks, Uncle Chase. You always make me feel better." He reached up and wrapped his arms around me to hug me.

"Anytime champ, anytime." Moments like this warmed my heart as we stayed sitting next to each other and watching the ducks. We took turns sharing a memory of Renee as we laughed and cried, then laughed some more.

An hour later I saw Grant's car pull up. Liam hung his head as his dad approached and I shot my brother a look that told him to go easy on the kid. His eyes were red and I could tell that he had been upset as well. He smiled softly at me as he approached, taking Liam in to get a feel for his mood.

"Can I join you guys?" he asked casually as Liam avoided looking at him. I nodded subtly and Grant sat on the other side of Liam. I debated whether to get up and give them some privacy but when I started to move my brother shook his head no.

"Liam, I would like to say I'm sorry for what happened earlier. I never should have yelled at you, and I'm sorry that I wasn't giving you my full attention." Grant held his posture stiff and continued. "I promise that it won't happen again."

Liam looked over at his dad and rested his head on his knee as he pulled his legs in and cuddled them.

"How can you promise that? You're always too busy with your job." Liam hid his face in between his knees.

"Not anymore." He paused as he waited for Liam to respond.

"You know why?" Grant leaned forward to try to make eye contact with Liam.

"Why?"

"Because I quit my job." Grant smiled a huge smile as Liam's head popped up.

"Really?!" Liam was excited as he looked back and forth between me and his dad.

"Really. I decided that I didn't need to keep working crazy hours and I didn't want to miss out on the things that were happening in your life. I want to be there for every moment, I don't want to miss anything." Liam reached over and hugged Grant so hard he almost knocked him over as Grant laughed.

"That's the best news ever dad. But what are you going to do for a job?"

"Well, it turns out that your school had a position open for a P.E. coach so I took it. I'll start when school goes back in the fall. Until then, I'm going to be the assistant coach for your little league team. Which means we'll get to spend a lot of time together!"

"Wow! That's great! Did you hear that Uncle Chase?" He beamed up at me with pure happiness in his eyes.

"I sure did. I told you, didn't I?" I smiled at him as I winked, knowing that Grant would wonder what we had talked about.

"Yeah, he figured it out." Liam laughed as his dad grabbed him and tickled him.

I said my goodbyes as I made my way to the truck and went back to work. Grant and Liam were skimming stones across the pond when I left and I was relieved to see their relationship getting stronger. I was proud of my brother for quitting a job that he loved in order to be the dad that his son needed. He was a great dad, he just needed to prove it to himself.

Seventeen
Mia

It was after two when I saw Chase come in and make his way to his office. Noah went back to talk with him but I had no idea what was going on. Chase had seemed upset when I saw him leave earlier but I didn't dare ask Noah about it. I was trying to lay low and let things settle between us before Noah started to think something really was going on with Chase and I.

The last few hours of my shift went by quickly as we got busy during happy hour. The tips were good and I was thankful that I would have some extra cash if needed. While I knew I would have steady paychecks, I felt uneasy about Damian going after Jade to try to find me so I didn't want to get too comfortable and not have a way to run if needed.

I wrapped up the last few tables I had been waiting on and closed their tabs as I waited for them to leave so I could clear their table. Noah had started taking over the new tables, the system we had created worked flawlessly. It was thirty minutes before my shift ended when I saw Chase come up front and sit at the end of the bar. I was about to walk over to wait on him when I saw Noah grab a glass and fill it before sliding it to Chase. I couldn't hear what they were talking about over the noise of the room, but it looked like an intense conversation as

Chase spoke to Noah. Before I could look away I felt Chase's gaze land on me and felt trapped in it.

There was something different in the way he looked at me. It wasn't anger, maybe more frustration? My body tingled as I held his gaze for another second before breaking it and looking away. I made my way under the bar top to avoid having to walk over to where they were talking and went to clean the tables that had just left. I was cleaning the last table when I saw Chase head back to his office. I loaded the few glasses into the bin and walked over to the bar and sat it on the back counter. There were only a few glasses in it so Noah told me to leave it there and he would take it back later when it was full. I double checked to make sure all of my tables were closed out and cleaned before I walked back to the break room to grab my purse.

As I walked through the door, I saw Chase walking down the hallway toward his office from the break room. There was still that look in his eye and something told me that something inside of him had changed. Maybe it was whatever he had left to deal with earlier? I couldn't imagine it was the one beer he had and hadn't even finished. He smiled when he saw me, a devilish look on his face. I tried to quicken my pace to get past him when he reached his arm out to the side, blocking my path.

"Where you going so quickly?" His voice was low and sexy.

"I'm done for the day. Just grabbing my stuff so I can get out of here." I took a step back as he took a step forward, his arm still extended to block me. I felt butterflies in my stomach as my body reacted to the physical contact with him as his arm was still touching me.

"Why? Do you have something more pressing to do?" He kept his voice low, drawing me in with each word.

Interesting choice of words as I thought about all of the things I would like him to press into me right now. I felt my face turn red at the thought and knew that he noticed.

"Do I make you nervous?" His finger reached up and gently caressed my jawline as I looked up and found him watching me.

"Nervous? No. Excited is more like it." The words were out of my mouth before I realized what I said. His eyes watched as the blush crept down my neck, my eyes focused on anything other than his face.

"Excited? Well, that's an interesting choice of words." His arm slid down the wall some to where his hand was low enough to reach mine. I watched nervously, waiting to see what he was going to do next.

"Excited...." he tried the word out on his tongue as he licked his lips. The movement caught my eye and I felt his gaze upon me as I stared at his mouth. I felt my lips involuntarily part as I wished he would lean in and kiss me.

"I'm pretty sure there's a better word for what you're feeling right now. Guessing by your body language, I would say that excited is an understatement."

There was something arousing about how he was talking to me and how he was taking control of the situation. It was different than how Damian controlled me. It was sexy. I felt wanted. I felt desired. I wanted him to keep going even though he made me so nervous. It was excitement mixed with anxiety mixed with arousal all in one.

"Okay, maybe more than excited." My voice was shaky and far from sexy, unlike his. He kept this smooth, sexy vibe and I was jealous that I could barely get words out right.

"I want to hear you say it. Tell me Mia, what are you feeling?" He smirked as he said it. His eyes met mine and held them in place as I read the challenge on his face. He was purposely pushing me and I could tell that it was exciting him as much as it was me.

"Aroused." I whispered as I looked down towards the floor. I could feel my cheeks heating as the words flowed freely from my mouth. My body tingled in response.

With the tip of his finger he gently raised my head and forced me to make eye contact with him again.

"Aroused." He bit his lip after saying it. "And how does that make you feel?" His eyes turned dark and I could see the desire in them.

"Wet."

I watched as he swallowed hard, caught off guard by my response. He slightly shifted his weight but kept the same position, blocking my path. He kept his eyes on me but remained silent which made my anxiety build. Had I said too much? Was he put off by how candid I was? All of a sudden it felt like our flirty game had ended.

"Like I said, I need to go." I pushed against his arm but the damn muscular thing didn't budge.

"So you're aroused and wet." He leaned in close and whispered in my ear, "What does it feel like?"

"You know what it feels like." I snapped, immediately frustrated with myself for allowing him this control. I thought I wanted it but now I was worried that it was only going to lead to my own embarrassment.

"I want to hear you say it," he pushed.

"I don't have time for this." I pushed harder against him, trying to move his arm so I could get by him. In a quick movement he turned me around so my back was up against the wall. He leaned in, resting his chest against mine, and pinned me against the wall with his forearms flat against the wall. "Say it."

My breathing quickened and a flush of heat took over my body as I responded to his touch. I tried to focus on anything other than the throbbing sensation that had started to build up.

"It feels like you could stick a finger inside me right now and find out just how wet I am." I whispered as I closed my eyes and tried to regulate my breathing. If that was what he wanted, fine, I would give it to him.

"What if I wanted to stick my tongue inside and taste it instead?" He whispered in my ear.

My eyes shot open finding him studying my face. I didn't know what to say, no one had ever talked to me this way before. And I found that I really liked it. Just as I tried to regain my composure, I felt his lips on my throat, slowly making their way to my collar bone. A moan escaped my throat as my hands made their way into his hair and I tilted my head to allow him better access.

"Do you want to feel my tongue inside of you?" He whispered as he pressed his body against mine. His hand slid down the wall and gently caressed over my breast while his legs spread my legs to hold me in place. In an instant I could feel just how ready he was for me. I moaned in response and heard a low growl in this throat.

"Say it out loud, do you want to feel my tongue inside of you, sucking and licking up all of the wetness?" He nipped my ear as he said it. The dirty words rolled around in my head while my body responded to them.

"Say the words Mia."

"Yes..." I felt like I was practically panting, I could come undone at any moment. The way he touched me mixed with the things he said to me were like a toxic combination and I wanted another hit.

"Yes what, Mia? I want to hear word for word what you want me to do to you." His lips continued kissing their way down my shoulders and hovered at the top of bra, teasing me as he pulled the fabric away from my skin with his teeth and ran his tongue over my nipple.

"I want to feel your tongue inside me. I want to ride your hard dick until you come inside of me. I want all of it." My breathing got heavy and faster as I grabbed his shoulders and arched my back, allowing him access to grab my ass. I felt his hands move over the fabric of my denim skirt, pulling it up in the process.

"Chase…." I whimpered as I allowed myself to give in to what was happening. Everything felt so good, I didn't want it to stop.

"Fuck, Mia." He groaned as he pushed his erection against my thigh.

The door opened as Noah walked in, stopping in his tracks as he saw us up against the wall. I immediately pushed Chase off of me and pulled down my shirt as I looked away from Noah.

"I thought you left?" Noah asked as he carried a crate of glasses to the back shelf. "Looks like I walked in on an interesting discussion." A smug smile sat on his face as he stared at Chase. Chase lowered his head and shoved his hands in his pockets.

"You walked in on nothing," I assured him as I made my way to the break room and grabbed my purse and keys. I was thankful they had both made it back up front as I made my way down the hallway and out the double doors. What had I just done?

Eighteen
Chase

"Want to explain what that was all about?" Noah asked as he sat the crate of clean glasses down behind the bar and wiped his hands on the front of his jeans.

"It was nothing." I looked past him to avoid making eye contact.

"Oh really? So, Mia is usually that flushed and flustered when you guys aren't doing anything, just talking? And, I'm assuming the bulge in your pants is because you're happy to see the new sampling glasses that just came in?" Noah raised an eyebrow in question. "Or maybe you're just happy to see me?"

I rolled my eyes and tried to hide the laugh that threatened to make its way out.

"You can play dumb and you can avoid talking to me about it right now, but we both know that you're going to give me the details of what just happened."

"And why would I do that?" I asked as I tilted my head to the side. I was dying to know the answer to this one.

"Because you tell me everything. Because you have a tendency of fucking things up with women and I always have to come to your rescue later. And honestly, it's easier if I can just fix shit before you get the chance to mess it up. Maybe I should just go finish whatever you "didn't start" with Mia. Save us all some time, have a little fun?" He wiggled his eyebrows suggestively and it took everything I had not to throw something at him.

Being best friends since we were six years old meant that he knew all of my buttons and exactly how to push them. I focused my attention on the tv across the bar to avoid giving Noah the response he was waiting for. He knew that I've had a crush on Mia since we were kids and now that she was back, he never missed an opportunity to take a jab at me about the only girl I wasn't able to get.

"Wow, I would have expected you to make some joke about kicking my ass by now." Noah commented, interrupting my thoughts. "She must really have a hold on your balls."

"First of all, no one has a hold on my balls. Second, me kicking your ass is never a joke- unless you want to hear the punch line." I smirked so he got the point.

Noah chuckled as he walked by and patted my shoulder.

"Tonight's going to be a slow night, why don't you take off and see what kind of trouble you find for me to bail you out of later?" Noah offered with a smirk.

"Sounds like a great idea to me, leaving your crazy ass to run this place. Call me in the morning after you've let it burn to the ground so I can call the insurance company and get started on the claim." I grabbed my cell phone from the counter and made my way out of the door as a group of college girls came in. I glanced behind me to see Noah's head perk up at the sight. He was absolutely hopeless.

I didn't have plans, which was odd for a Friday night. I could go to the gym and burn off some frustration or I could go home and obsess about what happened with Mia in the hallway. No matter how hard I tried, I couldn't shake the image of her letting me touch her. The way she responded to me was such a turn on. I didn't know how she would react, but she definitely surprised me. If I thought I had it bad for her before, it just got about ten times worse. I drove the short distance toward my house when a thought suddenly hit me and I made a U-turn. My plan was either going to work in my favor or bite me in the ass.

Growing up we all used to go to Paul's Pizza on the weekend and it soon became Mia's favorite. She was never big on going to parties and loved the nights when we would pick up a pizza and stay up late watching movies.

It was 6:15 and she had already been gone 45 minutes so it was a risky move, but one that I was willing to try if it meant that I could spend some time with her. I made my way to General Bob's and grabbed a bottle of the wine she was looking at the other day while I called in a to go order at Paul's. I wasn't sure what Mia had and didn't have at her apartment so I grabbed the basics- paper plates, napkins, and a corkscrew for the wine.

I was antsy while I waited inside Paul's for my order to be ready, counting down the minutes until I could try to see Mia. I didn't know if she was home, though I couldn't imagine where she would go. She wasn't very social since she had been back, especially since she was trying to keep a low profile. A young girl with freckles called my name as she smiled and handed me the box.

The drive to Mia's apartment was quick which I was thankful for. The traffic was never bad here but Friday and Saturday nights tended to be heavier with people getting out of the house and looking for something to do. I parked my truck and grabbed the box of pizza and the bag from General Bob's as I made my way to her apartment. I was as anxious as a teenage boy about to have his first kiss as I stood outside her door, trying to keep my hands from sweating as I knocked on her door and held my breath as I waited for her to answer.

132

Nineteen
Mia

It was 7:00 on a Friday night and I was wearing yoga pants and drinking wine out of a coffee mug. Had my life become pathetic or had I reached a new level of adulting? I wandered into the kitchen to look for suitable options for dinner. As I opened the fridge, I had hoped to find some sort of actual food, but instead I was greeted by milk, coffee creamer, and a half empty bottle of wine. I let out a sigh as I leaned against the open refrigerator door and debated whether to walk to the store to grab something to make for dinner, or to order takeout. I glanced down at my comfy clothes and decided takeout was the winner.

I closed the fridge and opened the drawer in the island that stored the takeout menus and began sorting through them when the doorbell rang. I stood still for a moment, waiting to hear a voice or for a sign that it might be someone at the wrong apartment. A few seconds later came another ring. I walked over to the door, determined to tell the person that I wasn't interested in whatever they were trying to sell, only when I opened the door I found that I was in fact, very interested.

Standing in front of me was Chase holding a pizza box and a bag from General Bob's. I looked at him with confusion, unsure of why he was there. He had offered to have a housewarming dinner but I had never accepted and we definitely hadn't made any plans.

"Can I come in?" He asked, interrupting my thoughts.

"Sorry, I should have called first, but I was worried you would say no and we really need to talk." He smiled and I knew I wasn't going to be able to say no.

"And what exactly do we need to talk about?" I asked with a sigh as I leaned against the open door. I was happy to see him but I didn't want him to know that, especially not after what had happened earlier. This was a slippery slope and I needed to try to stay on my feet as long as I could.

I saw him look down as he took in the outfit I was wearing and immediately wished I was wearing anything other than yoga pants and a tank top. Perhaps if I had been expecting company, I would have even put a bra on. I felt vulnerable with him checking me out but I squared my shoulders and tried to play the part of uninterested and unaffected. I continued to lean against the door, blocking his entrance as he looked past me to the wine glass on the counter next to the take-out menus.

"It appears I have a solution to your problem." He nodded towards the counter as he held onto the pizza box which I imagined was starting to get uncomfortable holding. It was big and bulky and he was still holding the bag in his other hand. He adjusted the angle at which he was holding the box and I saw the Paul's Pizza logo on the top of the box. I tried to hide a smile as I remembered our nights growing up, spending the weekends eating pizza and watching movies. It was sweet that he had remembered how much I loved Paul's Pizza.

"And what's that?" I asked with a sigh as I tried to feign interest. He handed me the pizza box and when I reached out to take it, he did some sly maneuver that turned me around so we were both inside the apartment.

"I played it safe and got a plain pepperoni pizza. I remembered that was your favorite growing up, so I hoped that hadn't changed. I mean, if you don't like pepperoni then this has to end now." He raised his eyebrows as he waited for my response.

"What has to end now?" I was confused. He was being sexy and charming and it made me feel drunk around him. Maybe it was the aftereffects from earlier still playing with my head.

"This flirty banter we started earlier. The start to our rocky but incredible relationship. The one with the mind-blowing sex," he said with a huge grin as he rocked back on his heels.

"There's no relationsh-," I started to protest but my words were cut off by his fingers over my mouth.

"Shhh, you're just hangry. Let's talk about it over pizza. Then we can move on to more important topics, like finishing our conversation from earlier." He was really in the zone tonight and I started to worry that I would end up giving in to his charm.

"You're so impossible." I mumbled as I closed the door behind him.

"That pizza better be worth all this." I walked past him and sunk down on the couch, curling my legs underneath me. I already knew that it would be, but still, I had to play the part. I couldn't lay all my cards out on the table this early on.

I watched as he maneuvered around the kitchen, unpacking the items he brought. Paper plates, napkins, wine, a corkscrew. He was prepared, I had to give him that. I waited on the couch as he brought two plates over with slices of pizza on them and sat them down on the table. He smiled as he went back to the kitchen and opened the bottle of wine. His brow furrowed as he looked around for wine glasses then turned back to me.

"There aren't any. I've been using a coffee mug." I nodded toward the one I left on the island. He smiled and grabbed another mug from the shelf above the sink and rinsed the one I was using. A few minutes later he sat the mugs of wine on the coffee table as he sat in the armchair across from me.

"You haven't answered me." I covered my mouth as I spoke in between bites of pizza. "What do we need to talk about?"

I reached for the mug to wash down the pizza when I was startled by how full the cup was. The wine was filled to the top, almost overflowing. I looked at him as he smiled again and nodded for me to have some wine while he chewed his bite.

"Thirsty?" I asked, looking for an explanation as to why the glass was so full.
"Liquid courage."

"Why do you need liquid courage?"

"It's for you, not me," he replied in between bites. "We're going to finish our conversation from earlier and I'm guessing you may need some liquid courage in order to do so."

"First of all, there is nothing to finish discussing. Second, I don't need liquid courage to talk about anything." I was lying and I knew that he knew it just as much as I did.

He stayed silent as he leaned back in the chair and wiped his mouth with a napkin as he finished his slice. There was a smirk on his face and it was driving me crazy.

"What?" I asked with more annoyance than I had intended to.

He continued to stay silent as he watched me. I felt like I was put on display and it made me feel anxious. I watched as his eyes roamed over my body and I wondered what he was thinking. He shifted in his seat and adjusted his jeans which drew my eyes to body. He was completely relaxed yet his muscular body looked rigid and solid. I remembered the feel of it on top of mine earlier in the hallway. The way his arms braced me against the wall, strong, yet gentle. It was a turn on to watch him take control of the situation and push me to tell him what I wanted. No one had done that before and I was still aroused by it. If I could rewind time I would go back to that moment in the hallway and play it on repeat, but in slow motion.

I licked my lips as I remembered the feeling of his lips on mine. How soft and gentle they were as they waited for my permission. My breathing changed as I relived the moments in my head, forgetting that he was sitting right in front of me while I continued on with my daydream.

A few minutes later my thoughts were interrupted by the sound of him clearing his throat. Startled, I looked up and made eye contact with him, knowing I had a frozen deer in the headlights look on my face. There was no way to hide what I had been thinking about as I felt the blush creep up my skin.

"Wanna share what you're thinking? Or should I guess based on how long you've been staring at my body and the flush in your cheeks?" His grin spread across his face as I forced myself to look away. I took a few big sips of wine, emptying my mug.

"May I?" he asked as he held up the bottle of wine, ready to refill my glass.

"Yes, please." I smiled a nervous smile.

"So the liquid courage is helping already." He chuckled.

"What makes you think that?"

"You're not being as feisty or looking at me like you want to rip my head off."

"Well you are pretty frustrating most of the time. Perhaps your personality flaw is leading to a drinking problem on my end. I maintain my innocence in this situation."

I watched as he got up and took the empty plates to the trash after I declined his offer for more pizza. Between the two slices I had and the wine, I was getting full, fast. I watched as he came back and sat at the other end of the couch instead of sitting in the armchair. My body instantly reacted to his presence and silently I wished that he would sit closer.

"I would venture to say that innocence would be far-fetched at this point, but I'm happy to play along," he joked. "However, the fact that you find me frustrating leads me to believe that I am in fact *frustrating* you."

"Here we go again." I sighed, taking a long sip of wine.

"Why can't you just admit that you're attracted to me?" He turned his body as he leaned toward me. "Given that you're not wearing a bra, and it's 80 some degrees out, I can tell for a fact that you're aroused at this very moment. Just like you were aroused earlier when we were in the hallway."

Embarrassed, I quickly grabbed one of the throw pillows and pulled it up to my chest.

"Attraction, my friend, is overrated." I took another sip and finished the wine left in my glass. "You can be attracted to lots of people but not want to do anything about it."

"So what is it about me that makes you not want to do anything about it?"

"I'm not really into one-night stands and I know what kind of guy you are. You like the challenge but once you get what you're after, you're done. You show up unannounced on a Friday night, I can only assume what you're really after." He sat in silence as he waited for me to continue.

"I haven't been with a lot of guys, Chase. And the last one I was with is trying to find me so he can kill me. I can't afford to let my guard down and let you in, only for you to run off after you get what you wanted. That's not fair to me." Apparently liquid courage was what I needed so I could tell him how I really felt.

I was scared to trust anyone again. And even though I had feelings for Chase and I was attracted to him, I didn't want to be another notch on his belt. I wanted it to be something more but I wasn't sure that I was even in a place to try to make it something more. No matter which way we played it, I was bound to be the one to get hurt in the end.

"You really think you know me that well?" He slid over closer to me on the couch. "I showed up here unannounced because I couldn't get you out of my head from what happened earlier. Trust me when I say that I had plenty of offers for tonight and I can have any of them with a quick reply to their text."

"That's not the point." Feeling frustrated I got up and took my mug to the kitchen sink. This was getting too complicated, too fast. I heard his footsteps behind me as I kept my back turned to him.

"What is the point?" He came up behind me and placed his hands on each side of my hands on the sink. I could feel the heat from his body behind me. All it would take was one small step backwards and I would be in his arms, leaning against his chest where it felt safe. I tried to focus on keeping my body rigid so I didn't give in to what my body really wanted.

Gently he moved my hair to the side and slowly kissed the back of my neck. I closed my eyes and soaked up the feeling while it lasted.

"What's the point, Mia?" he murmured as he ran kisses along my neck and onto my shoulders.

"That it's complicated. That it's wrong. That I'll be the one who gets screwed in the end."

"Baby if you want me to screw you, I have no objections to that request. I'll gladly screw you any way you'd like and as many times as you'd like. I'm just waiting for the green light." I could hear the flirtiness in his voice and knew that he was teasing me. He pulled away from me as he turned me around to look at him.

"I know that it feels complicated, Mia. I don't want you to think that I'm discrediting how you feel. But I have no intention of hurting you. I don't want to see anyone other than you. You're not a piece of ass that I'm after. This is more than that for me." His eyes searched mine, pleading for me to hear his words. "I know that you're technically still married and that it's scary to want to be with someone else, I get it. I really do. But I feel the way your body responds to me, Mia. And I know you feel it too."

"It's getting late. Thank you for the pizza and wine, I think it's time for you to go." I looked down to avoid having to see the hurt look on his face. I watched as he stepped back and ran his fingers through his hair in frustration.

"Okay, Mia. If that's what you really want, then I'll go. I promised that I would never try to push you or make you feel uncomfortable, and I meant it. But promise me that you'll take the time to think about yourself and what you really want. You deserve better than what you're allowing yourself to have, Mia. And at the end of the day, it's not me, that's okay. I'm still going to push for you to have the best, to have what you deserve."

He let out a deep breath as he walked past me, our hands grazed each other, and the door closed behind him.

I locked the door behind him and tried to get myself together. I was disappointed in myself for pushing him away when really I wanted nothing more than to spend time with him and let myself have all of the things he wanted to give me. I leaned my back against the door as I slid down it and sat on the floor thinking about what had just happened.

Twenty
Chase

Well, tonight definitely didn't turn out how I had hoped it would, though it's not like I was expecting for her to take down all of the walls she's built up and suddenly declare her undying love for me.

Frustration had started to build even more as every approach I made with Mia seemed to turn into a dead end. I tried to take things slow with her and be the best friend that I've always been, someone that she could lean on and trust. Then Noah reminded me that she would never see me as anything other than a brother.

So then I tried subtle flirting with her but that seemed to confuse her even more. For whatever reason, she refused to believe that I could be interested in her or that I would be flirting with her. Finally, I decided to lay it on even thicker to make sure she got the point, which she did, even if she didn't want to admit it. I saw the way her body reacted to my touch and to the things that I said to her. And for a fraction of a second, she responded to me and told me what she wanted. It was raw and dirty and such a turn on. I wanted nothing more than to give her everything she could ever ask for. I would go to my grave fulfilling every single one of her sexual desires if she would let me, there was no doubt about that.

But it was more than that. I wanted more from Mia. I wanted the girl that I grew up with and fell in love with. The girl who liked to cuddle on the couch while eating pizza and watching movies. The girl who would get the giggles and laugh so hard that she would snort. I wanted to protect her from anything that could ever hurt her and make her feel safe again. In the end, it didn't matter what I wanted if she didn't want those things in return. My mind was too busy to go home and obsess over what had happened so I made my way to The Vine.

It was fairly busy for a Friday night and Noah was behind the bar flirting with a blonde who appeared to be overly drunk and barely legal.

"Head outside. There's a taxi waiting for you." I nodded toward the door and watched her pouty face as she grabbed her purse and stumbled toward the front doors, nearly falling on her way out.

"Gee thanks." Noah muttered as he picked up a bar towel and wiped off the countertop after she left.

"Sure thing."

"I was being sarcastic."

"And I was keeping you from going to jail for over-serving Malibu Barbie and having to explain that you thought it was still consensual sex, even if she is passed out."

Noah grinned ear to ear, knowing that I was right.

"So, what brings you in on a Friday night, in such a delightful mood, I might add?" Noah questioned with one eyebrow raised.

"Don't want to talk about it. How bout you stop playing shrink and offer me a drink?"

Noah picked up a glass and worked the towel through it as he dried it before walking to the tap and filled the glass. He slid it across the bar as I reached out and grabbed it.

"I take it things didn't go well with Mia tonight?" He leaned back against the counter behind him and crossed one leg over the other.

"What makes you think I went to go see Mia?"

"Because you're in a shitty mood and you're only ever in this shitty of a mood when you don't get your way. What happened?"

I took a deep breath and let it out as I took a drink. The cold beer felt good going down.

"She has this guard up and I get it. I really do. But she's known me since the 3rd grade, you would think she would know what kind of person I am. I hate that I'm making this effort and she doesn't believe me. She's so determined that I'm just after sex and that she's the only one that will get hurt in this. I've tried telling her how I really feel but she doesn't hear me." I avoided looking at Noah as he watched me, listening to what I said as I regretted saying it out loud. I wasn't one who liked to tell others about my problems, but with Noah, it was different.

"She's been through a lot. I'm not going to tell you what she's told me because it's not my place to tell you but trust me when I say that you can't imagine what she's been through. Right now she needs a friend, Chase. I know that you are in love with her, but she isn't ready for that right now. I don't know that she even knows what love is. He broke her in more ways than one. She's going to need time to heal. And WHEN she gets into another relationship, she's going to need someone who understands and respects what she went through and who is willing to take things at the pace that she wants to go." He leaned forward and I could feel his eyes on me. I looked up at him as he continued.

"She doesn't know what any guy wants from her at this point. To think that you'd be any different is hilarious. You may walk on water with other women, but as far as Mia is concerned, she wouldn't care if you drowned. Right now she's focused on protecting herself and you need to respect that."

Noah was right. It wasn't anything that I hadn't already told myself but hearing it from him made me put it into a different perspective. If I really wanted Mia then I had no choice than to back off and hope that when she was ready, she would come find me. I didn't want to keep pushing her and risk pushing her away completely.

"Sometimes I hate talking to you about stuff." I glanced up at him, looking smug as he looked down on me.

"I know, but you know that I always give you the best advice." He winked and I almost snorted as I laughed.

"Oh really? Is that why just the other day you told me that I had to stop acting like her friend and start flirting with her if I wanted her to notice me? And now look where we are!" I pointed at him as I laughed and he held his hands up in defense.

"Hey, what can I say? I was going off of her having a sex dream about you, I thought it might help if you flirted with her."

"Maybe you should have told me about the dream before I unloaded my charm on her." I teased, hoping he would finally tell me about the dream.

"She never told me anything about it. I only know she had a dream about you because she was flustered about it and I had heard her calling out your name in her sleep."

"That's good to know." I felt satisfied to know that at least the dream version of me was having better luck with her.

"I wouldn't get too excited there champ, only her subconscious seems interested at this point and it only lasted all of two minutes. I'd hate for you to have to try to last long in real life." He ducked as I picked up the towel and whipped it at him.

I could hear him laughing from under the bar as he slid his way down and out into the open, escaping any additional attacks I might launch on him. I pulled some cash out of my wallet and slid it under my empty glass as I made my way toward the doors, nodding as Noah waved from one of the tables as I left.

Twenty One
Damian

I sat in my office and tapped my fingers impatiently while I waited for Hank to come in. This was not how I wanted to spend my Saturday night, but shit needed to get done. I looked down at my phone to check the time, again, when I noticed a new text message from Claire. My finger slid over the button to open the message when a picture of Claire's naked tits popped up on the screen. That was a nice surprise, to say the least, though it didn't calm my temper with Hank being late.

It was almost 6:30 and my blood pressure was rising as I counted the minutes that he was late. I reached into the bottom drawer and pulled out the new bottle of whiskey I had brought with me. I was just about to unscrew the top when I heard the front door open. I grumbled under my breath as I put it back in the drawer. There was a light knock on the door followed by Hank's big ass head peaking in.

"We said 5. It's 6:30." I glared at him as he made his way in and sat down across from me.

"I know, I'm sorry. My contact I've been working with was able to get some more information for me, that's why I was late." He crossed his leg over his knee and leaned back in the worn-out leather chair.

145

"It better be worth it," I warned as I waited for him to get on with it already. He was lucky I had given him a week to get the information before I threatened to pound his head into the concrete outside.

"We ran Mia Johnson through the system but kept hitting dead ends. As you know, she isn't using any of her credit cards and has been off the radar." *No fucking shit, Sherlock.* How the fuck did this guy ever make it through the academy? Did they not have standards anymore?

"Then we ran her social security number and found that she legally changed her name eleven years ago from Amelia Johnson to Mia Johnson." He smiled as he waited for my reaction. *Keep waiting, kid, keep waiting.*

"And why exactly do I care about that?"

"Because Mia Johnson isn't showing up anywhere, however Amelia Johnson is currently employed and renting an apartment in Haven Brook, Colorado." He smirked as if he just proved the earth was round. My hand twitched as it fought the urge to reach across the desk and smack it off of his face.

"Where is Haven Brook?" I asked as I thought back to whether she had ever mentioned her hometown while we were dating. It didn't ring a bell, so I assumed she hadn't told me where she was from. Just like how she apparently never bothered to tell me her real name either.

"It's a few hours from Denver. Small town but growing in size, especially over the recent years. They recently added some new apartments and some condos are going up later this year by the golf course they are adding as well."

I rolled my eyes as Hank spoke. Who the fuck cared about any of that? I asked him to find my wife, not plan my next vacation. I couldn't wait to be done with this asshole.

"I didn't ask for a fucking tour guide to tell me about the town, dumb ass." I sighed heavily as I rubbed my temple from the headache he was inducing. "Who's your contact?"

"I have a cousin who works in law enforcement in Eastern Point, it's another small town near Haven Brook. I decided to have him search Colorado since that's where her flight landed."

"How far is that from where she's at?" I looked down at my phone as another text message popped up from Claire. While I appreciated the dirty texts she would send me, she was starting to get too clingy. I slid my phone to the side of my desk and waited for Hank's response.

"It's about an hour away."

"Good. Tell him to drive out there and find her. He's not to approach her or have any contact with her. I want to know where she's at, what she's doing, and what her routine looks like."

I wanted to pack up right then and there and get on a plane to Colorado so I could end this bullshit right now but I couldn't do that. I had a charity dinner to attend tomorrow night that the firm was hosting and I was damned if I was going to try to explain to Ronnie why I wasn't going. He was already watching me like a hawk and stopped by the house unexpectedly to talk to Mia. It was getting harder and harder to come up with lies and I needed to be able to sneak out of town without anyone noticing I was gone. My plan would never work otherwise.

"I can't ask him to go down there, he has a wife and kids!" Hank threw his hands in the air.

I felt the vein in my temple throb as I glared at him. *Did he seriously just say no to me? Did he forget who the fuck he was dealing with?*

"He doesn't have an option. Either he gets down there and watches her for a few days and reports back to me, or I bring him on charges of obstruction."

"Obstruction? How so?!" Hank's voice rose along with my temper. I slammed my fist down on the desk, causing Hank to jump in response. I watched the look on his face change as I turned toward him.

"You don't think that I can link him to the missing money? Who knows, he might have even tried to bribe me to try to get you a lesser sentence." I raised an eyebrow as I challenged him. I didn't even know about his cousin until 5 minutes ago, it's not like I had any time to dig up any dirt on the douche bag.

"You dirty son of a bitch!" Hank lunged forward in his chair, knocking the pen holder over in the process. I watched as it spilled across my desk, regret on Hank's face as he watched it happen.

I didn't get the feeling that in general, Hank was intimidated by me. He was a cop and surely had dealt with far worse than the likes of me. However, Hank was intimidated by me because I was the ONLY lawyer who was willing to take his case when all others had declined, knowing they would never win. I planned to hang that over his head as long as I needed. He didn't need to know that I had been stuck with his case. He held out hope that I had taken it because I thought I could help him, and that was all that I needed to keep him hooked.

"You have no proof, and you know it!" His face was red with anger which amused me.

"Who do you think people are going to believe, Hank? A crooked cop who was caught on video stealing cash from his wife's work, or an upstanding lawyer who has a clean track record?" I raised my eyebrow even further to challenge him to correct me. I watched as he worked his jaw back and forth in frustration.

He leaned back in his chair as he shook his head at me, disgust on his face. I could care less. All I cared about was finding Mia and tracking her movements. I needed someone to watch her until I could get there myself and take care of things from there.

"So what's it going to be Hank? Are you going to call him and get me in contact with him, or do I need to start working on paperwork?"

He shook his head as he lifted out of his seat and pulled out his cell phone. I watched as he pressed a few buttons and put it on speakerphone as we waited for the guy to answer. After five rings I assumed it would go to voicemail when I heard a male voice answer.

"Hey Lenny, it's me." Hank let out a deep breath as he glared at me over the phone.

"What's up?"

"I need another favor. I have you on speakerphone. I'm at my lawyer's office, he's the one that we're trying to find the information on the girl for."

"Okay...." There was hesitation on the other line.

"His name is Damian and he's gonna tell you what he needs. You guys will be in contact from here on." Hank reached over and handed me the phone. There was silence from Lenny as he waited for me to talk.

"Lenny, I need you to drive down to Haven Brook and follow Mia for a few days until I can make it down there."

"And why exactly would I do that?" His attitude instantly pissed me off. Now was the time to play my hand and see what would happen.

"Because I know you took money from Hank, from what was embezzled. He's on the hook for a Class B felony, I wouldn't want to be linked to any part of that if I were you." There was an edge to my tone.

"Son of a bitch." He sighed heavily. "I didn't want to take the money. My wife is sick and the medical bills are piling up, we didn't want to lose the house."

Bingo. I had both of them where I wanted them. I had no idea that Hank had given him money. Bluffing paid off. I heard Lenny fall silent on the other end as he waited for me to play my hand.

"Then I guess if you don't want to do jail time, you better do as I'm fucking asking you." My tone was harsh and void of any empathy. I had my own problems, I didn't care about him or his wife.

"Fine. What do you want?"

"Drive there tonight. Watch her but don't approach her or let her know that you're there. I want to know where she lives, where she works, what she drives- I want to know everything. Who she talks to. Where she goes." I let out a deep breath frustrated that I had to give this incompetent moron step by step instructions instead of doing it myself.

"And find her phone number, I know she has a new one. I want an update from you as soon as you find her and we'll take it from there with step by step directions."

Silence lingered on the other end of the line and for a moment I wondered if he hung up on me. I prayed for his sake that he didn't. That would've been a fucking stupid move to make on his end.

"Got it?" My voice was deep and controlled as my knuckles turned white from how hard I gripped the phone.

"Yeah, I got it. Text me your info and I'll send you an update as soon as I find her."

There was an edginess to his voice as I heard the line disconnect before I had a chance to say anything further. He had no idea who he was dealing with. I tossed the phone back to Hank and nodded my head toward the door for him to leave.

A few minutes later I heard the front door open and close and knew I was finally alone in the office. I reached down and pulled out the bottle of whiskey. I waited for the familiar burn as it passed down my throat and watched the phone as I called Claire. The phone rang twice before she purred hello as she answered. I rolled my eyes as I stuffed the bottle back into the bottom drawer and closed it. I needed a release and with her I didn't have to work for it, which made it somewhat worth it to deal with her pathetic little show.

"Be naked with your ass up on the bed when I get there in 10 minutes." I hung up the phone as I left the office, the tension from the day soon to be relieved.

Twenty Two
Mia

It was slow for a Saturday night, even with the few tables that had made their way in for dinner. I dropped off a couple of beers at a table and scanned the room as I made my way back up behind the bar and looked for any sign of Jade. I hadn't heard the door chime that someone had come in, but I was so anxious to see her that I found myself obsessing over when she would get there. The last update I had received from her was a quick text message last night: yoga tomorrow at 6:30.

I had my back turned as I entered the order into the system and waited for the receipt to print. Out of the corner of my eye I noticed someone approach the bar and sit down, my body already on full alert. I didn't have to look behind me to know who was there. He had this natural ability to draw me to him without trying. A small smile formed on my lips as I tore the receipt off and slid it onto the mini clipboard and turned around to face him.

"Hey." His tone was happy though I could hear a level of uncertainty in it. We hadn't talked since I asked him to leave my apartment last night, and I had avoided him the majority of the day today when he showed up unexpectedly to work. I smiled and waited for him to smile back, unsure of what to do. There was an awkwardness between us and I hated it.

"Do you want something to drink?" I asked as I glanced behind me at the beers on tap, unsure of what he was in the mood for.

"Just water, please." I was surprised that he didn't want a beer but thought better than to ask him about it. I needed to figure out what the lines and boundaries were going to be between us and that meant that right now I needed to stay his friend and keep my distance. But how do you act like a caring friend while wanting to be more than friends, without acknowledging that you want to be more than friends? The door chimed behind me and I was thankful for a distraction from my thoughts. I leaned to the side to get a look at the door as I placed the glass of water in front of Chase, my eyes still focused on the door.

"How's it going today? You seem a little distracted."

I looked over to find him watching me with curiosity on his face. He has always had a way of reading me without me having to say much so it was no surprise that he would notice the change in me today.

"Jade is supposed to be here today. She text that she thought she would be here around 6:30 and she's supposed to meet me here. Every time I hear the door, I get excited that it might be her." I sighed as I watched another young couple walk in and make their way out to the patio area. "It feels almost surreal that she's going to be here soon. That I'll get to see her again and that she made it safely." I let out a sigh and slid my finger over my phone to check for any messages or calls from Jade. Nothing. I looked down at the time. 6:45. I felt my face drop as my anxiety started to rise. What if something had happened to her and she wasn't going to make it after all?

"I'm sure she'll be here soon. You know traffic sometimes gets jammed up on the way in, maybe she got stuck in it?" His voice was gentle which for a moment made me feel better.

"Maybe." I turned my head away to look out at the patio. Noah's head tilted back as he laughed at something one of the girls said as she ran her fingers up his arm. For a moment I was jealous that I would never have that kind of a life. My life would always be clouded by fear that Damian would find me. It had been three weeks since I had left but only a few days since he had gone after Jade looking for me which left me with little hope that he would give up on finding me.

The front door chimed again and I looked over to see Jade walk in, her eyes scanned the room as she looked for me. Once her eyes landed on mine, we both smiled and I let out the breath I had been holding. I quickly made it around the bar as she came running over and pulled me into a hug. For a moment nothing else mattered and no one else was in the room, just her and I. Happiness filled my heart as I held her, knowing that she was okay. My body trembled as the emotions continued to flow through me.

"Jade! I'm so happy to see you! You're really here!" I shrieked with excitement as she smiled back at me.

"I'm so happy to see you too, I've been worried sick about you since you left." She ran her hand up and cupped my cheek as she wiped away a tear that had made its way down my face. "This place is ADORABLE, Mia. I love it here!"

"You've only been here a few minutes, how can you love it already?" I laughed as I let go of her and walked the short distance to where Chase was sitting, watching us.

"Jade, this is Chase. Chase, this is Jade." I introduced them as Jade sat on the barstool next to Chase and they shook hands. I heard the door to the patio open and watched as Noah made his way up to the bar, unaware of Jade sitting next to Chase. He came around the corner and went to say something to Chase when I saw his eyes light up at the sight of Jade. I laughed as I watched him try to put together what was happening.

"Hi, I'm Noah." He smiled as he extended his hand out to Jade, completely oblivious to the fact that Chase and I were there as well.

"This is Jade," I offered as he turned to look at me, surprised that I was standing there.

"Ah, the best friend from Boston. Nice to meet you." He smiled the smile that usually melted girls' panties and I waited for Jade's reaction.

"Nice to meet you too." She pulled her hand back, completely unphased by the interaction. Usually women were smiling back at him and batting their eyes, but not Jade. I wasn't sure if she even knew he was still there. I let out a chuckle at the same time as Chase. Our eyes met and instantly we both burst into laughter, knowing that we were both thinking the same thing.

"What's so funny?" Noah looked between both of us, waiting for the punchline to our joke.

"Nothing." I smirked as I tried to avoid his look, afraid that I would laugh even harder if I made eye contact with him. In all of the years that I've known Noah, I have never seen him meet a woman who wasn't instantly into him. This was refreshing to say the least.

"Did you have any trouble getting down here?" Chase asked as he turned on the barstool toward Jade and shifted the focus from Noah's subtle rejection. Noah let out a soft sigh as he raked a hand through his hair and went to enter his sales into the system.

"Everything seemed to go fine. I didn't notice anyone following me and I ditched my cell phone in Boston before I got into the rental car." Jade reached over and squeezed Chase's hand for a second as she took a deep breath. "Thank you again for what you did for me with the rental car. I can't imagine how I would have been able to leave so easily if it hadn't been for your help."

"Of course, it was no big deal. Did you get the care package in the glove box?"

Jade let out a laugh as she nodded yes. "Yes, thank you."

"So, what was in it?" I probed, relieved that she was finally here. I watched her as she talked and tried not to focus on the fading bruises that were left on her body because of me.

"There were the essentials that came in very handy- cash, a few gift cards for gas, some snacks, and a few CDs." She tried to hide a giggle as we all waited for her to keep going. "The CDs were nothing but songs about hating men. I think my favorites were a toss-up between Miranda Lambert's Kerosene and Mama's Broken Heart." Laughter erupted as I tried to picture Jade driving by herself along the open highway, belting out country songs. As long as I had known her, she was always a rock kind of girl so I couldn't see her jamming out to country.

"Sounds like Marty." Chase smiled warmly.

"Well, you must be tired after driving for a few days. Do you want to go get settled in at my place? I should be home in a few hours but you can make yourself at home until I get there."

"That sounds great, thank you." She smiled as I pulled my keys out of my pocket and handed them to her. It felt really good to have her back in my life and to know that she was safe. I gave her directions to my apartment, followed by Noah's offer to personally escort her there, if needed, and watched as she walked out and headed for my apartment. My heart felt full that my best friend was back in my life and that she was safe.

The night continued by at a fast pace as Chase stayed working on something in his office and Noah stayed on the patio with the bachelorette party. The bachelorette party was heading out around 8:30 which left the place practically empty. Noah left with the girls and asked that I close by 9 and be out by 9:30. I practically squealed with excitement to get to leave early and go hang out with Jade. There was so much that I wanted to catch her up on with Chase and everything that had happened since we last talked. It felt like it had been such a long time since we were able to really talk to each other and I missed that connection we had.

At 9:00 on the spot, I went up front and locked the front doors, relieved to be done. As I made my way back toward the bar, I felt a vibration in my pocket and pulled my cell phone out to find a text message from Chase. For a moment, I had forgotten he was still back there and I hadn't told him that we were closing early tonight.

Chase: When Noah takes a break let me know.

Mia: He left 30 minutes ago to go with the girls from the bachelorette party. I just closed the front and plan to be out of here in 30 minutes. Might want to call him on his cell.

I sat my phone on the counter and grabbed the towel and cleaning supplies to clean the last few tables that had left. I quickly worked the towel across the last table, lifting the sugar packets to clean underneath them. As I moved them back across the table my arm bumped the bottle of cleaner, causing it to roll across the floor. It rolled quickly under another table, finally stopping further back than I could reach. I sighed as I pulled my skirt down a little then got down on my hands and knees to crawl under the table to get it.

"Fuck, Mia." I peered over my shoulder to see Chase standing behind me, arms crossed over his chest in frustration.

"Sorry, I didn't hear you come in."

"Do you have any fucking idea what you're doing?" He ran a hand down the scruff on his face as he let out a low muffled growl.

"Picking up the bottle of cleaner?" I offered my cheesiest smile as I stood up and sat the cleaner on the table between us.

"You can't wear a short skirt like that then be running around here on your hands and knees with your ass in the air Mia."

"Why not?" I chewed my bottom lip as I looked up at him, his eyes hooded. My stomach clenched and I reminded myself that I was venturing into more than friends territory the more I flirted with him. Even if it was subconscious.

"Because you make it really hard for me to not pull you over here and fuck some sense into you. Damn it, Mia," he growled.

"I didn't know anyone else was in here, I'll try to be more careful with cleaning up next time." I had hoped to lighten the mood but given that he didn't seem to be budging on his side, I picked up the cleaning supplies and carried them back down the hallway to put them away. I could feel his footsteps in line behind me.

"Look Mia, about last night-"

I held up my hand to cut him off. I had beat myself up about it all night last night and didn't want to get into it with him tonight. I just wanted to give it some time and hope that my attraction to him would subside. He deserved better than a woman who was hiding from her husband and may have to up and leave at any given moment.

"No Chase, we're not talking about last night."

"And why the hell not?" I could hear the frustration in his voice as I felt his glare on me.

"Because now isn't the time to try to discuss it. Things are complicated and I don't imagine they are going to get any easier." I sighed as I looked up at him. I needed to walk away and clear my head. To stop letting him look at me the way he was. The way that made me want to let down the wall I had been working so hard to build.

"Things are only hard if we make them hard. I like you. You like me. I find you attractive. You think I'm pretty hot as well. What is so hard about that?" He stepped to the side as I made my way down the hallway, expecting him to reach out to stop me. Surprisingly, he didn't. My stomach dropped a little bit and I scolded myself for wanting the physical contact from him.

"It's just hard, okay? I need to go finish closing." I walked past him and let the door close behind me as my heart ached for shutting him out. I fought so hard all of my life to find someone who would love me and now that I had someone who wanted to, I wasn't able to let them in.

I was finishing with closing up front when I felt my phone vibrate in my pocket. I stuffed the report into the deposit bag and zipped it closed as I pulled out my phone and looked at the screen. I had thought that it might be Chase, disappointment hitting me when the screen said Unknown instead. I debated on whether to answer the call since I didn't know who it was, then remembered that Jade's phone shows up as Unknown in my phone. I smiled as I slid the button to answer the call.

"Hey!" My voice was more cheerful than usual, the smile still prominent on my face.

"Hello, Mia." My blood ran cold as I stilled, Damian's voice paralyzing me. I must have heard wrong. There was no way that he would be calling me. How did he get my number? I stayed silent for what felt like hours when I was interrupted by the sound of his voice.

"Cat got your tongue?"

"How did you get this number?" I whispered, unsure of what else to say. Cautiously I looked around as I turned my back against the counter. My eyes continued to scan the room as I waited for him to talk.

"You know what's funny- when you get stuck defending a crooked cop and suddenly they have access to a lot of things. Like birth names and social security numbers that show where you're currently renting a new apartment," he taunted. "You know what's not funny? When your wife leaves you and you have to spend three weeks trying to chase her down."

I heard the tone in his voice as I remembered the fights we had right before I left. My skin felt cold as goosebumps ran up along my arms. Suddenly the warm evening night had an icy chill to it.

"That makes me fucking angry. And you *know* that I don't like getting angry, Mia."

"What do you want Damian?" I used the tone that I knew would work with him. The one that was direct and to the point, without sounding like I was actually standing up to him. It was what helped me to dodge fights that could have been a lot worse than they were. I needed to know where he was as much as I needed the air which suddenly felt too thick to breath.

"You know what I want. I want what is mine." He paused for a minute as silence filled the empty space. "I thought I had made myself very clear, there is no *you* without *me*."

His words were heavy and I could hear the weight of the whiskey on every breath. He would drink so much that it became harder and harder for him to speak as his words got jumbled and the alcohol numbed his body.

"Damian, just let me go. Please. You don't want or need me. You're happier without me." I pleaded as I slowly walked the short distance along the bar until I reached the window. I pulled my body back as I tried to stay hidden in the shadows while I looked around outside for any sign of him.

"You think you know what the fuck makes me happy?! You haven't made me happy in years," he scoffed. "This isn't about what makes me happy, Mia. This is about taking what is fucking mine and dealing with your behavior. I've warned you…." His voice trailed off as I continued to search the darkness.

"It would seem that you've forgotten your place, dear *wife*," He spit out the word wife as if it disgusted him. "You come back home, dress like a slut in your little denim skirt, and think that I won't find you? You're even stupider that I thought."

His words send a chill down my spine. I clutched a hand to my heart as I gripped the phone tighter, desperate to find him. If he knew what I was wearing, that meant he could see me. Even if I couldn't see him. My body trembled as the fear coursed through me, shredding every ounce of hope I had built up the last three weeks of surviving him.

A movement outside caught my eye and I leaned forward slowly, no longer worried about keeping myself hidden since he obviously knew where I was. Across the street sat a man on the bench at the bus stop with a cell phone in his hand. My heart raced as I stared at the figure partially hidden in the shadows of the night sky. I continued to watch in horror as he lifted his hand and waved at me. It was a slow, creepy wave. The kind of thing that haunted you in horror movies, only this was real life. I brought my hand to my mouth as I fought the urge to let out a scream.

The line was quiet as I waited for Damian to talk. Anxiety built as I watched him sit in the darkness, stalking me. My breathing became shallow as I strained to listen for any sign of movement on the other line, desperate for him to say something. He continued to sit at the bus stop, no effort to come over to where I was. The longer he stayed silent and didn't move, made me even more uncomfortable. He was being unpredictable and it was eating at me.

"Don't you know it's rude not to wave back?" His voice broke my concentration as it brought me back to the phone call.

The door to the back offices opened and I realized that I had completely forgotten that Chase was still there. I turned to look at him, thankful that I wasn't by myself. My eyes were wide as I kept my phone pressed against my ear and let out a shaky breath as I turned my attention to back to the window. All of a sudden the bus stop was empty. I leaned forward as I pressed the phone harder to my ear and searched the area, not seeing any sign of him. My heartbeat quickened as I tried to find him, unsure of where he had gone. Knowing that he was here and that he knew where I was, but that I had no idea where he was, made my stomach churn.

"Remember, you can run, but you can't hide." The line disconnected and I stared at it, bewildered. Then I realized that this was all a game for him. He could have come for me long ago and already ended this. He wasn't the kind of man who waited for the right time, he was reckless and careless when he didn't like something. But he had warned me the night that I left that this was a game for him; *how about a game of hide and seek? You TRY to hide, and I'll let you wait in fear before I come to find you.*

I knew that he liked the idea of torturing me, it gave him a sense of control and made him felt powerful. The physical attacks had gotten worse, but I started to fight back and he didn't like that. What I hadn't expected was that he would move on to playing mind games.

I felt Chase walk up beside me, concern on his face as he tried to assess the situation. I stayed staring out the window as I held my cell phone close to my chest.

"Mia, what's going on?" His voice was low as he looked out the window with me.

"He found me." I turned around and looked up at Chase, desperate to feel safe but not sure that I ever would as long as Damian was after me.

"Is he here?" Chases eyes went wide as he stepped past me and looked out the glass doors that led to the patio. Fear paralyzed me as I watched Chase go back and forth between the windows and doors, looking for a sign of Damian.

"Mia, is he here? What did he say?" There was an urgency in his voice and I struggled to try to focus on what he was asking, my mind still reeling from his words.

"He's here. He found me. He knows what I'm wearing. He's watching me." My words stumbled out of my mouth as I tried to get everything relevant out at once.

"Where is he, Mia? Did you see him?" Chase stood directly in front of me and placed his hands on my shoulders as he pulled my gaze into his. His eyes searched mine as if they would hold the answers that my mouth couldn't get out.

"There was a man sitting across the street at the bus stop. I couldn't see him very well. But he waved. This really slow, creepy wave." I tried to imitate it the best I could. "Then he told me it was rude not to wave back. I couldn't see the guy, Chase, but it had to be him, right?"

"Mia, get your things, we're leaving." His hand touched my lower back as he guided me. He stayed by my side as we put the deposit in the safe and grabbed my things before making our way to the front door. I felt relieved that I had him there with me so I didn't have to face Damian alone, but I was also terrified of what Damian might do to him. Guilt weighed heavily as I thought about how selfish I was being by allowing him to help me.

"I can't go home." I whispered as we walked to the front door. "He's coming for me. He'll kill me this time."

I looked down at the floor, sadness and despair taking hold of me. Just hours ago I had been so happy and excited, now I was back to where I had been three weeks ago. Jade! I had completely forgotten that Jade was at my apartment. The apartment that Damian said he knew about. What if he was there right now? Panic rose as I worried about Jade and how I would get to her before Damian could.

"You're not going home," Chase leaned forward to look outside before opening the door. He was on high alert, just like I was. "You're coming home with me so I can keep an eye on you and protect you."

"He knows where I live, Chase." My eyes looked past him into the darkness outside, wondering if he was out there waiting for me. "Jade is at my apartment." I swallowed hard as I lifted my head to look at him.

"We'll take care of it, Mia. Don't worry, you guys are safe here." He leaned forward and kissed my forehead, taking away some of the worry and stress that was suffocating me.

I took a deep breath as he opened the door and we walked the short distance to his truck as I looked around, waiting for Damian to come out of the shadows. I got in his truck and waited for Chase to close the door behind me while I checked my cell phone for any missed calls or texts from Jade. So far nothing. Chase opened the driver's side door and climbed in, locking the doors before starting the truck. I watched as he pulled out his cell phone and called Noah, allowing the call to go through the truck's blue tooth so he could drive.

The truck pulled forward and I nervously looked around, wondering which vehicle Damian might be in. Would he simply follow us and continue to stalk me? Would he ram the vehicle and push us off the side of the road like I've seen in movies? My mind was running wild while I listened to the phone ringing throughout the cab.

"You have the WORST timing. Someone better be dead." Noah muttered into the phone.

"Well, Damian's in town and found Mia. So how's that for bad timing?"

"What the fuck? What happened? Is she okay?" Noah's tone had immediately changed and I listened as it went from noisy to quite as he left wherever he was when he first took the call.

"She's fine, she's with me. I'm taking her to my place but we need to check on Jade. She's at Mia's apartment. He knows where she lives."

"I'm on it. Let me know when you guys get home."

"Will do. Get me an update on Jade ASAP."

"You got it."

The call disconnected as I sent up silent prayers that Jade would be okay. Guilt overwhelmed me as I thought about how hard she fought to make it out here, only to have Damian show up at the same time. Maybe she would have been better off staying in Boston, instead of uprooting her life to come to Haven Brook. It seemed anyone I cared about became an instant target for Damian and that thought killed me as I looked over at the man next to me.

Twenty Three
Chase

There was a brisk chill in the air that made me feel even more alert as I drove toward my house. I had no idea what Damian looked like, and frankly, I was kicking myself for not looking him up sooner. But having lived in Haven Brook all my life, I knew pretty much everyone who lived here, including the new families that had moved in over the past few years. It was rare that a single person moved into town, and when they did, the town talked about it. I had a feeling that I would immediately know Damian the moment I saw him, for that exact reason. He would stick out like a sore thumb.

The drive from The Vine to my house was short and usually only took me about ten minutes, but I decided to take the long way to make sure no one was following us. As I pulled onto the one lane highway that leads out of town, I felt Mia's eyes on me

"Where are you going?" she asked confused.

"I'm taking the back-way home to make sure we aren't being followed." I glanced in my mirrors repeatedly as I took the exit onto the dirt path that would eventually lead back to my house. The road was barely a road, more of a beaten path that some of the locals took when they wanted to go off roading. There were no streetlights and the closest house was miles away and not visible through the thick forest of trees. I knew these roads better than most who lived here and knew that the likelihood of encountering another car would be slim, unless we were being followed. I was more likely to encounter wildlife, which was another item added to my list of things to watch for.

The road was dark and quiet as we made our way along, the sound of dirt and gravel crunching under the tires filling the cab. I wanted to talk to Mia about what had happened but I didn't want to push her until she was ready to talk about it. Noah knew what had happened and why she left but he's never said anything to me about it, other than to allow Mia to tell me herself. And now, I needed to know what happened. In order to protect her, I needed to know what this guy was capable of.

"Growing up with Noah, I had to know all of the back streets and places to hide when he'd get into trouble," I tried to break the silence by offering an explanation of why I took this road. "Which you know with Noah meant we were traveling these roads every weekend. This road will actually take us to my house and I'll be able to see if anyone has been following us before we get there." I watched her shoulders rise and fall as she listened, knowing that her mind was still somewhere else.

The road wound around a few bends before it finally came to an end. I slowed as I approached the fork in the road and followed it to the right. The ten miles of dirt road had been clear of any other drivers and I hadn't seen any headlights in the area which meant we hadn't been followed. A few miles down the road and I turned left onto the road that wound up the side of the mountain, leading to my house. I loved that my house was secluded from the others with at least an acre between each house and the mountain as my backyard. It gave me the country feel that I wanted while being ten minutes away from the modern conveniences that I enjoyed.

I pulled into the paved driveway and looked around as I scanned the area before I pressed the button to open the garage. Once I made sure everything was clear I pulled in and waited for the garage door to close behind us before getting out and helping Mia out of the truck. I could feel the heat from Mia's body behind me as I entered the six-digit alarm code and waited for the beep to confirm it was turned off. She fidgeted with the hem of her shirt, a giveaway that she was nervous. While I was relieved to have her there with me so I could protect her, I felt bad that we hadn't had a chance to talk about what had happened last night. I had been trying to talk about it but she shot me down every chance she could. The alarm beeped, indicating that it had been turned off.

"Nice place," Mia commented as she stepped into the open space as we walked inside. She stepped to the side, out of the way, unsure of where to go.

"Thank you." I smiled as I set the alarm behind me. I wanted to make sure she felt safe with me, even if I never set the alarm except for when I left. "Let me show you around since you'll be here with me for a few days."

She smiled as she waited for my lead. It felt weird having Mia in my house, especially knowing that she would be living with me for at least a few days. I felt nervous like a teenage boy who was hoping to go to first base for the first time but not having any clue what to do. I ran my palms down the front of my jeans as I took a few steps into the open space that served as the living room and kitchen, looking around to see where to begin.

"So this is the living room," I pointed toward the couch and love seat that surrounded a distressed wood coffee table. The TV hung mounted on the wall above the fireplace which was next to the door that led to the garage. "and this is the kitchen. Obviously." I felt so awkward as if she couldn't tell that it was a kitchen. I wanted to smack my forehead for sounding like such an idiot. I watched as she walked by the island that separated the kitchen from the living room and ran her fingers along the smooth granite top. She leaned to the side to glance out the sliding glass door that led to the wrap around porch and I saw a shimmer of disappointment cross her face when she realized it was too dark to see anything.

"There's a full wrap around porch. This end has a hot tub and the grill, the front has a swing and a few rocking chairs that my grandpa and I used to sit in when I was a little boy," I explained as I turned on the porch lights for her to see outside. A soft smile formed when I mentioned my grandpa and memories of us hanging out with him when we were growing up crossed my mind.

"You've done a lot with this place. I barely remembered where it was when we were driving here, but now that I'm inside, it feels like we're ten years old again."

"My grandpa always wanted to fix it up and make it more modern before he died but he never got the chance. I started working on some of the renovations, like the porch and the fireplace, before he passed. He helped when he could, otherwise he would sit and tell me stories while I worked." Talking about my grandpa had never been easy for me since he passed but talking about him with Mia felt comfortable and easy.

"He would have loved all of this. You did a really good job." She squeezed my forearm gently as she walked away from the sliding glass door and waited for me to continue with showing her the rest of the house.

"Thanks, I really appreciate it. I figured the least I could do was finish the dreams he had for the place after he left it to me." I laughed a nervous laugh and waited for her response. Everyone had made me feel like I was some entitled prick that took his grandpa's house and destroyed it after he passed. Little did anyone know that my grandpa had left me the house, completely paid off, along with a hefty savings account to finish the projects that we had hoped to work on together. I worked hard at The Vine to earn my keep, even if I didn't have a mortgage to pay. It was a constant struggle to feel like I had to justify myself to others and prove that I worked just as hard as anyone else.

"I'm sure he was relieved to know that you would take care of it and continue to work on the things he didn't get a chance to do with you. There's nothing wrong with that, Chase." She paused to look up at me as I walked closer to her. "Anyone who really knows you, knows that you busted your ass to help your grandpa with this house, while also helping your mom take care of your brothers after your dad passed, AND while trying to start your own life. Anyone who tells you any different is an idiot and you shouldn't be surrounding yourself with people like that."

In just a few minutes she took the years of guilt and worry that I had been harboring and destroyed them with her words. No one has ever made me feel like I was a good person for taking over my grandfather's house and continuing his projects. This was one of the reasons why I loved her. She was always real and honest with me, and she had a way of making me feel good about myself when others tried to knock me down.

I smiled down at her and for a moment I felt that connection between us again. The one that no matter how hard I tried to avoid it, forced me to want to pull her into my arms and kiss her. Her face was filled with mixed emotions as I watched her smile then look away, unsure of where she should look.

"So this hallway leads to the bathroom and bedrooms." I nodded toward the hallway as we started to walk in that direction, hoping to get past the awkward tension that had filled the room.

"The guest bedroom is here on the right, the bathroom is across the hall on the left, and at the end of the hall on the right is the master bedroom and bathroom." I stepped to the side to let her look into the guest bedroom. Confusion crossed her face as she leaned in further and pulled back out, her eyebrows pulled in.

"The room is empty."

"Yeah, I don't have many guests."

"Oh. Well, no problem, I can sleep on the couch." She licked her lips as she tugged at the bottom of her shirt again.

"You're not sleeping on the couch." I turned her to face the master bedroom and gently placed my hand on her lower back to guide her in.

"Then where am I supposed to sleep?" She looked up at me inquisitively.

"In the bed." I shoved my hands in my pockets as I leaned against the door frame and nodded toward the bed.

"Chase, I am not sleeping in your bed."

"Why not?"

"Because I don't want to put you out and make you sleep on the couch."

"I won't be sleeping on the couch."

"Then where are you going to sleep?"

"In the bed."

"In the bed?"

"Yup."

"I'm not sleeping in your bed with you." She walked across the room and turned to look at me with her arms crossed over her chest.

"Why not?"

"Because that would be….. weird. Awkward. Hard…."

"How so?" I was really enjoying watching her squirm. It was cute. If she really didn't want to share the bed with me, that was fine, I would sleep on the couch. But I was having fun with the back and forth and watching her reaction to it.

"Because- it's just- it's hard."

"Most women find that to be a good thing." I raised my eyebrows suggestively. "Just saying."

I watched as her face turned a slight shade of pink as the blush made its way down her neck.

"You're impossible." The smile she tried to keep off of her face gently pulled up at the corners of her mouth before she looked away.

"What, are you afraid that you won't be able to keep your hands off me if we share a bed? Mia, I'm a man, not a piece of meat…"

I waited for a sarcastic answer to come out of her mouth but instead I saw a look of guilt on her face before she quickly looked away. While I hadn't expected that to be an actual reason for her to not want to share the bed with me, I was quite flattered to know that she felt that way.

"I'm kidding, Mia. Not to worry, we don't have to share the bed. However, you will be sleeping in it either way. I won't budge on that." I smiled as I pushed off from the wall and joined her in the middle of the room.

The bathroom was immediately off to the left as soon as you entered the bedroom and was a pretty decent size for how old the house was. I had remodeled the bathroom after my grandpa had passed away and gutted the entire bathroom. The old, outdated tub was replaced with a walk-in shower and the hard wood floors were replaced with gray rustic looking wood planks. Across from the shower was a full wall mirror that sat above a double sink with a few drawers beneath the counter. The counter ran along the length of the wall which created a four-foot space by the bathroom door that was open. Aside from a small wastebasket, there was nothing else in this space which made the bathroom feel more open. The remodel took longer than I had expected due to some water damage that I didn't know about, but it was one of my favorite projects that I had completed so far.

I watched as Mia took in the master bedroom and looked around. It wasn't a big room but was big enough to fit a king-sized bed that was centered along the wall with the bathroom and had a nightstand on each side. There was a huge bay window that took up the outside wall with three panes that curved outward with a plush bench seat and throw pillows beneath it. Growing up I would often find my grandma sitting on the bench seat crocheting or reading a book. Someday I pictured my future wife doing the same.

Across from the bed was a TV mounted to the wall above a chest of drawers. All of the furniture in the room was a dark oak color with light brown paint on the walls. The master closet was more space than I would ever need and was tucked away next to the dresser. Most women would probably complain about how small it was but I loved that I didn't have a ton of room to store unnecessary crap.

"Well, that's everything," I said as I watched her walk around the room and peek inside the bathroom. "Feel free to make yourself at home."

"Thanks, Chase, I really do appreciate it."

"Of course." I smiled warmly at her as the reminder loomed in the air about why she was there to begin with. It wasn't because she had finally given in and decided to be with me. It was because her husband had tracked her down and wanted to kill her, which instantly killed any thoughts I had about having Mia to myself in my house.

"I'm gonna go check in with Noah, I'll let you get settled in if you want." I didn't know how to make things any less awkward and hoped this would be a good chance to get away before it got worse. I knew she didn't have anything with her other than her purse but still, I wanted to give her some space to try to feel as comfortable as possible at my place.

"Thanks." She smiled nervously as she chewed her bottom lip, looking at the chair sitting next to the dresser by the window.

"Alright, I'll be in the living room if you need me." I tapped my knuckles on the doorway a few times as I made my way down the hall, leaving her to have the space she needed. Having her in my house might be even harder than I thought.

Twenty Four
Mia

The night flew by in a blur and my head was spinning as I sat on the edge of Chase's bed and tried to sort through what had actually happened. My worst fear, the one that I always knew deep down, in the back of mind, that it would come true, had happened. Damian found me. I shouldn't be surprised, though I had hoped that he would be too drunk to actually be successful. But then again, once Damian had his mind set on something, no amount of alcohol could stop him.

I sighed as I pulled my cell phone out of the front pocket of my denim skirt and checked the battery which was almost dead thanks to the constant missed calls from what I assumed was Damian. It was hard that Damian and Jade both showed up as unknown in my phone so I didn't know who it was that had called. Finally, Noah and Chase decided that it would be best if Jade called Chase if she needed anything since Damian didn't have his number. I sat my phone on the nightstand, next to my purse when I suddenly realized that I didn't have anything with me other than the clothes on my back and whatever might be in my purse. Anxiety started to loom over me as I thought about how crazy and foolish it was of me to come back to Chase's house. The idea of having someone else around made me feel safer, though the idea of sleeping in his bed made me feel nervous.

He had joked about me not being able to keep my hands off of him, and while he was joking, the blush on my face had given me away. I wanted to kick myself for the reaction he was able to draw out of me so easily. If I could just NOT be attracted to him, things would be so much easier. But as I was quickly learning, nothing in my life was easy right now.

I walked down the hallway and found him sitting on the couch with his cell phone in his hand. He looked serious and I wasn't sure if I should interrupt as I tried to sneak past him to the other couch.

"Hey." He smiled up at me as he slid his phone onto the coffee table and watched me sit down across from him.

"Hi." I pulled my legs up under me while trying to be as ladylike as possible in my skirt. "Have you heard anything from Noah on Jade?"

"I just got off the phone with him a few minutes ago. He checked out the apartment and everything looked fine. He offered to stay with Jade, she said no. He offered her to go stay at his place, she said no. He offered to buy her a pizza, and as you can guess, she said no." He laughed as he glanced down at his cell phone, a text message notification lit up the screen.

I pulled my eyes away. I didn't want to be nosy, even though curiosity was getting the better of me and I really wanted to know who the text message was from. It was a Saturday night and he was a single guy, I should have assumed that he might have a date. Instantly I felt bad for being there and for possibly ruining plans that he might have had to cancel.

"I'm sorry, I feel bad if you had to cancel plans tonight because of me." I nodded toward the cell phone on the coffee table.

"I didn't have any plans."

"Okay." I didn't know what else to say and the awkward tension from earlier surrounded us again.

"It's an alert that the pizza I ordered is out for delivery. I thought you might be hungry, and figured pizza might be a safe bet." He stood as the doorbell rang and I watched as he went to the door and peeked through the peephole before opening it.

A tall, lanky teenage boy with red curly hair tucked under a baseball hat that was too big for his head stood on the other side with a pizza in one hand and a small bag in the other. Chase smiled as he handed him the cash and told him to keep the change. He closed the door and carried the box and bag over to the island, tilting his head as he nodded for me to join him.

I got up and made my way to the island as Chase grabbed paper plates out of the cabinet and sat them in front of us. I waited as he opened the box, extending it toward me to take a slice. The kind gesture of him ordering food for us without asking made my heart full. He was always going above and beyond to take care of everyone else, it made me feel sad that he didn't have anyone to take care of him. I pulled the slice onto my plate and grabbed a napkin from the pile that was in the bag with the packets of red peppers and parmesan cheese.

Chase smiled as he carried his plate over to the coffee table and sat it down. I started to follow, feeling uneasy to just make myself at home, when I felt him watching me.

"You can go ahead and make yourself comfy on the couch. I'll bring us some water, unless you want something else. Beer? Wine? Tea? Whiskey?"

"Water is fine, thank you." I sat on the couch and pulled my legs up under me as I waited for Chase to come sit down before I started to eat. The couch was soft and worn in which made me want to curl up in it and go to sleep. Everything about Chase's house made it feel warm and homey. I felt like I could feel really comfortable there if I could ever get past my attraction to Chase. Everything I touched reminded me that he had touched it too and that thought played at the corners of my mind, entertaining ideas that I had been trying really hard not to have.

"Thank you for the pizza, this is delicious." I took another bite and allowed the fragrant aroma to fill my mouth and satisfy my taste buds. In all the years that I had been gone I was convinced that nothing would ever bring me back to Haven Brook, except maybe pizza from Paul's Pizza. I might even sell my soul for a slice.

"You're welcome."

We sat in silence while we ate and for once, it wasn't an awkward silence. I was relieved for that. I sat my empty plate on the coffee table and leaned back against the couch as I curled up into a soft throw pillow. Between my overly full stomach and the mental exhaustion from the day, I was ready to crash out right then and there. My eyes felt heavy as I laid my head back and closed them.

"Do you want to go get ready for bed?" Chase interrupted my thoughts as I fought the urge to give in and go to sleep. I knew he didn't want me to sleep on the couch but right now, I couldn't imagine that anything would be as soft or as comfortable as this.

"I don't think you can pry me from this couch. It's officially accepted me as its own." My eyes were still closed though I could sense that Chase was close from the light scent of his cologne. It was always light and subtle but my body reacted to it as soon as it smelled it, a smell that had been etched into my memory long ago.

"I don't think it would be hard for anything to accept you." His voice was soft and sincere, a gentleness that I didn't always see from him.

Reluctantly I pushed the pillow to the side and stood up, my body protesting as I moved away from the warmth and comfort of the couch. I smoothed down my skirt as I stood and remembered that I still didn't have anything with me other than what I was wearing. I frowned at the thought of sleeping in my skirt and tank top but it was better than stripping down to my bra and panties in front of Chase.

"What's the matter?" he asked, mimicking the frown I had been making.

"I was just thinking about how I don't have anything to sleep in that would really be appropriate." My voice trailed off as I ran my hands down the front of my skirt and tucked my chin.

"You can borrow something of mine. I have t-shirts and sweats you can wear, though they might be a little too big."

"Thank you. I'm sorry for being such a pain."

"Mia, you're far from a pain. I have several shirts and sweats, I think I can spare some for you to wear tonight. Don't worry about it." He smiled as we walked to the bedroom. I sat on the bed while he pulled a few things out of the closet, holding them up in the air then shaking his head and putting them back in the closet. A few minutes later he came out with a few shirts and a pair of sweatpants folded over his arm and handed them to me.

"Sorry, I tried to find the smallest shirts I could find. I'm hoping that you won't drown in these." He shrugged as he held them out to me. I tried not to laugh as I took them and made my way into the bathroom, closing the door behind me. It was cute that he was so worried about having clothes that would fit me when I was more worried about having clothes that would be too provocative.

I stripped off my tank top and skirt and folded them neatly before setting them in a pile under the counter. The shirt was a little baggy but it fit, and more importantly, it smelled like Chase. I pulled the drawstring on the sweats as tight as it would go and was pleased that they sat low on my hips without falling off. For a moment I felt comfortable and relaxed.

As I opened the bathroom door I found Chase by the closet, shirtless as he bent over to pick up his boots he had kicked off. He was wearing nothing but jeans and socks and I had an unobstructed view of his perfectly ripped body. I imagined he spent a lot of time working outside without a shirt as he had a sun kissed glow. I couldn't imagine how he stayed so lean and fit, with literally zero body fat, when all I've ever seen him eat is pizza. He must spend a lot of time at the gym or maybe he only eats bad when I was around.

He cleared his throat as he pulled up his sweatpants which sat low on his hips and showed off his taut muscles on either side of his abdomen. I had been so consumed with my thoughts that I hadn't paid attention to the fact that I had subconsciously watched him undress, or that he had caught me. I felt his eyes on mine as I tried to pull away.

"Ready for bed?" He came toward the bed and sat his watch on the nightstand next to his phone. It was awkward because I didn't know if he was really planning to sleep in the same bed as me and I didn't want to have expectations either way. Part of me hoped that he would so that I would feel safer, but part of me hoped that he didn't so I didn't feel any temptation to cuddle up against him in my sleep. I didn't want to have to make the decision or to ask him to sleep somewhere else, especially since this is his house and I was an unexpected guest.

"Yeah, are you?" I asked as I looked up at him as if he was going to make the decision on where to sleep.

"Sure am." He walked over toward my side of the bed as I climbed in and pulled the covers up over me. I watched as he bent down and fumbled around beneath the bed. I had no idea what he was doing but his head was next to mine as he smiled and continued to fumble around.

"Liam always ends up losing this." He reached further and finally grabbed whatever he was trying to reach. A beat-up baseball bat appeared next to him as he stood up and positioned it next to the nightstand. "Use this if anything spooks you or if you need it. I'll be on the couch so just yell and I'll be right here."

"Chase, you don't have to sleep on the couch." All of a sudden it felt like I knew what I wanted before I could stop my mouth from saying it.

"It's okay, I don't mind. I want you to be comfortable and to get some rest."

"I think I would actually feel safer with you in here, with me." There was a new level of nervousness in my voice and I couldn't tell if he picked up on it or not.

"Whatever you want, Mia. I don't mind sleeping next to you if that's what you want." His eyes were soft as he waited for my response.

"That's what I want." I reached over and pulled the covers back on his side of the bed as I watched him turn off the light switch by the door and climb into bed. The bed shifted as he climbed in and I realized that I had been wrong earlier. The couch wasn't the most comfortable thing in the house. This bed was. My body relaxed into the softness of the bed and I wondered how many women were responsible for wearing down the mattress to make it this soft. Having Chase next to me made me feel safe and allowed me to rest for a little bit without having to worry about Damian. It was reassuring that if he did find me at Chase's house, at least I had someone else here with me so I didn't have to face him alone. That thought had been floating around in my mind from the moment I got into Chase's truck and had kept me calm throughout the evening. I was thankful for a friend who took me in, no questions asked, and created a safe place for me.

Twenty Five
Chase

The soft snore of Mia sleeping made me feel at peace that she was getting the rest that I hoped she would get. I couldn't imagine what she was feeling after everything that had happened but I could see that she was struggling with how to process all of it. Throughout the night I watched as she checked her phone, silencing it as it rang. I didn't have to ask to know that it was Damian calling her repeatedly.

She seemed distracted and while I still wanted to talk to her and make sure she was really okay, I knew it wasn't the right time to do so. She needed to work through whatever she was trying to work through, and I sensed that part of it was her trying to figure out her feelings toward me and being alone with me in my house.

I had caught her watching me undress and part of me wanted to act on the look in her eye and satisfy every single desire she had. But now wasn't the time or place for that and I needed to remember that she needed me to be her friend, not her distraction. I had seen this plenty of times with other girls. They would be upset about something that had happened, didn't want to deal with it, and ended up in my bed. It's easy to trick yourself into thinking that you want something when you're so desperate to try to get away from something else.

Mia was still living in fear of Damian, even if she was comfortable at my house with me. I noticed how she flinched when the doorbell rang when the pizza was delivered. How she startled when she hadn't heard me walking toward her until I was already right beside her. She was afraid and she had every right to be. I just hated that there wasn't much that I could do to alleviate that fear for her. Until things were resolved with Damian, she wouldn't have any escape from that fear.

It was close to midnight and I still hadn't been able to fall asleep. It wasn't that I couldn't sleep having a woman lying in bed next to me, it was that I couldn't fall asleep knowing that *Mia* was lying in bed next to me. I had dreamt of this day for years, though never due to these circumstances. My body was tired and my eyes were heavy but my mind wouldn't shut down for me to go to sleep. I was never one to be scared of anyone or anything but tonight I found myself overly alert to every little noise. It was unlikely that Damian would be able to find her unless he tracked her cell phone, which was a possibility. I wasn't about to take any chances and assume that random noises couldn't be him.

"No…. please… stop… you're hurting me… please…. stop…I can't breathe…." I rolled over to look at Mia as she continued to mumble in her sleep. I gently tried to shake her to wake her up but her body felt limp and she didn't respond.

"Not my stomach. You're going to kill the baby. Damian, please stop. The baby."

My heart lurched forward in my chest as my mind tried to process the words she just said in her sleep. I desperately shook her, trying to wake her from the nightmare she was having, praying that it was only a dream.

"Mia, wake up." I shook a little harder and rubbed my hand up and down her arm. "Mia, you need to wake up. You're having a bad dream." My heart felt like it was going to beat out of my chest as I continued to try to free her from the dream.

She gasped and jolted forward on the bed, her hand clutching her stomach as her eyes scanned the room. I quickly reached over and turned on the light on my nightstand as I saw her turn toward me. Tears were rolling down her face as she searched mine.

"You're okay, Mia. It was a bad dream. He's not here." I reassured her as I scooted closer to her and wrapped an arm around her. "You're safe, he's not here."

I could feel her body tremble against mine as she cried, my heart continued to break for her.

"Shhhh…." I whispered in her ear as I held her as close as I could. I rocked her gently back and forth as I tried to comfort her.

"It's okay, Mia. I've got you. It's okay."

"Shhhh…." I wanted to comfort her as much as I could but I had no idea what to say to make her feel better so I continued to hold her and hoped that she would feel my love through my touch. I could feel her breathing slow down some as she took a jagged breath as she leaned away from me.

"I'm sorry. I had a bad dream." She wiped her tears away with the back of her hand.

"It's nothing to be sorry about. Are you okay?"

"Yeah. Sometimes he haunts me in my dreams." She let out a shaky breath.

"I can see that. Do you want to talk about it?" I tried to be as gentle as possible. I didn't want to push her, especially with how upset she was.

"What did I say in my dream?" She worked her lower lip back and forth through her teeth as she waited for my response. I didn't want to remind her what it was about if I didn't have to, why make her relive it while she was awake? But part of me felt like maybe she really needed to know so she could try to work through it.

"You sounded like you were fighting Damian." I sighed. "You told him to stop, that you couldn't breathe. Then you mentioned that he would kill the baby." I looked up at her, hoping that she would assure me that it was only a dream. A nightmare that lived in her subconscious and wasn't a part of her reality.

Her eyes filled with a sadness I had never seen in my life, not even when my dad died, or when my grandpa died. A sadness of someone who lost more than their share from someone who purposely wanted to hurt them. I wanted to reach out and hold her. Take her in my arms and never let her go.

"Mia…." My eyes pleaded for an answer.

"I wasn't trying to get pregnant. I mean, we weren't trying. I didn't mean to get pregnant. I was surprised that I could get pregnant." She folded her hands in her lap as she looked down to tell me what had happened. "I was 8 weeks along when I found out. We had just started to have problems, it wasn't anything like what it was when I left. I was hopeful that having a baby would fix things between us, make him love me again." A tear rolled down her cheek as her eyes continued to look down at the bed.

"He wasn't happy about the baby. He accused me of getting pregnant by another man, insisted that I had an affair. I couldn't believe it. This was a few days after he had hit me for the first time." She looked up and met my eyes for a quick second before she looked away again. It killed me that she allowed herself to feel so much shame for this.

"We got into a fight that night and of course, he had been drinking. He had pinned me to the wall and had his hands wrapped around my throat to where I couldn't breathe. I didn't think about it, I just brought my knee up and caught him in the groin. He let me go and I fell. I was worried about the baby as I tried to crawl away from him while catching my breath. He was pissed that I had kneed him and he caught me in the hallway and kicked me a few times in the stomach. I knew then that the baby was gone."

I felt my jaw clenched as she told the story, my knuckles white from gripping the sheets in anger. How could a man ever hurt a woman like that? Before I had hoped to find Damian so I could stop him from hurting Mia. Now I was obsessed with finding this prick so I could make him pay for what he did to Mia.

"Mia, I am so sorry." I didn't know what else to say. There were no words that could ease her pain of what she physically went through at the hands of her ex.

"Thank you." She took a deep breath and looked up at me. "I know it sounds horrible, but in a way, I'm thankful that I lost the baby. It just means that he can't hurt it."

I nodded and pulled her in for a hug as she started to cry against my chest. I wrapped my arms around her as tight as I could without hurting her and allowed her to let herself fall apart. My heart was broken for her.

"Mia, it doesn't sound horrible. It sounds like a good mother who wants to protect her baby from harm. It wasn't your choice what happened to you or to the baby. He's a terrible man and one day he will pay for what he's done. Trust me."

I could feel her body relax into mine and after a few minutes her breathing evened out. Gently I rubbed her back in circles, the way my mom used to do when I would have a bad dream when I was little. Fifteen minutes later I heard the soft sound of snoring and knew that she had fallen asleep in my arms. Part of me didn't want to let go of her, but I knew that she would sleep better laying down than to stay curled up in my arms all night. Gently I rolled her to her side and pulled the covers up over her. She looked small and frail as she laid in my bed, swallowed up by clothes that were too big for her. I reached down and placed a gentle kiss on her cheek as I rolled over and laid down next to her. I was exhausted but after hearing what had happened with Damian, I wasn't about to go to sleep and leave her vulnerable. Reaching over, I grabbed my cell phone from the nightstand and googled Damian Stone. I had a few hours to kill which meant I had time to learn everything I could about the little douche bag.

Twenty Six
Mia

I opened my eyes and tried to adjust to the darkness of the room, trying to figure out where I was. Disoriented, I looked around and saw Chase asleep next to me with his arm sprawled out across my abdomen. I remembered crying and having him comfort me, but I didn't remember falling asleep. Then it occurred to me that I must have fallen asleep on him and he rolled me over so he could get some sleep.

I slowly slid his arm off of me and laid it down by his side as I quietly got out of bed and went to the bathroom. All of the water that I drank during dinner had finally worked its way through me as I fumbled with finding the light switch. I crossed my legs as tight as I could while my hand made its way across the wall, relieved when I found the switch and turned the light on. The bathroom tile was cold on my feet as I sat on the toilet, trying to be as quiet as possible to not wake up Chase. I flushed the toilet and prayed that I wouldn't wake him up as I quickly washed my hands and took a glance in the mirror. My hair was a mess and my blue eyes were red and puffy from crying. Not the best look by any means.

I tiptoed back to bed and slowly got in. The bed shifted with my weight and I held my breath as I slid under the covers, trying to keep my movements small so I didn't wake him. After ten Mississippi's I took a deep breath and rolled onto my side to check my phone. The clock reads that it's 4:00 in the morning and I wondered how long I had been asleep. I had lost track of time earlier and didn't know how long I was up with Chase after my nightmare.

My stomach churned as I thought back to that night and the fight that cost my unborn child its life. I hadn't told anyone that I was pregnant, except for Damian. Chase was the first person I had ever talked about that night with. It was one of the hardest things I had gone through with Damian because I couldn't get past the guilt of costing someone else their life. An innocent baby died because of me. I couldn't get past the sadness of not being able to protect my own child against their parent, something that I vowed to do after the childhood I had. A heavy disappointment had hung over me and I had forced myself to make peace with it because there was no other choice. I would never wish for a child to die, especially the way I lost mine, but a small voice in my head told me that my child was better where they were, in a place where no one could ever hurt them again. I rolled onto my back as I let out a sigh and felt the bed shift as Chase changed positions. From the corner of my eye it looked like he was still asleep.

"You ok?" he asked groggily with his eyes closed.

"Yeah, sorry, I was hoping not to wake you. I needed the restroom."

"You can wake me any time. But I wasn't actually sleeping so you didn't technically wake me."

"Why weren't you sleeping?" Concern filled me as I worried that his inability to sleep was due to me being there.

"I wanted to make sure that you were safe." There was a tenderness to his voice that pulled at my heart.

"I'm sorry. I feel bad that you're not getting sleep because of me. I'll be fine, you should get some sleep."

"Trust me, I'm fine without sleep. I would rather that you get sleep."

"You sure you're ok?" He pressed.

"Yeah, I don't usually sleep well lately so I tend to be up throughout the night." I explained with a shrug even though it was too dark for him to see it.

"You slept pretty good while you were laying with me, wanna try that again?" There was a hint of flirtiness to his voice that I had missed. I playfully swatted at his arm, embarrassed that I had fallen asleep on him earlier.

"Seriously though Mia, it's ok to let yourself be vulnerable with me. I would never hurt you. I'll go to my grave trying to prove that to you."

"I know, Chase. I appreciate how much you care for me."

"Then why do you fight me so hard on wanting to be with you? I can prove to you however you want or need me to that it's not just about sex with you Mia." He gently rubbed his hand over my arm. "I mean, I definitely want to have sex with you, don't get me wrong." He laughed. "But I want more from this, not just sex."

"Why do you want me?" The words were out of my mouth before I could think about it or stop them.

"Why wouldn't I want you?"

"I'm not the sexy, flirty girls that you go out with. I'm not some successful businesswoman. There's nothing about me that stands out or makes me different."

"Mia, you are everything that I could ever want in a woman. You're gorgeous. You're sweet. You're caring. You're giving. You're rowdy as hell when you want to be. You keep me on my toes. And you're the definition of sexy. You don't need the slutty clothes or the over the top hair and makeup to make you sexy. You're sexy wearing my t-shirt and sweats, Mia. If you need proof of that, I'm happy to show you." He reached down and adjusted his sweats as he raised an eyebrow. "Trust me, it's not easy having you in my arms and not being able to actually touch you."

I giggled as I cupped my hands over my mouth and looked down at the bed where the covers were hiding him. Slowly he lifted the covers and I saw the outline of a bulge in his sweatpants. My eyes went wide as I looked up at him. He subtly licked his lips as he dropped the covers over himself again and rolled onto his side to look at me.

"If time is what you need, Mia, then time is what I will give you. But please don't walk away from this because you have some absurd idea in your head that you're not good enough for me."

"I tried to be sexy once with Damian." I don't know why I felt like telling him this but for whatever reason I felt like I wanted to open up to him and finally let someone in. "I had cooked dinner and when he came home, I greeted him wearing nothing but an apron and high heels. He took one look at me and told me that I looked ridiculous and to go put some clothes on as he took his dinner to his study and closed the door. I was so nervous before he got there, it was the wildest thing I had ever done. After that I was so embarrassed that I never wanted to do anything like that again. It's hard to feel like you're sexy when someone is always telling you that you aren't, you know what I mean?"

"He's an idiot. But then again, we already knew that." He smiled and chuckled. "Do you know what I would do if I came home and found you wearing nothing but an apron and high heels?"

"What?"

"I would pick you up and carry you into this bedroom, laying you down on this bed so I could look at how sexy you look while I take off my clothes. Then I would slowly go down on you and show you that you taste better than anything you could make in the kitchen. I would fuck you with your apron on until you couldn't take anymore Mia. And then we would go eat the delicious meal you made, get some energy back, then I would spend the rest of the night making love to you."

"You make it sound so easy." I tried to slow my breathing as I clenched my thighs together, turned on by the erotic picture he just painted for me.

"Mia, it is easy," he said gently. "He's taken plenty from you already, don't allow him to rob you of your self-confidence. There's an incredibly sexy woman in you and I'm dying for her to come out and see what she wants."

I thought about what he said and how his perception of the world is so different than anything I've been used to for the past few years. I yawned as I felt the tiredness start to take over again. Before I could think about what was happening, I felt Chase grab me and pull me into him, my back perfectly nuzzled against his chest.

"What are you doing?" I asked over my shoulder as I made no effort to move.

"Making sure you get some rest. Now go to sleep."

A smiled formed on my face as I allowed myself to relax against him, our breathing synchronized. Soon after I felt the change in his body as he drifted off to sleep, a soft snore filled the air above my head. I wished I could turn around and watch him as he slept, knowing that he would look as peaceful and beautiful as he did when he was awake. My eyes grew heavy as my body gave in and I fell asleep cuddled up against his warm body.

Twenty Seven
Mia

Sunday and Monday went by relatively quick while I spent time at Chase's house even though I was still anxious about where Damian was hiding. I would get a few calls from unknown numbers but didn't bother to answer them. If they were Damian, which I figured they were, he didn't bother to leave a message, which was fine by me. Sunday morning we stopped by my apartment to check on Jade and I grabbed a few things that I needed. Everything looked fine and Jade assured us that she wasn't afraid to stay there by herself. We made sure she had Chase's number programmed into her phone if needed before we left and ran to the store for some groceries for the next few days. I had no idea how long I was going to be staying with Chase but neither of us seemed to want to rush my departure.

By Tuesday morning we were both feeling antsy being cooped up in the house for a few days so Chase suggested a drive over to Lakeside. While we could have been productive and gone into work, we decided to spend a few days away from the office and clear our heads while enjoying some fresh air. Noah assured us that he had it handled and they had a temp who came in to help when needed who had been looking for some work which gave us a good excuse to take a few days off.

Lakeside was smaller than Haven Brook and I don't think it had grown any since the day I was born. It was a cute small town with a beautiful lake that we used to fish for trout in growing up. The drive out to Lakeside was relaxing as I rolled my window down and hung my hand out of the window, allowing the warm breeze to dance over my body. I closed my eyes as I leaned my head back against the seat and felt the warm sun on my skin. For a moment I left all of my worries behind me as I got lost in the peaceful silence as Chase drove.

An old George Straight song played softly on the radio as the sound was muffled by the sound of tires crunching over gravel. I opened my eyes and smiled when I saw the lake in front of us. It was even more beautiful than I had remembered with green grass leading to the bank and tall trees casting the perfect amount of shade by the water's edge.

I waited for Chase to turn off the truck before I swung my door open and hopped out. It was so quiet and peaceful, not a single other person there except for us. I looked over at Chase as he smiled at me and walked with me to the shady spot in the grass that we used to hang out at when we would come here.

"This feels like I'm back in high school." I plopped down on the grass and stretched my legs out in front of me as Chase sat down next to me.

"Yeah, it really does." He plucked a few pieces of grass and ran his finger up and down the blade as he looked out at the water.

"Thanks for bringing me out here today."

"Of course. It's nice to get away from it all sometimes."

Silence filled the space between us as we looked out at the calmness of the water. I would come here a lot growing up when I wanted to get away from my mother. She would always pretend to freak out, claim that I had ran away, just so she could get attention. Chase and Noah would always end up making their way out here and would claim they came to go fishing and didn't know I was here. They've always looked out for me, as long as I've known them.

"Sometimes I wish I could just live at the lake." I sighed as I took in a deep breath of fresh air. "Never have to worry about anything again."

"I don't know about that." He looked at me out of the corner of his eye and I could see the start of a smirk.

"What's that supposed to mean?"

"Well I'm sure after a few days even the fish would smell better than you. And then no one would want to come here because some smelly girl ruined the atmosphere for everyone else." His grin spread across his face as he turned toward me.

"I would not smell!" I playfully reached across and swatted his chest as his hand caught my arm. An electricity zinged between us and I considered pulling my arm away as he gently pulled me forward. We were close enough that I could smell the cleanliness of the soap from his morning shower. I took a deep breath trying to inhale as much of him as I could as he tilted his head and brought his face closer to mine. Slowly I lifted my head and turned into him, planting a soft kiss on his lips.

The kiss was tender and left me wanting more as I felt him slowly pull away from me and move his arm away from mine. I instantly missed the physical contact and wondered what had made him pull away. Secretly I wondered if I actually did smell worse than the fish even though I had a nice long shower that morning.

"I'm sorry, Mia." He looked at me as he spoke softly.

"For what?" I leaned back on my arms and tried to distract my body from the longing it felt to reach over and touch him again.

"For kissing you."

"Is it because I smell worse than the fish?" I tried to lighten the mood as he laid down next to me and rested his head in his hands.

"Do you think you smell worse than the fish?" He arched one eyebrow as he looked up at me, a smile making its way back into his gorgeous face.

"Not particularly. But you're the one who pulled away, so who knows?"

"You don't smell worse than the fish," he chuckled. "I was just trying to be respectful and not step over the line."

One thing that I really admired about Chase was that he was a real gentleman and I always knew that I could trust what he said. But part of me wanted to see what it felt like to just give in and stop being afraid. To have one reckless moment and live life without worrying about the repercussions.

"I appreciate that, thank you." I leaned forward and pulled my legs in toward me as I played with the grass nervously. "But I didn't mind it." I bit my lip as I avoided looking at him. It was the first time I was genuinely admitting that I was interested in him and part of me worried that I would still be rejected.

"Oh yeah?"

"Yeah." Another deep breath. "I don't want to constantly live my life in fear, Chase. I just want to live in the moment for once. To act on impulse. To feel like I'm actually living. To kiss you and feel you against me." My voice trailed off as I tried not to get too far ahead of myself.

"It's okay to want those things, Mia. You deserve to have a life that isn't lived in fear." He sat up and scooted closer to where I was sitting. I could feel the fabric of his jeans against my bare leg, sending shivers through my body.

"Tell me what you want, Mia." His voice was soft and low as he reached over and gently used his finger to turn my head toward him.

"I want you." My eyes searched his as they looked for him to assure me that he wanted the same. There was a darkness that shadowed his as I watched him lean into me and close his eyes as he pulled me in for a kiss.

My lips parted as they accepted his tongue, eager to explore my mouth as one hand made its way into my hair while the other slid down my back and pulled me down onto the grass. I wrapped my arms around his neck as I pulled him closer to me as his muscular body hovered over mine. My senses were overwhelmed with my body wanting more of him.

I started pulling at the hem of his shirt to pull it over his head as I heard him chuckle as he rolled off of me and took his T-shirt off. His perfectly toned body was within my reach and my fingers ached to touch him.

"Aren't you a little minx?" he teased with a wink as he tossed his shirt to the side.

"I've waited a long time for this."

"Same here." He leaned down and kissed me again as he wrapped his arms around my waist and rolled me on top of him. I shifted my position and was pleasantly surprised when I felt the bulge beneath me through his jeans. My eyes went wide as he smiled and licked his lips.

"Your turn." He nodded and waited, though I had no clue what he was waiting for.

"My turn? For what?"

"You wanted my shirt off, now I want yours off." There was something so incredibly sexy about the way that he said it. Maybe I was just high on endorphins, everything he said sounded sexy.

I watched as he watched me reach down and lift my tank top over my head and toss it to the side as I stayed straddling him wearing a black lacy bra and denim shorts.

"Very nice. I like it." He reached up and ran a finger along the lace trim on top of the cup that barely covered my breast.

"But I think I would like it even more if you took it off."

"I thought this was supposed to be fair- you remove a piece of clothing, I remove the same piece?" I joked as I tried to build up the confidence to do it.

"Well, we can play it that way. But you do have more clothes on than I do, which means I'll be naked before you. And I'm already bare chested, you're not."

“Fine.” I sighed as I tossed my hair over my shoulder and leaned my head back as I reached behind my back and unclasped my bra. I slowly pulled each bra strap down my shoulders as I held the cups in place with one hand, watching his reaction as I teased him. His eyes were fixated on my every move and I found myself getting more turned on by it. His hands slowly made their way up my hips and along my stomach as I let go of the bra and allowed his hands to cup my breasts.

I could hear him moan as he gently rubbed each one as I tilted my head back and leaned against his legs that were propped up. His fingers rolled each nipple as he leaned forward and sat up, taking his time licking my neck down to each breast and pulling a hard nipple in.

My body felt on fire with every touch, I wanted more. I looked at him as I parted my lips and leaned forward for a kiss. Taking control, I gently forced him back on the ground as I worked his belt buckle free underneath me. I slowly kissed his jawline down his neck as his hands continued to work their magic on my breasts and my hands worked to unbutton his jeans. I could feel his erection bulging through the thick fabric and I yearned to have him inside of me.

One swift movement and he had rolled me over and laid me on my back once again while I watched him jump up and unzip his pants. He watched me as he kicked his boots off and slid his jeans down, stripping him of everything but his boxers. My legs slightly spread as I watched him come toward me, a hunger in his eyes.

His lips softly kissed my stomach as he slid my shorts down, pulling my panties along with them. I laid completely naked in front of him as he slowly looked me up and down before meeting my eyes.

“You’re so damn beautiful.” He whispered as he reached down and pulled off his boxers, his thickness taking up the majority of his hand. Slowly he laid down beside me and gently kissed me as he pulled me closer to him.

“How do you want it?” he murmured between kisses.

“I don’t care as long as it’s inside of me.” I moaned as I heard a low growl from his throat. I felt his arms pull me onto him as he laid on his back and braced me with his legs. I watched him as I slowly lifted myself as I reached down and guided him inside of me. A hiss escaped his lips as he shut his eyes and his hands gripped my hips tighter. I stilled for a moment while I allowed my body to adjust to his size before I started to rock back and forth, creating a perfect friction.

We watched each other as I rode him through to my release which was the most intense orgasm I had ever had. I studied his face as he closed his eyes and he chewed his lip as he got closer. His fingers dug into my hips as I continued to push down on him and followed the changes in his body as he tried to hold off as long as he could before letting go and climaxing. His body shook beneath me and a smile crossed my face, satisfaction that I was able to take him over the edge. Exhausted I collapsed onto his chest as he kissed my forehead and rubbed my back. We didn't say anything. We just allowed ourselves to get completely lost in the moment as we stayed entangled in each other.

The drive back to Chase's house was quiet as we held hands the entire way back, both too tired to talk about much after spending the day soaking up the sun and making love. The sun was beginning to set as my stomach rumbled, a gentle reminder that we still needed to eat dinner. As we pulled into the garage I noticed a strange look on Chase's face as he looked around before putting the truck in park.

"What's wrong?" I asked as I looked around, unsure of what was bothering him.

"It's probably nothing, but the alarm should have beeped twice when we pulled in, and I only heard it beep once."

"What does that mean?"

"It means that the alarm was turned off. A single beep indicates that a door is opened, or in this case, the garage door was opened." He looked around while the garage door stayed open and the truck was still running. It felt like he was ready for a quick getaway if we needed one and that made me feel uneasy as I wondered if Damian had figured out where I was after all.

"Is it possible you missed the first beep because the windows were rolled up when we pulled in?" I asked with hope in my voice.

"It's a possibility. But I have the alarm system linked to my blue tooth, so I hear the beeps in the truck as well."

My eyes darted around the garage as I looked for any signs that someone had been in the house. I had only been staying there for a few days so it wasn't likely that I would be able to tell if anyone had been there but I continued to look anyways.

"Look, we don't need to panic yet. I'll call the alarm company and confirm if the alarm was set before we left. That will put us at ease once we know for sure." He pulled out his phone and held it to his ear as he waited for them to answer.

I stared out the window as I chewed my fingernail, anxious for Chase to get confirmation of whether the alarm had been set. His home had felt so safe to me from the moment I walked in the door and now I felt like that could easily be stripped away from me. It had only been a few days since Damian had called and even if he hadn't followed us the first time we came to Chase's house, it didn't mean that he hadn't followed us at some point since then.

"Okay, thank you. I appreciate your help." Chase let out a big sigh as he pressed the button to end the call and turned in his seat to look at me.

"They confirmed that the alarm was turned off when we left earlier and hasn't been set since then. I must have turned it off earlier when we left, thinking that I had set it."

It made sense but it still made me feel uneasy. I tried to remember whether I had seen him set it before we left. Did I hear it beep? Did I see him set it? I couldn't remember.

"You ready to go inside?" he asked as he turned the truck off and took the keys out of the ignition. I nodded as I got out and followed him inside as I looked behind me one last time.

Dinner was quick and easy which was nice given that we were both still tired from the day. Around ten we decided to call it a day and went to bed. Within minutes of my head hitting the pillow I was out and floating around happily in a blissful dream.

The clock on the nightstand showed 3:00 am as I was startled awake. I sat up and tiredly rubbed my eyes before looking around. The tv was still on with an infomercial about vitamins playing. Everything looked fine but I still had an overwhelming uneasy feeling. Slowly I scanned the room again when a dark shadow in the corner caught my eye.

My heart started to race as I peered into the darkness and found the outline of a person sitting in the chair by the window. I held my breath as I waited for them to move. It was too dark to see much other than a shape but it looked large enough to be a man. Large enough to be Damian. I felt my body stiffen as I waited for him to make his way over to the bed and attack me, but he just stayed sitting there. Every second felt like it was moving in slow motion as I continued to wait.

A shadow moved along the wall and I squinted to try to see what it was. Was it his hand? Was it a gun? My breathing quickened as I felt the adrenaline rush through me as I gripped the blankets around me. What was I supposed to do? Should I wake Chase and risk Damian hurting him? Should I take off and run out of the room so Damian would follow me and leave Chase alone? My mind tried to go through the options as quickly as possible when I felt Chase move on the bed next to me. I looked down as he looked up at me with a smile on his face. Once he noticed the look on mine his mind registered something was wrong as his eyes darted to where I was looking. I nodded toward the chair as I pulled the sheet up to my chest and pushed myself further back against the headboard as if the feel of the soft material would comfort me. Chase quickly rolled over and pulled the gun out of his nightstand, pointing it at the chair as he flicked on the light.

My eyes immediately focused on the chair and my heart dropped when I saw that there was nothing there other than a few throw pillows, and some laundry that was piled up on top of the pillows. My hand clutched my chest as I looked over and over, unable to process how it could have looked like a man when it was really just a pile of laundry on top of pillows. I let out a long sigh as I leaned back against the headboard and listened as Chase made his way through the rest of the house, checking to make sure everything was okay.

"Sorry, I think my mind was trying to play tricks on me tonight." I offered as an explanation as he put the gun away and climbed back in bed.

"Not a problem at all, I'm glad we were able to check things out to make sure they were okay." He leaned over and gently kissed my cheek.

"I never knew laundry could be so terrifying."

I heard him chuckle as he adjusted his pillow and laid next to me, propped up on his elbow.

"Not to worry, we can work on it in the morning. I'm sure you're wanting some clean clothes to wear since you've run out of what we brought from your apartment."

"Yeah, that would be nice. Sorry for leaving them under the bathroom sink. I was trying to be as out of the way as possible."

"What are you talking about?"

"My dirty clothes. I've been leaving them in a small pile under the counter in the bathroom, so they are out of the way."

"Mia, there are no clothes under the sink. The clothes you've been wearing are the clothes that are piled up on the chair. The clothes that startled you."

What was he talking about? I hadn't put any clothes on the chair. Everything had been folded and piled neatly under the bathroom counter, out of the way. I looked over at the chair and tried to figure out what exactly was on it but it was hard because everything looked like it was balled up in a messy pile. I looked over at Chase as I expected him to tell me it was some weird joke he had played on me but he kept looking at me as if I was the one who was losing it. Maybe I was?

"Why did you put my clothes on the chair like that?" There was so much confusion, none of this made any sense. Maybe he didn't want my clothes piled on the floor so he moved them? But why didn't he just tell me and I could have put them somewhere else? And why was he acting like I was the one who put them there?

"I didn't touch your clothes, Mia. They were like that when we got home earlier. I thought maybe you put them there because you were getting ready to do laundry."

"I didn't move my clothes. And I wouldn't have put them on the chair like that." I pointed toward the chair as I chewed my lower lip, unsure of what was happening.

"Are you sure?" His tone was calm as he reached over and held my hand. The look on his face made me feel like he thought I was crazy.

"Of course I'm sure." My tone came out more defensively than I had imagined but none of it made any sense to me.

"Okay, I'm sorry. I wasn't trying to accuse you of anything, Mia."
"I'm sure because that right there," I nodded toward the chair, "is something that he would have beat me for if he saw it. Damian didn't allow anything to be untidy, dirty laundry included."

I looked up at Chase as he gently squeezed my hand.

"He knows I'm here."

Twenty Eight
Damian

It had been nice to hear Mia's voice the other night when I called. Not because I missed her but because I enjoyed hearing the fear in her voice as she pathetically begged me to leave her alone. Wah wah wah. Cry me a fucking river. It was after seven on Wednesday night and I was irritated as fuck as I waited for Lenny to send me the last bit of information that I needed so I could get on the road and get to Haven Brook. This had gone on long enough and I was ready to put an end to it.

I had already printed the information that I needed on where Mia's apartment was and Lenny was supposed to be getting me the additional information that I asked for on Chase, the stupid prick who was trying to sabotage my plan. Leave it to Mia to go running to someone for help and making this even harder. Why couldn't she get it through her head that I wasn't going to stop until I had what was mine? Had I not made it clear?

This morning I had called into the office and convinced Doris I was too sick to come in to work. I faked a cough as many times as I could and pretended to be drowsy when she asked if I wanted to speak to Ronnie to let him know. There was a mandatory meeting that afternoon that I would miss but I didn't give a flying fuck. I needed people to think I was out sick so no one would notice if I was out a few more days as I left town.

The sooner I got to Haven Brook, the sooner this could all be over and I could be done with Lenny and Hank. As smart as Lenny should have been, he was still fucking up little things when he could. Part of me knew that it was simply to spite me. Like letting Mia see him at the bus stop when I told him to make sure she didn't see him. Lucky for him I was quick on my feet and played it off as if it was me, waving at her, which added an additional level of fear that I was disappointed that I hadn't thought of sooner. I didn't bother to worry too much about Lenny- I just needed him to finish the things I had asked of him, then he would get what was coming to him.

I glanced over at the printer as it finished printing the items I had sent over when I heard the doorbell ring. Who the fuck was there? I sure as hell hadn't been expecting anyone. I tried to ignore it as I heard it ring again. And again. And again. My temper rose as I pushed back my chair and stormed out of my office and flung the front door open.

"You don't look sick to me." Ronnie stepped inside and tucked his hands into pockets as he looked around.

"Yeah, well, I am." I leaned into the open doorway, leaving a path for him to go back the way he came. "What do you want?"

"I came to check on you. Doris said that you called in but she didn't give me much information, so I figured I would come see how you were doing since you missed a mandatory meeting this afternoon. Figured you ought to be on your death bed and I should come say my goodbyes." His eyes narrowed in on mine and I could tell he wasn't planning on leaving until he got whatever it was he was after. Apparently stubbornness ran through our veins.

"I haven't felt well all day. Fever. Cough. Stomach cramps. Throwing up. You know, the typical flu stuff that knocks you down for a few days."

"Interesting.... I don't usually wear jeans, button down shirts, or steel toed boots when I have the flu. Most people tend to live in sweats when they are that sick." He shrugged and looked into the kitchen.

"Where's Mia?"

My eyes darted up to his as I tried to come up with an excuse of where she was. I could lie and say that she was already in bed but I doubted that he would believe she went to bed this early. I could say that she was sick too but he would want to check on her. I could say that she was out of town but I couldn't remember if I had used that excuse with him recently or not. I felt him staring at me as he tried to read me, something he had done since I was a boy and had started getting into trouble at an early age.

"She's out."

"Out where?"

"With her friend. I don't know where they went."

"You don't know where your wife went?" His eyes narrowed as his brow furrowed. "The one that basically has to check in with you every time she goes to the bathroom. And you don't know where she is?"

I felt my blood pressure rise as quickly as my anger. I wasn't prepared to have to talk about Mia tonight nor I had I expected my nosey ass uncle to drop in and ask about my estranged wife. Fuck!

"I didn't feel good enough to care. Now can you just leave so I can rest?" I ran my hand through my hair as I sat on the arm of the couch and nodded toward the door.

"Damian, something is going on and I want to see Mia." He sat on the couch and planted his feet in front of him as he waited for my answer. "Now." His tone was stern and it pissed me off. Where the fuck did he get off coming over here uninvited and demanding to see my wife?

"She's not here so that's not really a possibility. Why don't you go and I'll leave a message for her to call you when she gets back?" There was an edginess to my tone and I knew he would pick up on it. It wasn't the first time I had ever challenged him and it wouldn't be the last time.

He stood up and sighed as he looked me square in the eye.

"Did she finally get tired of dealing with your drunk ass and decided to leave you? Is that what happened?"

My nostrils flared as my jaw clenched, anger coursed through me as I stared at him. How dare he fucking ask me that. He stared back at me, a challenge in his eyes as he waited for me to say what we both already knew. Problem was that he didn't need to know what had happened or that she had left me. And now that he knew, that was another problem that I needed to solve. I took a deep breath and tried to unclench my first that was balled up at my side.

"I knew it wouldn't be long before she came to her senses and left you. It was only a matter of time." He shook his head and as he turned to face me my fist made contact with his temple and knocked him to the ground. Everything played out before me in slow motion as his head whipped back and he fell backwards, his head hitting the edge of the coffee table on his way down.

There was a pool of blood that had formed around his head while his body laid lifeless on the hardwood floor. I watched as I waited for him to move, ready to deliver another blow if that was what it would take to keep him down. My breathing was heavy as the adrenaline rushed through me, giving me the high that I had learned to love so much. There was something about being in control that just really got to me. I could feel it in my blood and it felt almost as good as the few times I had partied too hard in law school and fueled myself with cocaine to make it through.

After a few minutes of Ronnie staying sprawled out on the floor I decided to move on with my night and started throwing the things I needed into the car. I debated what to do with Ronnie as I couldn't just leave him there in case he eventually came to and decided to go run his mouth to someone about what had happened. That wouldn't be good. There weren't any other options as I drug his limp body through the garage and loaded it into the trunk. It would add on a little extra time to find a place to dump him but at least it would get one thing marked off the list.

I grabbed my cell phone off of my desk and grabbed the file with the printed information that I needed. A quick pat of my pocket confirmed that I had my care package to keep me awake for the drive out there.

There wasn't time to bother with eating or sleeping until all of this was done and over, and the sooner, the better.

I climbed in the car and waited for the garage door to open before backing out. The night sky was already dark, much to my relief. If I could get a head start while it was still dark then I had a better chance of no one knowing that I had left. I didn't need anyone else putting their nose in my fucking business.

The two-lane highway was nearly deserted this time of night, especially since we lived in the suburbs and there wasn't much traffic out here to begin with. I leaned back against the leather seat as the line of trees whipped past me so fast they were nothing but a blur. I needed to dump Ronnie's body further out so if it washed up somewhere it would be harder for them to find if he was reported as a missing person.

I was twenty minutes away from the next town and considered whether to dump Ronnie's body or wait for another town. If I dumped him now then it was still close enough that they might find and identify him easily. If I waited then I ran the risk that he might come to, if he wasn't already dead. I didn't care enough to check before I stuffed his fat body into the trunk.

The exit was quickly approaching as I saw the sign for it on the right. As I debated whether to take the exit something darted out onto the road in front of me, forcing me to jerk the steering wheel hard to the right to avoid hitting it. I knew better than to over correct but there was nothing that I could do about it as I felt my body jerk to the side as the car spiraled down the steep side of the hill and plunged headfirst into a tree. The airbags deployed immediately upon contact and my head was whipped back and forth from the impact. There was a loud ringing in my head as I reached up and tried to push the airbag out of my face before it suffocated me. The car was stuck with the hood wrapped around the tree and the back end up in the air which forced me further into the airbag. I reached over and fumbled with the armrest until I got it open and pulled out a ball point pen, praying it would work. I quickly stabbed at the airbag, deflating it as I gasped for air.

I had to get out as I looked around for the best way to do so. The car was totaled which made the doors hard to open since the frame had been crushed in. I fumbled with my seatbelt as I slowly got it undone and tried to steady myself from falling forward. There was a heat under my feet as I struggled with the door handle, unable to push it open. Panic started to flood me as I saw flames under the hood of the car. My hands worked at the door handle again but the lock was jammed. I desperately searched around for something to break the window with as I watched the flames get higher as they moved in closer. I was running out of time, only seconds before the car would be completely engulfed in flames. I let out a deep breath as the heat spread over me and darkness took over.

Twenty Nine
Chase

The door slammed shut as Mia walked out my front door and didn't bother looking back. This wasn't the way that I had wanted to start the morning I thought as I rubbed a hand down the scruff of my jaw. I was exhausted with the past few days wearing on me.

Mia hadn't been the same since Tuesday night with the whole laundry fiasco which lead to some tension between us all day Wednesday when I didn't freak out about it the same way she did. There was no sign that anyone had been in the house so it made it hard for me to believe that Damian would find where I lived, break into my house without my knowing, move Mia's clothes around, then sit and wait for her to freak out about it. From what Mia had told me about the guy I didn't imagine he was going to just sit on the sideline and play games with her. None of it made any sense to me. If he was there, why hadn't he physically come for her?

By Wednesday evening she was still obsessed over Damian being at the house and kept insisting that he must have been there while we were at the lake. I assured her that I had already checked in with the security company and no one had been in or out of the house the entire time we were gone. I could tell that she still felt uneasy about it but there wasn't anything else I could do to try to prove it to her.

I hated to see her so afraid. It broke my heart. I wanted to offer her the peace and comfort she had a few days before she ever got the call from Damian but there was nothing that I could do now. I knew that she was just as exhausted as I was. Hell, probably more, from not sleeping at night. She was in this state of defense, constantly waiting for something to happen.

This morning was no different other than she seemed to reach a new level of irritability with me and decided to go back to her apartment so she could have some space and clear her head. I hated the idea of her being alone, even if Jade was still staying there with her. It made me feel better having her near me so I could protect her if needed.

I leaned back against the couch as I felt my cell phone vibrate in my pocket as I fumbled around and pulled it out. A new text message from Mia came through.

Mia: I made it to my apartment.

I was happy to hear that she had made it home safely, especially since she had refused my offer to drive her. I had never met anyone as stubborn as Mia, especially when she was mad. My fingers moved quickly as I sent a response thanking her for letting me know. I kept it short and simple which felt like what she wanted right now.

The house felt different without Mia there which made me miss her. There was no way that I could just sit around all day in a quiet house and think about her so I grabbed my keys and headed into work. I needed something to keep myself busy and help pass the time.

Noah was in a good mood when I got there which was a pleasant surprise given the attitude I had been getting from Mia the past few days. I stayed in my office the majority of the morning, catching up on things from the few days I had been out. Thursday's were always slow which was a nice break while I got caught up. By 2:00 my head was killing me from the lack of sleep and excess caffeine I had downed at my desk. I still didn't feel like going home but needed a break from work stuff so I took the time to mess around on the internet.

There wasn't anything in specific that I was looking for but somehow I ended up logging into my home security account online and pulled up the entry log for Tuesday. I stared at it for a few minutes as I looked at the general log which showed when the alarm was turned on and off over a 24-hour window. It felt like I was missing something but I just couldn't put my finger on it.

Just as I thought I was onto something I heard Noah open the door that led back to the offices and call for me. I let out a deep breath as I got up to see what Noah wanted, leaving the screen open on my computer.

Hours later I finally made it back to my office after helping Noah with the evening rush after Stacy, our temp, had gone home sick at last minute. While I loved to stay in my office and work the numbers, sometimes I really loved being up front and interacting with people. There were quite a few groups of college kids that came in tonight, laughing and hanging out, that reminded me of hanging out with Noah and Mia. We got into a lot of trouble but we sure had fun doing it.

I could hear Noah putting the deposit in the safe as he finished closing everything up front. It felt late even though it was barely 9:00, but I was ready to go home. I went to turn my computer off when I moved the mouse and the screen to the security system page popped up. I had been so busy up front that I had forgotten that I was looking for something.

Part of me wanted to say forget it and go home, knowing there wasn't anything I would find out of the norm anyways. A bigger part of me told me that I needed to look into it more. I sighed as I sat down at my computer and clicked the tab for a detailed report for Monday and Tuesday since we had been home all day yesterday. A 4-page report popped up as I moved my mouse over the print icon and selected it. I didn't have the energy to look at it now but wanted to have the physical copy in case insomnia kept me up again tonight and I needed something to read. A few seconds later the printer spit out the pages as I grabbed them on my way out of the office and went home for the day.

Thirty
Mia

"Do you want another cup of wine?" Jade asked from the kitchen as I watched her refill her coffee mug.

"Sure." It was getting late and my mind wouldn't slow down about everything that had happened since Tuesday night. I had tried to sleep but it was pointless, which left me in this overly tired dog state that Jade was left to deal with.

I hadn't planned to come back to my apartment at last minute but after I talked to Jade and told her what had happened, she insisted that I get back here as soon as possible so we could talk about it. That was why I loved her, she was always there for me regardless of what the problem was.

Chase and I had been tense with each other all day yesterday and when I realized that it was going to be the same today, I left. I knew that he didn't really understand the things that had happened with Damian, I don't think anyone really did. But it was so frustrating to me that he wouldn't listen to me or take me serious about Damian being in his house.

We'd spent the day on Wednesday analyzing why Damian would come in and move my laundry around and at one point, Chase had actually laughed when I said- to mess with me! I felt like I was going crazy and it didn’t help that it felt like Chase agreed with me. I just needed him to be on my side. To take me serious. To help me figure things out. I knew that it didn’t make sense why IF Damian was there, he didn’t just come find me and attack me. But I had heard the tone in his voice that night. I knew the game he wanted to play. And I knew that he was going to keep playing it until he could drive me away from everyone that could try to protect me. If he made me look crazy enough, people would walk away and he would have his chance. No one would notice if I was missing at that point because no one would care anymore.

I smiled up at Jade as she handed me the mug filled to the top with cold white wine. I wasn’t sure that there was a wine that went well with Chinese take-out but neither of us bothered to complain as we ate and sipped our wine. It was too late to bother with cooking and we had spent so long talking and catching up that we hadn’t noticed the time earlier. It was nice to hear about Jade’s adventures through Haven Brook as she applied for different jobs and had a few run ins with the locals. It was a good distraction to keep my mind off of Chase and I was happy that she hadn’t been sitting in the apartment by herself this week, hiding from Damian.

“You feeling any better?” Jade asked between bites of Kung Pao chicken.

“My head hurts and I feel like I’ve been hit by a train. Except that train is my life.”

“I’m sorry. I really wish there was something I could do for you.”

“Thanks. Me too.” I took a bite of my food and scraped the chopsticks along the bottom as I fished out the last piece of shrimp from the container. I leaned forward and sat the empty carton on the coffee table as I steadied my other hand to keep from spilling the wine.

“It really sucks about you and Chase. I was really starting to like him.”

“So was I. But technically I knew better than to let anything happen between us. It was really stupid to let my guard down the way I did.” I pulled my legs up under me as I leaned back against the couch and took a sip.

“Why do you say that?”

"Because I'm not in any position to be dating. I'm technically still married." I threw my hand up in the air. "My actual husband is trying to find me so he can kill me and I'm off having an affair with my high school crush. I don't think that spells successful relationship."

Jade let out a soft laugh as she leaned forward and put her empty carton on the coffee table next to mine.

"I don't think that's how things are supposed to work," she said softly as she looked up at me, "but you shouldn't have to deny yourself what you really want, just because you married someone who won't let you go. You deserve happiness, Mia. You deserve love." She gently squeezed my leg and smiled.

"Thanks, Jade. I really appreciate having a friend like you." My hand reached down and squeezed hers.

"You mean sister." She winked as she stood up. "And this sister needs the bathroom. I'll be right back."

I giggled as she made her way to the bathroom and looked down at my phone. There were no messages from Chase, and no calls or messages from Damian which was odd. Then it occurred to me that I hadn't had any calls from him all day. I scrolled through the missed call log and found the last call from him was yesterday at 4:07. That was odd. My blood ran cold as I tried to think about why all of a sudden he would stop calling. Was he done playing the game and ready to find me? I was still staring at my phone when I heard Jade walk into the room, stopping next to the couch where I was sitting.

"Um, Mia?" Her voice was shaky.

"Yeah?" I looked up at her, concern on my face from her tone. She stared down at her phone as she covered her mouth with her other hand. My stomach was in a knot, knowing something bad had happened. Was it Chase? Was it Noah? Did Damian get to them?

"Damian..... he..." She let out a slow breath as I watched as her hand trembled. "He's dead." Her eyes looked down at mine as I let her words sink in.

"What?" I stood up and looked at her as if she had just told me the Earth was flat. If this was supposed to be a joke, it wasn't funny.

"Someone forwarded me the news story. He was killed in an accident last night. Just outside of Boston."

The room started spinning as I reached out and held onto Jade's arm. I couldn't hear the words she continued to say, everything was blocked out by this loud humming that took over and made my head feel like it was about to explode.

"It says that the car hit a tree at high impact which forced the car to be wrapped around the tree before it caught on fire. By the time rescue workers were able to put the fire out, it was too late for any survivors. They are still working the scene to recover what they can." Jade sat her phone down on the coffee table and looked at me as she held onto my shoulders.

"Mia, are you okay?"

"He's dead?"

"Yes."

"Like dead- dead?"

"Yes."

"So.... all of this... is over?" Hope filled my eyes as I blinked back tears. I didn't know if I was upset that he had died the way he did or if they were tears of relief that this was all over with now. It felt too good to be true.

"It's over. He can't hurt you anymore, Mia."

My hands covered my mouth as my body trembled and I dropped to my knees. Jade sat beside me and pulled me into a hug as I cried. So many things were going through my head as I tried to process all of them. It made sense now why he hadn't been calling me. How could he if he was dead?

I thought about calling Chase to tell him that Damian was dead but didn't feel like I had the energy for it. For now I just wanted to focus on myself and how I felt about everything before I started to pick up the pieces of my life.

Thirty One
Chase

Friday mornings should be happy and filled with excitement for the weekend. Mine was dreadful with a headache that continued to pound through the Tylenol that I had hoped would alleviate it. I had already been at the office for an hour and tried making myself productive with no luck.

Last night had been a waste as I barely made it home before crashing on the couch the moment I sat down. I didn't bother with dinner or looking over the reports as my body demanded to sleep. After getting some solid sleep last night I didn't feel as worried about the security system report I had printed out to look over at home but since I was caught up with nothing else to do, I printed another copy and looked over it at my desk.

An hour later and I had looked over it what had felt like 1000 times. The lines were starting to blur which meant I needed to step away and take a break. As I started to push the report off to the side I noticed a line at the very bottom of the second page that didn't have any markings on it, meaning I hadn't paid attention to it when I was highlighting and marking through things as I went through it.

I pulled it up closer to my face and looked at the time stamp on Tuesday- 1:35. My mind scrambled as I tried to think of where we were at that time. Were we leaving the house to go to the lake? I put the papers down for a minute while I closed my eyes and tried to retrace our steps. We had run errands in the morning and then came home to make sandwiches to take with us to lake. That was before noon because Mia suggested we do it mid-morning so we didn't get too hungry and miss lunch. We got to the lake around 12:30 and ate lunch around 1 after we had fooled around. So how was there an entry at 1:35 if we were at the lake?

There had to be some sort of mistake. I quickly turned to my computer and logged into my account as I searched for that entry. I clicked on the 1:35 entry and read the details that popped up below it.

MANUAL OVERRIDE

What the hell? I ran a hand down my face as I stared at the words. My brain was trying to make sense of it but nothing was happening. I picked up my cell phone and called the security company as my foot tapped anxiously under the desk.

"Thank you for calling Force Field Protection, how may I help you?" A chirpy woman's voice answered on the other line.

"Yes, I need some clarification about an entry on my account. I'm not sure that there hasn't been an error."

"Yes sir, I'd be happy to help you with that. May I have your account number and name?" Her robotic mannerisms made me more and more frustrated as I provided the information she asked for and responded to her questions. Finally she asked for the specific entry and had me hold while she pulled it up.

"Okay, I see that at 1:35 on Tuesday, you called in for assistance with turning off the alarm. It was a manual override on our end after we verified your security information."

What. The. Fuck.

"Do you have a record of the call? Did it confirm my name?" I asked as I struggled to figure out who would have been able to call and change it.

"Yes, it shows that you called in and that you also requested to update the password on file for future manual overrides." Her voice was hesitant as she reacted to my tone.

"I'm sorry, it's been a long week and I haven't had a chance to catch up on sleep. Can you remind me what the password was updated to?" I asked as calmly as I could even though I was far from calm.

"Damian."

My heart dropped as I heard it. Mia was right. Damian had been in my house. He had played the security company and convinced them that he was me so he could get into my house and mess with her. My blood was boiling as anger shot through me. I wanted to find him and put his head through a wall. I didn't realize I was still on the call until I heard her voice come through and interrupt my thoughts.

"Would you like to change it again, sir?"

"No, thank you." I hung up before she could say anything more. I had what I needed and would deal with the password thing later. Right now my mind was focused on Mia. I had to see her and tell her. She wasn't safe. I didn't want to scare her by showing up unannounced so I sent her a quick text to let her know that I was on my way and that I needed to talk to her. I didn't care whether she wanted to see me or not. I needed to make sure she was safe.

I nearly flew out of my office as Noah's head whipped up and looked at me with surprise. I didn't have time to explain it, I just needed to get to Mia.

"I'm going to Mia's. Call in ten minutes, if I don't answer- send the police." He looked at me like I was crazy, which I probably was.

"I'm serious. Do it!" I banged my fist on his door a few times and took off down the hallway and out the door. I had to get to her before he could.

Thirty Two
Mia

Chase: I need to talk to you, heading your way.

I sat my phone down on the island and picked up my cup of coffee, savoring the rich flavor as it made its way down my throat. Last night was a long night and I looked like shit to prove it. If I was going to deal with Chase this early in the day, I was going to need some caffeine.

Jade had run out to the store to pick up the necessities that we were running low on. Wine. Ice cream. Coffee. Frozen pizza. Like I said, the necessities. She hadn't been gone long which would give me some time to talk to Chase by ourselves. I didn't know if he was at work or at home when he had text so I didn't know how long it was going to take him to get there. There was a knock on the door and I smiled as I sat my cup down. There was my answer.

I opened the door and my heart dropped as I stared at the person in front of me. Rough hands wrapped around my throat, pushing me back into the apartment as the door was kicked shut. I struggled to breathe as I clawed at the arms that held their grip on me as I tried to break free from their hold.

"Hello, Mia." His voice was hoarse, the smell of whiskey fresh on his breath. My feet no longer touched the floor as he lifted me up and threw me against the wall next to the fridge. His hands let go as I slumped down onto the floor, forcing my lungs to take in the air they needed. I looked up at him as he paced the area in front of me like a caged animal.

In all of the years I had been with Damian I had never seen this side of him. He was acting so primal and animalistic that it scared me. There was a large gash across his forehead that was still bloody along with burn marks under his chin and along his throat. He continued to pace in front of me as he kept wiping his at his nose. I stayed balled up against the wall as I watched the man I used to know stare at me like I was a trophy animal and he was going hunting.

"Is *this* what you wanted?" He asked as he spread his arms out in front of him and glared at me.

"To live some pathetic life on your own? To leave me? To make me look like a fool back home?" His voice grew louder and boomed throughout the room. I flinched at the sound.

"Do you know the things that I had to do to get here, Mia? Do you know the sacrifices that I had to make? How many hours I drove last night with NO sleep, just to get here to finish things off?"

I stayed silent as my chest heaved. My pulse rang in my ears as I tried to figure out what to do. I watched him continue to pace in front of me as he wiggled his nose and wiped at it, leaving a smear of blood above his lip.

"Of course you don't. You're so selfish. All you ever care about is yourself. But guess what? That's all about to end." He took a few steps forward as I heard a knock at the door. Panic filled me as I saw Damian's head turn toward the door before looking back at me.

"Expecting someone?" He raised an eyebrow as he walked to the door and flung it open. I watched with fear as I saw the look on Chase's face when Damian answered the door. He stepped back then ducked down as Damian swung at him and missed.

I got to my feet as quickly as I could, still struggling to catch my breath. I could hear Damian grunt as Chase swung and made contact with Damian's face, forcing him backward. Chase's eyes looked over me quickly before turning his attention back to Damian. I turned and ducked around the other side of the island as they scuffled toward me, swinging at each other along the way. I knew Chase was strong but I was worried about just how strong Damian was with whatever drugs appeared to be in his system. If he survived and walked away from a car accident a few nights ago, he was pretty much capable of anything.

I reached for my phone and started to dial 911 when Damian pulled out a gun from the back of his jeans and grabbed Chase in a headlock. My eyes went wide as I watched him push the gun against Chase's head while his other arm maintained its grip around Chase's neck.

"Put down the phone. NOW!" His voice boomed loudly as I tossed my phone on the island and raised my hands in surrender as I backed myself up against the kitchen sink.

"You don't want to push me, Mia, I'll put a fucking bullet in his head right now." He was constantly moving which made me nervous that he would accidentally pull the trigger. I looked at Chase as he looked at me and I saw worry lines on his face. It was in that moment that I knew this wasn't going to end well.

"I'm not pushing you, Damian." I took a step forward. "Why don't you just let him go? It's me that you're here for." Another step.

"Mia- don't," Chase said through gritted teeth as Damian's hold around his neck got tighter. My stomach churned as I watched Chase, helpless in Damian's hold.

"This has nothing to do with him. It's about me." I slowly rounded the corner of the island as Damian watched me. "You and me, Damian. Remember?"

His eyes went soft and for a moment I saw the man that I had once fallen in love with. There was a movement behind me and I realized that the door was still open from when Chase came in. I watched as Chase looked at me then looked to the far right before shifting his eyes back to the door. I had no clue what was going on as I slowly stepped to the side as Chase tried to direct me.

There was a loud sound that echoed through the apartment as I whipped my head around and found Noah in the doorway with a gun drawn. I looked around frantically as I searched for who had shot the gun- Damian or Noah. Within seconds Noah was standing in front of me with his gun still aimed at Damian who had released his grip on Chase as he stumbled to the ground.

"You okay man?" Noah called over to Chase who was bent over, trying to catch his breath.

"I'm good." He slowly stood upright and looked down at Damian before kicking the gun away from his hand.

My heart was racing as I watched Noah and Chase go over to Damian and check his pulse before Noah pulled out his cell phone and called 911. Chase came toward me with a look of concern on his face as he looked me over again. My throat was still sore from where Damian had grabbed me and I was pretty sure I would have a few bruises tomorrow from being thrown against the wall. I was lucky that Chase came in when he did, before it got worse. But I felt terrible that he ended up in the middle of it.

"I'm so sorry," I whispered as I began to cry. He rushed to my side and pulled me into his arms as I held onto his shirt, feeling the comfort from his touch.

"I didn't mean for you to get hurt." I stammered between sobs.

"Mia, I'm fine. I didn't get hurt." He leaned back and looked down at me. "Are you sure you're okay? Did he hurt you before I got here?"

"I'm okay." My hand reached up and touched the sore spots on my throat as his eyes followed. "I'm really thankful that you came in when you did. I don't know what he was going to do next. He was acting so strange, almost like he was on drugs." I shuddered as I recalled the way he stared at me as he paced back and forth in front of me.

"Me too." He leaned forward and kissed my forehead.

"What did you want to talk about?" I asked as I looked up at him, suddenly remembering his text about coming over.

"It's a long story but I wanted to apologize to you for not believing you when you said he had been in my house. I called the security company after I found a weird entry while we were at the lake." He sighed as he walked with me over to the couch and we sat down. It wouldn't be long until the place was storming with cops and paramedics and I wanted to make sure we had a chance to talk since it had sounded important.

"What did they say?"

"They had on record that I had called in to request help with the alarm and that they had manually overridden the system after verifying my information. Turned out that I had also updated my password to Damian." He chuckled as he looked over at me.

"I'm sorry that I didn't believe you."

"It doesn't make sense though." My mind tried to wrap around how he could have been at Chase's house in the afternoon on Tuesday and then back in Boston by Wednesday, which was when he had the accident. It was possible that he was never in Boston and someone else had wrecked his car but the wounds on his face seemed pretty consistent with an accident.

"Oh my God." My hand covered my mouth as goosebumps ran up my arms.

"What is it?"

"He was never here. That's why he was 'playing the game'- he wasn't here until this morning. He was stalling, making me think he was here when he wasn't." My head was spinning as I tried to piece together all of the pieces of the psychotic puzzle.

"Why do you say that?"

"Because he told me earlier that I didn't know the things he had to do to get here or that he had been driving all night last night with no sleep. And his face looked like he was in an actual accident. It all makes sense now."

"What accident? I'm so confused." He leaned back against the couch as I turned my body toward him.

"Jade found out last night that Damian had been in a car accident just outside of Boston. The car had wrapped around a tree and caught fire so they didn't think there were any survivors. Last night Jade and I thought Damian had died, but apparently he actually survived the accident and drove all the way to Haven Brook without stopping."

"Then if he wasn't in my house, then who was?"

"I have no idea. Damian was good at manipulating people. It could have been anyone." I watched as the room began to swarm with cops and paramedics.

Noah talked to the first officers that came in and I could see him point to Damian as he talked before looking over at Chase and I.

"How did Noah know to come here?" I asked as I watched a female office approach us.

"I was coming to warn you about Damian but I didn't get a chance to tell Noah so I told him I was coming here and to call me in ten minutes. If I didn't answer, then he needed to call 911." He stood up and walked off with the male cop that came to speak with him.

I sat on the couch and answered questions for what felt like hours as I watched the forensic team move around Damian's body. Soon they had collected what they needed and loaded his body onto the gurney as they zipped up the body bag and wheeled him out. It was comforting to know that this chapter of my life was finally over. There were no questions or doubts in my mind, I finally had all of the answers that I needed and was ready to move on with my life.

Epilogue
1 Year Later

I looked up at the handwritten letter that was taped to the mirror in the bathroom, my daily reminder of where I truly came from. A year ago I was fighting for my life and trying to get away from the one man who had promised to always love me. Now I sat and watched as Jade slipped on her black stiletto heels and smoothed down her red floor length satin bridesmaid gown. She smiled warmly at me in the mirror as my fingers worked the last bobby pin into place. My nerves were starting to get the better of me so I sat back in the chair and read the words that had been calming me since I first read them 11 months ago.

Dearest Mia,

I hope this letter finds you and that you are doing well. I wanted to bring it to you in person but it didn't seem like the right thing to do. The right thing to do would be to forget about the letter and tell you in person, but my hands are shaking so bad trying to write this that I doubt my mouth would have been able to work properly if I tried to tell you in person.

You've been on my mind these past few months, ever since I saw you run out of the woods. I knew you were in trouble and the cop in me wanted to help you. But there was something different about you, something that I didn't know would impact me so deeply until I realized who you were.

And I'd like to say that the moment I saw those blue eyes look at me, I knew who you were. My mind knew what my heart couldn't accept. I'm sure you're wondering what I'm talking about, and I promise, I'll get to the point soon. You had mentioned that you grew up in Colorado, though you never said where. What you didn't know is that I had also grown up in Colorado. When we drove to the hotel I only said that Arlene and I were from Colorado, but I didn't tell you that I grew up in Eastern Point, which as you know, is very close to Haven Brook.

I spent a lot of time in Haven Brook as I was growing up and right after high school I met a girl named Bonnie. I fell madly in love with her and wanted to give her the moon and stars- whatever her beautiful heart wanted. And I tried. I tried constantly to give her what I thought would make her happy, but as you know, the list of things that made her happy was never ending.

Bonnie wanted to move to LA and pursue an acting career but I didn't have the money for us to go. She threatened to leave and even though it broke my heart, I told her she should do what she needed to do, so she could be happy. A few weeks later she told me that she was pregnant and had given up on the LA idea. I was so happy and ecstatic, I couldn't believe that I was going to be a father! I found a second job and started putting money in savings so I could buy us a bigger house. Bonnie found out about the savings and became irate that I would put money into savings for a child I didn't know, but I wouldn't do it to help her get to LA. I tried to reason with her but she left me. Called it quits and left.

I tried desperately to get in touch with her, to ask for another chance. I didn't want to miss out on being part of my child's life. A month had passed before Bonnie finally talked to me and it was to tell me that she had met a director who was going to help her get her acting career started. I asked her about being there so I could help with the baby and she told me that she had an abortion. She felt that if I wasn't supportive of her dream to be an actress, then she wasn't going to allow me my dream of being a father.

She left and I never heard another word from her.

My world had felt like it was collapsing around me. My mother had moved to Haven Brook to try to help me get on my feet again after Bonnie took all of the cash I had been saving for the house. Soon after that, I met Arlene and she was the one who saved me from myself. She convinced me that I had a life worth living and showed me how to love again. We moved to northern Colorado shortly after and I never looked back.

I ignored the letters from my mom as she talked about how Bonnie had come back with a stomach as big as a watermelon, and how Bonnie's little girl looked just like me when I was that age. My mother never gave up on the idea that you were mine and she's sent me updates throughout the years. When you graduated high school. When you moved to Boston. When you got married. She always found a way to stay updated with what was happening in your life.

When I heard you use your real name at the airport, I couldn't believe it. The woman my mother had been telling me about for 25 years was standing right beside me. My heart felt like it was going to give up on me that day and I thought- well at least you got to meet her before you died!

Never in a million years would I have ever imagined that you were mine. It's always felt too good to be true so I never wanted to allow myself to consider it when I would get the updates from my mom. If I allowed myself to believe it, and then it wasn't true, I didn't think I would survive it. My world felt like it had ended the day Bonnie said she had chosen to kill my baby than to allow me to be happy. That's not something that's easy to recover from.

I'm sorry that you grew up thinking that your father walked away and didn't want you. Please know that I have always wanted you. From the moment you were just a thought in my mind, I've always wanted you. I regret not believing my mom. I regret not coming to find you sooner. There are so many regrets, but never will I ever regret meeting Bonnie. Without her, I wouldn't have you.

I know that this doesn't make up for the 25 years of your life that I've missed but I would really love the opportunity to try to get to know you if you'd let me. If not, I understand and wish you the best.

All my best,

Joe

A single tear rolled down my cheek as I read the letter that always made me cry. To feel so much love from someone in a letter- it was mind boggling to me. A huge part of me wished that my mom would never have done what she did to Joe and that I would have been able to grow up knowing my father. How different would my life have been?

I stood up and smoothed down the white lace of my dress as I glanced at the bump that stretched it tight across my stomach. I tried to suck it in and giggled when I realized that it was still there. Gently I rubbed a hand over my swollen belly and closed my eyes as I thought about how lucky I was to be carrying his baby.

"You ready?" Jade's head popped in from behind the door as she reached her hand out for me. I pulled up the fabric behind me and carried it in one hand as I followed Jade down the hallway. The sun was getting ready to set and I was anxious to see Chase. My heart beat faster while I counted down the minutes before I would see him.

Outside I could hear as the music started, a soft sound that floated in through the open door. This was it. This was the moment I had been waiting for. I smiled as Joe walked over to me and held out his arm for me to take it. I wrapped my arm in his as he leaned over and kissed my cheek.

"You look absolutely beautiful. He's a very lucky man." He patted my hand gently as we slowly started walking toward the sliding glass door that led out to the patio. There were lights strung along the rail of the porch and all throughout the trees. Fresh rose petals were scattered along the path that led me to Chase and left a fragrant smell as I slowly walked through them. Everything looked beautiful and for a moment I couldn't believe that this was our backyard, it looked so formal and elegant, while keeping the simplicity of the backyard wedding that I had always dreamed of.

I smiled as Jade and Noah walked down the aisle in front of me, holding hands when they thought no one was looking. They had been dating for a few months but neither of them were ready to label it so we all pretended like we didn't know what was happening. We turned the corner and I could see Chase standing in front of the chairs that were filled with our family and friends. Liam was by his side, standing proud as he held the rings on the pillow. The mountain served as the backdrop behind them with shades of green and yellow illuminated by the setting sun.

Chase's family sat in the front rows while the family I never knew I had until a year ago, sat on the other side of the aisle. I smiled as Arlene watched us walk down the aisle and patted Jean, my grandma, as tears rolled down her cheeks. There was a happiness that overwhelmed me as I felt like my life finally felt complete. The music started to fade as I stood next to Chase. Joe's face lit up as he smiled up at us with tears in his eyes, our arms still wrapped together. I tried to force back the tears that threatened to ruin my makeup when they asked who gave me away and Joe proudly said, her father.

I took Chase's hands in mine as we looked deep into each other's eyes and repeated after the minister. Finally it was time for us to say our own vows and I felt the lump in my throat grow bigger as I listened to Chase speak as he wrapped his hands around my stomach.

"Mia, I have loved you since the day I met you. You are the most incredible person that I've ever met and your strength continues to surprise me. Your life has never been easy but you've always looked on the bright side of things and tried to make the best of everything. I'm so proud that someday you're going to teach our daughter how to do the same." He gently rubbed my tummy as a tear slid down my face.

"I promise to love you forever and to protect both of you, for the rest of my life. You will never have to want for anything because I will live all of my days making sure that you have everything your heart could ever desire. You make me the happiest man in the world and I'm so lucky that I get to call you my wife." He pulled me in and wrapped me in his arms as he leaned down and kissed me. Somewhere in the distance I could hear the words 'you may now.... continue to kiss the bride...' as laughter floated around us. My heart felt full as my husband and I started the beginning of our happily ever after.

232

The Cradle Will Fall
Samantha Baca

234

235

One
Noah

"Just put the knife down, please. You don't want to hurt her." My voice was unusually calm and steady given how I felt anything but calm. My eyes darted around the room, following her every movement as she placed the tip of the knife under Jade's throat while pulling her hair to keep her head tilted back. I swallowed hard, desperate for a way to get in between her and Jade. One quick movement could be fatal for Jade, so I had to stay calm. Her life depended on it.

I tried to lean forward slightly without drawing too much attention. If she would just step out of the shadows, I could see her face and know who I was dealing with. My hands felt sweaty as I ran them down the front of my jeans, making sure I was ready for whatever might happen.

"You don't know what I want," she rasped, her voice barely above a whisper. She shifted in the darkness, taking a step backward with Jade still in her grip.

"Don't take her, please, just let her go," I pleaded as they slipped further into the shadows. Within seconds I no longer saw Jade's face. I reached out to grab her as the knife swung out and sliced my wrist. I watched as the blood ran down my hand and puddled by my feet, the life in me slipping away into the same darkness.

"If you really love her, then you must die for her." Her voice floated above me as I stumbled further into the darkness until it was pitch black around me. Jade was gone and within seconds, so was I.

I sprung forward in bed, gasping for air the way I always did when I had one of these dreams. They were almost predictable at this point and began soon after Jade and I had started seeing each other again. It seemed the closer we got, the more often the dreams would come. Almost like some sort of bad omen for us to be together and settle down.

I glanced down beside me; Jade's hair was fanned out across her pillow as she slept. She had changed so much since the day I first met her, the short black hair with red streaks through it was now blonde and almost touched her ass. While I loved the black hair, I was digging the blonde these days. That was Jade though, always keeping me on my toes, as wild and unpredictable as they come.

I reached down and gently pulled the blanket up over her back, the room a little more chilly than normal with the recent storm that had rolled through. Winters in Colorado could be rather brutal, and this year was starting out to be a tough one. Usually, I would have adjusted the temperature before going to bed but we had been a little busy and needless to say, hadn't noticed the cold.

I glanced over at the alarm clock beside my bed, groaning silently when I saw it was already five in the morning. I could either lay in bed and toss and turn for another hour until Jade and I had to get up for work, or I could just give in and get up. Reluctantly I rolled over and slid out of bed, careful not to wake her up.

The hardwood floors were cold beneath my bare feet as I walked down the hallway and turned up the heater. I programmed the coffee maker for 6:30 and made my way to the guest room that I had recently been using as a workout room. It's a funny thing when you get involved in a committed relationship, suddenly you need different ways to burn off some stress when you don't sleep with random women anymore.

An hour later and I was finishing my kettlebell routine when I saw Jade lean against the doorway, hair still tousled, wearing nothing but one of my worn-out T-shirts that barely covered her ass. I sucked in a deep breath, her beauty constantly taking my breath away.

"You're up early again, everything okay?" She walked over and sat on the bed against the wall and looked at me, concern filling her emerald green eyes.

"Yeah, just couldn't sleep." I shrugged as I opened the closet door and put the kettlebells away. The room was barely big enough to function as a guest room without having the constant clutter of my expanding collection of workout gear.

"Another bad dream?" She tilted her head to the side and watched me. I let out a deep breath and went to sit by her on the bed. She leaned into my chest as I wrapped an arm around her and held her.

"Yeah."

"Do you want to talk about it?" I could hear the tiniest bit of hope in her voice, each time she asked it was less and less with each time I said no. There was no way that I could bring myself to talk to her about the nightmares I was having about someone trying to kill her.

"Nope. But thanks." I squeezed her shoulder gently and planted a kiss on her forehead.

"Well, in that case, I'm going to jump in the shower. I can't afford to be late today, we have a new teller that I've been assigned to train so I have to make a good impression." She hopped off the bed and lingered for a moment in the doorway, looking back at me over her shoulder. "But I do have a few minutes to spare if you wanna join me."

I saw the look in her eye and jumped off the bed, chasing her down the hallway as she squealed and ran ahead. Within seconds my T-shirt was pulled over her head and flung backward at me as she kept running the short distance to the shower, her bare ass and butterfly tattoo greeting me as I caught up to her. My hand reached out and grabbed her before she slipped away and darted into the shower. The hot water started to fog up the glass of the shower door, her eyes watching me as the water ran down her body. It was like a game of cat and mouse and I never got tired of playing it with her. Jade was carefree and playful, and it was one of the things that drew me to her the most. That and her ass.

What was supposed to be a quick shower turned into a long, cold one as the hot water ran out by the time we were ready to actually shower. I let Jade finish up first so she could have the last of the warm water while I took a much-needed cold shower. Being with Jade was pretty much the equivalent of being on Viagra, she could keep me going for hours.

I was in the kitchen pouring our coffee into travel mugs when she walked in wearing a black and white polka dot skirt with a black silk shirt. It was always such a mind fuck for me to see her get dressed up for work, looking professional, and completely put together when I got to see the wild side as soon as she got home. I couldn't lie, it also made for some freaking hot role-playing in the bedroom.

"You look nice, should I be jealous of this new hire?" I joked as I tightened the lid on her mug and handed it to her.

"Relax, it's a woman." She rolled her eyes as her heels clicked across the floor as she walked to the fridge and grabbed a yogurt for breakfast.

"Well... I've never been known to be one to complain...." I winked as she suggestively licked a spoonful of yogurt into her mouth.

"You're impossible." She shook her head and took another bite.

"A guy could fantasize."

"Oh really? So that's your fantasy? Me with another woman?"

"Well, I would be there too, of course." I shot her a playful look as she rolled her eyes again, a smile spreading across her face.

"So you, me, and Cindy Belmont." She ate her last bite of yogurt and sat the spoon in the sink. "I can always ask if she's interested while I'm training her. Just gotta pick the right time. Maybe after money laundering but before armed robbery?" Her eyes danced wildly as they watched mine as she toyed with the idea, teasing me every step of the way.

"Wait- what did you say her name was?" I heard her say it the first time but there was no way that she had actually said that name. My stomach felt uneasy as I waited for her to confirm.

"Cindy Belmont." She tilted her head to the side as she walked past me to throw her empty container away. "Why, do you know her?"

I swallowed hard and tried to think of how to answer that. Did I know her? No. Did I fuck her? Yes. She was a one-night stand that I had the night that Jade and I got into a fight and called it quits. That was six months ago, right after Chase and Mia's wedding and I hadn't seen or heard anything from Cindy since it happened. There was no fucking way that the woman I slept with from a one-night stand was the same woman who was now going to be working with my girlfriend, was there? I cleared my throat and walked past her to the sink, desperate to hide the look on my face.

"Doesn't sound familiar, no."

"Well, I guess I should go or I'm really going to be late."

"Okay, text me on your break." I smiled as I felt her arms slide around my waist and hug me from behind.

"Are you feeling okay?"

"Yeah, I'm fine. Why?" My heart was racing as I was anxious to get away from her long enough to find out whether or not the Cindy she was going to be working with was the same Cindy I had slept with. While it shouldn't have been an issue given that we had broken up, I hadn't been honest with her about whether I was with anyone else when she asked me about it when we got back together.

"Because you didn't follow that sentence with your usual, 'send me some nudes.'" Her voice was low as she mocked me saying it.

"You know I never say no to those." I turned my head to smile at her as she stayed wrapped around my back.

"And you know I don't take them." She swatted my ass then turned to walk away.

"I'll talk to you later," she called over her shoulder as she walked out the door.

"Sounds good."

The door closed, leaving me running late for work and distracted with a problem I didn't want to have to deal with.

Two
Noah

"You're in early for a Monday." Chase leaned against the doorway and crossed his arms over his chest.

"I'm surprised you're here at all, isn't Mia supposed to pop any day now?" I kept my attention on my computer and didn't bother to look up to make small talk. There was too much on my mind and I needed to clear it before I had to go upfront and be around other people in a few hours.

"Any day now." He ran a hand down the scruff on his face, evidence that he hadn't taken the time to shave this week.

"So what are you doing here? Shouldn't you be at home helping her practice her breathing or something?" My brow furrowed as I stared at my computer, not finding anything on Cindy. I didn't know why it was bothering me so much that she was back in town given that we had only had one night together, but something kept eating away at me as I thought about her working with Jade. Was this what it felt like to be with someone who finally made me worry about getting caught doing something that I knew I shouldn't have done?

"Practice her breathing? Really?" He pushed off the wall and walked around to my desk, looking over my shoulder at the computer.

"Who is Cindy Belmont?" He leaned down and peered at the computer screen to read the name and the very few Google results it came up with.

"No one." I pushed the keyboard away from me and leaned back in my chair as he took a step back and looked down at me.

"What's up Noah? And stop with the whiny bullshit, just tell me what's going on."

Chase and I had one of those love/hate brotherly relationships which worked out well given he had been my best friend since we were little and we now ran a brewpub together. We had the natural ability to call the other out on their shit and knew when something was going on, which unfortunately for me, meant that he knew something was going on.

"She's a new girl at the bank, Jade's training her today."

"Okay- so what's the problem? Why are you Googling her?" He pulled his brows together in confusion.

"I slept with her." I let out a heavy sigh as I finally said the words out loud to someone else.

"You cheated on Jade?" His tone was harsh as he stared at me, waiting for me to confess just how badly I fucked up.

"Yeah... No. I don't know?" My head was a mess as I had spent the last hour asking myself the same thing.

"How do you not know? If you slept with someone other than Jade, you cheated on her. It's pretty simple."

"What's pretty simple?"

I looked up to see Chase's younger brother Grant walk into the office and smile as he looked back and forth between the two of us.

"Noah isn't sure whether he cheated on Jade by sleeping with someone else," Chase explained as he leaned against the wall beside me, Grant sitting down in the chair in front of my desk.

"You cheated on Jade? Really bro? She's literally the perfect girl for you, why would you do that?"

I threw my hands up in exasperation and shook my head.

"I didn't cheat on Jade. I slept with someone else six months ago, when her and I had that huge fight and broke up. It was a one-night stand that meant nothing."
"Okay, then I'm confused- why are we talking about it?" Grant pulled his eyebrows together.

"We aren't." I leaned back against the cool leather of my high back chair and shut my eyes.

"So you slept with her while you guys were broken up, it was a one-night stand, and now she's working with Jade. Am I missing anything?" Chase looked over at me and waited for an answer.

"Jade asked me when we got back together if I had been with anyone else during the time we were broken up. I said no."

"Fuck." Chase exhaled and shook his head, realizing what the problem was.

"Double fuck." Grant leaned back in his chair and gave me a sympathetic half-smile.

"So now I don't know what to do because the girl I had a one-night stand with six months ago just mysteriously showed up in town and is working with my girlfriend. I mean, what am I supposed to do? Do I come clean and tell Jade before she possibly finds out, or do I just ignore it and pray that Cindy keeps her mouth shut and forgot about me completely?" I looked back and forth between them, hopeful that one of them would have a logical answer for me.

A few minutes of silence passed as they exchanged a few unsure glances before Chase finally spoke.

"I say don't tell her. What's the likelihood that she'll find out anyway? If this girl was interested in anything with you, she would have made a move back then. I don't think there's any reason to hurt Jade when you guys have come this far in your relationship."

"I agree, nothing good will come from telling her." Grant shrugged his shoulders before a smirk crossed his face. "And on a different subject, is Cindy cute?"

"Gross! You don't want Noah's sloppy seconds." Chase laughed as he pushed off the wall and pulled his phone out of his pocket.

"What?! It's a small town and Noah has slept with pretty much every girl here. It's literally impossible to find someone he hasn't slept with."

I tried to keep a straight face but failed as I joined Grant in laughing at how true that statement was. There really weren't that many girls in town that I hadn't already been with, but that's also because not many new people move here, and I started at an early age. I looked up at Chase as he stared blankly at his phone.

"You okay, Chase? You look like you just saw a ghost." I chuckled as I leaned forward and waited for him to snap out of the daze he was in.

"Yeah, I'm fine. Mia's water just broke." He slid the phone back into his pocket and looked at us as if nothing had happened.

"Are you just going to stand there or are you going to get your wife to the hospital?" Grant asked as he stood up and looked at Chase. A few seconds passed before Chase registered the words.

"Shit! It's time!" A look of panic crossed his face as he patted down his pockets for his car keys before spinning on his heel and running out the door. Grant and I exchanged a look before bursting into laughter.

"You laugh now, one day that'll be you, my friend."

"I don't know about that. Jade's not looking to settle down and we're taking it slow. Who knows what the future has in store for us?" I looked away and pretended to be doing something on my computer to take the focus off of me. Grant had always been like a little brother to me growing up and had the same annoying knack for reading me that Chase did.

"What do you want? Do you think someday you might want to get married and have kids?"

"Honestly, I don't know." I sighed and pushed back from the computer when I realized that Grant wasn't going anywhere nor was he going to let this conversation go. The problem was that I had thought a lot about my future lately and that probably scared me more than anything.

"It's okay to want more out of life. Sometimes I think about trying to meet someone new and seeing where it could go. I know Liam misses Renee and while I would never want to try to replace her, I think he would like to have a woman in our lives again. I can't give him back the mom he had, but that doesn't mean that he doesn't deserve to know that kind of love as he grows up." His eyes filled with tears as he looked away and my heart broke for him the same way it did the day Renee lost her battle to cancer.

It was coming up on the 3 year anniversary of her passing and Liam was starting to test his dad the way all ten-year-olds do. While I couldn't imagine trying to find love again after everything Grant went through, I knew him well enough to know that he was also looking out for his son. It was a delicate balance that Grant was constantly working to maintain as he did the best he could to raise his son on his own.

"Sometimes I think that I want that life." I sighed and looked down.

"What life is that?"

"The whole happily ever after. Getting married. Having kids. I see Chase and Mia together and they make it look so easy."

"They are good for each other and when you find someone like that, it does feel easy. Just like what you've found with Jade."

I looked up at him and saw the words written on his face that he didn't have the heart to say.

"I have to tell her what happened, don't I?"

He nodded his head in agreement as he gave me another half-smile. I let out a deep breath and leaned back. I knew it was only right to tell Jade what happened, she deserved to know if we were going to try to build a life together. But the thing that I feared the most was what she would say when she found out. Would she curse me out and be pissed at me then get over it? Or would she be the Jade that I knew and thank me for telling her the truth before walking out and leaving me forever? My heart clenched as I knew the answer.

"Well, on that note, I should get out of here before you need to get upfront to open." He stood up and pushed in the chair. "If you talk to Chase, let him know that I'll get the tool bag from him later."

"Did you need to borrow tools? I have mine out in the truck."

"If you don't mind, that would be great. I would just steal his but they're in his truck which is now gone." He laughed and waited while I leaned back and dug the keys out of my pocket before tossing them to him.

"Thanks, I'll bring them back this afternoon."

"Sounds good. I'm gonna head upfront, you can just leave my keys on the desk when you're done." I walked by and clapped him on the shoulder as we walked down the hallway together.

"You deserve to find love again, don't ever forget that."

"So do you, Noah. Let me know how it goes when you tell her." He chuckled softly as he walked away and for a moment, I felt like myself again.

I wasn't the guy who was romantic and thinking about love and starting a family. I was the guy who was constantly with a different girl and getting my balls chopped by the guys for my reckless behavior. I took a deep breath and prayed that the day would be busy so I could keep my mind off of the things I wasn't ready to deal with.

250

Three
Jade

It was mid-morning and I felt like I had been talking for hours in a one-sided conversation. It was rare that we ever had new hires at the bank, and this was the first one that I was responsible for training. I had expected it to be more of a question and answer type setting while she preferred a lecture instead which meant I had been the only one talking all morning. I constantly tried to engage her in the conversation and ask if she had any questions, but she was yet to interact with me.

"Okay, we've covered a lot. Why don't we take a 15 minute break then we'll get started again?" I smiled and picked up the pages of the training binder that we had already covered and moved them to a small pile on the corner of the desk.

"Thank you! This baby is sitting on my bladder, so I really need the bathroom." She stood up and out of nowhere a very pregnant belly greeted me.

"Of course. See you in 15 minutes." I smiled awkwardly as she walked off and made her way to the bathroom. She had on a loose shirt with a flowy skirt that hid her bump as she walked away but part of me wondered why I hadn't seen it before then.

I stood up and smoothed down the front of my skirt before walking to the break room to fill up my water bottle. It felt nice to stand up for a few minutes and stretch my legs. My body was sore from sitting idle for so long that I couldn't wait to get home and do some yoga. I thought about texting Mia to see if she would want to get together and do some light yoga with me when I saw Cindy come out of the bathroom and make her way toward the break room. I smiled as I walked past her, sitting my water bottle on my desk before heading to the bathroom.

The day felt long and tedious just sitting there and going over every single page of the training manual. I finished up and walked back to my desk, surprised to see her sitting there, waiting for me.

"Alright, I thought it might be a nice little break to take a few minutes to get to know each other before we jump back into the training. Is that alright with you?"

"Sure." She smiled meekly as she sat on her hands and crossed her ankles in front of her.

I took a deep breath and turned to face her, worried that this was going to be like talking to a wall. She was very quiet and didn't strike me as the kind of person who had a lot to say.

"So, are you new to Haven Brook?"

"Yeah, I just moved here."

"Oh yeah, where did you move from?"

"Eastern Point, it's about an hour away. My family still lives there."

"What made you want to move here?"

I hated small talk more than anything and here I was, trying to find something to talk about with this girl who looked like she'd rather do anything else in the world than sit here and talk to me. This is what good employees and trainers do, I reminded myself.

"Well, I kinda want to find this guy that lives here."

"Oh yeah?" I raised my eyebrows as I waited for her to tell me more.

"Yeah, we had a thing one night six months ago, and well, as you can see...." Her voice trailed off as she giggled and rubbed a hand over her stomach.

"Does he know that you're pregnant?" I smiled as she looked down adoringly at her stomach.

"Not yet. I didn't have his information when I left, it was all so quick before I had to go. But I know he grew up here so I don't think he would have left." She sighed heavily. "At least I hope not."

She reminded me of an innocent girl who fell in love for the first time and it brought a wave of happiness over me.

"I'm sure he's still around. What's he look like? Maybe I know him?" I leaned forward on my desk and watched her shift nervously across the desk from me as her eyes lit up with excitement.

"Oh my, well, he's gorgeous. Like really, really gorgeous. He has jet black hair and these really pretty eyes. They're kinda brown but also kinda green. It's weird, it's like they're two colors mixed into one."

"Hazel?" I tilted my head and watched her reaction as the word flowed off my tongue.

"Yes! That's it- they're hazel. Gosh, this baby is making me lose all of my smartness." She giggled and I smiled back, fighting the urge to tell her that wasn't a word.

"He sounds very good looking."

I watched as her eyes lit up and silently wondered just how many guys in Haven Brook fit that description, knowing the answer that I didn't want to accept. There was only one.

<u>Four</u>
Noah

"She is beautiful. Congratulations you guys." I stared down at the most beautiful teeny tiny baby wrapped up like a burrito with a handful of blankets. My heart felt so heavy and full that I had to blink several times to force the tears back.

"Hey guys, can I come in?"

My head lifted to the sound of Jade's voice as she quietly opened the door to Mia's hospital room.

"Get your butt in here and meet your niece!" Mia exclaimed excitedly. I looked over and caught a glimpse of the look her and Chase shared as they watched me hold their daughter.

"Oh my gosh!" Jade squealed quietly as she looked over my shoulder at the baby while washing her hands in the sink behind me. I laughed when I watched her struggle to stay focused on drying her hands as she rushed to hold the baby. A paper towel flew by my head, missing the trash can, as Jade reached her arms out in front of me for the baby.

"Can I help you?" I teased as I pulled the baby in closer to my chest. She raised an eyebrow while pursing her lips, a look I could never take seriously when she was mad because she was so damn cute.

"Wilder, if you know what is good for you, you'll hand over that baby," she warned playfully, reaching in to take her.

"Fine, but you have to sit first. You're too antsy, I'm not going to risk you hurting my niece." I slowly got up, clutching the baby to my chest to keep her safe. Never in my life had I ever held something so delicate and fragile.

"Alright, move out of my way." She smiled excitedly as she sat down and held her arms out for the baby. I gently leaned forward and waited until I could feel Jade's arms around her before I pulled back, still keeping my hands right under the baby just to be safe.

I watched as Jade's eyes lit up the moment she looked at her, taking my breath away. For a moment I imagined what she would look like seeing our baby for the first time. I shook my head to clear my mind of the image and kissed her forehead before stepping to the side of her to pick up the paper towel and throwing it in the trash.

"She's perfect. Absolutely perfect." She looked up at Mia with tears in her eyes as they shared a silent moment that lead to both of them crying. It was getting to be too much in this room, too heavy with all of the emotions flying around me.

"Thank you," Mia and Chase said at the same time, looking at each other and laughing afterward.

"Have you guys picked a name?" I asked, hoping to lighten the mood some. I watched as they looked at each other and Chase smiled at Mia as he nodded and smiled. Mia turned to us and sat up straight with a proud smile on her face.

"Guys, we would like to introduce you to Rylee Rose Walker." Her

smile beamed across her face, Chase's arm wrapping tight around her shoulders as he placed a tender kiss on her cheek.
"I love it!" Jade looked down at the baby and gently rubbed her cheek with her finger. "Hello, Rylee Rose. I love you so much already, sweet girl."

"It's a beautiful name you guys."

"Thanks, we wanted something meaningful and Rylee means courageous. We changed the spelling to make it more unique, but we think it fits her already."

"It definitely fits her, Mia. She's going to be courageous just like her momma."

"Knock, knock. Is it safe to enter?" Grant's voice called out from behind the door and we all laughed at how no one felt safe entering the room of a new mother.

"Come on in, brother." Chase smiled as Grant and Liam came around the corner, a pink teddy bear in Liam's arms as he stayed close to Grant.

"Hey buddy, would you like to come in and meet your cousin?" Chase looked over at Liam and smiled as he slowly walked over to where Chase was sitting on the bed next to Mia.

Jade smiled sweetly as she slowly stood up and carried the baby over to Chase, giving Liam a few minutes to get situated on the couch next to the bed. Grant sat beside his son and I saw a look of pain on his face as his son reached out and carefully pulled the tiny baby close to his chest and rested her on the pillow they placed on his lap. I could never imagine what it felt like to be Grant, to start my life with someone who I planned to spend forever with only to have that pulled out from underneath me before it even got started. Everyone knew that Grant and Renee had wanted a big family, he wanted three kids, she wanted four. Seeing his son holding a newborn baby, knowing that he wouldn't have a sibling of his own had to kill Grant deep down inside.

The thoughts of Grant's life and what all he was missing out on flooded through my head and took me back to the same nagging questions that I had been having for months now. Was I ready to finally settle down and did I really want to get married? Were kids going to be part of my future? I had a wonderful childhood growing up but I've never felt like I was destined to be a dad, and quite frankly, I wasn't sure that I wanted to be one. But now something was different. I remembered the feeling of Rylee's tiny, delicate body in my hands, and all of a sudden, I wanted more than anything for Grant to find love again and have the family he dreamed of. And I wanted it for myself as well.

My heart started racing as I realized what was happening and suddenly, I wanted to get down on one knee and propose to Jade before running her home and knocking her up. The hospital had to have been putting some mind-altering drugs through the vents that made people delusional. That was the only explanation.

"You okay?" Grant looked over at me, breaking my attention with his question. My cheeks felt red and flushed, my throat suddenly dry.

"Yeah. I'm good."

"We should probably get going and give them some time with Rylee." Jade nodded toward Grant and Liam as she picked up her purse and slung the strap over her shoulder. She looked at me in a way I hadn't seen before and for a moment, I could swear that she looked upset with me.

"That's a good plan, want to follow me home? We can go grab something for dinner or I can order a pizza, just let me know what you prefer."

"Actually, I think I'm going to stay at my place tonight." Her lips were pursed as her arms crossed across her chest. I had only seen this look a handful of times, but I knew enough to know that this wasn't going to end well. Why was she so upset with me? She seemed fine until she came to meet the baby. Was it because we weren't moving forward in our relationship and she was mad because she wanted a family and thought that I didn't? A hundred questions came flooding through my mind as I thought about what I should say with everyone watching us.

"Is everything okay?" I went with the safest response I could think of on the fly.

"Yeah, I'm fine. I just need some space. I have a lot that I need to think about."

Shit. This was definitely about the baby. It had to be. I rolled my eyes and took a deep breath as I silently cursed her for making me look like a pansy in front of the guys but if she needed a big song and dance, I would give it to her. Hell, she could ask for the moon and I would try to find a way to get it for her.

"Look, Jade, I think there's something that we need to talk about." I moved my eyes slowly to the door, hoping she would take the hint and move our conversation to the hallway. If I was going to bare my soul and look like a total pussy at least it would be in the presence of doctors and nurses that were used to men wallowing in front of women since this was the maternity ward.

"I think there is." Her lips were pulled in a tight line, her jaw set. The look in her eye told me everything and I knew at that moment that this was no longer about her wanting to have a baby. This was about Cindy. She knew.

I tried to brace myself for the slew of profanities I was sure were about to come from her mouth but was surprised when she stayed quiet and stared at me, waiting for me to talk. I wanted to come clean and tell her about Cindy, I really did. But for whatever fucking reason, I wasn't able to. I glanced over at Grant, my eyes pleading for him to give me some sort of advice to help me through this as he subtly nodded his head. "Jade….. I um….." I cleared my throat and tried to ignore everyone as they stared at us. "I think you should move in with me. Permanently." I blew out the breath that I was holding and saw Grant's head drop to his chest as he slowly shook his head no. Chase arched an eyebrow before looking away and quietly whispering something in Mia's ear.

"I don't think that's a good idea."

"Why not?" I knew that I didn't really want to know the answer but I asked anyway. It felt like it was impossible to avoid asking. It was like a band-aid that was wrapped too tightly around an oozing wound. You had to pull it knowing that it was going to hurt like hell every inch of the way.

"I think you know why." She shifted her weight and a sadness crossed her face. I swallowed hard as my heartbeat raced.

"Jade, please," I whispered.

"You should have told me. You should have told me when it happened and not let me accidentally find out. Did you think I was stupid?" Her brows pulled together as she glared at me.

I licked my lips and lowered my head, my eyes closed to avoid having to see the look on her face. When I opened them, she was gone.

<u>Five</u>
Jade

"You don't have to stay on the phone with me, you should get some rest or go snuggle that sweet girl of yours." I wiped my nose with the tissue that was falling apart from using it so much. I took a ragged deep breath and held my phone closer to my ear, desperate for the comfort that Mia was providing on the other end.

"Chase is snuggling Rylee so I have some downtime and honestly, I need something to distract myself for a little bit. I've been so consumed with the pregnancy and everything else that I feel like I don't even know what's going on around me. And I really want to know." Her voice was gentle as she said that last sentence and I felt myself starting to cry all over again.

"Jade, what happened? Talk to me."

"Do you remember that big fight that Noah and I had a while back? The one right after your wedding?"

"Yeah."

"Well, I asked him after we got back together if he had been with anyone else while we were broken up and he said no. He asked if I had been with anyone, and I said no." I took a moment to try to collect myself as I had been playing this over and over in my head since Cindy had told me about the guy she came here to be with. Mia stayed quiet as she waited for me to go on.

"I trusted him. Even though I knew deep down that I shouldn't. He's Noah- everyone wants him and he's always getting with a different girl. Why did I think that it would have been any different when we broke up for two weeks?"

"Did he tell you that he was with someone else?" She spoke softly and I wasn't sure if it was to try to help keep me calm or if it was to let Chase and the baby rest, but either way, I was thankful for it as it actually did calm me down some.

"No. But I'm 99.9% sure that he was with someone else."

"What would make you think that?"

"We have a new hire at work, a girl that just moved here from Eastern Point. She said that she moved her to find the guy she had a one-night stand with."

"Did she say that it was Noah? Because there are a lot of guys in Haven Brook that are known to have one-night stands. Chase's youngest brother, Wyatt just got himself into some trouble with the same thing." Mia sighed and I let out a soft laugh as I knew just how much trouble Wyatt was getting into as he was coming to Noah for help every other weekend.

"No, but she didn't have to. She described the guy as gorgeous with black hair and hazel eyes. How many guys do you know that look like that here?" My voice was laced with a little too much sarcasm and I hated myself for how jealous and insecure I sounded. Part of me wanted to just ask Noah about it and be a grown-up, mature person, but the other part of me felt so hurt and betrayed that I couldn't find it in me to be that.

"Well, that is pretty hard to say- yeah, I'm sure she was talking about someone else." Mia sighed as I heard her shushing in the background.

"Yeah, it definitely is." I shifted my weight on the couch and grabbed my wine glass from the table, taking a big sip, enjoying the feeling of the cold liquid as it ran down the back of my throat. "I can let you go, Mia, I don't want to keep you from your family."

"Oh, shush."

"Okay, I'm going to let you go. I'll talk to you in a few days, see how you guys are doing and if you need anything."
"I was shushing you, Jade."

I started laughing and could hear Mia join in on the other end.

"Okay, so let's go ahead and agree that Noah slept with another woman who has come back into town and wants to be with him. You don't know for sure that she slept with him when you guys were broken up, it might have been before you guys ever got together. Noah is completely in love with you, Jade. There's no way that he's going to leave you for some girl that he had a one-night stand with." Her voice was so positively reassuring that I didn't want to break the news to her.

"She's six months pregnant and came back to make things work with the baby's daddy." I closed my eyes and sunk lower into the couch as I brought my wine glass up and held the cold glass to my swollen eyes. I wasn't one to cry but for whatever reason, this really broke me. I couldn't figure out if I was more upset with Noah for not telling me about the other girl after it happened, or if it was because I knew that he would leave me to be with her. He may not love her but he would do the right thing.

"Oh my god." She let out a heavy breath leaving us both sitting in silence for a few minutes.

"What are you going to do?"

"What can I do? I can't be the person who stands in the way of a father being part of his child's life. I have to walk away." A sob escaped my throat before I could stop it.

"Oh, honey…. I wish I was there with you right now, you shouldn't have to go through this alone."

"Thanks, I'll be fine though. I just need to get out whatever it is that I'm feeling right now and then move on."

"Is it really that easy?"

"No. But when you truly love someone, sometimes you have to let them go. And as hard as it will be, I have to let him go, Mia. Maybe he was never mine to begin with." Tears rolled down my cheeks and for once I didn't bother trying to wipe them away. My heart felt like it was breaking and any questions I had regarding where things were going with Noah and I were quickly answered.

"Don't make any decisions tonight. You're upset, and you have every right to be. Take some time to let yourself think about how you feel and then talk to Noah. Just because he's having a baby with someone else doesn't mean that you can't be part of his life."

"I know. I just feel so betrayed by him. I asked him and he said no. Then I have to find out from some girl that I'll be working with 5 days a week? How am I supposed to be able to work with her and NOT think about them having sex?"

"I get it, I would feel the same way if some girl from Chase's past came back into our lives. But Jade, you forget that you are an AMAZING woman who is capable of so much. You're not a jealous, vindictive person. Once you take some time to process everything and talk to Noah, you're going to be just fine. She's not a threat to you honey."

Mia's words really hit and I was so thankful that she took the time to talk to me because it was just what I needed. She was right, I wasn't this person. I needed to think about how I felt about everything and sit down and talk with Noah. No one could decide our future except for us. There were plenty of families that were blended, beautiful messes, and if we had to- we could be one too.

"Thanks, Mia. You truly are the best. I appreciate you being there for me tonight."

"Of course. You sure you're going to be okay?"

"I'll be just fine, I promise."

"Alright. Well I better get going, Ry just woke up and she's hungry. It hasn't even been 24 hours since she was born and all this girl wants to do is eat." She giggled and I smiled, though part of me felt sad that I wouldn't be able to share this first with Noah. He would share all of the firsts regarding a new baby with a woman he doesn't even know.

"Go feed that sweet girl, and text me if you guys need anything." I smiled as I hung up and put my phone on the coffee table before laying back against the pillows and closing my eyes. There was a lot to think about and I needed a clear head before I even attempted talking to Noah. I heard my phone buzz on the table and ignored the new text message from him. He had been sending them all night but I gave up reading them for now. A few deep breaths and I could feel my body relaxing as I drifted off to sleep on the couch.

<u>Six</u>
Noah

I sighed as I sat my phone down on my desk and glared at the clock. It was 8:30 and Jade hadn't responded to a single text that I had sent. I felt so anxious after leaving the hospital that I decided to come into work in an effort to avoid showing up at her apartment and begging her to talk to me. I knew that she needed space but I found it increasingly harder to give it to her. I looked down and checked my phone again, the message still showing as delivered, not read.

It was close to closing time so I grabbed my phone and shoved it in my pocket as I went up front to help the new girl wrap things up for the night. I had hoped to have her better trained before Mia went on maternity leave but for whatever reason, we fell behind schedule which meant I was working a lot more hours than I usually did. And now with Chase taking a few weeks off to be home with Mia and the baby, I was going to be covering his side as well. Maybe the extra work would be good for me and keep me distracted until Jade was willing to talk.

I had been replaying the scene in the hospital over and over in my head all night. She was furious with me for not telling her and while I assumed she knew what happened with Cindy, I was too much of a coward to say anything to her about it. Never in my life had I ever regretted a one-night stand as much as I regretted that one. Jade and I had just broken up and I had been out drinking to blow off some steam. Cindy was a beautiful girl, thick and curvy with long brown hair that had wrapped nicely around my fist as she straddled me and told me all of the filthy things she wanted to do to me. I had to admit, I was pretty impressed with her dirty talk but even more impressed with her take-charge attitude, including when she surprised me with a blow job that ended with her rolling a condom on my dick before sliding me inside of her as she rode me.

A night of fun, while I was in a dark place, was now costing me something that meant more to me than anything else ever could. I knew I should have told Jade and it had been eating at me that I didn't have the balls to tell her this morning when she mentioned her. I knew who it was the second I heard the name. We didn't have anyone named Cindy in Haven Brook and what was the likelihood of someone with the same name showing up to work with Jade and being someone totally different? It was my luck that I would finally find someone to fall in love with only to have it ruined by a night of drunken stupidity.

I walked through the door that led from the back offices into the restaurant and made my way to the bar area off to the left. Julia was busy waiting on a few tables when I saw a woman sitting at the bar. I slid around the corner and grabbed a coaster from the back counter before turning around and placing it in front of the woman.

"Hey, what can I get you?" I asked as my eyes slowly made their way up from the countertop to the curvy brunette sitting in front of me. My heart stopped as I looked at Cindy who was smiling at me with a hint of mischief.

"Hey, stranger." She smiled as she folded her hands on top of each other on the bar top in front of her.

"Hey." My mind raced as I thought of what to say to her. The hardest part was that I didn't want to say anything to her. I felt furious with her as I looked at her, thinking about how if it wasn't for her, Jade would still be talking to me.

I took a deep breath and leaned back against the counter behind me, careful not to accidentally bump the handles on the beer tower behind me.

"It's been a while." Her eyes watched me cautiously.

"Yeah, it has been a while. You back in town for a quick visit?" While I already knew the answer since she was working with Jade, I wanted to hear from her what her actual plan was.

"I actually just moved here. So I'll be here for good." She smiled and looked down at her lap before looking back up at me.

"Well, I'm sure you'll like it here. It's not that different from Eastern Point." I pushed off the counter, ready to be done with the conversation. "Did Julia already take your order or was there something I could get you?"

"Just water is fine. I don't drink these days."

Something about the way her tone changed made my stomach drop. She scooted off of the barstool and stepped back, revealing a very round bump under the white sweater she was wearing with thick leggings. My eyes followed her hands as they ran over her stomach and cradled it.

"It looks like we have some talking to do." Her voice was quiet even though it sounded like it was screeching through my head. My eyes looked up at her, a mix of emotions on my face.

"We used a condom."

"Yeah, well, they aren't always effective. Obviously." She pointed at her stomach and smiled.

"Are you sure that it's mine?"

In an instant, the smile she had on her face quickly turned into a scowl as she stared at me like I had just asked the most ridiculous question she had ever heard.

"I'm not that kind of girl, so it DEEPLY bothers me that you would even ask that question." Her jaw was clenched tight as she gritted her teeth, each word filled with anger.

How the fuck was I supposed to know what kind of girl she was? I barely knew her for twenty minutes before she was using her mouth to roll a condom on me before fucking me senseless. She was a good lay, I would admit that, but it irritated me that she felt so entitled to something more given we didn't even know each other.

"I'm sorry, I didn't mean to offend you. But as you remember, we didn't know each other before that night and this is the first we've talked since then, so surely you can imagine how well I know you and how well you know me." My eyes drifted past her as Julia walked by, carrying a tray of empty glasses to the back as she cleared her last table. It was almost nine and time to close up.

I looked back at Cindy who stayed staring at me, waiting for me to say something. It felt like a trap and I had no clue what she was expecting. This wasn't the first time I had heard of a girl coming back, claiming she was pregnant from a one-night stand but I never thought I would be on the receiving end as the guy.

"So, what is your plan?" I asked, hoping to speed this process along.

"Well, I think we need to sit down and talk about stuff. This baby will be a part of your life and we need to figure out what that looks like."

"What do you mean what it looks like? Like joint custody after it's born?" My brows furrowed together.

I watched as her nostrils flared, the sweet girl I had met six months ago replaced by the angry pregnant woman in front of me.

"I was hoping that you would be the kind of guy who did the right thing from the start. Like go with me to my prenatal appointments and ultrasounds. Help me decorate the nursery. Pick out names together. You know, the stuff people usually do when they're having a baby."

"In all fairness- you're just now telling me about a baby that you've known about for six months. That makes it kind of hard to do the right thing. We can find some time later this week or this weekend to sit down and talk about living arrangements for the baby and you can give me the dates for your appointments and we will try to be there." I squared my shoulders and waited for her response.

"Who is we?" Her eyes pulled together as she glared at me.

"My girlfriend, Jade. She'll be a part of this as well." I had decided then and there that I wasn't about to let this ruin what I had with Jade. I prayed that Jade would let me talk to her and beg her for forgiveness for putting us in this predicament to begin with. Even if she didn't, I wanted Cindy to be fully aware that there was another woman in the picture and that this wasn't going to be her and I falling in love and starting a family together. We had one night of fun that resulted in a major responsibility which I was willing to accept, but that didn't mean that I had to end things with Jade.

She pursed her lips together and continued to glare at me.

"Well then, I guess WE will all talk soon. Here's my phone number and where I'll be staying if you come to your senses and decide you want to give this another shot. You know, be a good daddy for your child." She rolled her eyes as she turned on her heel and walked out the front door. I looked down at the paper she had handed me and debated whether or not to tear it up. It didn't matter either way. Nothing mattered until I talked to Jade and explained my side to her. I wrapped up closing and jumped in my truck, heading to Jade's apartment.

It was after 9:30 when I got there which felt like it took forever, yet it wasn't enough time for me to figure out what to say to her. She already knew that I had slept with someone else, that much was clear now from the conversation we had at the hospital. And given that she worked with Cindy, she also knew that she was pregnant. Jade wasn't stupid and I wasn't about to treat her like she was.

I made it up to her apartment rather quickly and knocked on the door, wondering if I should have called or text to let her know that I was coming over. Not that it would have mattered given that she hadn't read any of my other messages I had been sending all night. I took a deep breath before knocking again, debating on whether to leave or keep pushing my luck to try to get her to open the door and talk to me. A few seconds later I heard the locks click as the door slowly opened. I expected her to stand there and yell at me or slam the door in my face but surprisingly she moved to the side and nodded her head for me to come in.

"I thought for sure you were going to slam the door in my face," I admitted as I stepped inside and slipped out of my jacket before laying it on the back of the barstool behind me. Her apartment was bigger than most in the city and totally felt like Jade. Instead of a traditional dining room table, she had opted for a high-top table and barstools where we had spent a lot of time playing poker with Chase and Mia after she moved in. Her kitchen flowed into the living room, which always felt lively with the bright colors scattered around the room with rugs, pillows, and paintings along the wall. It fit who Jade was perfectly and my heart sank when I saw the puffiness around her eyes, knowing she had been crying. The room that usually felt bright and cheery now felt dark and gloomy.

"I'm not that immature, Noah." She sighed as she walked past me and curled up under a blanket on the sectional couch that took up the majority of the living room. I walked over and sat down beside her, desperate to talk things out with her and find the happiness we had this morning before everything had gone to hell.

"I know that you're not." I ran a hand through my hair and looked at her as if she would magically say the words to make everything better. As much as I knew this was my fault and I needed to be the one to make things right, I had no idea how to actually do that. The only thing that I knew how to do was flirt with women and lure them with my sexual abilities. I seriously doubted that it would work for me in this situation.

"I'm so sorry Jade. I screwed up and I'm sorry." I waited for her to answer as she looked over at me, the pissed off girl from the hospital making another appearance. I groaned and leaned back against the couch, pulling a bright yellow pillow into my side as I prayed that maybe it would force some happiness into the room.

"Noah, I'm trying very hard not to strangle you right now."

My eyebrow arched as I watched her pull her bottom lip in between her teeth and glare at me. On the surface, Jade looked pissed. But there was something in her eyes that went a little deeper, something that showed me how hurt she was. Not that I was happy that she was hurting, but I knew that if she was hurting then it meant that she still cared about me and that there was a way for me to save what we had. Going on a whim I decided to try a different approach and prayed that it wouldn't blow up in my face like everything else had today.

"Well, I'm not usually into that but we can give it a try. Erotic asphyxiation sounds a little kinky but I'm down for it if you are." I winked and waited to see what her reaction was. Her eyes gave her away as the green turned a shade darker before she got up and stormed into the kitchen. I had seen that look before and knew that she wasn't as mad at me as she was trying to let on.

I got up and followed her into the kitchen, standing directly behind her as she stood at the sink and filled a glass with water. I slowly kissed behind her ear, her hair pulled up into a messy bun on her head. I could feel her body responding to me as I kept alert to make sure the water wasn't thrown in my direction if she changed her mind.

"It's not going to work, Noah." She sighed as she turned around and pushed me away with one hand, taking a few steps away from me. I could see the frustration on her face as she warred over whether she wanted to stay mad at me or not.

"Are you sure about that?" I stepped closer, keeping my eyes on her as I closed the distance between us. She watched me as she tried to act like she wasn't feeling the electricity between us, stepping to the side before I could fully close the gap.

"Yeah, I'm sure," she snapped, crossing her arms over her chest before she tried to step past me again.

It was a bold move but honestly, I've done worse. I stepped directly in front of her, forcing her palms to hit my chest as she tried to avoid contact. I could see her pull her bottom lip in as her eyes darkened. Most guys would take it as a warning to back off and leave her alone, I took it as a challenge. I smiled coyly as my hands slowly reached forward and gently pushed her backward by her hips, her body resisting every step we took. Within a few short steps, her back was up against the kitchen counter, my arms pinning her in on both sides.

"So what? You want some sort of angry sex? You want me to tell you all the things that you do that piss me off while I fake an orgasm?" She jerked her head to the side, her eyes squinted in anger. Fuck. I knew she was mad but this was a side of her I hadn't seen before. And honestly, the more she spoke to me that way, the more my dick twitched. I might not be good at apologizing and begging for forgiveness, but I was good at worshipping her and showing her how much I fucking wanted her.

I took another step toward her, invading more of her space as she leaned her arms back against the counter to avoid touching me. Her words were telling me all of the reasons she was pissed at me while her body was screaming for me to give her the release she desperately wanted. Her shoulders were pulled back as her head looked away from me in annoyance, her pelvis slightly tilted toward me. I smiled as I moved closer, lining myself up so she could feel how hard I was through her thin yoga pants.

She let out a small gasp as her eyes darted toward me before looking away again.

"Since when have you ever faked an orgasm with me?" I whispered as I leaned close to her ear and softly kissed her neck. "Last I remember, you have at least 2-3 without me even trying." I leaned up and playfully nipped at her earlobe. I could feel her breathing change and knew that I was getting to her.

"But...." I leisurely ran my tongue down her neck and over her collarbone, feeling a faint shiver from her beneath me.

"If you want me to stop..." My tongue hovered right above the black lace of her bra that peeked up over her tank top, "just say the word."

Her body was still as my head lingered by her full breasts, the rise and fall starting to hypnotize me.

"Noah..," she warned as I bit the fabric and slowly tugged it down, exposing her nipple. I looked up at her under hooded eyes as she watched me, desire flushing across her face. I knew Jade well enough to know how her body reacted to me when she was turned on. When her hips softly rotated, allowing me direct access, I knew she wanted this more than she would ever admit.

"Just say the word, Jade." I pulled her nipple into my mouth, forcing her back to arch in response. I would be willing to bet that she was soaking wet for me already which made my dick feel like it was going to burst at any moment with all of the buildup. Her head fell back as she allowed me to work my tongue over her other nipple, both breasts on full display for my pleasure.

"Tell me, what do you want?" I ran a hand up and firmly grabbed her breast, flicking the nipple with my thumb as I planted kisses up the side of her neck. Her body swayed with mine, responding to every touch.

I pushed into her again, showing her just how much I wanted to be inside her already as a soft moan escaped her throat.

"I'm still mad…" she whimpered with closed eyes as her hands wrapped around my neck and through my hair.

"Good," I growled, ready to get her naked and be inside of her already.

"Good?!" Her eyes shot open, anger on her face as she reached out to push me away.

"Yeah, because I'm about to fuck it out of you." I gave her the cockiest smile I had before leaning in and kissing her as my hands worked to get her shirt and bra off in record time. My eyes lowered to take in the sight of Jade before me, her beautiful body full of perfection. Her hands braced against me as I trailed kisses down her stomach before sinking to my knees and pulling her pants down, slowly taking her panties with them.

I looked up and watched her as I leaned forward and licked her slit. Her hand grabbed my hair as she bit her lip, watching as my tongue pushed in and out of her. I let out a chuckle as her hips started to grind against my face, her hand fully wrapped in my hair, pulling it harder the closer she got to climax.

"Spread for me, baby," I commanded as she slowly stepped to the side, spreading her legs. I ran a hand up her calf and grabbed her thigh, pulling it up over my shoulder immediately giving me more access as I pushed my face closer. I could feel her body responding as her breathing quickened and she pushed her hips down to get more pressure where she needed it. I smiled and groaned as I grabbed her other leg and pulled it over my shoulder so her pussy was right in my face as she leaned against the cabinet behind her. I flicked my tongue back and forth inside her, sucking up all of her wetness while focusing on her clit.

"Noah... Noah..." she panted heavily, my name never sounding more arousing than it did at that moment. I knew she was right there, ready for a release as I sucked harder, pushing her over the edge. Her body clenched as she dug her heels into my back, her body shaking in response against my tongue.

I waited until her body stopped quivering before helping her to her feet. She looked down at me as I slowly stood up and stood in front of her. I wanted to be inside of her, to forget everything that had happened today, and just make love to her. She watched the pained expressions on my face as she reached up and cupped my cheek, stroking it gently with her thumb. I closed my eyes and felt her pull me closer to her as she wrapped me in a hug and held me, everything I had weighing on me slowly slipping away.

"I am so sorry, Jade. I can't say it enough." I shook my head as the mood shifted and a darkness fell upon us.

"I know you are," she whispered, still holding my face.

"I should have told you. I never should have even slept with her, but I was drunk and upset, and there's no excuse. I messed up. I fucked everything up."

I pulled back and ran a hand down my face as I turned away from her. She didn't deserve any of this. She deserved so much more than what I was giving her. I heard rustling behind me and knew that she was getting dressed. While I enjoyed going down on her and giving her the release she needed, I knew that it didn't solve any of the problems that were still surrounding us.

"You did fuck up, Noah. But only with not telling me. We weren't together when you slept with her and I knew that. I'm not mad at you for sleeping with her- don't get me wrong- I'm not happy about it either. But I can't hold it against you for sleeping with her when we were broken up. We hadn't been together that long before we broke up so I get it. I knew who you were before we started dating, that's why I asked you if you had been with anyone while we were apart." She looked into my eyes and I was relieved that she was willing to have an honest, mature discussion about this.

As hard as it was to talk about, I was thankful that we didn't have to have a ton of drama. I would spend the rest of my life making this up to Jade if she would let me, I had no problem admitting that I had made a huge mistake that hurt her tremendously.

"I was really hurt when we broke up. I didn't know how to deal with it and next thing I knew, I was going back to old habits." I shrugged as we made our way over to the couch and sat down.

"I know." She gave a half-smile as she nodded in agreement.

"I never meant to hurt you, Jade. I swear. When you said her name this morning, I couldn't believe that it was the same person. I was stressed all day trying to figure out what to do. I wanted to tell you because you deserved to know, but at the same time, as cowardly as it sounds, I didn't want to tell you because I wanted to protect you from the pain that I ended up causing with all of this." I watched as a tear slid down her face, my hand desperate to reach over and wipe it away for her.

"I was pretty blindsided when I sat across from a very pregnant woman who was going on and on about how she moved here to be with the man she loves and is having a baby with. When she described him as gorgeous with black hair and hazel eyes, I knew it was you."

"I'm so sorry that you had to find out that way. She showed up at The Vine tonight and I'll admit, I was pretty fucking surprised to see that she's pregnant."

"She showed up at your work?" Jade's eyes narrowed.

"Yeah, right before closing."

"Did she know you worked there from when you guys got together before?"

"No, we didn't bother talking about anything personal. I was out drinking with Wyatt and we were at Malarkey's when I met her."

"How did she know you would be there?"

"I have no idea. It's a small-town thing, people know everything about you whether you want them to or not. All she had to do was ask around a few places and someone would point her to The Vine."

"That's true, I guess." She sighed as she leaned into the cushion and stretched her legs across the couch. I reached over and lifted them up as I scooted over and rubbed them for her.

"So, what does all of this mean? I mean, you're having a baby with a woman you don't even know." Her eyes searched mine, looking for an answer to a question she hadn't asked.

"I don't know, honestly. She wants me to be there for all of her appointments and to help set up the nursery and stuff. I've never been in this situation before so I'm not sure what I'm supposed to do. Chase shot daggers at me earlier when I asked if he should be at home helping Mia practice her breathing before she went into labor, so obviously, I have no fucking clue what to do with pregnant women." I smiled as Jade laughed and for a moment, everything between us felt like it was going to be alright.

"Did you tell her about me?"

"I did, I told her that we would find time soon where we could all sit down together and figure everything out. I mean it, Jade, just because I'm having an unexpected baby with another woman, that doesn't mean that I want anything between us to change. And honestly, I really meant it earlier when I said that I thought you should move in with me."

My hands started sweating as I realized what I had said before I took a moment to think about it. At the hospital, I didn't know if I actually wanted Jade to move in with me or if I was just saying it because I was feeling desperate. Now that it came out of me so naturally, I felt like maybe I was ready for the next step in our relationship. Jade studied me nervously as she thought about my proposal to live together. I knew that I had lost her trust but I was willing to do whatever it took to earn it back.

"Are you sure that we're ready for that?" There was a hesitation in her voice that killed me and I hated that she had to doubt everything about our relationship because I made a terrible mistake and kept it from her for six months.
"I'm ready for it. Are you?"

She let out a deep breath as she looked around the apartment. I braced myself for her to say no. I couldn't blame her.

"Can we just keep doing what we're doing? Where I stay at your place sometimes, and you stay at mine? I'm not ready to give up my apartment just yet, it's the only thing I have that is really me. I love this apartment and IF something were to happen, I wouldn't want to be stuck trying to find something else."

"Fair enough." I smiled, trying to hide the disappointment I felt that she wasn't ready to give up her life so freely like I had wanted. When I thought about it, that was exactly what I was asking her to do. Give up everything she had worked for her since she came here on her own, and come live with me in my house. If the question was reversed, would I be willing to walk away from everything I had worked so hard to build for myself? My stomach hardened as the answer stared me in the face.

"I'm sorry Noah, I know you're disappointed. I just don't want us to do something out of impulse because there's suddenly other changes around us." Her voice was soft as she ran a hand up and cupped my cheek.

"It's okay," I whispered as I pulled her across the couch and wrapped my arms around her.

Seven
Jade

Yesterday felt like a whirlwind of a day, between training a new girl at work who just happened to be carrying my boyfriend's baby, to Mia having her baby, to Noah and I working things out. There was a lot packed into a very small window which explained why I woke up this morning feeling like a truck ran me over a few times.

I worked on getting my hair pulled up into a sleek ponytail before applying another coat of mascara to my overly tired-looking eyes. Growing up my mom could always tell the days that I truly didn't feel well because my eyes would change from a dark green to a grayish color, and today they were definitely gray. I quickly applied some red lipstick and gave myself one more glance before grabbing my purse and heading off to work.

Noah and I had spent a few hours last night talking through everything which seemed to help my overall mindset about what had happened. There was so much going through my mind before he got there that once I saw him at the door, I was almost relieved to just deal with everything right then and there so we could get it over with.

I wanted to be mad at Noah. Furious at him. But every time I thought about it in my head I kept reminding myself that the only thing he actually did wrong was lie to me about whether he had slept with anyone while we were broken up. I had already accepted that I had no right to be mad at him for the things he did when we were broken up, especially when I was the one who had decided to break up with him. Neither of us knew at the time whether we would get back together, our lifestyles too restless for each other. We weren't the type of people who wanted to settle down and I was already feeling the itch to go somewhere and do something different.

People have always said that I'm such a free spirit, that I have it in my blood to wander and roam without wanting to be tied down. The truth is that I grew up with a single mom who moved us every time she would start to get close to someone. If there was the opportunity for a real relationship to develop, we were out of there before the thought could even process in their mind. She would always say that it's always best to leave before you get attached. You can't get hurt if you don't stick around to let them. Leave them before they can leave you.

Those were the things that I grew up learning and to this day I've yet to have an adult relationship where I've stayed long enough for it to turn into something. Until now. Now I have Noah and for the first time in my life, I don't want to run. I don't want to get out before it's too late. Until yesterday I was playing around with the idea of what our future might look like someday.

I pulled into the parking lot of the bank and glanced into the rearview mirror, giving myself a quick mini pep talk before I had to walk in those doors and see the woman who had caused so much havoc in such a short period of time. I opened the door and grabbed my purse and cellphone from the middle console, seeing a text message from Noah. I smiled as I opened it.

Noah: Good morning, beautiful. Have a wonderful day and don't forget to send me some nudes on your break.

I laughed as I rolled my eyes and sent back a quick good morning message before tossing my phone back into my purse. I pulled my shoulders back and walked into the building with the confidence of a woman who didn't just find out that her boyfriend was having a baby with her coworker.

Relief settled over me as I made my way to my desk and noticed that Cindy wasn't there yet. I opened the bottom drawer and sat my purse inside, tossing my keys on top. This morning had been such a rush that I hadn't given myself time to make coffee and I instantly regretted it. I wandered off to the break room after closing the drawer, making sure my purse was secure. There weren't a ton of coffee drinkers here that didn't bring their own coffee from home so the likelihood that someone would have made a pot of coffee was slim. I walked into the break room disappointed when the coffee pot sat in its usual spot, empty. I sighed and decided to give up on the idea, my motivation for anything pretty lacking at the moment.

As I started heading toward my desk I noticed someone bent over, leaning toward the bottom drawer where my purse was. I tried to walk as quietly as I could, keeping my heels from clicking too hard on the tile floor. As I got closer I noticed the brown hair before Cindy popped up, startled. My eyes narrowed together as I crossed my arms over my chest and glared at her, waiting for an answer.

"Hi!" Her face flushed red as she tried to sit upright as quickly as possible as she tried to shut the drawer with her foot. I tilted my head to the side, one eyebrow arched, as I watched her do it. Her face turned a darker color of red as she stood up and moved away from my desk, coming around to the other side where she is supposed to sit.

"Is there a reason that you're going through my personal things?" I walked past her and stood on the other side of the desk, placing my palms flat on the desk as I leaned forward and waited for her to answer. She shifted uncomfortably in her seat before looking up at me and making eye contact.

"I'm sorry, I was looking for a notepad so I could take notes." She looked away and I knew she was lying. Hell, I knew she was lying the moment I caught her red-handed.

"Like that one?" I nodded to the notepad and pen that were sitting neatly on the desk in front of her that I had purposely sat out the night before.

"Oops. Guess I should have looked here first."

I let out a deep breath as I tried to focus on being professional and not reaching forward to rip her head off like I really wanted to.

"Look, Cindy, we need to have some boundaries and those will include you respecting my personal space. If you need something, you need to ask before you go helping yourself." I stared at her as she nodded slightly before looking away.

I sat down and leaned over to look inside the drawer to see what she could have been messing with. My purse looked exactly the same as how I had left it and nothing else looked like it had been moved. My desk was always clean and organized which meant she didn't have a lot of time to snoop around in the few minutes I was gone. I closed the drawer and opened the one above it, pulling out the training material that we hadn't finished the day before. As my irritation with her increased so did my regret for not making coffee.

It was almost nine which meant the lobby would be opening soon. I could try to run quickly to the back to make a pot of coffee or I could wait it out and see if any of the customers asked for coffee, which would mean someone would end up making a pot. It was a gamble since we weren't usually busy on Tuesdays but I didn't trust Cindy by herself at my desk so I had no choice but to skip it.

I spent a few minutes sorting through the training materials on my desk while having Cindy review her notes from yesterday in an effort to stall until I could get my head straight and work with her. The door chimed up front and out of the corner of my eye I watched as the receptionist walked back to her desk as someone followed behind her.

I expected the person to head to the teller line or sit in the waiting area for a loan officer, instead a pair of steel-toed boots stood beside my desk. As I slowly looked up, the smell of coffee floated around me.

"Hey, beautiful. Thought you might need this today." Noah sat the to-go cup of coffee on my desk and sat on the corner of it, out of the way from the pile I had created. Behind him, I saw Cindy's eyes go wide with the shock of seeing him at my desk and I wondered if she knew I was the girlfriend he had told her about. I smiled as I stood up and wrapped my arms around his neck, hugging him a little too tight for it to be appropriate in the workplace.

"Thanks, baby. You have no idea how badly I need this today." I pulled back and smiled, genuinely happy to see him while not giving a damn that Cindy was now glaring at our interaction.

"No problem. Anything to keep my girl happy." He reached forward and gently pinched my chin between his fingers before slightly looking over his shoulder to acknowledge Cindy.

"Morning."

"Good morning," she replied tightly before shifting her attention back to her notes.

"Well, I better get going. I have a lot to do with Chase being out this week on his little vacation." He rolled his eyes as I playfully swatted his shoulder.
"He's not on vacation, he's being a good husband and helping Mia with their beautiful new baby." I smiled warmly at him before second-guessing talking about babies with the situation sitting in front of me. While I didn't want to keep Noah from being involved in his child's life, I also didn't want Cindy overstepping into ours. And given I was already irritated with her for going through my personal stuff, this

made everything feel even more awkward.

"Either way." He chuckled and stood up, planting a kiss on my forehead. "See you tonight?"

"Sounds good," I whispered, wanting to keep our relationship a little more private with Cindy so close.

"Bye, Cindy," He called out over his shoulder and walked out the door.

I sat down at my desk and pulled myself closer, reaching for the coffee and taking a sip. Within seconds I could feel the heat flowing through my body, calming me in the process.

"Alright, let's get started." I grabbed the pile that we needed to get through as Cindy's head whipped up, a pissed off look on her face.

"You two seem happy, have you been together long?"

The way she asked the question had my blood boiling.

"Noah and I are very happy, and I'm sorry, but my personal business is none of yours." I looked at her as I picked up my coffee cup and took another sip. I may not have had a lot of romantic relationships in my life but I've had plenty of times where I've had to stand up for myself which made dealing with Cindy easy.

"Well then I'm sure he's told you about our situation and how we will all be involved, so I guess that does make your personal life my business."

"How so?" I leaned forward resting my forearms on my desk while straightening my posture.

"Because Noah will want to be in his child's life and that means that as the mother, I get a say in who is in his. I may not want someone toxic around my child." She jutted her jaw forward and rubbed a hand over her stomach.

"Look, there are a lot of things that the three of us will need to discuss soon. However, this is not the time or the place to do so. If you're unable to keep your personal life separate then maybe you should look at another job that allows you to do so." I took a deep breath and leaned back against my chair. "I will not continue to train you if this is going to continue to be an issue."

I watched as the color drained from her face and she lowered her hands to her lap.

"I really need this job."

"Then I suggest we make an effort to work together."

She nodded her head yes in agreement as I took another long drink of coffee, thankful to have a little ammunition on my side today.

<u>Eight</u>
Noah

I leaned down and checked on the food in the oven before opening a bottle of wine as I waited for Jade to get here. Last night was a long night and even after I left her apartment feeling better that we had talked things out, I still felt like I needed to prove my love to her in so many ways. Especially since I was completely head over heels in love with her and we hadn't actually said it to each other yet.

I had skipped out of work an hour early after our regular temp, Stacy, offered to pick up some hours with Chase and Mia being out of the office. I loved Stacy and she had worked with us for so long that I trusted her to run the place as much as I trusted Chase. She would watch over Julia tonight which left me confident that the two of them would be just fine without me. And the worst-case scenario, I was just a phone call away if not.

It was almost 5:30 and Jade should be there any second. I poured the glasses of wine and sat them on the table that had already been set with candles and a basket of bread in between the plates and salad bowls. I pulled the chicken parmigiana out of the oven right when the doorbell rang and called for her to come in over my shoulder while I dealt with the hot pan. I sat it on top of the stove, sliding the oven mitts off when I turned to go open the door since I hadn't heard the familiar sound of Jade's heels across the floor as she came in.

As I spun around I was stopped in my tracks by Cindy standing in front of me.

"Cindy? What are you doing here?" My brows pulled together as I watched her look past me to the table I had worked hard on setting up for my romantic dinner with Jade.

"You said to come in."

"I thought it was Jade. What are you doing here?" I crossed my arms over my chest and watched her as her eyes filled with tears.

"I'm sorry. I should go." She turned to leave. Part of me wanted to let her but the other part wasn't a complete dick.

"Why are you here?" My tone was softer as I leaned against the counter behind me, watching the door for Jade.

"I didn't know where else to go, I don't know anyone in town. I just needed a friend." Her voice was low as she looked down at the ground and played with the drawstring on her coat.

"Okay, so what's going on?" I was starting to lose my patience the longer she moped in my kitchen, knowing that it would ruin the ambiance I had worked so hard to create for Jade if she walked in and saw her here.

"I don't think Jade likes me and I thought maybe we could talk about it?"

I blew out a frustrated breath as I pushed off from the counter and looked at her.

"Look, I'm more than happy to talk to you about this later. Right now isn't a good time."

"You're right, I shouldn't have just come over unannounced." She let out a heavy sigh as she turned to leave, almost running into Jade on her way out the door. I watched as Jade's face changed the moment she saw Cindy, the anger flickering in her eyes as she looked between the two of us.

"We'll talk later, thanks again." She smiled warmly as she walked past Jade as she stepped inside, leaving plenty of room for Cindy to leave. The door closed leaving an awkward silence behind. Jade glared at the door before turning her attention to me.

"Jade, I'm so sorry-"
"Don't." She put her hand up to stop me.

"But-"

"Noah, did you do all of this?" She gestured to the romantic dinner beside me.

"Yes." I swallowed hard, praying that all of this wasn't ruined after all. I watched as Jade sat her purse on the coffee table and kicked her heels off before she came running over to me, wrapping her legs around my waist and pulling me in for a kiss. I wrapped my arms around her as our lips stayed pressed against each other, feeling the comfort from her body as she wrapped it around mine.

"You surprise me, Mr. Wilder." She leaned forward and kissed me again before unwrapping her legs and sliding down to the floor. Her ponytail swayed from side to side as she shook her head back and forth in amazement as she walked around the table and took in the details.

"Oh yeah?"

"Yup. I would have never imagined you to be a candlelight dinner kind of guy." She smiled up at me as she stood behind the chair, her eyes filled with happiness. My heart started to go back to normal as I allowed myself to relax with her, fear of the evening being ruined by Cindy dissipating.

"I'll be whatever kind of guy you want me to be." I ran a hand across her lower back where her silk blouse was tucked into her black dress slacks.

"I just want you to be you." Her eyes searched mine as she reached a hand up and gently stroked my cheek. I raised my hand to hold hers before placing a kiss on it.

"Have a seat and I'll get dinner served before it gets cold." I pulled out her chair and waited until she was seated before I scooted behind her to grab the pan of chicken. Thankfully, everything was still hot and fresh, just like my mom assured me it would be. I had heard the change in her tone when I had told her what I was trying to do. She contained her excitement the best she could before squealing for me to call her tomorrow to let her know how everything went.

I sat the plates on the table in front of us with a generous serving of chicken parmigiana and noodles accompanied by steamed asparagus. Jade's eyes went wide and she tried to hide her surprise when she realized that I had actually cooked and not ordered takeout. I ignored the giant pile of dirty dishes in the sink as I grabbed the salad from the fridge and brought it to the table.

"Noah, everything looks and smells delicious. This is amazing!"

"I'm happy you like it. Now let's just hope it tastes as good as it looks," I joked as I sat the rest of the salad down on the counter behind me and joined Jade at the table.

We ate in silence as we enjoyed the wine and every now and then I would hear her moan as she took a bite that she enjoyed. I tried to keep myself distracted and focused on eating instead of thinking about how hot she sounded as she enjoyed the meal. If I would have known that she could sound that fucking sexy while eating, I would have started cooking for her a long time ago. It would give a whole different meaning to appetizers and four-course meals.

"Oh my gosh, I am so stuffed. This was one of the best meals I've ever had." She leaned back against the chair and smiled at me as she lazily brought the glass of wine to her lips and took a sip. I licked my lips, jealous of the glass she was holding, and adjusted my jeans to give me some relief from the tightness she was creating.

"I'm glad you enjoyed it." I mimicked her and leaned back against the seat as I finished the wine in my glass.

"There's a lot that I enjoy with you."

"Same here." My eyes darkened as I thought about how much I wanted to enjoy her. Right here.
Right now.

"You cooked so, I'll clean up." She scooted her chair back and stood up, grabbing her plate and salad bowl from the table.

"I don't think so." I stepped beside her and grabbed them from her, sitting them on the counter. "The dishes can wait, I'll do them later."

"Noah, that's silly. I can help clean up," she protested as she put a hand on her hip and looked at me. Her eyes were back to dark green and not the gray they were when I saw her this morning. I loved that she was back to her sassy, sexy little self.

"I know you can, but tonight is about me showing you how much you mean to me." I slid an arm around her waist and pulled her into me, smelling the coconut smell of her shampoo.

"You don't have to do all of this, you know that right?" She pushed back and looked at me like I was crazy for wanting to show my love to her.

"I know that I don't have to. I want to." I looked down and studied her face as confusion settled in.

"Hasn't anyone ever done something like this for you before? Shown you how much they care about you?"

"No," she whispered before she looked away.

"Jade, you deserve to have someone show you how much they love you every single day."

Her eyes whipped up to look at me, panic on her face. Now was the moment that we both had been cautiously avoiding. The moment where the way we felt about each other would be more than just trying to show each other. It would be saying the words that we purposely avoided at all costs. The words that you couldn't take back once you said them.

"I love you, Jade."

Nine
Jade

I was by far the worst person in the world. Who lets their boyfriend make a romantic candlelight dinner and says I love you for the first time, and not say it back? The evening had progressed into a calm, relaxing night as we cuddled on the couch but I couldn't help but wonder what Noah thought when he told me he loved me and I didn't say it back.

Did I want to say it? Absolutely. One hundred percent. But something deep down wouldn't let me. Was it the fear my mom instilled in my sister and I from the time we were little to never let ourselves fall in love so easily? Or was it the result of watching my sister die at the hands of an abusive man that promised to love her and yet beat her every day from the time they said I do.

Maybe it wasn't any of that. Maybe it was that I walked in on Cindy inside Noah's house unexpectedly when I got here. Everything about Cindy felt like a trigger for me. No matter how hard I tried, I just didn't like her and didn't trust her. I could feel my shoulders getting tense from the thought of her, Noah's body responding to it right away.

"Everything okay?" He leaned to the side and looked at me as I stayed tucked into his side under his shoulder.

"Yeah, I'm fine." I gently rolled my shoulders a few times hoping it would help alleviate the tension.

"Do you want to talk about it?" His voice was soft in my ear as he held onto me, my body starting to relax into his. I let out a sigh as I debated whether I wanted to talk about it or not. Either way, I knew that we needed to if we wanted things to keep moving forward in our relationship. Now wasn't the time to have blocked communication or to keep things from each other.

"Why was Cindy here earlier?" I kept my gaze on the tv for fear of looking like a totally insecure and jealous girlfriend.

"Honestly, I don't know. I sure as hell wasn't expecting her. I thought it was you when she knocked and I told her to come in."

"What did she say?"

"Nothing really, just that she needed a friend to talk to." His voice trailed off and I knew there was more.

"Talk about what?" I turned slightly and looked up at him.

"She thinks that you don't like her."

"I don't." My answer was cold and blunt but there wasn't a need to try to sugarcoat it. I felt his chest move as he tried to stifle his laughter at my bluntness.

"I know that it sounds immature and petty but I don't like her. And not just because you slept with her and she got pregnant, I just don't trust her."

"Why not?" His eyes searched mine with genuine curiosity, making me feel comfortable having this discussion with him.

"This morning after I got to work I stepped away from my desk for a few minutes and when I came back I caught her sitting at my desk, going through my bottom drawer where I keep my purse."

His eyes got dark, his jaw clenching in response.

"Did you ask her about it?"

"Absolutely. She insisted that she was looking for a notepad to take notes with, then I pointed out there was one on the desk where she sits."

He nodded his head as he looked off across the room toward the door.

"I was very direct with her and told her we needed to have boundaries, that she wasn't to go through my stuff."

"Good. I'm sure that will help. Maybe it was just a misunderstanding?" I could hear the faint sound of hope in his voice that this wasn't as big of an issue as I was making it into.

"That's not all." I scooted away from him and turned to face him. I needed his full attention before I told him the rest.

"Okay.... what else happened?"

"After you left, she made a snide comment about how happy we seemed and asked how long we've been together." I blew out a deep breath before continuing. "I explained to her that we are happy but that my personal business is none of hers. She got REALLY defensive about how she's having a baby with you so that makes my business her business because she may not want toxic people in her baby's life."

I watched as Noah leaned back against the couch and pinched the bridge of his nose as he closed his eyes. His chest rose and fell heavily as he let out a sigh.

"I'm so sorry that you're getting caught up in all of this, Jade." His eyes met mine, sadness to them that wasn't there before.

"It's fine, I'm a big girl. I can handle myself."

"So what happened after that?"

"I explained to her that it was a place of business and that if she couldn't keep her personal business separate then maybe she needed to find a new place to work. Her attitude seemed to change after that and she told me she couldn't afford to lose this job. The rest of the day she was quiet and ended up leaving an hour early because she said she wasn't feeling well."

"Well, I can see why she would think you don't like her." His eyes lit up as he tried to hold his laughter inside. Playfully I reached over and swatted his chest.

"Oh stop it, I'm not that mean!" I tried to keep a straight face before my laughter mixed in with his as he pulled me over to him, tickling me until I was straddling his thighs.

"You are, in fact, very mean." He eyed me suspiciously, his hands maintaining a firm grip on my hips so I couldn't try to get away.

"Am I?" I licked my lips as I slowly lowered myself further down on top of him and ran my tongue up the side of his neck before playfully nibbling on his earlobe. I could feel the stretch of his jeans underneath me as I slowly rocked back and forth, his body reacting to every movement.

"I don't know that you wanna start something you can't finish." His voice was gruff in my ear as his hands helped guide my hips into the fluid motion as I continued to grind against him.

"Who said anything about not finishing?" Slowly I reached down and unbuttoned my silk blouse, taking my time with each button while my hips continued grinding lower against him. I could feel his erection bulging beneath, growing bigger by the second.

His eyes watched my every movement as I tossed the shirt to the side and reached back to unclasp my bra. I chewed my lip as I took my time sliding the bra strap down each arm, carefully holding the bra in place against my breasts. Without warning his hands flew up and grabbed the bra, throwing it to the side and freeing my breasts that were inches away from his face. I giggled as he swatted my hands away and ran his up my stomach and under each breast before slowly leaning forward and running his tongue over my nipple.

I leaned back, resting my hands on his thighs as he continued sucking my nipples and caressing my breasts. I could feel the pressure starting to build up, the need to feel him inside me growing stronger with each lick. I leaned forward and wrapped my arms behind his neck, pulling his hair as I tried to find a release. I needed out of these dress slacks and for him to be inside of me already.

I took a jagged breath and slowly pushed off, his eyes wild as they watched my every move. I stood in between his legs as I slowly unbuttoned the top button of my dress slacks, my hand firm on the zipper as I pulled it out down. As I was about to slide them down my legs I saw a reflection in the mirror of someone watching through the sliding glass door behind us.

I gasped as I quickly turned around, one hand covering my breasts while the other grabbed my pants to keep them up.

"What's wrong?" Noah jumped up beside me, his eyes quickly searching the room.
"Someone was outside watching us! I saw their reflection in the mirror, they were at the back door." I pointed to where I had seen them then quickly grabbed my pants before they fell down again.

Noah took off running past me and flung open the front door while I quickly grabbed my clothes off the couch and got dressed. A few minutes later Noah came back inside, out of breath as he closed the front door and locked it.

"Did you see anyone?"

"No, but a car took off as soon as I went outside. I tried to run after it but I didn't get a good look. It was a small car, a sedan of some sort. Red. That's all I got." He walked over and checked the sliding glass door before closing the blinds and coming over to the couch.

"A red car?" My stomach sank when everything started to click.

"Yeah, that's what it looked like. Why?"

"Cindy drives a red car."

Ten
Noah

I looked out into the open field, the sun starting to set behind the mountain casting a warm glow. I took a deep breath as I forced all of the worries and doubt out of me as I exhaled. People were starting to arrive and my hands were sweating as I looked back and saw the rows of white folding chairs creating an aisle that Jade would soon be walking down.

In the crowd I spotted my mom and dad, making their way toward the front row. Off in the distance, Chase was playing a quick game of catch with Liam and Grant, all of them dressed in black tuxedoes. The music started floating overhead as the pastor made his way up to the altar and stood next to me. Soon everyone had taken their seat and at the end of the walkway, I could see the wedding party lining up.

Chase and Mia were first in line as they pushed the stroller with Rylee in it, too little to actually throw rose petals, but still the most beautiful flower girl I had ever seen. Liam walked quickly down the aisle, holding onto the side of the stroller as he ignored the whispers from everyone around him on how handsome he looked.

Soon the wedding party had all made their way down the aisle and fanned out next to me as we turned our focus to Jade. The music changed and I listened carefully for the song she chose to come on. There was nothing. Just silence. I leaned forward and tried to see past the rows of chairs, looking for her.

Slowly she stepped forward, her face as beautiful as ever with her hair pinned perfectly upon her head. Her dress was stunning and showed off her curvy body including a pregnant belly. I swallowed hard as I looked beside her and saw Cindy. Suddenly music played overhead but it wasn't Jade's song. It was dark and ominous as it slowly got louder. I could see panic on Jade's face as she looked for me, reaching out her hand for me to come get her. I started to run toward her as everyone got up from their seats and started walking toward me, getting in the way.

My parents reached me first, my mom desperately clutching at her throat to try to stop the bleeding while my dad gasped for air, blood soaking his shirt. My eyes were wide with horror when I saw the knife wounds. Panic filled me as everyone around me started to drop dead on the floor, Chase and Mia cuddled together as she tried to rock Rylee whose face was covered in Mia's blood. No one was safe. Liam. Grant. Jade.

I watched in horror as Cindy smiled at me, a sharp knife in her hand as she grabbed Jade and drug her backward. I ran as fast as I could, darting in between chairs and dead bodies, desperate to get to Jade. The harder I ran, the bigger the distance was that separated us until there was nothing around me but dead loved ones as Jade disappeared with Cindy.

I felt ice-cold fingertips run across my chest as my eyes flew open, forcefully pushing them away. Jade jolted up, startled, as her eyes watched me with horror.

"I'm sorry..." I said as quickly as I realized that it was Jade that was touching me and that I had been having another nightmare.

"Are you okay?" She continued to watch me as she kept her distance on the other side of the bed.

"Yeah. I was having a bad dream, I didn't mean to scare you." I blew out a breath and sat up, leaning back against the headboard.

"It's okay, I could hear you panicking in your sleep. I was trying to wake you."

"Thank you." I reached over and gently patted her hand.

"I know that you don't ever want to talk about them, but I really think that you should. This is the 5th or 6th one that you've had while I've stayed over in the past two months. Something is obviously bothering you, Noah." Her eyes pleaded with mine. I patted the empty space on the bed next to me, relieved when she slid over and cuddled up against me.

"I've been having nightmares." I paused as I quickly debated whether I should even be telling her this. "About you."
I waited for her response, worried that she would take it the wrong way. Was there a right way?

"Okay. What happens in the dreams?"

I blew out another breath and ran a hand down my face.

"Terrible, horrible things." I closed my eyes and leaned my head back against the headboard.

"Noah...." I could hear the warning in her voice and had to laugh that she could be so bossy with getting me to tell her when most girls would be upset to find out that they were the source of my nightmares.

"It's different things. Someone takes you and I can't see who it is. They threaten to kill you. They've tried to kill you. They kill my family. They burn down my house while you're in it. Everything always leads back to them hurting or killing you and I can't do anything about it. This one was worse though."

"What happened in this one?"

I shook my head and looked away.

"Noah, what happened in this one?" She turned sideways and took my head in her hands, forcing me to look at her. "Tell me what happened."

"We were getting married. Everything was beautiful. White chairs spread out across the green field, the mountains in the distance with the sun setting. Everyone was there, my family, our friends. Everyone had walked down the aisle and I was waiting for you. But you never came. Then the music changed and you were in the back being held hostage by Cindy. And everyone around me was dying. My mom's throat was slit. My dad was stabbed. Chase. Mia. Rylee. No one was spared. I was trying to get to you but every step I took I only got farther away as Cindy smiled and pulled you further away from me as she held the knife that killed everyone."

Her eyes were soft as she pulled me towards her and wrapped her arms around me. She held me tightly as she kissed my face, planting kisses all over before landing on my lips. I could feel the weight of my dream lift off me the longer she held me, calmness settling over us. She pulled back and held my head in her hands, smiling at me.

"Thank you for telling me." She sighed but never let go, even as a quick flash of sadness crossed her face.

"Those are terrible dreams and I'm so sorry that you keep having them. I'm even more sorry that they're about me." She laughed and I felt the pull of a smile across my face. "But they are just dreams Noah, no one is ever going to take me away from you. Ever. Okay?"

I nodded yes as she wrapped herself around me again and at that moment I knew that I never wanted to be with anyone else.

"I should have said it earlier and I'm sorry that I didn't, but I love you too, Noah. I love you more than you could ever know."

I wrapped her in my arms and pulled her as close as I could, wanting to feel every tiny bit of love that we were sharing at that moment. If I could, I would have bottled it up so I wouldn't have to worry about ever losing it. If only I would've known...

Eleven
Jade

"How has it already been two weeks? I could swear you just had Rylee yesterday." I leaned closer to the bundle of blankets and took a deep breath, filling my lungs with the sweet smell of baby.

"I know, it's crazy! I was just telling Chase that we needed to have you and Noah over soon to catch up. Things have been so busy with the baby that I haven't been able to see straight and I know he's been looking forward to getting back to work. It would be nice to have a distraction too." Mia sighed as she leaned back against the couch and watched as I rocked Rylee back to sleep.

"It would be great to hang out with you guys, I miss seeing you all the time."

"I miss seeing you too."

"Should I put her down or is she okay to sleep on my shoulder?"

"She's fine where she's at unless you'd rather put her down. In that case, we can put her in her crib in the nursery."

I wrinkled my nose and frowned as I slowly sat down on the opposite end of the couch from Mia and sunk into the pillow while Rylee stayed sleeping on me. Mia let out a soft laugh, the lines under her eyes creasing in response.

She looked gorgeous for being a new mom who wasn't getting any sleep and I prayed that someday I would be able to look as good as she did. Her naturally blonde hair had been cut into a short bob that framed her face perfectly with side-swept bangs that made her baby blue eyes stand out. She was already beautiful but I thought motherhood had changed her for the better. There was a new softness that hadn't been there before.

"So, tell me what's new. Chase said that Noah is going with Cindy to her next ultrasound on Monday- how's everything going with that?"

"It's fine, I guess." I shrugged and debated how much of the Cindy drama I wanted to get into.

"Just fine?"

"He's putting a lot of effort into trying to be there for her and it feels like she's taking advantage of the situation."

"How so?" Mia's voice was gentle and lacked the judgmental tone I had gotten used to hearing from Cindy for the last few weeks.

"She uses the baby against him for everything. It's like she knows that he wants to do the right thing and be in the baby's life so she constantly threatens to take that away. He's been late to work a few times to show up at appointments that she doesn't tell him about until the last minute then claims that he didn't want to go or he would have been there on time. It's just hard watching him jump through hoops for her."

"Wow. I heard she was a little crazy but I didn't know that it was that bad." Mia smiled sympathetically as she leaned her head against the couch.

"Yeah, crazy might be an understatement." I shifted on the couch and gently patted the baby's back to keep her asleep. "Mia, are you sure you don't want to go lay down? I'm off the rest of the afternoon and don't mind watching Rylee so you can get some sleep while Chase is at work."

She looked exhausted and I suddenly felt bad for asking to come by last minute after I was told to take a half-day for the extra hours I had worked last week with getting Cindy trained and on a teller drawer. I didn't think twice before accepting their offer. I was out the door and on the phone with Mia before I even opened my car door.

"No, I'm okay. I'm always tired but I never get to visit with anyone. Trust me, I need this." She smiled as she tried to fight a yawn. Guilt flooded me as I realized how bad of a friend I had been for not checking in on her sooner. I had intended to give them time to get settled in with the new baby before coming by but the sadness on Mia's face when she said she doesn't get to visit with anyone made me regret not coming by sooner.

"If you're sure..." I eyed her carefully, waiting to see if she would change her mind.

"Yes, I'm sure." She playfully swatted at my leg and smiled.

"So how's Chase doing with all of the baby stuff?"

"Good, he's just as exhausted as I am. But he's been great at helping me with everything. He gets up with us in the middle of the night and handles the diaper changes since I'm the only one that can feed her. Granted we have bottles and breast milk in the fridge but neither of us wants to bother with warming it up in the middle of the night when I can just feed her and be done with it."

"It's nice that he's stepping in crand helping. Not many guys actually do that."

"Yeah, I got really lucky with Chase." She smiled and I looked away, hoping to hide some of the disappointment on my face as I thought about how great of a dad Noah was going to be. Only it wasn't with me.

"Are you okay?"

"Yeah." I took a deep breath and tried to gather my thoughts to keep from having a total meltdown. "I just keep trying to figure out what it's going to look like for us when Cindy has the baby and Noah has new responsibilities to handle. He's said that he wants me in the baby's life but Cindy has made it clear that she doesn't. It's been a little rough to figure out what my place is in all of this."

"When is she due?"

"She'll be 7 months in a few weeks. I only know because she scheduled her appointment for Valentine's Day and asked Noah if he wanted to grab dinner with her when they were done."

"Seriously? That's ballsy. And rude." Mia shook her head as I nodded along with her in agreement.

"Well, at least you still have some time before you guys have to decide on anything. Who knows, maybe Cindy will lighten up by then."

"Yeah, you never know." My mind drifted as I thought about what could change in the next few months as I held Rylee against me and wondered what Noah's baby's life would be like if I stayed in the picture. While I loved Noah and wanted to build a life with him I also had to take into consideration that I could complicate this innocent child's life simply by being a part of it. The last thing that I wanted was for this child to know drama and fighting because of me and their mom not being able to get along.

Twelve
Noah

It was almost four and Cindy was supposed to be meeting me at The Vine before we went to her ultrasound. I was thankful that Chase was back in the office this week and that today had been rather slow and uneventful for a Monday. I heard the door chime up front and glanced up to see blonde hair bouncing in a ponytail as the sun beamed in through the glass, obscuring my view of the actual person.

My heart beat faster as I excitedly waited for Jade to make it through the lobby but as soon as she stepped further into the room my heart sank when I saw it wasn't Jade. Standing before me was Cindy with hair as blond as Jade's, cut and styled the same exact way that Jade wears hers. I looked her over and noticed that she was wearing a pair of maternity bootleg jeans with a black lace shirt, similar to what Jade recently wore. The frumpy clothes she had been wearing since she moved here were now replaced with form-fitting clothes similar to Jade's style.

She grinned mischievously as she spun around in a slow circle, waiting for me to take it all in.

"What do you think?" She beamed as she held a hand up to her blonde hair and waited for my response. I tried to think of a quick response but the frown on my face gave it away before I could answer.

"You don't like it?" She threw her hand on her hip as she stared at me.

"I didn't say that I didn't like it. It's a lot to take in." I spoke cautiously as I had been doing more of the past few weeks. The back door opened as Chase came out, stopping in his tracks at the sight of her.

"Hey Chase," she purred, "you like my new look, don't you?" She pouted her mouth and batted her eyes as he glanced at me with a -what the fuck- kind of look on his face. I slightly shrugged my shoulders since I didn't have any fucking idea.

"Hey... look at that." He raised his eyebrows and avoiding saying anything more. "I need to talk to you about some of the recent orders, can you stop by my office tomorrow morning when you get in?"

"Sure thing." I nodded to him as he made his way back to the offices and shook his head as he left. Lucky bastard. "Well, we better get going so we're not late."

I grabbed my phone from the counter behind me and stuffed it in my pocket as I started walking towards the door.

"I'm not going anywhere until you tell me that you like my new look."

I spun around to see Cindy standing in the same spot, her arms folded across her chest as she stared at me, pissed off.

"What does it matter if I like it or not?" I took two steps toward her, pulling my shoulders back as I towered over her.

"Because it's important to me to know what you think." She looked shocked as she batted her eyes up at me.

"What I think is that it was stupid to bleach and color your hair when you're pregnant, but that's not really what you wanted to hear, now is it?" My mind was still trying to process why she would do this in the first place as I tried to fight the anger of the possible harm she put the baby in as she sat there with chemicals in her hair for hours while they stripped her brown hair to the almost platinum blonde it was now.

"You don't seem to have any issues with Jade having blonde hair." Her lips trembled as she said it, tears threatening to overflow from her eyes.

"Jade isn't pregnant with my child. And what Jade does to her look is not your concern. Maybe you should focus on taking care of yourself and this baby, and less on Jade." My tone was sharp as I turned around and stormed out the door, hearing the heavy footsteps as she followed behind.

I had never been to an ultrasound before and was thankful that she was far enough in the pregnancy that they didn't have to do much to get a good image of the baby on the screen. I sat back in the cold metal chair beside the bed she laid in, neither of us speaking to each other on the way over. The ultrasound tech squirted some gel on her belly and started moving the wand around as she adjusted a few things on her screen. I looked up at the tv mounted on the wall above me and felt my heart skip a beat when I saw the very recognizable image of a baby.

"There we go, there's your baby." The tech pointed to the screen as she flipped a switch and the sound of the heartbeat floated around us. My hands started sweating as I watched the baby move on the screen, a few big movements along with some small ones. I looked over at Cindy and stared at her pregnant belly in complete awe that my baby was inside of her and that I was getting to see it on the screen.

"When did you say your due date is?" The tech squinted her eyes as she leaned closer to the computer.

"April 7th." Cindy's eyes darted to the screen above my head as the tech wrote something down on a notepad beside her.

"Is there something wrong?" I asked cautiously as Cindy avoided looking at me.

"Not necessarily. We may have the wrong conception date in our system, I'm just looking back at other notes from her last visit."

I sat in silence, confused by what the tech was saying.

"Can you confirm the date of your last period?" She looked at Cindy, waiting for an answer.

"I, um, I don't remember. But I definitely got pregnant in July."

"Well the conception date listed does show a possible July or August conception date but the actual size of the fetus suggests that it was late August or early September. The baby is not measuring on track compared to the estimated gestational age based on the date of your last period."

My head was spinning as I struggled to make sense of everything.

"In plain English- what does that mean?" I leaned forward, resting my elbows on my knees as I looked up at the tech, hoping she would spell it out for me.
"It means that based on when she said she had her last period she should be around 7 months pregnant but the size of the baby is measuring around what we would see for someone who is 6 months pregnant."

Cindy let out a shaky breath as she stared at the tech who was gently using a towel to wipe the gel off of her stomach.

"I know when I got pregnant. It was over the Fourth of July when I came down here for the weekend." She cast a steely glance at me before turning her attention back to the tech. "Maybe we need a new tech who knows what she's doing and can accurately measure our baby."

I watched as a hardness came across the tech's face as she took in Cindy's accusation. While Cindy swore that she hadn't been with anyone else, part of me wondered if she hadn't been lying all along. We walked out with a handful of ultrasound photos and a follow-up appointment two weeks later to confirm the due date with the doctor based on how much the baby should grow during that period. It was either that they had the wrong conception date and Cindy wasn't as far along in the pregnancy as she claimed, or there was something wrong with the baby's growth. I chewed the inside of my cheek nervously as we drove back to The Vine in silence. The sky was gray as new clouds started moving in with the promise of a harsh winter storm.

I hopped out of the truck and made my way around to the passenger side to help Cindy down. It irritated me that she refused to drive herself to these appointments knowing damn well that she wasn't able to easily get in and out of my lifted truck. You would think that she would want to drive herself so she had the comfort and safety of her own car but she didn't.

"Hey, do you think I could hold onto one of the pictures from today?" I asked as I shoved my hands into my pockets and hoped that she would say yes without questioning why I wanted them. Her eyes lit up as she smiled and handed me the handful of pictures.

"Thanks, I can get them back to you soon. I just wanted to have one to show my parents." I lied straight-faced as she continued to beam.

"Go ahead and keep them, I know where to find them if needed." She smiled as she ran a freshly manicured finger down my chest and swayed her hips as she walked to her car and left.

I rolled my eyes as I went back inside to check on things before heading out. When I walked inside I found Jade sitting at the bar with Chase and Mia beside her as she cried. I rushed over, confusion on my face as I wrapped my arm behind her waist and looked at Chase. He gave me a tight smile as he stepped back from the counter, giving me some space.

"Jade, baby, what's wrong?" Her green eyes looked up to meet mine as fresh tears filled them.

"I lost it..," she stuttered before she started sobbing again. Mia wrapped her arms around her from the other side and whispered in her ear.

"Lost what?" I tried to keep my voice calm and supportive as I desperately waited for someone to clue me in on what was going on.

"The locket...." She sucked in jagged breaths. "The one my sister...gave me...before she..." Her voice cut off and I knew exactly what she was talking about and why she was so upset. She had shown me the locket a few times early on in our relationship and I knew how sentimental it was to her because it was the last thing her sister had given her before she was murdered. My heart squeezed tight in my chest as I gently turned her toward me and pulled her into my arms. I wrapped her as tightly as I could as she cried harder, Chase and Mia patting me on the back as they made their way out from behind the bar and carried Rylee to his office.

"Baby, I'm so sorry. We'll find it, I promise," I whispered in her ear as her body crumbled beneath me from the weight of losing the only thing in her life that was important to her.

Thirteen
Jade

The sun was almost completely set by the time I got to my apartment after leaving The Vine, having spent an hour there looking for the missing locket in Noah's office. I couldn't remember the last time I had seen it with everything being so crazy around me lately and panic had set in the moment I dumped everything out of my purse and still couldn't find it. I finally gave up and decided to go home and keep looking around my apartment, thankful that Noah was on his way to help me and would be bringing pizza and wine.

I climbed the last few steps and was walking toward my apartment when I looked up and saw someone standing with their back toward me, trying to open the door to the apartment next to mine. The apartment had been vacant for a few weeks after the incredibly loud party animal had finally been evicted. I was relieved to see him go and prayed that someone quiet was moving in instead.

I was about to say hi and introduce myself when the woman turned around and faced me before I could. My jaw dropped when I saw Cindy smiling at me, her hair a light blonde color, similar to mine.

"What are you doing here?" My confusion overrode my manners as I realized how rude I might have sounded after I said it. Her brows pulled together in response, a look of disappointment replacing the smile quickly.

"I'm moving into my new apartment, what does it look like?" She looked over her shoulder at the suitcase that sat behind her next to a few boxes stacked next to the window.
"You're moving in? To that apartment?" It was like my worst nightmare was coming true right before my very eyes.

"Yeah... that's why I'm holding the key." She rolled her eyes as she turned back to the doorknob and turned the key, opening the door to a furnished apartment that looked almost identical to mine. The only thing different was the bright colors I had used to make my space more personal, and that the layout was flipped to the opposite side. I peeled my eyes away from the apartment, trying to force myself to think about anything other than the woman standing in front of me that was trying to look like me and would now be living in the same apartment next door to me. My stomach dropped as a dark thought crossed my mind that she was actually trying to be me.

"What happened to your old apartment?" I leaned my shoulder against the small wall that separated our apartments and crossed my arms over my chest. Even with the thick scarf and heavy jacket, I felt a chill go through to my bones.

"I needed something bigger than a studio apartment for the baby. And I figured this would be perfect since Noah is over at your place half the time anyway, he would be close by to help with the baby. It was either this or move into his house. How crazy would that be?! The three of us living under one roof and raising a baby?" Her laughter reached a pitch that I'd never heard from her as she leaned her head back, laughing hysterically. I stayed watching her in disbelief as I heard footsteps approaching behind me.

"Hey, Noah! I was just telling Jade the exciting news about my new apartment. Did you want to come check it out?" She looked past me as I felt Noah's hand on my lower back, the tension in his body radiating toward me.

"Your new apartment?" His tone was stern as he kept his glare on her, his hand never leaving my body.

"Yeah, I was just about to get my stuff moved inside but you guys can come in and check it out if you want. Figured we'd be spending a lot of time here so you might as well make yourself at home right away." She smiled as if she didn't have a care in the world as Noah and I kept our stoic expressions. It felt like watching a horrific accident; you didn't want to see it but yet you couldn't look away.

"Maybe another time." Noah slowly pulled his hand away from my back as he turned his body toward me, blocking Cindy with his back.

"Let's get inside and eat before the pizza gets cold." His voice was quiet as he spoke, calming me from the meltdown I felt was coming. I nodded my head yes as my fingers felt around in my pocket until they found the keys and opened the door.

"Be careful moving stuff around and call downstairs if you need them to help you." His words were more of a warning than anything as he glanced over his shoulder at Cindy before gently leading me into the apartment with his hand on my lower back.

Once we were inside I heard the door click shut before Noah slid the deadbolt in place and sat the pizza down on the counter. We both stayed quiet as we worked to get out of the layers of clothes we were wearing, the tension around us thick.

"Did that seriously just happen?" I asked as I looked at Noah, hands on my hips. "Did she change her looks to look like me and then move into the apartment next door to me?! The same exact apartment as mine?!" My voice rose quickly, Noah wrapping me in a hug and holding me as he whispered in my ear.

"Watch what you say, these walls are super thin," he warned as he rubbed my back gently. "Remember how much we heard when that asshole next door was living there, she's going to be able to hear things just as easily."

"I can't believe it. It's like she's trying to take over my life. She would take you too if she could." I kept my voice low as I stepped back and looked up at Noah. The day had been long and draining with this taking the cake.

"She will never be you and she will never have me. Even if I wasn't with you, she still wouldn't have me." He leaned forward and kissed my forehead before grabbing my hand and leading me to the pizza.

We ate in silence as he worked to get the bottle of wine open, a much-needed treat for the night. The tension in the room subsided quickly as we cuddled on the couch and watched an old movie on the tv before getting the energy to look for the locket. My heart had been broken since I first noticed it was missing, part of me wondering if I had actually lost it or if my head was just too chaotic to remember where I had put it.

"I think it's officially lost," I muttered as I pushed myself up from being on my hands and knees looking under the bed with a flashlight. My body was sore from the constant stress I had been under lately, amplified by the weird positions I had been putting myself in trying to find the locket.
I closed my eyes as I leaned forward, slowly stretching as I bent down to touch my toes. My body tingled as I pushed myself deeper into the stretch, forcing the muscles to remember the yoga that I used to do daily. I smiled as I felt Noah come up behind me and gently grab my hips, lining himself up perfectly with my ass.

He slowly worked his hips as he teased me with a grinding motion, keeping his grip on me to keep me from falling over as I started laughing.

"Hey, I was trying to stretch!" I stood upright and playfully swatted at him as he moved in closer, a hungry look in his eye.

"Not to worry, I plan to stretch you as far as you can go." His voice was low and deep, pure sex dripping from every word.

"Oh really? Is that a threat or a promise?" I arched my eyebrow as I licked my bottom lip and locked eyes with him.

"Both." He studied me like a hunter would their prey, watching every move I made as he slowly pulled his T-shirt up and over his head. My eyes trailed over his muscular body as my fingers longed to reach out and touch him. I took a few steps backward, keeping my eyes on him as he moved towards me with determination. I felt my body change with every move he made, turned on by the way he looked at me. Suddenly the back of my legs bumped into the chair next to my dresser leaving me nowhere to go.

Noah's lips curled upward into a mischievous smile as he saw that I was trapped. My chest rose and fell heavily as I watched him creep closer, almost within reach. At last minute I ducked underneath his arm as he reached out to grab me and slid past him before he spun around and wrapped his arms around me, tickling my sides as he carried me over his shoulder to the bed. I giggled, his fingers continuing to tickle me as he climbed on the bed, dropping me on the soft mattress before climbing on top of me.

"You really thought you could get away that easy?" The smile on his face was one of the sexiest things about him as it lit up his hazel eyes.

"I gotta make you work for it, you can't just have me whenever you want," I teased as I blew a stray strand of hair off my face. His eyes got darker as he reached down and grabbed my hand, pulling it down to feel the bulge in his jeans.

"Baby, I will work you harder than you can handle," he growled as my fingers grabbed him through his jeans.

"Prove it." I licked my lips as I felt him twitch in my hand, my need to have him inside of me growing stronger.

He quickly rolled off me and kept his eyes on me as he took off his jeans and boxers. I let my eyes drift over to his massive cock as I lazily ran my fingers along the top of my bra. His fingers wrapped tightly around his shaft as he watched me, stroking up and down as my fingers pulled my bra down and traced over my pebbled nipple. My back arched in response, my breathing increasing to match his strokes.

"Fuck, Jade, you're gonna make me come just from watching you." He climbed up on the bed and pulled my leggings down before pushing my panties to the side and sliding a finger inside of me. I gasped at the welcomed intrusion, the wetness spreading as he moved his fingers inside of me. Within seconds my panties were gone and he was stroking himself while fingering me.

"I need you now, Noah," I begged as my body inched closer to orgasm.

"Now..," I panted as his fingers rubbed in circles over my clit. I reached up and ran my hands in his hair, pulling it as my body went over the edge, convulsing around his fingers.

"Fuck, you're so beautiful when you come." He pulled his fingers out as he slid himself inside of me, my body stretching to accommodate him. He stilled for a moment, allowing me time to adjust before he slowly rocked back and forth, closing his eyes as he increased his speed. I lifted my hips to let him in deeper, a groan from him in response as he plowed deeper inside of me. My legs wrapped around his waist as my hips ground into him, the headboard banging against the wall with each movement.

"We can't be too loud," I whispered as I nodded up toward the wall behind us. "Cindy is on the other side, remember?"

"Let her hear us. I want her to hear you moan as I fuck you, knowing that it will never be her."

His words stirred something deep inside me and a feeling of pride flowed through me as I realized how much he really did love me and that I didn't have to be jealous or insecure about Cindy.

He shifted his weight and lowered himself so he was rubbing against my clit. I could feel the pressure build as I watched him watching me. Harder. Deeper. Faster.

"Don't stop, right there..."

"That's it baby, come for me..."

"Noah...."

"Say my name baby, say it louder. Let her hear you as I make you come again. Say it baby," he coaxed as I screamed his name over and over, our bodies melting into a giant puddle of satisfied bliss as we climaxed together.

<u>Fourteen</u>
Noah

"How's Rylee doing? She's almost at the one month mark, right?" I leaned against the doorway to Chase's office, desperate to get my mind off of Cindy and the baby without much success.

"She's good, getting bigger every day. Mia is taking her for her wellness checkup today, but yeah, she'll be one month old on Saturday." He smiled proudly and my heart felt happy that Chase finally had the life he had always wanted.

"Does Mia still have the ultrasound pictures from when she was pregnant?" I scratched my head, feeling awkward for even asking. I still couldn't shake the thought that something might be wrong with the baby after the ultrasound tech said the baby wasn't measuring on track for how far along Cindy should be.

"Yeah, why?" He pulled his brows together as he leaned back in his leather chair and studied me.

I blew out a breath and ran a hand through my hair as I sat down in the chair across from him.

"The ultrasound tech said that the baby doesn't look like how a baby should look right now in the pregnancy."

"What does that mean?"

"Fuck if I know? She tried explaining it but Cindy got really defensive and kept arguing that she knew when she got pregnant."

"Did she think something was wrong with the baby?"

"She didn't say that, and she didn't seem to act like there was. We have another ultrasound at the end of the week, right before her 7 month prenatal appointment. They want to check the baby again and see if it's grown in the two-week period from the last one."

"So the baby is just measuring behind?" Chase ran a hand down his face before grabbing his cell phone and typing quickly while I talked.

"I guess so. The tech said that it looked like the baby would have been conceived late August or early September. Cindy is adamant that it was when she was down here for the Fourth of July which would make her close to seven months, the tech thinks the baby is closer to six months." I leaned back against the chair and waited while Chase did something on his phone.

"I know it might be hard to tell since you don't have a picture to compare it to, but this is Mia's from when she was six months pregnant with Rylee. Did the baby look like this?" He extended his cell phone to me, a Facebook post with the caption of baby Walker at 6 months. I got up and went to my office, grabbed the ultrasound photos from my desk drawer, and sat back down in front of Chase. I laid the photos on his desk as a smug smile crossed his face. He sat his phone down next to them as we craned our necks to look at them in comparison.

"I don't know, these look pretty much the same. Does it change much by seven months?" I asked as I stared at the pictures, trying to find anything that would help.

"Here, let me see. I think we posted monthly updates so there might be one from seven months." Chase pulled his cell phone in front of him and scrolled through posts until he found what he was looking for and sat his phone on the desk between us again.

We stared at the pictures, looking back and forth between the phone and the pictures, frustration evident when there was no apparent difference between the ultrasound photos. I pushed away from the desk and let out a heavy sigh as Mia walked into the office, balancing Rylee in her car seat on her arm.

"Hey, what's going on?" she asked as she looked down at the ultrasound pictures on Chase's desk then looking back and forth between us. "It's a long story." I looked up at her apologetically, not having the energy to go through everything again.

"Humor me." Her eyes lit up as she looked to Chase knowing that he would give in and tell her.

"Cindy claims to be almost seven months pregnant but the last ultrasound shows the baby measuring around six months. We were trying to compare the ultrasound photos to the ones on Facebook of Ry." Chase smiled as Mia bent down to kiss him before setting the car seat down next to Chase. She leaned over the table and studied the ultrasound photos, picking one up to see it closer.

"It's hard to tell by just looking at these but the baby does look a little small. You can't go based on that though because you can't see the actual size of the baby, especially since it's zoomed in for the scan. But babies tend to plump up more around 7 months and this one isn't. When does she have her next prenatal appointment?"

"This Friday."

"Well, they should be checking her fundal height which should give a better idea of how far along she is."

"I'm sorry, her what?"

"Fundal height. It's a measurement from the top of the uterus to the pubic bone and it should be close to the number of weeks pregnant. For example, if she is close to 28 weeks pregnant, the fundal height should be around 26-30 centimeters. Are they doing another ultrasound as well?"

"Yeah, right before the checkup."

"That's good, I'm sure they'll be able to confirm everything then." She sat on the edge of the desk as Chase wrapped his arms around her waist from behind. "Why is Cindy having so many ultrasounds anyways? Is she high risk?"

"I have no idea, I just go where I'm told to go."

"You should ask and see. If she's high risk then it would be good for you to know what they're monitoring her for and be prepared."

"I guess I don't know much about all of this, do I?" I blushed as I looked away, embarrassed that I already felt like a failure as a father. "It's all a learning process, my friend." Her eyes were sympathetic as she smiled. "Speaking of which, Cindy came by the house yesterday to ask me about labor and delivery. I hope she shared all of the gory details with you like she promised she would."

I could hear the teasing tone in her voice but my blood ran cold when I processed what she said.

"Cindy came by your house?"

"Yeah, she said that you told her to come talk to me." Mia paused as she looked at me, reading the expression on my face. "It wasn't a big deal, I didn't mind talking to her. I wish I would have had a heads up that she was coming, but it worked out better anyway when she helped me with Rylee."

"Mia, I NEVER told Cindy to come talk to you. I've never even talked to her about you guys." My heart started to race as I thought about Cindy alone with Mia and Rylee in the house.

"She made it seem like you suggested it. And then she said that us girls could spend some time talking about babies while you and Chase were at her apartment building the crib." Mia's eyes went wide as she looked back at Chase. "You guys weren't building the crib?"

"No, I was with Grant and Liam. We had baseball practice like usual. I'm sorry, I would have told you if I was going somewhere else Mia."

"Why would she lie to me? She acted like everyone was friends, I just thought maybe I wasn't that involved yet because I'm always at home with the baby."

"I don't know but I'm not liking the way things are going. Something's not right." I reached down and pulled my phone out of my pocket, sending a text message to Jade to see where she was. I knew she should be at work but with the way the day was going, anything was possible at this point.

"I agree, something doesn't feel right. I felt like something was off the other day when I saw that she had changed her hair to look like Jade." Chase's words struck a nerve as he said what I had been trying to deny all along. I shot him a stern look.

"What?" he asked, holding his hands up in defense. "I can't be the only one who finds it creepy that some random girl shows up out of the blue, knocked up, and within a few months she is literally doing everything that Jade does."
Mia and I sat in silence while Chase looked between us.

"Oh, come on! She works at the same place as Jade. Colored her hair the same color as Jade. Drives a red car like Jade. Started dressing like Jade. Slept with the same guy as Jade…. Am I missing the connection here?"

"And now she lives next door to Jade." I lowered my eyes as I heard their gasps. Chase was right, things were getting eerily similar.

"What the fuck?" Chase stared at me with complete shock on his face.

"Yeah, she just moved into the vacant apartment next door."

"You mean she is living right next door to Jade? As in they share a wall?" Mia's voice was shrill as she glanced down to make sure she hadn't woken Rylee up.

"Yes. Apparently, she told Jade that she needed something bigger than the studio she was in, and she thought it would be easier for me to help with the baby since I'm always at Jade's house when she's not at mine. And to top that off, she made a joke to Jade about how it was either live there or move in with me." I swallowed hard as I took in the gravity of the situation.

"Wow. I can't believe it. This is so creepy." Mia shuddered as she stood up next to Chase.

"Maybe I just need to talk to her? Like really talk to her and find out what the problem is?" I glanced down at my phone as a new message from Jade came through. I frowned as I read it.

"What's wrong?" Chase asked.

"Jade is on her way here."

"Why?" Mia questioned as she bent down to adjust the pacifier in Rylee's mouth as she started to stir.

"I don't know. Guess we'll see when she gets here."

"So what are we supposed to do now with Cindy?" Mia asked as she turned away from the baby who had fallen back asleep.

"What do you mean?"

"Well, I have to see her again soon, am I supposed to act like everything is normal and fine? Should I cancel on her?"

"Why are you seeing her again?"

I watched as Mia swallowed hard before answering.

"She's bringing something back that she borrowed."

My eyes narrowed as I waited for the bomb to drop.

"What did she borrow Mia?"

Her eyes were wide as she looked away, avoiding having to look at me. I stared at her while waited, clearing my throat to remind her that I was still there. Her eyes slowly lifted and made contact with mine.

"She has the photo album from our wedding. She said that she was working on a surprise gift for you and needed a recent picture of you. Those were the only ones that I had."

I closed my eyes and pinched the bridge of my nose as I heard footsteps down the hall as the door opened. I stood up and walked into the hall as Jade was heading toward me, tears on her face.

"Baby, what's wrong?" I pulled her tightly into me as she cried against my chest. She was still dressed for work but I noticed her badge that she used to get in and out of the building wasn't attached to her pocket like it usually was.

"They fired me." She sniffled as she pulled back and looked up at me, her eyes a light shade of gray.

"What? Why?" I stepped to the side as I heard Mia and Chase walk into the hallway behind us.

"I was accused of bullying and harassment, creating a hostile work environment, and showing favoritism with other employees."

My jaw clenched knowing who was responsible for this.

"That's bullshit." I shook my head knowing that there was nothing that I could say that would make this any better.

"I tried talking to them but they said that they have to take the accusations seriously and that they had noticed the tension between Cindy and I. Given that she was the one who went to them to file the report, they claim they had no choice other than to fire me."

"Jade, I'm so sorry." Mia came around from behind me and wrapped her in her arms as Chase and I looked at each other. I was furious as I thought of the things I planned to say when I saw Cindy.

"I'll be back." I looked straight at Chase, seeing Jade's head whip up from Mia's shoulder as I stalked off down the hallway.

"Noah, where are you going?" Jade called behind me as the door closed, silencing her pleas for me to come back.

It was after five which meant that Cindy should be home by now given that the bank closed every day at four. I veered in and out of traffic, my anger building the closer I got. As I made my way up the stairs I felt my pocket vibrate and pulled out my phone to see a message from Chase confirming that Stacy would close up tonight and they were taking Jade back to their house. I shoved my phone back into my pocket as I reached Cindy's door, pounding loudly with my fist.
Her car was downstairs in the parking lot which meant she was here. I waited a few seconds before pounding again, my hand slipping when the door flung open, Cindy's eyes wide as she stood on the other side.

"Noah, what's wrong?" Her voice was high, eyes filled with concern as she stepped back and allowed me to come inside. I slammed the door behind me as I stood in front of her, glaring.

"What the fuck is wrong with you?" I towered over her, looking down with fury on my face as I watched her reaction.

"What are you talking about? Maybe I should ask what the fuck is wrong with you?" She stepped away and walked over to sit on the couch, plopping her feet up on the old wood coffee table in front of her.

"You got Jade fired. That's what's wrong."

"I had nothing to do with that." She arched her eyebrow and I immediately wanted to wipe that smug look off of her face.

"Really? Because it seems like you were the one who filed the report claiming that she was bullying and harassing you."

"I didn't file a report. I completed the required paperwork for my thirty-day performance evaluation that asked me about my experience. I was honest like they asked me to be." She crossed her arms over her chest and stared at me.

"Jade has never bullied you and you know it."

"Yeah well, she wasn't the most pleasant person to work with either."

"So you got her fired because you don't like her?"

"She got herself fired because she doesn't know how to be nice to other people."

"You seriously have issues. If you think that you can move to a small town like this and treat people that way, you've got another thing coming. Whatever this bullshit act is that you have going- just stop now. I don't have time for it and quite frankly, I'm not interested."

"So what? You're just going to walk away and abandon me and your unborn child for some girl that's an easy lay?" She stood up and walked toward me, pure evil on her face.

"I never said that I was walking away from my child, I said that you need to learn how to treat people if you want to make it in this town. And trust me, Jade wasn't the easy lay." I looked her up and down as my eyes lingered over her stomach. Her face turned a dark shade of red and for a moment I expected to see smoke come out of her ears.

"You really need to have more respect for the woman who is carrying your child." She pulled her shoulders back as she stepped closer.

"I never asked you to." My blood was boiling and it took everything inside of me to remember that she was a woman. You don't put your hands on a woman. Never put your hands on a woman.

Within seconds she was on me, wrapping her arms around my neck as she forced her lips onto mine. I quickly stepped back, pushing her away with my arm as I glared at her.

"What the hell was that?" My eyes narrowed, her face falling at my reaction.

"I don't know why you keep trying to fight this thing between us, Noah. We're going to be together for the rest of our lives, bound together by this baby. It just makes sense that we should be together. You know, for the baby."

"Is that what this is all about? Us being together?"

"It just makes sense that a child should see their mother and father together. In love." Her last word fell on her lips as a whisper.

"Cindy, I'm not in love with you. I'm having a child with you but nothing more. Do you understand that?" I took a deep breath and watched as she slowly started to calm down.

"But you could love me, if you just tried." She looked up at me under thick lashes, her eyes pleading with mine.

"I'm in love with Jade, Cindy."

"So you think. But she's not the person you think she is. I've seen a side of her that's cold and vengeful. You don't want someone like that in your life. I could make you so much happier than she ever could." She rubbed a hand over her stomach as she stepped closer.

"I'm not here to talk about my relationship with Jade. I'm here to talk about us and set boundaries in place. If we're going to try to raise this baby together then we need to respect each other and stick to those boundaries. Okay?"

She slowly nodded her head yes, taking another step forward as I took a step back.

"My relationship with Jade will remain private. You will leave her alone and stop showing up at Mia's house unexpectedly. If and when I want to have you involved in my personal life, I will let you know. Once it gets closer to the baby coming, we'll sit down again and talk about what things will look like at that point. Until then you can keep me updated on doctor's appointments and I'll do my best to be there." I looked sternly at her, waiting for her to object but she didn't.

"Okay." She pursed her lips and folded her arms over her chest as I nodded my head and walked out the door, slamming it behind me.

Fifteen
Jade

I rolled over and found the sun filtering into the room through the sheer curtains, Noah's dark hair looking lighter from the warm glow it cast on the pillow. It felt weird to get up and not have a job to get ready for. I let out a deep breath as I rolled over and slid out of bed, making my way to the kitchen to start a pot of coffee. It was still early but I was restless and had struggled to stay asleep most of the night, even with having Noah next to me. Usually having him in bed next to me would calm me but for some reason, nothing could calm the uneasy feeling that seemed to be lingering around.

I sat on the soft rug on the floor and closed my eyes as I slowly reached up and stretched, taking in a deep breath and slowly exhaling. My body was stiff and rigid, fighting every stretch as I pushed myself further into them. If I could force my body to give in and relax, maybe my mind would do the same. My eyes were still closed when I heard footsteps down the hall as Noah made his way to the living room.

"Maybe I should start staying over more often if this is the view in the morning."

I heard the sound of the coffee pot as he sat it back down and looked over my shoulder to see him shirtless leaning against the counter as he sipped his coffee while watching me. I chuckled as I turned back around and focused on the stretch, spreading my legs further apart in a wide V in front of me as I laid my torso flat against the rug and extended my arms above my head.

"Then again, maybe I'll just stay at my own place so I don't have to worry about walking around with blue balls every time you decide to do yoga," he joked as he walked past me and sat on the couch.

"Very funny." I laughed as I finished the stretch before I got up and sat next to him. "You never have blue balls so don't start acting like you do now."

"See for yourself." He held his coffee cup in one hand while he pulled the waistband of his sweats out so I could look inside. Feeling a bit rowdy I reached my hand inside and grabbed him, feeling him jerk in response as the coffee sloshed in the mug.

"Hmm, not blue." I bit my lip as I pulled my hand away and stood up, swaying my hips as I walked to the kitchen to look for something to make us for breakfast.

I was leaning against the refrigerator door when I felt Noah come up behind me and wrap his arms around my waist. A smile crossed my face as I felt the bulge in his pants against my butt, loving that there was rarely ever a moment that he wasn't turned on around me. He ran a hand up my stomach and over my chest as he kissed my neck. I closed my eyes as a whimper escaped, my body finally starting to relax.

"What do you want for breakfast?" I asked with my eyes still closed, enjoying his hands as they roamed my body.

"You."

I giggled as I playfully bumped him with my butt, his hands quickly grabbing my hips and holding me in place.

"You always want me," I teased. "What kind of food do you want?" I closed the door to the refrigerator and turned around to look at him. He slowly backed me up against the cold steel of the fridge as he pinned me against it and leaned his body on mine. His eyes changed and I watched with curiosity as he looked at me, searching for something.

"Move in with me." His words were soft and full of sincerity.

"What? You don't want me to live with you, it's too soon." My head was spinning as I thought about what he was asking me. I loved Noah but there wasn't any way that he was serious about us moving in together right now with everything going on.

"There's nothing that I want more, Jade. I want to wake up every morning to your beautiful face, and fall asleep every night inside of you."

"You're such a romantic." I playfully rolled my eyes at him knowing that I loved being with him more than anything. Maybe that was what had kept us together this long? Incredible, mind-blowing sex that neither of us could get enough of.

"I never claimed to be romantic, just good in bed. And we both know there haven't been any complaints in that department." His eyes danced wildly as they watched me squirm beneath him as his finger ran down my stomach and over my hip before reaching down and spreading his palm across my pussy.

"No complaints indeed," I whispered as my body froze beneath his touch.

"Then move in with me. Please." He leaned closer and lightly kissed my neck as his hand continued to play with me over my thin pajama pants. "We practically already live together, we sleep over at each other's place every other night."

"But, Noah," I murmured, ready to give in.

"No buts, just move in with me." His hand moved as he dipped it inside of my pajamas, moving my panties out of the way as he worked two fingers inside of me. My body came alive as he slid in and out of me, kisses creating a trail of fire as he planted them across my shoulder and down my chest.

"Are you using sex to try to lure me to the dark side?" I panted as my body responded to his touch, my back arched as my legs started to tremble.

"Whatever it takes to get you there," he whispered in my ear as his fingers rubbed my clit harder, my body on the verge of orgasm.

"Yes! Yes! Yes!" I screamed as my body gave in, his fingers clutched by the tight convulsions as I spasmed against him. I leaned my head against his chest as he chuckled, my hands wrapped around his neck.

"You cheat." I grinned as I said it knowing that he was feeling pretty cocky about it.

"Hey, you said yes, there was no cheating on my end."

"I was lost in the moment, I didn't know what I was saying yes to." I looked up at him with playful eyes, surprised to see the love reflected back at me in his.

"Well, if you move in with me, I can promise to give you an orgasm every morning and two every night." He ran a finger across my cheek as his eyes pleaded with mine.

"Okay," I sighed.

"Okay what?" He tilted his head as he waited for my response.

"I'll move in with you." I let out a nervous breath. "But I want a minimum of four orgasms a day." I quirked a brow as I tried to hide my smile.

"Done." His lips were heavy on mine as he kissed me, lifting me into his arms before carrying me back to the bedroom.

342

<u>Sixteen</u>
Noah

"You all done there, champ?" I leaned across the table and handed Liam a napkin to wipe his mouth as he finished his last bite of cheeseburger. While cheeseburgers weren't originally on the menu at The Vine, they had been a consistent item shortly after Grant had quit his job over a year ago and needed to feed Liam after school. For a while, they were living with Grant's mom so she could help take care of Liam while Grant was at work but after he quit his demanding job and took a position teaching PE at Liam's school, he decided it was time to be out on their own again. The last month The Vine had seen a significant increase in cheeseburger sales which confirmed Grant had in fact moved out.

"Yeah, I'm stuffed." He pushed the plate toward the center of the table and leaned back the way I'd seen his dad do over the years. I let out a soft chuckle when I noticed how much Liam was a spitting image of his dad and quietly wondered how much of me my own child would have in them. Would people think the same thing? Would they see the same little quirks and traits in my kid that they saw in me when I was little?

"Good. You know we have other stuff than just burgers and fries, right?" I eyed him suspiciously, knowing his answer before it came out.

"I'm good. I'm a meat and potatoes kind of man."

I leaned back in my chair as laughter forced its way through my body, filling the silence around us. Liam smiled, completely proud that his response got such a rise out of me.

"I'm sorry, I won't push the other stuff on you anymore. I didn't know you had become such a distinguished man with set tastes," I joked, still laughing.

"I'm almost eleven, so that makes me one year closer to being a man." He sat upright in his chair and attempted to puff his chest out while I looked away and chewed my lip to keep from laughing.

"Hey, um, Noah, can I ask you a question? You know, man to man?" He raised his eyebrows as he said the word man.

"Sure, what's up?"

"My dad said that you're having a baby."

"Yeah, that's true." I nodded my head while I waited for him to ask his question.

"But it's not with Jade, it's with another girl."

"That is also true." My brow furrowed as I wondered what he was trying to ask.

"So you love Jade and you guys live together now, but you're having a baby with another woman. Is she carrying your baby because Jade can't?" He titled his head at me in confusion.

I blew out a breath and shifted in my seat, wishing Grant was out here with us instead of talking to Chase in his office. How was I supposed to talk about this with Liam? I had no clue what he knew and didn't know about girls or sex or one night stands but I sure as hell didn't want to be the one to teach him any of it.

"No Liam, she's having my baby because there was a night where we were together, but Jade and I were broken up."

"So, if you like a girl and you want to hang out with her, does that mean that you have to have sex with her? Like if she wants to be your girlfriend, do you have to have sex?"

"No, you don't ever have to have sex with anyone that you don't want to." I ran a hand down my face feeling like this conversation was starting to get out of control and heading in a direction that Grant wouldn't be happy about.

"What's going on Liam? Where are these questions coming from?"

"Well, there are these two girls at school that I really like and my buddy Luke said that he heard that they both like me too and that they BOTH said that they want to be my girlfriend. I just don't know that I'm ready for all of this." He sighed and leaned forward, resting his elbows on the table as he looked at me. "You gotta help me, Noah, you know what it's like to have all the ladies wanting you."

I ran my hand across my face, attempting to hide my laughter without success. Liam scowled at me before I saw the corners of his mouth twitch before giving in to a full-blown smile on his face. Soon we were both bent over laughing so hard that Liam would snort and send us further into hysterics. I felt a hand clap my shoulder and turned to see Grant and Chase standing behind me, smiling.

"What's so funny?" Grant asked as he spun a chair around and straddled it backward.

"You know, the usual girl problems." Liam waved his hand dismissively before whispering something to Chase who had taken the empty seat next to him.

"Oh really?" Grant eyed me as his tone changed, forcing me into another bout of laughter.

"Relax, I've got this." I patted his knee as I turned my attention back to Liam.

"Alright little man, here's how you solve your problem. First, you decide which of the girls you like the most and you make an effort to find out if she likes you too. Second, you don't try to date two girls at the same time. It will be nothing but trouble. And third, you don't wait to see which one wants you before you decide which one you want. That's the pussy way of doing things and everyone involved deserves better than that. Treat the girl with respect and remember that you both need to be in agreement before even talking about sex." I winked as I saw Grant fling his arms up in the air beside me.

"Wait- What?!" His eyes narrowed at me as Liam sunk further in his chair and Chase tucked his chin in to hide his laughter. "What the fuck kind of conversation did I just walk in on?"

"You might want to watch the language." I gritted between my teeth, nodding toward Liam, hoping it would lighten Grant's mood.

"Really? From the guy who just told my son not to be a pussy?" "Alright, fair enough." I looked over at Liam and he nodded subtly. "Liam here was confused about my situation with Jade and Cindy. He wanted to make sure that just because someone is his girlfriend, that it doesn't mean that they have to have sex. I was just confirming that he doesn't have to have sex if he doesn't want to. And," I looked sternly at Liam, "it's something that he should wait for until he's ready. I get that he's a meat and potatoes kind of man now, but sex is a huge deal and it can have serious consequences with adult responsibilities."

"Like you and Cindy." Liam smiled proudly.

"Yup. So if you don't want to be a father at your age, you need to really think about it before you start having sex. Don't be afraid to talk to us, we have plenty of years of experience between us so we're pretty much experts at sex and relationships."

Laughter erupted around me as Liam shook his head and walked away, heading to the gated-in patio out back. I was thankful that the mood had shifted and Grant no longer looked like he wanted to murder me.

"Sorry about that, he caught me off guard by asking and I wasn't sure how you would want me to answer."

"It's fine, the kid has to learn at some point, and honestly it's not like he won't hear the town talk about how you've slept with everyone here." Grant nudged me with his elbow.

"Those days are over my friends. I'm a one-woman man now." I leaned back and laced my fingers behind my head.

"Yeah? So which woman are you with? The one you moved in with you or the one you knocked up?" Chase joked though I could hear the underlying truth in it.

"Jade is the girl for me. And yeah, Cindy will be there because of the baby, but that's it. I've already talked to her and reset expectations."

"I don't think it's going to be that easy. I think Cindy wants more and going by what I have seen from her so far, I don't see her stopping until she gets it." Chase reached forward and pointed at me. "You need to be careful with her, there's something about her that I just don't trust."

"I agree with Chase. Sorry, but I think you have bigger issues with her than you think."

I didn't want to admit that they were both right but I hadn't been able to stop thinking about what had happened after I went to her apartment to talk to her. The way she looked at me when she tried to convince me that I could love her the way that I loved Jade had made me uncomfortable. But the way she didn't even flinch when I accused her of trying to be Jade made me even more uncomfortable. My palms started sweating as I ran them down the front of my jeans.

"It's fine, I can handle it." I looked between them feeling their doubts cast upon their face, a reflection of what I felt inside.

"This is real life, Noah. It's not all rainbows and orgasms. It's not the bullshit games that you used to play with women. This is an innocent child involved and the possibility that you could lose the first woman you've ever loved. If that doesn't mean something to you then I don't know what will." Chase shook his head as he stood up and walked off to the back offices.

I hung my head and let out a sigh as I glanced over at Grant. I knew that Chase was right but I wasn't ready to admit to myself so it felt like a fucking attack coming from him.

"What? You don't have any salt to add to the wound? Any jokes about how I'll likely fail as a father?" I pushed knowing that I was purposely trying to start a fight so I would have something else to focus on.

"Oh I have plenty, but I'll save it for another time." He pinned me with a look that told me everything was about to get real.

"Noah, stop acting like an immature little asshole and figure out how to do the right thing for everyone. If you love Jade and you want to be with her, then make some grand gesture."

"I thought I did by begging her to move in?"

"Really? That was your big gesture? Asking her to move in with you when you guys are practically living together anyway?"

"It felt like a big step." I let out a heavy breath as I took in his words.

"It was, but if you want to keep her in your life you have to do something even bigger. You have to assure her that she's the one that you want in your life, that nothing else will ever take your love from her. Things are going to change, and soon. That baby will be here before you know it and when it gets here, your life is going to be completely changed. You're going to constantly be with Cindy and that's going to make Jade feel insecure and probably a little jealous. That baby is going to take so much of your time and attention that you won't have as much to give Jade. She's going to pick up on it and your absence will be felt by her, whether you acknowledge it or not. What we're saying is you need to be working on your relationship with Jade right now and fuck everything else. If you can't get to a new level with Jade that makes her feel like she is wanted and needed in your life, you're going to end up losing her when the baby comes."

"So what am I supposed to do?"

"I don't know. I can't tell you what to do. You're the only one who can figure out what you want from your relationship with her. Maybe it's asking her to marry you. Maybe it's talking about the future and letting her know that you want to someday have kids with her. I really don't know."

"That's it! That's what I'm going to do!" I slammed my fist down on the table excitedly as my eyes looked up at Grant, thankful that he talked me into what I needed to do.

"What? What are you going to do?" His forehead wrinkled as his brow arched.

"I'm gonna ask her to marry me."

Seventeen
Jade

"So what are you going to do now for a job?" Mia asked as she cut the last few pieces of cucumber and tossed it in the salad bowl on the island.

"I told her she could work at The Vine until you get back from maternity leave." Noah snuck up behind me and wrapped his arms around me. I leaned back against him, inhaling the light scent of his cologne as I slightly tilted my head toward his neck out of habit.

"You better be careful, I'm not afraid to clear this island and eat you for dinner, Ms. Alyson." He nipped at my ear as he kept his whisper low enough for only me to hear. I felt a blush creep up my neck as I gently pushed my hips back and rubbed my ass against him. His fingers dug into my hips as I heard a sharp intake of air as I looked playfully over my shoulder and bit my lip.

"Don't make promises you can't keep, Mr. Wilder." I pulled my bottom lip in between my teeth before smiling and releasing it. He softly reached up and ran the pad of his thumb over it, a look of desire on his face. I heard a low grumble from deep inside his chest before Chase opened the sliding glass door and rolled his eyes at us.

"Seriously? Can't you guys keep your hands off each other for two minutes?" he grumbled as he poked his head in.

"Stop, it's cute," Mia teased over her shoulder before turning toward him to wash a carrot in the sink. "There was a time when you couldn't keep your hands off of me."
"I remember quite vividly. And I believe that might be how miss Rylee got here." He nodded to the playpen in the corner of the living room where she slept peacefully.

"Those were the days," Mia whispered under her breath as she turned back to the island and gave me a sad look.

Chase slid the door open and sat the barbecue tongs on the counter behind him before grabbing Mia from behind and tickling her as she giggled.

"6 days. 9 hours. 23 minutes," he said loud enough for everyone to hear. Mia looked up over her shoulder and frowned at him.

"Until what?" she asked.

"Until it's been six weeks and you're officially cleared. Then I plan to give Noah some baby practice while they watch Ry for us so I can spend the entire night and the next morning making love to you because damn if six weeks isn't a hell of a long time to go without being with you." He planted soft kisses along her shoulder as she giggled and blushed.

"Come on Noah, this meat isn't going to cook itself. Grab some beers and make yourself useful." Chase grabbed the tongs from the counter and turned to head back outside, smacking Mia firmly on the ass on his way out. Noah laughed and shook his head as he grabbed the beers and followed him. After the sliding door was closed I pulled out the barstool and sat across from Mia while she cut up the carrot and tossed it in the salad.

"You guys are as cute as you were when you first started dating."

"Thanks, I feel very insecure about everything right now and keep thinking that he's going to get bored and start looking for someone else already."

"Are you kidding? You guys are married. He loves you..."

She sat down the knife and planted her palms flat on the island as she looked at me. She didn't have to say the words for me to see that she was terrified that he would cheat on her like her ex-husband had.

"Mia, he's not Damian. He adores you. And Rylee. And he probably would have taken you here on this island if we weren't here," I joked watching the smile cross her face. "Trust me, I don't think he's going to be too strict with that countdown." I laughed and felt relieved when she joined me.
"I know he loves me and he loves Rylee but I don't know that he still wants me. My body isn't the same and honestly, I'm so exhausted from the baby that I don't know that I would even want to have sex. What if I disappoint him?" She extended her arms out and shrugged.

"Do you want to know what I see when I look at you?"

"Probably not." She rolled her eyes as I tossed a discarded carrot top at her.

"Well too bad because I'm going to tell you anyway. I see a woman who has gained so much confidence in the past two years. I see a woman who is strong. Who is determined. Who has a beautiful body that has some majorly sexy new curves. And seriously, I'm not sure that Chase knows that you have a face anymore because every time I see him, he's staring at your boobs." I looked pointed at her chest as she looked down at the sweater that was pulled tight against her chest.

"He does not!"

"He does. It might be a new fetish for him, who knows." I shrugged and laughed as she swatted at me, the blush creeping up her face.

"Don't be so hard on yourself, Mia, he still loves you and I can tell that he's still very much turned on by you." I smiled to reassure her as she smiled back at me.

"I guess I can say the same for you and Noah?" She called over her shoulder as she opened the fridge and pulled out a tray with cut lettuce, tomato, and onions.

"Yeah, things are good between us. For now." I sighed and lowered my head as I picked at the magenta-colored nail polish that was starting to chip.

"What's that supposed to mean?" She sat the tray on the island beside the salad before reaching back in to grab a bowl of potato salad.

"I don't know. I guess things aren't necessarily doomed so to speak but I can't sit here and expect that things will stay the same when Cindy has the baby. I know that things are going to change, I just don't know how much. Maybe instead of taking steps forward, I should be taking steps back."

"Are you regretting moving in with him?" She pulled out the other barstool and sat next to me, leaning back to check on Rylee before getting comfortable. I glanced out the kitchen window and saw Noah and Chase, their heads back laughing at something while their breath formed clouds of smoke in front of them from the cold air. It felt weird to me that they wanted to barbecue in the middle of winter but apparently, Chase was in the mood and didn't care how cold it was.

"I don't necessarily regret it but I also haven't bothered terminating my lease yet either. Which is stupid because I can't afford to keep paying rent when I don't have a job." I blew out a frustrated breath and looked at her. "I don't want to end up being the roommate that he has sex with because it's convenient and he's too nice to kick me out after his life with Cindy starts when the baby gets here."

Mia's face fell, mimicking the way my heart dropped to my stomach after I said it. I had been questioning everything for weeks now but I hadn't been honest with myself about what I was actually afraid of. I had fallen in love with a man who was now about to fall in love with someone else. His child.

It was a different kind of love and I knew that, but it would be stupid of me to think that he could handle everything at the same time. There was no way that he could still be with me and grow in our relationship while also devoting time to his child. That meant that when the child got here, our relationship would be cemented where it was and I wasn't sure that it would ever be enough for me.

"The baby will definitely change things, I'm not going to lie. It's going to be hard and he's going to be focused on the baby and nothing else for a while. But if you can be patient and supportive until he gets a hold on everything, I really do think you guys can have an awesome relationship. Have you guys talked about the future? Getting married? Having kids of your own?"

"No, it all felt like it was too soon to talk about that stuff then bam, Cindy shows up and now it feels weird to talk to him about having a kid of our own when he's having one with someone else." I played with the forks on the table in front of me, not ready to make eye contact with Mia. Her hand reached over and softly touched my arm.

"Jade, you're not your mom. It's okay to let your guard down and be happy with someone. Her past is not your future."

My eyes shot up towards hers as tears filled them, threatening to spill over. My mind raced as it thought about what she said, no time to respond to her as I saw the guys walking to the door with plates full of meat in their hands. I felt like a deer in the headlights as Noah looked at me, his smile immediately replaced with concern when he saw the look on my face. I slid off the barstool and rushed off to the guest bathroom, locking the door as I slid down it and held my face in my hands.

A few minutes later I heard a soft knock at the door.

"Hey, is everything okay?" Noah's asked quietly. I stood up and glanced in the mirror before I opened the door.

"Yeah, I just needed a moment."

His eyes searched mine as he leaned against the doorway and crossed his arms.

"You sure you're okay?"

"Yeah, I'm good." I forced a smile hoping he would take it and let it be. He quirked a brow as he kept studying me. I let out a deep breath as I dropped my shoulders and looked at him.

"It's not a big deal, really. It's not important. Let's get back out there before dinner is cold."

I went to step in front of him when he reached an arm out, stretching it across the doorway to block me. His hazel eyes darkened as he watched me, the fabric of his hoodie stretching tight across his muscular chest.

"Jade, don't you know by now? If it involves you, then it's important."

There were genuine love and sincerity reflected in his voice which killed me knowing that I had to end this thing between us, breaking both of our hearts in the process.

Eighteen
Noah

"You've been awful quiet tonight since dinner, you sure you don't want to talk about what's bothering you?" I reached across the middle console of the truck and placed a hand on Jade's leg as I focused on the back road that would eventually lead to an old abandoned farm with acres of land around it. I loved coming out here and just lying in the bed of the truck, looking at the stars, and forgetting the rest of the world even existed.

"Yeah, I've just been doing some thinking."

Her head leaned back against the headrest while she looked out the window into the darkness that surrounded us.

"I'm here if you want to talk, you know that. Right?"

She had been acting so different with me tonight and I couldn't put my finger on what had happened while she was inside with Mia. She was pulling away and the thought of losing her was starting to feel more real. Nothing had worked to get her to talk to me and I felt desperate to try to get through to her. I needed her more than I needed air at this point.

She nodded her head in agreement as she continued to stare out the window, her hand reaching up to wipe away a tear as it slid down her cheek. I sighed heavily as I pulled the truck over on the side of the road and turned in my seat to look at her.

"Baby, please talk to me. Something is wrong, I can clearly see it on your face." I reached over and wiped another tear as it fell. My chest felt tight and something told me that I wasn't going to like what she was about to say.

"I think we should stop seeing each other." Her voice was stern as her lip trembled, her eyes still focused on the darkness outside the truck. I closed my eyes and leaned my back against the cold door. This can't be happening. Not now. Not when everything was heading in the right direction. Suddenly I felt the weight of the world on my shoulders, the happiness I had felt earlier when I bought the engagement ring dissipating. I opened my eyes and looked at her as she slowly turned toward me, tears rolling down her face.

"What brought this on?" I asked calmly, trying my best to keep the raw emotion I felt out of my voice.

"There's a lot of change coming, and soon. I don't think that our relationship is in a place to withstand that level of change."

"I think that we can push through whatever comes our way if we're in this for the right reasons. I know I am." I watched her face fall and felt bad at the insinuating tone that made its way through.

"Do you really think that we're in a place to handle moving in together and a few months after that, you having a baby with another woman?" She pulled her brows together and frowned.

"I do. Because there's nothing that I want more than you, Jade."

"You say that now but a baby changes everything, Noah. Look at how much it changed Chase and Mia-- and they're married. It still had a major impact on their relationship and they were a lot further along in their relationship when she got pregnant than we are."

"So what? Do you want to get married? Have a baby? What is it that's missing that would make you feel like our relationship is where you want it to be?"

"Time." Her eyes pierced mine as the word hung in the air between us.

"Jade, I know that having the baby come soon is scary. I'm not gonna lie, I'm freaking the fuck out about it. But just because I'm having a baby doesn't mean that I can't have you too. I can love you and be with you while also being a dad to a baby. Every relationship has its ups and downs, Jade, but if we give up every time things get a little hard there would never be a lasting relationship. People would just bounce from one relationship to another, never planting any actual roots to build something lasting with someone else."

I watched as her chest fell and she lowered her eyes. Suddenly I knew what it was really about.

"Jade, is all of this about us and me having a baby? Or is it about your childhood and watching your mom run from every relationship she ever had before things got too complicated?"

She lowered her head into her hands and I watched her body shake as she cried. I slid over as close as I could to the middle console and reached over and grabbed her, pulling her into me as I tried to comfort her.

"You don't have any idea of what my childhood was like or what relationships I've been in." Her breath was ragged from crying but her words were sharp with anger.

"I know what you've told me, I can't be faulted for not knowing more if you don't open up to talk to me," I spoke softly and gently to avoid sounding like a total asshole. I knew from the few times that we had talked about her childhood that her mother had constantly bounced from relationship to relationship, getting what she could from the guy before moving on when they wanted a commitment. Jade had always said that's why she is as wild and free-spirited as she is now, she never learned how to actually settle down and stick with something or someone. I felt her pull away from me as she sat back against her seat and wiped her face with both hands.

"Well we're talking now and I'm telling you that I don't think this is going to work. We should cut our losses and move on."

"Is that what you want?" My stomach churned as I waited for her answer, praying that she would come to her senses.

"Yes."

I blew out a deep breath as I turned forward in my seat and started the truck. I glanced in the rearview mirror out of habit, knowing that no one ever came down this road that dead-ended at the abandoned farm. As I was about to pull forward I caught a glimpse of a car parked off in the distance behind us that I hadn't seen when we first pulled up. It was too dark to see it clearly, let alone confirm who was in the car. Frustrated enough with how the night had ended I sped off in the opposite direction, not giving a fuck about who was in the car.

Nineteen
Jade

Can I get you anything else?" I slid the receipt onto the table next to the full glasses of water as the elderly couple shook their head no and continued with their meal. It was my second day working at SlowMo's and I was slowly starting to adjust to waitressing again. I reached up and adjusted my ponytail as I stood behind the register waiting for another table to come in and keep me occupied. It was slow for a Friday but then I found that it was slow pretty much every day in Haven Brook compared to the fast-paced environment of the night clubs I worked at when I lived in Boston.

It had been two days since I saw Noah after he dropped me off at my apartment and didn't look back. I saw the hurt in his eyes when I told him that I wanted to end things between us. I knew that it would hurt him but I didn't expect that it would kill me. All night I kept trying to convince myself that it was the right thing to do. If you love someone, let them go. I guess I just thought that he would put up more of a fight. When he didn't, my heart broke even harder and I started to question whether he was actually as invested in the relationship as I was.

The bell chimed as the front door swung open, a huge bouquet of red roses blocking the face of the man delivering them as he made his way to the counter. A sudden feeling of excitement burst through me when I thought they might be from Noah and there might still be a chance to save the relationship that I swore I didn't want.

"Can I help you?" I asked as I tilted my head to the side to see his face behind the flowers.
"Um yeah, I have a delivery for..... oh golly, the name was right here. Hold on a minute." He tried to hold the massive bouquet in one hand as he fumbled with a clipboard with the other. I reached over and grabbed the vase from him, sitting it on the counter beside him. He smiled up at me as he used both hands to hold the clipboard, scrolling down the page with his finger until finding the name he was looking for.

"Arlene. Arlene Bennett." He smiled and raised his eyebrows as he waited for me to confirm who she was. I let out a disappointed sigh as I leaned back and called for Arlene. A few minutes later she came up to the front, a hand covering her mouth when she saw the display of roses on the counter. I signed for the flowers and watched as he waved and walked out the door.

"Oh my goodness, these are just beautiful." She looked up at me, beaming, as she lightly ran her hand across the fragrant flowers.

"They are." I smiled and watched as she found the card tucked inside a heap of baby's breath. She pulled it out and a beautiful smile spread across her face as she read it, clutching it to her chest and looking up at me when she was done.

"You know, Joe has never missed a single Valentine's Day since we've been together. Every year there's a different flower that he chooses for the bouquet. It's been a while since he's done roses, but this year is our 25th anniversary and roses were the very first flower he ever gave me."

I loved hearing love stories that had happy endings and had learned a lot about Arlene and Joe's love story through Mia as she spent time getting to know the father she never knew about until a few years ago. I had totally spaced that it was Valentine's Day and the thought of it sunk me even further into depression. Until now I just knew that it was Friday and that Noah was going with Cindy to another doctor's appointment after the ultrasound. I wanted to follow up with Noah to see how everything went but I no longer had a right to know. Everything felt weird and different, and I had no one to talk to about it. Even though Mia was my best friend, I didn't feel right talking to her about Noah when he had been her best friend since they were little.

I patted Arlene's shoulder and smiled as I walked off to check on the rest of the tables, leaving her to enjoy the roses. I still had four hours left in my shift which felt like it was going to drag on forever until I got to go home and wallow in self-pity.

It was an hour until my shift was over when I heard the door chime and smiled when I looked up to see Chase, Mia, and Rylee come in. I nodded toward a booth in the back as I finished clearing the plates from a table that just left.

"Hey guys! What's my favorite little family doing here on Valentine's Day?" I smiled as I slid into the booth next to Mia, stealing Rylee as she sat her on the table in front of her.

"We thought it would be a nice treat to come for some peach cobbler," Mia said as she slid further into the booth, giving me more room to sit and play with the baby.

"We do have the best," I cooed as the baby looked up at me and smiled. "How many do you guys want?" I asked without looking at them.

"Just one is fine, we're sharing so it will be more romantic." Chase winked at Mia, her eyes rolling as he said it. I chuckled as I caught the interaction out of the corner of my eye.

"We definitely want two." She looked playfully at him before turning back to him. "He's crazy if he thinks he's getting a piece of my cobbler."

I glanced up to see Chase's expression change at the innocent innuendo his wife offered without noticing.

"Mmm baby, I've already had your cobbler but that doesn't stop me from wanting more." He wiggled his eyebrows suggestively at her as he leaned back and stretched his arm across the top of the booth.

"You're lucky you're cute." She playfully tossed an empty straw wrapper at him, hitting him in the forehead.

"I'm more than cute. I'm sexy."

"Alright, that's enough of the lovefest." I passed the baby back to Mia as I slid out of the booth and smoothed down my apron. "I'll go put in the order for two cobblers, you guys try to keep your hands to yourself while I'm gone."

I heard them laugh as I walked away, shaking my head. It was cute to see people flirting and in love but in my current situation, I wanted nothing to do with it. I glanced at the clock on the wall and saw that it was almost time for Cindy's appointment. Part of me wished that I could ask Chase and Mia about it to see how Noah was feeling about going to it but I knew that I couldn't. I needed to focus on getting through my shift then I could go home and work out until I burned off some of this anxiety and tension that seemed to linger around me.

Twenty
Noah

My foot tapped impatiently as I sat in the padded worn-out leather chair next to Cindy as we waited for the ultrasound tech to come in. I saw Cindy's eyes glare in my direction as she blew out an irritated breath.

"If you don't want to be here then you shouldn't have come." She turned her head to look at me.

"I didn't say I didn't want to be here. I'm here, aren't I?"

"Well, you could be a little more enthusiastic about it instead of sitting there tapping a hole into the ground with your foot."

I rolled my eyes and looked in the opposite direction as I continued tapping.

"Is there somewhere else you need to be instead?" She asked with an obvious jealously in her voice.

"Like I said, I'm here with you, aren't I? You don't need to worry about anything else." I leaned back against the seat and rested my hands on the cold metal armrests. Her mouth opened to say something else as the door opened and an older man with thinning gray hair walked into the room and looked at us. Her mouth closed and for once I was thankful for the interruption.

"Hello, I'm Doctor Edison. I'll be doing the ultrasound today since there have been some questions about the due date and size of the fetus." He extended a hand which I shook before leaning back into my seat.

I watched as he guided her on lifting her shirt before squirting the cold gel on her stomach. A few seconds later the baby appeared on the screen and I felt that same pull in my chest as the first time I saw it. He moved the wand around her stomach and stopped every few seconds to type something into the computer behind him. His brows pulled together as he pushed his bifocals back up his nose and leaned closer to the monitor, squinting at something.

I sat quietly, waiting for him to give us an update on the baby while Cindy looked more anxious than usual. Her hands were clenched tight around the metal bed frame as he removed the wand from her stomach and sat it in the holder next to the computer.

"Alright folks, it looks like the baby has grown some since the last ultrasound, which is great news."

"Perfect. Then everything is on track with my original due date," Cindy blurted out, talking over him before he could continue. His eyes narrowed at her as he shook his head and dismissed her.

"Not exactly. While the baby did grow, the baby is still measuring a full month behind."

"That's not possible, I know when I got pregnant. Maybe the baby is just naturally small?" Her tone was aggressive as she sat up straight in the bed and stared at the doctor.

"Some babies are smaller than others, but that's not what we're seeing here."

"Just give it to me straight doctor," I said as I made eye contact with him and ignored Cindy as she turned her glare to me. "What does it mean?"

"It means that there is a very healthy baby that is measuring on track for six months, not seven. I am very confident that the original conception date and due date are incorrect given the measurements and development of the baby that I saw today compared to the scan that was done two weeks ago."

"So that means," my voice trailed off as he gave me a knowing look.

"That means that this baby was not conceived in July. I would say it was conceived closer to the end of August or beginning of September."

I blew out a breath of relief as I ran a hand down my face, trying to process what all of this meant. I could feel the heat radiating from Cindy as she looked furiously at the doctor. I needed absolute confirmation that this baby wasn't mine but now was not the time to demand a paternity test from her unless I wanted to have some sort of medical device lodged up my ass.

"I know there's been some back and forth and discrepancies so I'm curious as to why this wasn't found on an earlier ultrasound?" I was playing the game the best way I knew how.

"I actually tried to pull copies of the original ultrasounds but we don't seem to have any in the system." He turned to look directly at Cindy. "Where were the other ones done? I can reach out to them to request copies of the original scan that was used to date the pregnancy."

The color drained from her face as her jaw dropped and for once, she was speechless.

"I um, I did them back home, before I moved here. I'll call and ask them for a copy."

"Just tell me the name of the clinic and I can request them since you're now under our care." He clicked his pen and held it over the paper on top of her chart, waiting for her to give him the information.

"I don't remember. I'll have to look for it when I get home," she replied through gritted teeth.

"Well, once we have those it will be easier to try to figure out what happened and why they would have given you a due date that doesn't match where the fetus is now in development." He shrugged and turned to face us on the swivel stool he was sitting on.

"Can you get a better idea based on her fundamental height?" I swallowed hard, praying that I remembered what Mia had told me about the measurements they could do that would confirm how far along she was. I watched as he stifled a laugh and turned to cough to cover it up.

"We can check the fundal height, but it's not 100% accurate either. It just gives us an idea of how big the uterus is and should more or less match to how many weeks pregnant a woman is."

I wanted to smack myself in the head for getting the name wrong and sounding like an idiot. I glanced at Cindy as she squirmed on the bed nervously. Something felt wrong and I needed to know what she was keeping from me. The doctor stood up and stood next to Cindy as he fumbled around in his pocket before pulling out a wound up tape measure and raising his eyebrows in question. She nodded and looked away as he felt around the top of her stomach with his fingers until he found what he was looking for and placed the end of the tape measure under his finger. I looked away to give her privacy as he pulled it lower and looked at the measurement.

"26 centimeters." He looked between us before turning around to write the information on the paper he had been using for the other notes.

I swallowed hard as my fists clenched. I turned to glare at her, panic on her face as she read my reaction. Tears started rolling down her face as she watched me get up and walk out of the room, slamming the door behind me.

Twenty One
Noah

I heard footsteps running behind me as I stalked off toward my truck, the snow starting to stick to the ground as it fell.

"Noah, wait!"

I gritted my teeth, my jaw tight, as I turned around and stared at Cindy. Her face was red and splotchy as she bent over to catch her breath from running after me.

"You have some fucking nerve." I shook my head at her, looking away to keep from saying anything more.

"Please, Noah, let me explain!" She reached for my arm, gasping when I jerked it away from her.

"Fine. Explain." I crossed my arms and leaned against the truck.

"It's complicated, I don't know why these doctors keep getting everything wrong. I swear, the doctors back home told me that I got pregnant in July, after I had been down here. These doctors must have outdated equipment or something?" Her voice rose an octave as her eyes danced wildly as she rambled on. "This baby is yours, Noah. I'm not that kind of girl who just sleeps around, you have to believe me." She put a hand on her stomach and rubbed it.

"Not that kind of girl? You were sucking my dick in the first five minutes after we met. You pulled me into the bathroom at the bar. You hiked up your skirt as you bent over and asked me to fuck you. So what kind of girl should I think you are?" I tilted my head and watched as her face turned red from embarrassment.

"I felt something with you Noah. And I know it's crazy to say you believe in love at first sight, but I do. I really, really do. You weren't just some random guy that I saw in the bar." She looked up at me with fresh tears in her eyes. "I knew you were the one, that's why I gave myself so freely to you."

I shook my head and pushed off the truck I had been leaning against when she startled rambling.

"I want a paternity test. Now. Before the baby is born." I looked at her sternly so she knew that I wasn't joking.

"That's crazy! This baby is yours Noah, we don't need a test to prove it."

"Everything in that appointment today says otherwise. You want me to go on believing that this baby is mine? Get the test."

"It would be stupid to do the test while I'm still pregnant. It could hurt the baby. Why would you want to hurt your baby?" Her eyes watched me cautiously as she wrapped her arms protectively around her waist.

"People get them all the time and the baby is fine. Either get the test on your own, or I'll get a court order. I want the results by next week." I glared at her as I swung my door open and climbed in, slamming it shut as she stared at me with her mouth open. I sped off, anger flowing through me as I headed off to deal with the next problem on my list.

The snow was coming down even harder by the time I pulled into the parking lot of Jade's apartment, a sure sign that this storm was going to be worse than they had predicted. I put the truck in park and made my way up the stairs, hoping she was actually home. I didn't see her car in the parking lot but that didn't mean she wasn't parked in the back lot.

I rang the doorbell and shoved my hands down into my pockets, shivering against the cold. A few minutes later I was getting ready to ring the doorbell again when the door opened and a shirtless man covered in tattoos opened the door. I blinked several times as I tried to figure out why a half-naked man was answering her door, let alone a guy I grew up with and couldn't stand.

"What's up, Noah?" He raised his arms above his head and held on to the door frame showing off a washboard stomach as he stretched.

"Is Jade here?" I asked annoyed.

He smugly looked over his shoulder toward the bedroom and turned back to look at me with the smug look still on his face.

"She's um, busy." He raised his eyebrows.

I was already feeling the anger from my encounter with Cindy so this was just adding fuel to the fire. I had known Chaz since elementary school and we spent most of our adolescence in chest matches over girls. For once, I wasn't in the mood to engage him.

"Fine, tell her I stopped by." I turned and walked off as I heard him chuckle before closing the door. This was not the romantic Valentine's Day I had planned.

Twenty Two
Jade

"Were you just talking to someone?" I asked Chaz as I walked into the living room, drying my hair with a towel. Work had been a rather slow day but I still couldn't wait to get home and wash the smell of greasy food off of me. The storm had hit early which left me thankful that I got home when I did. I glanced out the window and saw the snow coming down harder than it was before I jumped in the shower.

"Yeah, Noah came by looking for you." His tone was even as he watched for my reaction. My eyes darted up to his, my reaction apparent as he read the anger on my face.

"Sorry, you were in the shower. And... I kinda wanted him to feel a little jealous." He shrugged his shoulders as he walked to the fridge and pulled out a cold beer.

"That wasn't your call and I don't need you playing high school games, trying to make him jealous." I grabbed my cell phone off the kitchen counter and walked off to my room, closing the door behind me.

I wanted to talk to Noah, to see how things went with the appointment today but I felt so nervous about asking him. I didn't know where we stood, whether we were even friends still at this point. I held my phone in my hand, looking down at his name as my finger danced in circles, debating whether to push send or not. I climbed on my bed and curled up against a pillow as I chewed my nail while waiting for him to answer. What if he got the wrong idea when Chaz answered the door? Did he think I was already seeing someone else? Why had he shown up here unexpected anyways? The noise in my head grew louder as the ringing continued.

A few seconds later his voicemail picked up and I blew out the breath I had been holding. I sat my phone down beside me and shook my head in frustration for being so naive to think that he would actually want to talk to me after I broke up with him and then him finding a half-naked man in my apartment. I scooted down on the bed and stared up at the ceiling, contemplating my life decisions this week when I felt my phone vibrate against my butt. Excitement coursed through me when I picked it up and saw Noah's name.

"Hey," I practically whispered, smacking myself in the head for being so weird about it.

"Hey. I saw a missed call from you."

My stomach clenched as I heard how short he was with me, no warmth or flirting like usual.

"Yeah, Chaz told me you stopped by so I was calling to see what you had come by for."

Please say me... my brain pleaded as I waited, knowing full well that wasn't what he had come by for.

"Oh good, I'm glad your new boyfriend passed along the message."

I smirked when I heard the jealousy dripping through his voice.

"Yeah, he did. So what's up Noah? Why were you here?"

Now I could have played this the mature way and just been straight with Noah, letting him know that Chaz was far from being my boyfriend. He was only in my apartment because I quickly realized that I wasn't going to make nearly enough at SlowMo's to afford this apartment on my own. I had no choice but to find a roommate, and that roommate happened to be eating lunch at SlowMo's while I was working. I honestly didn't care who it was as long as they could come up with $400 by the first every month.

Part of me was still mad about everything that had happened this week and it actually felt good to hear Noah sounding jealous of another man given how jealous I had recently become of the girl he was having a baby with.

"I thought we could talk." He sighed and I could hear the phone shift against the stubble I pictured on his face.

"What did you want to talk about?"

"Does it even matter? We haven't been broken up a week and you already have another man answering your door half-naked Jade." There was a heavy mix of anger laced with jealousy and sarcasm in his voice that drove right to my core. Instantly I was seeing red.

"Really? You have the nerve to judge me for having another man in my apartment DAYS after we broke up when you had your dick in another woman HOURS after we broke up the first time?" My voice rose with my anger as I sat up and hung my legs over the side of the bed.

"Maybe this was a mistake," he bit out.

"Yeah, maybe it was." I slid my finger across the screen, hanging up before I tossed the phone down next to me as the fury raged through me. Who the hell did he think he was? The pot or the kettle? A few seconds later I felt my phone vibrate on the bed and without looking, I picked it up and answered.

"What?!" My chest rose and fell heavily as my feet tapped against the beige carpet beneath my feet.

"Woah. Did I catch you at a bad time?" Mia's voice came through the line making me regret not looking to see who was calling before I answered.

"I'm so sorry, Mia." I let out a heavy sigh and closed my eyes.

"Everything okay?"

"Yeah, I just got off the phone with Noah."

"So did he tell you?" Her voice trailed off quietly.

"Tell me what?" I didn't want to get into the details with Mia, to tell her that we were both acting so incredibly immature that we didn't get around to actually talking.

"The baby isn't his."

My heart dropped. I closed my eyes and brought my hand to my mouth as I forced myself to process what Mia had said.
"What? How does he know?"

"The ultrasound confirmed that the baby is still measuring around six months, not seven. Noah asked the doctor to check the measurement of her uterus and it agreed with the ultrasound. He said that Cindy started freaking out and begged him to believe her that the baby was his. He told her he wanted a paternity test."

"Oh my god. That's so crazy." My words were soft as I felt all of the anger I had felt minutes ago quickly disappear as I listened to Mia.

"Is she going to do the test?"

"He said that she said no, she didn't want to do it now and risk hurting the baby. But you know Noah, once his mind is set on something he doesn't give up. He's already been talking with a lawyer to get a court order for the test as soon as the baby is born."

"Will he have to do that?" I didn't know anything about family court or how to prove paternity but I knew that Noah was going to make sure he was fully prepared for whatever came his way.

"Honestly, I don't know. Everything is kind of in the air right now, we haven't heard anything from him since he called Chase earlier."

"Wow, I still can't believe it. So what's going to happen now with him and Cindy?"

"I don't know." She let out a heavy sigh at the same time I did. "Noah will probably do what Noah does best and continue to be the best dad he can be until it's been proven that it's not his baby. I don't think he could live with himself if he walked away and didn't do the right thing, and then some crazy bizarre turn of events happens and he finds out he actually is the dad. That would just kill him if he thought that even for one second, he didn't do his absolute best for his child."

I smiled knowing that what Mia had said was true. I leaned back against the pillow while we talked for a little bit, finally letting go of some of the anger and tension that had been building. The conversation had shifted to Rylee which was a nice distraction. Things felt easier when I had walked away from Noah knowing that he was having a baby with Cindy and needed to give the baby his full attention. But if what Mia said was true, that meant that things were different now. Noah might not be having a child at all. Cindy may not be a part of his life like she had planned. So what did this mean for us? Was there hope that we could actually be together without any obstacles getting in the way?

Twenty Three
Noah

I leaned back against the headboard and watched as the ring I bought for Jade spun in circles around my pinky, reminiscent of my life at the moment. How had things gone from good to absolute shit in less than a week? It was like someone took the threads that were holding everything together and unraveled them until there was nothing left.

My phone vibrated across the top of my nightstand, catching my eye as it slid around the wooden surface. I didn't have the energy to deal with whoever was calling this late and even if it was an emergency, there had to be someone more equipped than me to deal with it.

The ring continued to spin around my finger when my phone started to vibrate again. Annoyed I reached over and sat the ring on the nightstand as I picked up the phone. Either whoever was calling came to their senses and hung up before I could answer, or I had been so lost in thought that I hadn't paid attention to when it started ringing. Or maybe it was because it hadn't stopped ringing so there was no break for me to process. The screen showed eight missed calls, all back to back in the last two minutes.

I opened the missed call log and found Cindy's name listed for each call. It was after midnight which made me worry that something might be wrong with the baby. She didn't know anyone in town so it would make sense that I was the one she would call for help. I clicked on the last missed call and was getting ready to hit send to call her back when my phone started vibrating in my hand with another call from Cindy.

"What's up, Cindy. Is everything okay?" I climbed out of bed and stuffed my wallet back into my pocket in case I needed to leave.

"Everything's fine, why do you ask?" Her voice sounded strangely calm for someone who had been repeatedly calling me in the middle of the night until I picked up.

"Because you called like eight times. Back to back. In the middle of the night." I yawned as I sat back down on the bed, relieved that there was no need for me to go anywhere.

"I needed to talk to you, I don't like how we left things earlier."

"So you thought calling me nonstop this late was the way to get me to talk to you?"

"Well, I figured it was a good time since you were still up. And given the noise coming from Jade's apartment with her new roommate, I figured maybe you needed a friend to talk to."

"How did you know I was still up? And what noise are you talking about?" I felt my jaw set as I waited for her to confirm what I already knew. Jade was already sleeping with someone else.

"The lights were still on, silly." She laughed playfully before continuing like we were best friends. "You know, those kinds of noises. The noises that got us in the situation we're in."

I rolled my neck until I heard the familiar pop as I tried to get some relief from the mounting tension.

"I'm not in the mood to hear about Jade and honestly, I'm too tired to get into anything between us. So unless there's some sort of emergency, I'm gonna go and ask that you don't call me again. I'll reach out to you when I'm ready to talk." I paused as I waited for her to protest, surprised when she didn't. "And Cindy?"

"Yeah?" There was hope in her tone as I said her name.

"Stop driving by my house. People in this neighborhood don't take well to people who don't belong here. I wouldn't want anything bad to happen to you." I let the threat of my words linger in the air, a smug smile forming across my face as I heard the faint gasp on the other end before I hung up.

I felt an uneasiness as I sat my phone down, unsure of what I needed to do next. While sleep was the logical thing to do, I knew my mind was too busy to actually let it happen. I stripped off my clothes and took a hot shower, hoping the water would wash away everything that was wrong and give me the clean slate I needed. There wasn't much that I actually wanted to fix, and the only thing that I did want to fix was the one thing I had no control over.

I scrubbed my face and body vigorously as I focused on what I wanted, and more importantly, what I needed. Things with Cindy didn't need my attention right now. Whether she was lying about the baby being mine or not was irrelevant. I had already talked to the lawyer that my family had known since I was in diapers and he had walked me through the steps I would need to take to request the paternity test. Right now it was a waiting game, there was no reason to force her to get the test when there was a risk to the baby. Once the baby was born then I could request the paternity test through family court and go from there.

I had spent hours trying to process how I felt about the baby not being mine and part of me was fucking relieved that I wasn't having a baby with Cindy but the other part of me wasn't ready to fully accept it and cut ties with her yet. What if the reports were wrong and it really was my child? The thought of not being there from the very start for my own child gnawed away at me faster than a woodchuck with a fresh pile of wood.

Even if the baby was mine, that didn't mean that Cindy and I had to be together. I strongly believed that we could raise the child together and figure out how to co-parent. What I couldn't wrap my head around was Jade. I had tried talking to Mia about what happened with Jade after we left their house and everything fell apart but she didn't know what had happened either. She didn't divulge the details of what they had talked about, but she was just as surprised as I was when Jade called it off and broke up with me.

The water started to get cold as I turned the handle, feeling the cold air of the room surround me as soon as I stepped out of the shower. The storm had already been worse than they predicted and at this rate was expected to drop another twelve inches by the morning. While I was used to heavy snowstorms growing up in Colorado, we hadn't seen one this strong in almost a decade. I shivered as I quickly dried off and slid into the warmth of thick pajama pants before pulling a hoodie over my head.

I felt calmer after taking a thirty-minute shower even though my mind was no less chaotic than it was before. The only difference was now I knew what I needed to do to win Jade back and I wasn't going to waste any time with sleeping.

The morning came faster than expected as I lost track of time working through every last detail of my master plan. My body felt heavy from the lack of sleep so I padded across the cold wood floor and started a pot of coffee, making sure to brew it stronger than usual. I walked back over to the couch and sat down, looking at the papers spread across the coffee table with the notes I had been making. My phone vibrated and I blew out a breath as I rolled my eyes and picked it, silently cursing that it better not be Cindy.

Jade: I think we need to talk. Can I come over?

Relief rushed over me as my fingers began moving quickly, asking her to give me thirty minutes before she came over. I was anxious to see her and find out what the fuck Chaz was doing in her apartment but I needed to hide what I was working on first.

The coffee had already finished brewing when I heard the doorbell ring, sitting an extra cup on the counter as I ran over to answer the door.

"Hey," I said as I opened the door and smiled, stepping to the side so she could come in and get out of the cold. She smiled back as she wiped her feet repeatedly on the welcome mat, getting rid of any excess snow that had stuck to her boots from outside. I watched as she pulled her gloves off before reaching up and pulling her beanie off, a wave of blonde hair falling down her back. It had only been a few days since I had seen her but I forgot just how breathtakingly beautiful she was.

There was a brown paper bag tucked up under her arm, a heavenly aroma filling the room which forced my stomach to grumble in response. I eyed the bag cautiously, knowing what was inside. She looked up and caught my eye, a smug smirk crossing her face as she tucked the bag tighter against her body as she turned away. She looked over her shoulder at me playfully as she walked in and sat on the couch, my eyebrow arched as I followed her.

"You better not be showing up to my house this early in the morning just to tease me with things I can't have," I warned.

She let out an exaggerated sigh as she fell back against the pillows on the couch and held the bag on her lap. There was the fun, flirty side of Jade that I had fallen in love with and had been missing ever since the stuff with Cindy started to interfere.
"I'll tell you what, you share some of your coffee, and I'll share some of my burrito." She patted the bag as she pulled her bottom lip between her teeth and slowly let it go.

"You can have the whole damn pot," I ran the pad of my thumb over her lip, freeing it from her teeth as I walked over to the counter, "Just stop biting your lip."

I heard a soft giggle behind me as I shook my head and poured two cups of coffee. When I turned around to walk back, Jade had sat the burritos on the coffee table and was staring at something in the middle of the table, a somber and serious look on her face.

"What's this?" She reached forward and picked up the engagement ring, holding it between her fingers as she studied me. I closed my eyes and shook my head, frustrated that I hadn't remembered to put the ring away with everything else.

"You weren't supposed to see that." I sat her cup on the coffee table in front of her and sunk down on the couch, taking a sip as I felt the scalding hot liquid burn its way down my throat. The pain was worth it to avoid having this conversation.

"You didn't answer my question." Her voice was quiet but her tone direct. She turned slightly to look at me, still holding the ring in the air.

I sat my cup down on the table in front of me and scrubbed a hand down my face, trying to think of how to tell Jade that I was planning to propose to her before she broke up with me. Everything had changed and shifted which left me feeling uncertain of whether it was even worth talking about right now. There were so many other things we still needed to discuss. Things like Chaz. In her apartment.

"It's a ring." I turned and looked her in the eye, challenging her. She licked her lips the way she does every time she gets nervous, much to my satisfaction. At least I wasn't the only one squirming in my seat.

"I can see that. Why do you have an engagement ring?"

"Because Jade, I was planning to ask you to marry me. To start a life with me. To show you that no matter what was happening with Cindy and the baby, you still came first." I looked away when I saw her flinch from the change in my tone.

She stayed quiet as she looked at the ring and sighed, leaning forward to sit it down on the table where she had found it.

"I'm sorry Noah, maybe I shouldn't have come here." She ran the palms of her hands down her jeans and stood up.

"You came here for a reason, Jade, let's just talk and get everything out in the open. If you still don't want to be with me, that's fine, but I at least deserve to know what the fuck actually happened."

"I told you what happened Noah, I told you that I was leaving so you could be with your child. It wasn't that I had stopped loving you. I loved you so much that I was willing to walk away from you so you could be the father you wanted to be without having someone complicate it for you, you selfish prick." She plopped back down on the couch and glared at me before picking up her burrito from the table and nodding at mine. "Eat your damn burrito before it gets cold."

I let out a chuckle, thankful that she hadn't decided to walk away, again. We ate in silence while taking sips of coffee to wash it all down until there was nothing left to fill the awkward silence between us once we were finished. She leaned back against the couch and closed her eyes.

"Why was Chaz in your apartment?"

I watched as her lips pursed in a thin line as she thought about how to answer me. I braced myself for the blow that was coming as my fists clenched at my sides.

"He's my new roommate." She turned to look at me, studying my face as confusion spread across it.

"He's what?"

"My roommate."

"Why do you need a roommate?"

"I took quite a pay cut from what I was making at the bank, I didn't have a choice."

I leaned forward, resting my elbows on my knees, and looked at her.

"You could have come to me, I would have found a way to help you."

"Seriously? You're going to help me with paying my rent each month after we break up? You're a good guy, Noah, but no one is that nice."

"Try me."

"It's just ridiculous to even think that! You have your own bills to pay and possibly a baby on the way, you can't possibly afford to pay $400 a month towards rent for someone that you're not even dating."

"Jade, I would pay your whole fucking rent if it meant you didn't have him as your roommate," I gritted through my teeth, the tension in my body coming back.

"Why? What's your problem with him?"

"I don't trust him, Jade, and I don't think you should either."

"Are you that jealous?" She raised her eyebrows as if this was the most insane thing she had ever heard.

"Abso-fucking-lutely I'm jealous, why wouldn't I be?" I studied her as she took in my words. "But aside from that, I wouldn't trust him with anyone. Not just because it's you. Did you even question him or interview him before you asked him to move in with you?" My heart was pounding in my ears the more my anger escalated at the thought of Chaz living with her. Her chest fell and I watched as she looked away and chewed on her fingernail.

"Jade, did you find out anything about him before he moved in with you? Or did you just take the first person that responded to your ad?"

"I um, I didn't run an ad." She slowly looked at me, still chewing her fingernail.

"So you just approached a random stranger and asked him to live with you?" I could hear the stern tone in my voice as her eyes looked panicked.

"I didn't go seeking anyone out, Noah. It wasn't like that. He was eating lunch, I was his waitress, he was complaining about needing to find a new place to live and I muttered something about needing to find a roommate then we just started talking and found a solution to our problems." She gave me a pointed look.

"Whose idea was it for him to move in?"

I watched as she looked away, avoiding eye contact with me. "Jade..."

She blew out a long, steady breath before turning her attention back to me.

"His."

I dropped my head into my hands and shook my head.

"What's the big deal, Noah? What has he done that's so bad that I should know about?"

"He's not a good person Jade, I grew up watching him manipulate people and take advantage of women the moment his family moved here from Eastern Point. And honestly, nothing good comes from that town. His family has swindled people out of money, forced their way into partnerships that should never have been formed, and everything they do is shady."

"Okay, I get it. I shouldn't have let him move in with me, I should have asked around about him before making a decision. But what am I supposed to do now? He's already paid this month's rent and I really need that money."

"The offer to move in with me is still on the table."

"You're relentless." She shook her head as she struggled to keep the smile off of her face when she saw mine.

"Yeah, but deep down you still think I'm adorable."

"Maybe." Her lips twisted up into a smile as I reached over and rested my hand next to hers.

"Maybe is all I need," I growled as I pulled her over to me, enjoying the sound of her giggle as I tickled her sides. There was still a lot we needed to work out but for now, I wanted to just live in the moment, and that moment was filled with beautiful laughter.

Twenty Four
Jade

I had spent Saturday morning at Noah's, trying to work things out between us but when I left that afternoon I still felt like I didn't know where we stood with each other. We were friendly yet flirty. Friends but not lovers. Definitely not enemies. There didn't seem to be a clear definition of what we were and I hated it. I wanted to be able to move forward but I didn't know which direction I was supposed to go.

The evening was quiet, Chaz was already gone when I had gotten back from Noah's earlier. There was nothing from him to indicate when he was planning to be back, and I felt stupid for feeling like I needed him to check in with me. He was a roommate, not a prisoner.

I was relieved to have some time to myself in the apartment but Noah's warning about Chaz kept ringing through my head, forcing me to doubt whether I made a good choice with letting him move in. Either way, it was too late now, I had already agreed to it and he had moved in. I could technically ask him to leave, give him a month to find a new place, but I also desperately needed his half of the rent.

The storm outside had finally started to calm after it dumped another six inches of snow on the few feet that had been accumulating since yesterday afternoon. Mia and I were supposed to have dinner together but that had been canceled so neither of us would have to go out in the cold. I felt restless as I paced the kitchen, debating on whether to cook or order food in. While cooking would distract me more, I worried I would be too distracted and end up burning it. I gave up, ordered a pizza, and poured a glass of wine while I watched the light snow as it fell outside while I waited.

Forty minutes later my doorbell rang, the savory aroma of pizza filling my apartment as I opened the door. I tipped the kid double since he had to come out in the bad weather to deliver and sat the pizza on the counter after he left. I took a deep breath as I opened the lid, my mouth watering in anticipation. I reached in, pulled out a slice and took a bite, lifting the trail of cheese that had fallen against my chin into my mouth when I heard the doorbell again.

I sat down the slice and wiped my face with a napkin as I walked over to the door, expecting it to be the delivery guy who had forgotten something. My stomach dropped when Cindy greeted me from the other side, I wasn't in the mood to deal with her tonight.

"Hey, Cindy. What's up?"

"I really hate to ask, but I was wondering if you could help me move something I'm trying to get the nursery set up before the baby gets here, but I can't lift anything heavy and I really don't know who else to ask since Noah isn't talking to me."

I saw the look in her eyes when she mentioned his name, the sadness that lingered when she acknowledged that he wasn't talking to her. I didn't want to help her but deep down inside I knew that it was the right thing to do. Aside from the handful of reasons that I didn't like her, I wasn't the type of person that would deny someone help when they needed it.

"Sure. Let me grab my phone and keys, then I'll be right there."

"It shouldn't take more than a second," her voice pleaded with mine and I felt thankful that she didn't seem to want me in her apartment any longer than I wanted to be there.

"Okay," I sighed, "Let's go."

I closed the door to my apartment behind me as I followed her outside and into her apartment. I had only seen inside for a brief second when she first moved in but now that I was inside and looking around, a feeling of dread rushed over me as I took in the room around me and heard the click as the door shut behind us. I wanted to turn around and look at Cindy, to see where she was, but my eyes were glued to the wall that we shared where picture frames were hung neatly around a black metal Family sign. The sound of the lock clicking into place followed by the slide of the deadbolt forced my attention away from the photos and over to Cindy.

"Do you like them?" she asked as she walked over and stood next to me, rubbing her stomach as she admired the collage on the wall. Each frame had a picture of Noah and I in it, however all of my pictures had been replaced with pictures of Cindy. The majority of the pictures were from Chase and Mia's wedding, however, a few were recent and I recognized them immediately. Noah and I at Liam's birthday party. Noah and I at Chase and Mia's for dinner. Noah holding Rylee. Noah at work.

"They're nice…" My voice trailed off as I struggled with what to say.

"I wanted to make sure that the baby had plenty of pictures on the wall to look at as they grow up, so they can see how happy mommy and daddy have always been." Her smile spread clear across her face as she beamed at the wall. I licked my lips nervously and tucked a stray piece of hair back behind my ear. I wanted desperately to get out of there.

"So, what did you need help moving?" I turned to face her, hoping to bring her back to the task at hand so I could be done and get back to the comfort of my own apartment while I tried to forget this was on the other side.

"I would say your body, but that would just sound crazy!" She let out a hysterical laugh as she threw her head back and snorted. I watched, my eyes wide with horror, as she continued.

"Well, if you don't need my help then I guess I can just let myself out." I forced a smile and kept my voice light, trying not to draw any attention to myself as I slowly started walking to the door.

"Yeah, I'm afraid it's not that easy, Jade." Her laughter stopped as she gave me a pointed look.

"What's not?"

"You leaving. I simply can't let you do that."

"Why not?"

"Because, if I let you go, you'll just keep getting in the way." She stepped closer to me. "And I'm sick and tired of you being in my way."

"Cindy, I'm not trying to be in your way. I just want to leave and go back to my apartment. I have no reason to stay here when it obviously upsets you so much." I tried to take another step towards the door, forcing my brain to flip the order of the apartment so I could guide myself to maneuver backward as I kept her focused on my words. "You don't get it. As long as you're around, Noah isn't going to stop chasing you. And if he's always chasing you, then he's not going to be around for me and this baby."

"Noah and I broke up, Cindy. I'm not keeping him from you."

She watched me through narrowed eyes as I took the tiniest of steps backward, trying to get to the door without drawing too much attention.

"Then why were you at his house this morning?" she spat out angrily.

How did she know I was at his house? Had she been watching me? Or had she been watching both of us?

"I went by to give him back the key to his house that he had given me."

"The key that SHOULD HAVE BEEN MINE." She took a few steps closer, closing the distance between us faster than I had anticipated which meant the window I had for getting out the door without her catching me was getting narrower by the second.

"Do you get it now, Jade? He's willing to give you everything you want, and yet you still don't want to be with him. You don't love him. You don't want to be with him. But I do, and I can't because as long as you're around he will continue to keep trying to win you over. So now I'm stuck making sure that never happens."

"What exactly do you plan to do?" I rolled my eyes for even asking the question, but she had already closed the space between us, and I was out of ideas for how to get out without causing a commotion. She was close enough that I could smell the garlic on her breath from the container of takeout on the counter behind her. Any possible escape options would now have to be heavily weighed given that she was pregnant, and I had no desire to hurt a pregnant woman or unborn child.

"I haven't decided what your ultimate fate will be just yet, but you won't be going anywhere any time soon. For now, it will look like you just up and left. And once Noah is over it, and we start building our life together, I'll figure out what to do with you."

"So you're going to lock me in your apartment until Noah falls in love with you?" I arched an eyebrow, getting a look of anger immediately in response from her.

"Exactly."

I rolled my eyes and turned, reaching for the doorknob. Whatever she thought she had planned wasn't my problem anymore. I had no desire to hurt a pregnant woman so I sincerely hoped she wouldn't force me to do so.

"Yeah, I'm leaving. Good luck with everything, Cindy," I said smugly as I felt the knob turn in my hand seconds before I felt the impact of something heavy making contact with the back of my head, forcing me to the ground.

Twenty Five
Noah

I was feeling more and more anxious as the hours went by and I still hadn't heard from Jade. We had agreed to get together Sunday morning for brunch but after she hadn't responded to my first text this evening, I started to worry that she might stand me up. Things weren't necessarily back to normal between us yet, but I had felt like we were on the right path when she left earlier today. It was almost nine o'clock and I had been texting her for over three hours with no response. I was starting to get worried. It wasn't like her to completely ignore me, even if she was mad at me.

I picked up my phone and called Mia, remembering that they were supposed to have dinner together tonight when Chase asked if I wanted to have a guys night while the girls gossiped. Last I knew it had been canceled, but maybe I was wrong and she wasn't answering because she was at Mia's. After the fifth ring, I was getting ready to hang up when I heard her answer.

"Hey Mia, I'm sorry it's late. Is Jade there with you?" I tried to keep the panic out of my voice while also not sounding like a completely whipped pussy.

"No, we decided to do dinner another night. Why? What's wrong?" Her voice was filled with concern which meant she had already picked up on mine.

"I haven't heard from her in a few hours and I'm starting to get worried."

"Have you been calling her?"

"No, just texting. I called once but it went to voicemail."

"Did you make her mad?"

I chuckled as I clearly saw Mia's face with her arched eyebrow as she asked the question, knowing that was a good likelihood. I sighed heavily and ran a hand through my hair as I asked myself the same question.

"I don't think so? If I did, I have no idea what I did this time."

"I know things have been off between you guys, maybe she just needs some space," Mia spoke softly, the way she always did when she didn't want to hurt my feelings.

"Maybe. But she seemed fine when she was here earlier."

"She was there? At your house?"

I let out a laugh at her reaction.

"Yeah, why is that so hard to believe?"

"It's not, sorry. I just didn't know she was planning to go over there. When we talked on the phone last night she was pretty fired up about your guys' phone call."

"She actually surprised me when she asked to come over this morning.

But by the time she left, we were laughing and joking just like we used to. She even agreed to have a late breakfast with me tomorrow."

"Brunch, Noah, the word is brunch." She giggled, knowing how much I hated the word.

"Fine, we were supposed to have BRUNCH and shit tomorrow," I joked.

"Does that make it feel manlier to you?"

"Fuck yeah it does."

We both laughed for a few seconds before turning our attention back to the reason that I had called.

"So what should I do? Do you think I should go to her apartment to check on her?"

"Honestly, I wouldn't. I know Jade and if she's purposely not answering you, she won't be happy about you showing up unexpected."

I could hear as she covered the phone, talking in the background.

"I'll go check on her and update you after I've talked to her."

"Absolutely not, Mia. I'm not having you go out in this weather, this late at night."

"You don't have a choice. I'm a big girl Noah, and believe it or not, I actually know how to drive both at night and in bad weather. I did live in Boston you know?"

"Chase is going to fucking kill me..."

"You're right about that." I could hear him in the background and rolled my eyes, hating the thought that Mia had to do this because of me.

"Can I at least meet you at your house and drive you over? That way I know that you're safe?"

"I'll be fine. Just stay where you are and keep your phone handy. I'll send an update when I have one."

"Thanks, Mia."

I heard the click as the call disconnected and held my phone against the bridge of my nose as I closed my eyes and prayed that everything was fine and that I didn't just send my best friend's wife out in bad weather at night for some stupid reason, like Jade's phone died. I sat on the edge of the couch and waited impatiently for an update.

Twenty Six

Jade

My eyes fluttered open as I tried to move my arms, feeling them bound behind my back. I looked around the room, recognizing the setup of Cindy's apartment as I heard footsteps in the back bedroom. Music was playing faintly in the background as she sang along. My head was killing me, whatever she had used to knock me out had left a terrible headache behind. I tried moving my legs and felt the tightness of the rope around them, pinning me in place to the wooden chair that I was sitting on.

I blew out a heavy breath through my nose, my mouth gagged by the bandana that was tied behind my head. Apparently, she wasn't joking about me not leaving this apartment. I tried again to wiggle myself free as the rope refused to give. My body sagged in response as I saved my energy and stopped trying for the moment. I needed to be smart about this if I wanted to escape, and I needed to give Cindy more credit than I had since I never would have imagined she would be capable of pulling this off. In hindsight, I should have trusted my instincts earlier and left the second things didn't feel right. Hell, I should have said no to begin with. Being a nice person wasn't always what it was cracked up to be.

The sound of the music in the bedroom started to get louder as I heard her footsteps approach. She walked into the kitchen and her eyes lit up when she saw that I was awake, her fingers working to turn the music down on her phone.

"Oh good, you're awake," she cooed as she walked over and watched me like I was some sort of caged animal that might bite if she got too close.

I watched her every movement as she walked behind me and untied the bandana, not taking it out of my mouth, just untying it from the back.

"Can you be a good girl and not scream?"

I nodded my head yes slowly, desperate for her to get it out of my mouth.

"You sure? Because these walls are pretty thin and I know for sure that you're a screamer." She leaned forward and wiggled her eyebrows suggestively at me. I forced a deep breath in through my nose, trying to force myself not to throw up on her. A few seconds later she slowly pulled the bandana away. Even if I wanted to scream, no one would hear it. Her apartment was the very last apartment at the end of the building and unless Chaz had made it home, no one would hear unless they were inside my apartment.

I took a few deep breaths after the bandana was gone and studied her as she pulled another wooden chair out from behind the table and slid it in front of me, sitting down to face me. As she sat in front of me I noticed a necklace around her neck and looked down to see the locket my sister had given me. The locket that I had cried over for weeks after it went missing. Looking back at the day I found her snooping through my desk, I should have known that she had taken it when I couldn't find it. The anger raged inside of me as I stared at it, something that was so sacred and special to me, now tainted by her touch.

"Let me go, Cindy," I warned as I stared into her icy cold eyes. "Now."

"Aww, that's cute," she mocked me as she faked a smile. "You really think that you can just get whatever you want, don't you?"

I ignored her question as I looked past her, not giving her the satisfaction of making eye contact as she searched my face.

"What is it that big, bad, Jade wants? Huh? Because it sure as hell isn't the man who is bending over backward to give you the world. You are so selfish and entitled, you don't even realize what a good thing you have." She shook her head and looked at me. "Sorry, had."

"I guess I should be asking you the same question. What is it that Cindy so desperately wants and can't have? Besides the love of a man that will never be hers." I pursed my lips as I glared at her, my anger starting to rise.

"You have NO idea what you're talking about. Once you're out of the way and he sees how hard you were to please, he'll be desperate for someone like me to love him. To show him how good it can be without having to constantly work to try to make someone happy who doesn't even know what happiness is."

"And you know what happiness is? You've had a love that was so grand, it taught you how to be exactly what he wants and needs?" My voice was laced thick with sarcasm as I watched the color drain from her face.

"I know that he deserves a hell of a lot better than you."

"Yeah, I could say the same." I arched my brow and tilted my head. I may be bound to a chair but that didn't mean that I didn't know how to deal with jealous, insecure girls like her. I had been doing it my entire life and was raised by one.

"You'll learn to respect me and to watch what you say around me." Cindy stood up and slammed her chair down beside me, forcing me to flinch from the sound. I watched as she walked off down the hallway and slammed the bedroom door shut behind her. I closed my eyes and leaned my head back as I tried to figure out how to get myself out of this mess.

Twenty Seven
Noah

"Mia, is she alright?" I didn't bother with saying hi as I rushed to answer my phone when I saw it light up with Mia's name.

"She wasn't home."

"Are you sure?" I knew it sounded stupid but I had no idea where Jade could be if she wasn't at home, and sure as hell wasn't at my place.

"Yeah, I rang the doorbell 3 or 4 times and waited, there was no answer."

"That's strange."

"I'm sure it's nothing. Maybe she went to bed early and just didn't hear it. Or maybe she went to the store. You know Jade, she's never one to stay still for too long." There was hope in Mia's voice that I found myself clinging to.

"Yeah, maybe." I got up and paced the small distance between the living room and kitchen as I tried to figure out where she could be.

"Noah, give it up for tonight. I'm sure she's fine. I'll try to call her in the morning and I'll let you know once I talk to her. Get some sleep."

"Yes, mother," I teased with a smile before hanging up.

It was driving me crazy that I hadn't heard from Jade all night and I tried not to let the nagging feeling that something was wrong get under my skin. I walked to the fridge and pulled out a cold beer, thankful that there was still one left given that I hadn't been to the grocery store since before the storm hit. Something else to add to my to-do list in the morning before I set up brunch for Jade.

I had planned everything out and spent the day going over all of the details for tomorrow after Jade left. The meal was planned out and a grocery list made with the items I would need. While I technically should be sleeping given that I was exhausted from not sleeping last night, my mind couldn't stop thinking about whether she would say yes tomorrow when I officially asked her to marry me. She had already seen the ring so the surprise of it was out of the way, though I didn't know whether that actually worked in my favor or not. She didn't give away much of a reaction but I could swear that for a split second, I saw her eyes light up. If the circumstances were different, I could imagine that she would have been excited to have me propose and there would have been no doubt that her answer would be yes.

I leaned back against the couch and took a long swig of my beer as I felt my phone vibrate next to me. I reached down, my fingers trembling with excitement that it was Jade and Mia was right about her being busy or asleep. As I unlocked the screen my face fell when I found a text message from Cindy instead.

Cindy: I'm really sorry. I don't know how to get you to talk to me but I really think that if you would just hear me out, everything would be okay.

I slid my finger over the button to erase the message and sat my phone down. No matter what was happening between Jade and I, there was nothing left for me to say to Cindy. I was a master at reading people and the way she reacted at the doctor's office with the ultrasound confirmed that she had been lying and that the baby wasn't mine. All that was left to do at this point was to wait for the baby to be born so we could do a paternity test to confirm.

Twenty Eight
Jade

The light trickled into the room as I slowly rolled my head forward, the pain from it hanging down while I slept was excruciating. Add to it the pain of getting whacked in the back of the head by some heavy object and the headache was unbearable. I looked around the room, trying to find Cindy, hoping she had left and I would have time to try to figure out how to get myself out of this mess.

It was Sunday morning so the likelihood of her going anywhere was slim. She didn't have work and if she set foot inside of a church I was pretty sure it would immediately burst into flames. Suddenly I found myself picturing it and shook my head to clear the terrible thoughts as they forced their way further into my mind. Heavy footsteps padded down the hallway and I let out a soft sigh knowing that she was still there and not about to burn in hell like she deserved.

I tried finding a clock to check the time, remembering that I was supposed to meet Noah at his house for brunch at eleven. Anxiety started to build as I thought about how he would feel if he thought that I had stood him up after we had talked yesterday and he had hinted at having a very special surprise for me at brunch today. I chewed the inside of my lip to keep the tears from my eyes as my heart silently broke at the thought of the pain it would cause him when I didn't show up.

Maybe if anything, Cindy would have come to her senses this morning and would decide to let me go. They say pregnancy makes some women do crazy things, maybe that included holding people hostage in your apartment while confessing your undying love for their boyfriend. I watched as Cindy walked into the kitchen, a red flannel robe loose over her flannel pajamas that barely covered her stomach as it forced the top up and left a sliver exposed. Her hair was piled high into a messy bun on top of her head and she had bags under her eyes as if she hadn't slept well. That would make two of us. She kept her focus on digging through the refrigerator as she pulled things out and sat them on the counter between the fridge and the stove. Next, she reached for the cast iron skillet that was sitting on the counter and glanced at me before sitting it on the stove and turning the gas on. The look that she gave me forced me to wonder if that's what she had used to knock me out. It made sense given that it was sitting on the counter, close to where she had been standing last night.

She poured oil into the pan and shook it back and forth, forcing the liquid to coat the inside. I watched as she aggressively opened the carton of eggs and banged each one on the side of the counter before dropping the raw egg into the skillet. A few minutes later she tossed in a handful of cut veggies from a Tupperware container she had pulled out from the fridge and added a handful of shredded cheese to the top.

"We're having omelets for breakfast," she said angrily as she looked over her shoulder at me.

"None for me, thank you." I kept my voice soft so as to not anger her further.

Too late. Her head whipped around as she glared at me.

"You're too good for the breakfast I'm making for you?"

"No, not at all. I'm allergic to eggs." I offered a tight smile that didn't reach my eyes. She studied me as she held the spatula in the air, one hand on her hip as she thought about what I said.

"What happens when you eat them?"

"I... can't breathe." I was reluctant to tell her for fear that she would use this information to actually try to kill me, but I also risked her getting so offended that I didn't eat them, that she still forced me to eat them and indeed, killed me.

"Interesting," she whispered as she pulled her bottom lip between her teeth before turning back to the skillet and flipping the omelet.

I sat in silence as I watched her finish cooking her eggs before sitting down across from me to eat them. My stomach grumbled in response to the smell, remembering that I hadn't actually eaten dinner last night. I could feel as my arms started to go numb, my body desperate to be free of this position. Just to stretch for a quick second and regain some of the blood flow would be heavenly.

Cindy got up and walked to the sink, sitting her plate and fork down before turning around and looking at me. There was a look of excitement on her face and I had no idea what she was thinking but deep down I knew that it wasn't going to be good.

"I'm going to go shower, then we'll get started. We have a lot to get done today." She smiled as she turned and walked down the hallway to the bathroom, the sound of water running a few seconds later.

I desperately tried pulling at the rope again, using everything I had in me to try to force it to give. Even just a small amount, I could try to make it work. There had to be a way to get out of this rope. After a few minutes of struggling, I was out of breath and my muscles were burning. I leaned against the wooden back of the chair and let out a frustrated growl. Never in my life had I ever felt so physically helpless. I looked around the room and studied everything, looking for anything

411

that I could use to try to cut the rope with.

Aside from the collage of photos on the wall, there wasn't much else in the apartment in way of decorations. The apartment had come fully furnished, just like mine had, however it didn't look like Cindy had bothered with adding any additional decorations since she had moved in. Off in the corner of the kitchen was a knife block that was tucked too far back for me to try to reach without getting caught. I definitely wouldn't be able to grab it with my hands given that they were bound behind a chair and the space on the counter was small with the cabinets hanging above. If I had more time I could try to nudge it free with my head and see if I could knock the block over, remove one or two with my teeth, and then turn around and grab it with my hand, slicing it perfectly through the rope and freeing myself.

Oh, who the fuck was I kidding? This wasn't some cheesy Hollywood action flick with unbelievable stunts that lead the good guy to defying all odds and miraculously escaping the bad guy. This was real life and there was literally a negative 1% chance of that plan actually working. I shook my head in irritation as Cindy walked back into the room, her wet hair wrapped in a towel on her head.

"What's the matter?" she asked curiously as she watched my discomfort as I tried to adjust myself in the chair.
"Nothing, I'm just uncomfortable from not being able to move."

"Oh, well that's not a problem. I plan to untie you in just a few minutes so we can get on with our day and get the stuff done that we need to." She smiled as she pulled her hair down from the towel and quickly rubbed the towel over her hair before combing it.

I was confused as to what she thought we had planned for the day but relieved that it would include her untying me. Once I was free I could fight my way out of here and be done with this bullshit.

"What exactly are we doing today?" I asked as I continued to move my hands behind me, thankful for the movement as they started to go numb again.

"Well, first, you're going to text Noah and break things off with him. For good." She gave me a look equivalent to that of a teacher catching students passing notes in class.

"I can't do that."

"Doesn't matter. I'll do it then. Either way, you're breaking up with him."

"I mean, I can't do that because I don't have my phone. Remember yesterday when you convinced me that I didn't need it because we would be quick? I don't think Noah is going to buy it if I break up with him from your phone."

"Well then, we'll just have to go get your phone, won't we?"

"Just untie me and I'll go grab it." My voice rose a tiny bit, giving away the hope that had started to bloom inside.

"Yeah, sure. Like I'm that stupid." She rolled her eyes and sat down the comb she had been using on her hair. "I'll go next door and get it."

"The door is locked."

"So then I'll knock and ask Chaz to get it for me."

"He won't. He doesn't know you."

"Trust me, I have my ways." She jerked her head, forcing her wet hair over her shoulder as she walked past me and opened the door. I waited to hear the click as it shut and was surprised when I noticed that it was still open a sliver and she hadn't noticed. I pushed myself as far to the side as I could without falling over as I struggled to hear what was happening outside. I could hear the faint footsteps through the wall and knew that Chaz was home. A few seconds later the door opened.

"Can I help you?" His deep voice vibrated through the walls.

"Hi, I'm Cindy, I live next door." She paused and I watched as she pulled the door shut the rest of the way when she must have seen that it wasn't closed all the way.

"Anyways, Jade is helping me build some furniture for the baby's nursery and she accidentally left her phone inside and asked if I could come grab it for her."

"Okay, go ahead and come on in. I think I saw it next to the pizza she left out on the counter last night. Is she okay?" There was a protective concern in his voice and hope filled me that he would act on his instincts and demand to come to Cindy's apartment to check on me. But then again I didn't know the guy and if what Noah said about him was true, I couldn't imagine that he had that much empathy in him to actually give a damn.

"Yeah, she actually stayed the night with her boyfriend last night. I heard them fighting earlier in the evening then there was some pretty loud making up before they went back to his place, if you know what I mean."

I could hear her giggling as my blood pressure started to rise.

"Here's her phone. Did you need anything else?" Chaz asked, completely dismissing her comment about Noah and I.

"I think that's it. I'm sure I'll be back if there's something else."

"Yeah, sure. Or maybe Jade can just come get her stuff herself."

I could hear the tension in his voice and knew that if I didn't act now, I would miss an opportunity. I didn't peg him as being the kind of guy who would ever hurt a woman, but at this point, I needed a man with huge muscles to come in and save the day, as lame and sexist as that sounded. I could hear their footsteps as they walked back to the door and knew the window was quickly closing. Without giving it another thought, I started screaming as loud as I could, which was rather hard given how dry my mouth was.

I was still screaming when I saw the door fly open, Cindy's eyes wide with anger as she slammed the door shut and stormed over to me. Within seconds I felt the impact from her fist crashing into the side of my face, forcing my head to whip to the side in response.

"What the fuck do you think you're doing?" she growled, keeping her voice low enough for me to hear as she towered over me and glared at me.

The pain spread across my cheek and up toward my eye as I slowly turned around and gave her the dirtiest look I could muster.

"You do that again and I will make your life even more of a living hell," she warned as she looked me up and down and walked past me, sitting my phone on the table. "I'll give you a few minutes to calm down before I untie you. I wouldn't want anything unfortunate to happen to you."

416

Twenty Nine
Noah

It was afternoon when I looked down at my phone again, disappointed that there were no texts or missed calls from Jade. The champagne sat in a bucket of melted water while the food was cold and looked like it had seen better days. The same song had played for the tenth time as the romantic playlist of her favorite songs looped back around. And the most depressing thing to fill the room was the thought that I had finally won her heart and thought that today would be the day that I finally asked her to marry me.

A text message came through from Chase, asking when they could come by to congratulate the happy couple. I shot him a quick text telling him that happy endings only exist in fairytales which meant it wasn't possible for me given that I was living in a nightmare. He offered to come by and hang out if I wanted to talk but it didn't feel like there was anything that was going to change my mood so I told him not to bother.

An hour later I was finishing up cleaning the kitchen and throwing out the spoiled food when my phone vibrated with a new text message. I sat the trash bag down next to the island as I picked up my phone and saw Jade's name. A tingle of excitement washed over me as I took a deep breath before opening it.

Jade: Things are over between us. Please don't try to talk me out of this decision, we both know it's best if we go our separate ways. You need to be there for Cindy and the baby. I'll be leaving town to make this a cleaner break from each other.

My stomach clenched as I read the words over and over, hoping that something might change each time I read them. That I might have read it wrong the first time and instead of breaking my heart, she was actually confessing her love for me. That I wasn't the only one who felt like they were drowning in a sea of misery.

I exited the message and slammed the phone down on the island as I stormed off to my weight room. I had too much pent up frustration and steam that I needed to burn off the only way that I knew how. Well, the only way that wouldn't get me into another Cindy situation.

Thirty
Jade

The day felt like it had dragged on forever as Cindy paced back and forth around the room, staring at her cell phone in her hand as she muttered under her breath about why Noah hadn't texted her back. My stomach had been sour ever since she had shown me the text message she had sent to him from my phone, confirming that I never wanted to see him again. My heart ached when I thought of what Noah must be feeling right now, especially after I had seen the engagement ring at his house yesterday.

Things with Noah had changed drastically over the last few months and a huge part of me was desperate to see where things could go with us. Part of me questioned whether we would be moving along at the same pace in our relationship if everything with Cindy had never happened. If he wasn't being forced into having a baby with another woman, would he still be interested in settling down? I saw the way he beamed when he held Rylee and the way his eyes lit up when he talked about the cute little things she did when he was with her so that made me think that maybe Rylee was also responsible for the change in him.

My arms were starting to ache even more and my butt was killing me from sitting in the same position for so long. I was desperate to be able to move, to sit in any other position than this one.

"Cindy, do you think I can get up to use the restroom?" I tried to keep any hint of anger out of my voice as I prayed that she had at least one tiny human bone in her evil pregnant body. She looked over at me, barely taking her eyes off of her phone, while she thought about what I was asking.

"Seriously, unless you want me to pee on your chair, I need you to untie me and let me use the restroom." I watched as she looked back toward the bathroom, still doubting whether she should let me go. "Cindy, we live in the same apartment. You know as well as I do that there's no way for me to escape from the bathroom. There's a tiny little window in there that even a child wouldn't fit through. I just need to use the bathroom, and I would love to stretch my legs for a minute."

"Fine. But I'm making sure that you're not going to try anything." She walked past me and sat her cell phone down on the kitchen counter behind me and opened a drawer before slamming it shut. A few seconds later I felt the rope loosen around my feet then the rope around my hands fell to the floor. I wanted to reach forward and stretch, to allow my body to get the blood flowing back to where it had been cut off, but the sound of her cocking a gun behind my head kept me completely still.

"Get up and walk slowly to the bathroom," she instructed.

I glanced out of the corner of my eye as I started walking toward the bathroom and saw her holding a small black handgun pointed at my head as she walked behind me. Any plan I had for trying to overpower her and escape had been quickly smoldered.

I walked slowly to the bathroom, thankful to be free from the chair and moving my legs which were achy from sitting so long. As I stepped inside the small guest bathroom, I went to close the door when I felt it hit something and bounce open. I looked down to see Cindy's foot blocking the door from closing, her face smug as I looked up at her, confused.

"Can I have some privacy?" I asked even though I already knew the answer.

"I don't see why you would need it. It's not like I haven't had to sit here and listen to you moan while you and Noah fuck each other. So no, you don't deserve any privacy when you openly flaunted your relationship with him to make me jealous." She pointed the gun toward the toilet and nodded for me to do my business. A blush crept up my neck as I thought about her listening to Noah and I having sex.

I took a deep breath as I struggled with what to do. I desperately needed to use the restroom, but I was beyond uncomfortable doing so in front of Cindy while she watched me. It was completely embarrassing and humiliating but as I watched her, my eyes silently pleading with hers, I knew that she wasn't going to budge. She was determined to degrade me and humiliate me any way she could. Slowly I pulled down my pants and underwear, and squatted down onto the toilet seat, careful to keep my legs closed as I used my hand to shield myself from her view. My heart was racing as I watched her stare at me, a smirk on her face as she watched me struggle to keep what privacy I could as I used the bathroom. I finished quickly and flushed the toilet as I turned away from her and pulled my pants up in record time. I washed my hands and dried them while she watched my every move, the gun still fixated on me.

She stepped out of the way as I walked to the door, allowing me to walk in front of her as we walked down the short hallway back into the living room and kitchen area. I contemplated whether to run for it, take off and pray that I could make it to the door before she could fire off a round, but part of me didn't put it past her to have a good aim.

"I came in second in a marksmanship contest back home, so trust me when I say that I will have a bullet in the back of your head before you even reach the door," she warned as if reading my thoughts. I walked the rest of the way and turned to face her once we were in the living room. I didn't want to voluntarily go back and be tied to the chair if I didn't have to, but I also had no idea what Cindy had in store for me. It wasn't like she could just keep me here forever.

"Sit." She pointed to the chair with the gun and raised her eyebrows as she waited for me to move.

"Do you really feel it's necessary to keep me tied to the chair? You said it yourself, you can put a bullet in the back of my head before I even make it to the door." I gave her a knowing look as I challenged her to question her own ability. One thing I learned growing up in a home where nothing was ever stable was that manipulation could get you where you needed to go.

"Maybe I just like to see you suffer," she snapped at me, tapping her foot on the carpet as she waited for me to respond.

"Maybe. But I don't think that's it." I let out a dramatic sigh as if I was already bored with the conversation. I saw her expression change to curiosity and knew that I had her exactly where I wanted her.

"Oh really? And why would you think that?" She shifted her weight and tilted her head to the side. "What if I want nothing more than to watch you suffer?"

"Then you would have done something besides tie me to a chair. You've had me in your apartment almost 24 hours now. If you were going to do something, you would've done it."

"Don't act like you know what I will and won't do. You don't know me at all. You don't have any idea of what I'm capable of."

"Maybe not. But I can see that you're a good person, Cindy. You don't want to hurt me or make me suffer. You just wanted me out of the way with Noah. I get it. But you're not a mean person Cindy, you don't like to hurt people if you don't have to."

Her expression softened as I saw her shoulders drop some as if the words that I spoke somehow lifted a weight off her shoulders.

"So, do you think that we can agree that I won't try to run if you don't tie me to that chair again? You can shoot me if I try to." I forced a smile as I waited for her to give in and accept what I was offering.

"Fine. But if you get anywhere near that door or try to scream again, I'll put two bullets in your head." She walked to the counter and picked up her cell phone as she sat the gun on the counter where her phone had been.

I let out a heavy sigh as I walked over and sat on the couch, hoping that I would figure out a way to get out of this mess. The longer I was here, the harder it was getting.

424

Thirty One
Noah

"Do you want to talk about it?" Chase asked as he stood outside my office and leaned against the doorway. It was too early on a Monday morning to have to think about any of this, especially since I hadn't slept well last night and started having nightmares about Jade again.

"There's nothing to talk about. She said it's over, so it's over." I slammed my mouse down beside my computer and pushed my chair back as I stood up.

"So it's over? Just like that?" Chase stepped back to let me pass as I walked by without looking at him.

"Yeah, just like that," I snapped, grinding my jaw.

"What the fuck happened to you?"

I whipped around and turned to face him as anger flashed across my face, our bodies inches away from each other as I balled my fists at my sides.

"You have a lot of nerve, you know that?" I growled. "You think you get to come in here and question me about my relationship, or lack of one? She left ME, Chase. What do you expect me to do? Chase her? Force her to be with me? She doesn't want to be with me so I have no choice but to let her go."

He squared his shoulders as he took a deep breath and I waited for the first punch to be thrown. We rarely ever got in each other's faces like this but when we did, it almost always came to blows.
"Maybe if you would fight harder for her, she wouldn't have left."

"You think I didn't fight for her? You have no fucking idea how hard I've been fighting for her! She found the fucking engagement ring and she STILL left!" My voice boomed through the narrow hallway and I was thankful that no one else was around to hear it.

"She knew you were going to propose?" He took a step back and crossed his arms over his chest.

"Yeah, she had seen it Saturday morning when she came over to talk. I had cleaned everything else up before she got there but I forgot about the ring and she found it." I let out a heavy breath, feeling the anger slowly leave my body.

"What did she say?"

"She asked me what it was for. We didn't get into it, I wanted to try to keep everything a secret for Sunday. But then she didn't show up and sent me a text saying she was leaving town so we could have a clean break." I leaned back against the wall and tilted my head backward as I looked up at the ceiling.

"I'm sorry. I didn't know that she already knew about the ring. I thought maybe she just assumed that you weren't ready to settle down, that's why she didn't show up. Mia thought maybe Jade was worried that you were trying to force things to work because you were stressed about everything with Cindy."

"Has Mia talked to her?" My heartbeat started to race as I hoped that Mia might have some information as to what was going on with Jade.

"No, she hasn't heard from her. She tried calling her all day yesterday, but she hasn't answered. We just assumed that maybe she was upset about everything that was happening between you guys and that's why she hasn't been answering. We know that she probably feels out of place with everything, given that Mia and I have known you for so long. Jade has never kept it a secret that she's felt out of place with the childhood stories we share and that we've all known each other most of our lives."

"I don't know what to do." I sighed heavily and looked him in the eyes. "What do I do? How do I make her see that she's the only person that I want?"

"I don't know. But I wish I did." He smiled sympathetically at me as he leaned against the opposite wall. We both stayed silent for a few minutes, both at a loss of words.

"Maybe it's not too late," I blurted out.

"What's not?"

"Fighting for her." I pushed off from the wall and felt my face heat up as a smile stretched across my face. "I'm going to keep fighting until I can make her see how much I love her. If she still decides it's not enough after that, then I'll at least go to my grave knowing that I tried."

"I know that look on your face, what are you about to do?" he asked as he followed me to my office.

"True love has no boundaries my friend, and I'm about to show her just how true my love really is."

I chuckled as he lowered his head into his hands and groaned.

"You got things covered here today?" I asked as I grabbed my cell phone and keys off my desk.

"Do I have a choice?" He raised his eyebrows as he watched me fly past him out of the office and down the hall.

"Nope," I called over my shoulder before the door slammed behind me.

Thirty Two
Jade

It was after nine in the morning when I heard Cindy calling in to work, complaining that she was feeling under the weather and wouldn't be able to make it in. I had no idea what she had planned and figured that she would just tie me to the chair again while she went to work. The fact that she had called in instead made me worry about what she had in mind since she couldn't afford to call in every day just to stay here and make sure I didn't leave. My nerves were starting to feel fried when I thought about how much longer all of this could keep going on.

Last night had been different and thankfully she hadn't tied me up again after our quick talk about her being able to put a bullet in my head if I tried to leave. I was allowed to sit on the couch and go to the bathroom when needed, with her escorting me, of course. But aside from that, I wasn't allowed to do anything else. A single glass of water to last me the entire day and a few sandwiches to count as lunch and dinner. By the time night fell, she was tired and cranky, which meant she wasn't easy to manipulate and I had been bound to the chair again for the entire night.

My body was sore this morning, but I was relieved to not be tied up to the chair for a little bit while Cindy ate her omelet and I nibbled on the toast she gave me. I was feeling optimistic that maybe today would be the day that I could get through to her and convince her to let me go but part of me knew that wasn't going to happen. I knew that I could manipulate her based on what I had been able to do so far, but she was far from stupid, and I wasn't that skilled with manipulating others.

Shortly after she called in, I saw her grab the rope from the kitchen table and head toward me. Dread filled my stomach as I eyed it.

"Come on, let's go. To the chair." She stood next to it and held out the rope as she waited. I contemplated whether or not to push my luck. To tell her no. As if reading my mind, she reached behind her and grabbed the gun, pointing it at me until I got up and walked over to the chair. A few minutes later I was bound to the chair again, my energy feeling depleted.

"I'm going to go take a shower, and I need you to make sure you're on your very best behavior," she mocked as she wrapped the bandana around my face, forcing it into my mouth before tying it tightly behind my head. I let out a frustrated breath through my nose and glared at her as she walked around and leaned forward to look at me. "There we go, that should do." She smiled a smug smile and walked off down the hallway, the sound of the shower turning on a few seconds later.

I leaned my head back against the back of the chair and closed my eyes. This was pure hell and I needed to find a way out of it. The sound of water from the bathroom softly filled the room and I was thankful for a break from having her in the room with me. Her energy was toxic, and I felt like it clouded my brain, making it almost impossible to think of a way to outthink her and get out of this mess.

My eyes were still closed as I tried to focus on clearing my mind when I heard faint voices outside. I opened my eyes and tried to lean as far forward as I could so I could try to hear better. My heart skipped a beat when I heard Noah's voice.

"Hey, Chaz, is Jade home?"

"She hasn't been home since I got here Saturday night."

"What do you mean she hasn't been home since Saturday night?"

I could hear the anger in Noah's voice as he got louder which worked in my favor as I continued to listen.

"I mean that I haven't seen her in the apartment since Saturday night. She's not here."

"Did she leave a note or anything?"

"Nope."

I heard the door shut and disappointment flooded through me. Noah was so close yet there was nothing I could do to tell him I was in here. I pulled as hard as I could against the ropes, the thick material cutting deeper into the marks that were already on my wrists from the last time I tried this. I screamed as loud as I could under the bandana, forcing as much air out as I could but nothing actually came out. I was starting to panic as I pulled harder, almost knocking myself and the chair over. I heard heavy pounding and stilled.

"What?" Chaz's voice was filled with irritation.

"I know she's in here. I don't know why you're lying to me, but I know she's here."

I heard a loud thud as the door slammed against the wall.

"Jade! I know you're here, just come out and talk to me. Please. Jade!" I heard Noah's voice fading as he walked around inside my apartment. A few seconds later I heard banging as he knocked on my bedroom door.

"Jade, please open the door and talk to me. I know that you're upset about something and I really want to talk about it."

My heart was aching as I heard him pleading with me through the door, not knowing that I wasn't on the other side.

"I will do whatever you need me to, so you'll forgive me. Just tell me what it is, and I'll do it."

Tears ran down my face as I screamed into the bandana and tried to pull against the ropes. I was shaking so hard that I hadn't noticed Cindy come in until she was standing beside me, scowling as she watched. Her attention shifted to the wall that we shared, and she walked closer as she heard Noah's voice from the other side.

"I'm not leaving until you talk to me Jade, I know you're in there. I'm not giving up on us, not until you tell me to my face that I'm no longer the man you love."

I closed my eyes and lowered my head as the tears continued to run down my face.

"Looks like we need to fix this little problem, don't we?" Cindy walked back over to me and forced my head up by yanking my hair down and holding it tight so I couldn't move my head.

I tried to keep listening to what was happening on the other side of the wall, but I couldn't hear Noah's voice anymore. A few minutes later I heard a door slam closed and knew that he had left. Cindy's lips turned upward into a devious smile as she heard the sound and turned to glare at me before letting go of my hair. I took a deep breath and tried to force myself to relax but was caught off guard when Cindy was behind me again, pulling my hair down and forcing my head back into the same position.

I watched as I caught a glimpse of something silver out of the corner of my eye. Within seconds I felt something cold skim the back of my neck and heard the scissors as they cut through my hair. She turned to look at me, holding a massive amount of blonde hair in her hands before dropping it to the floor beside me.

434

Thirty Three
Noah

Irritation continued to course through my veins as I left Jade's apartment, the image of Chaz's smug smile still fresh in my mind. I pulled into the parking lot of The Vine and put the truck in park as I contemplated what I wanted to do. I had never been in this kind of situation before and it was driving me crazy that I couldn't figure out what to do. Everything I did seemed to be the wrong thing. If this was what love was actually supposed to be like, I now understood why most people complained about how hard it actually was.

I leaned forward and rested my arm on the steering wheel as I thought through the options I had. I could go inside and try to work, pretending nothing had happened while I obsessed over Jade all day. Or I could go see the one person who knew the most about love and even more about heartache.

Fifteen minutes later I pulled up in front of Grant's house, knowing he would be home since the school he worked at was closed because of the weather. I knocked on the door as I pulled my beanie down lower on my head as the cold wind blew past me sending a chill through me.

"Hey, what's up?" Grant stepped back as he opened the door for me to come inside.

"Sorry to just drop in." I wiped my feet several times on the doormat before going in to make sure my boots didn't track in snow. "I was hoping we could talk?"

"Is this a beer at ten o'clock in the morning talk or will coffee do?" he called from the kitchen as I closed the door behind me and followed him inside.

"Coffee would be great, thanks."

I heard footsteps running down the stairs and looked over to see Liam fly around the corner in the flannel pajamas that Jade had bought him for Christmas.

"Good morning, Liam," I said as he came in and hopped up onto the barstool at the island, pouring himself a glass of orange juice before turning and waving at me as he drank it.

I took a seat at the kitchen table and watched as Grant and Liam moved around each other as Grant made coffee and Liam slipped around him to sneak a donut out of the box on the counter before running off to the living room. I chuckled and shook my head, knowing that Liam was exactly the same as how his dad was at his age.

A few minutes later the coffee finished brewing and Grant brought two cups over to the table and sat across from me as he handed me my cup. He slowly sipped his while eyeing me over the rim, waiting for me to spill it on why I was at his house on a Monday morning when I should be at work.

I wanted to dive right in and tell him everything, brainstorm ideas with him on how to fix everything, but the problem was that I didn't even know what I was trying to fix. Jade left me and I honestly didn't know why. He let out a heavy sigh as he took another sip before setting his cup down in front of him and leaned back against the padded chair and watched me.

"I don't know where to start," I muttered as I kept my eyes fixated on the coffee mug in front of me on the table.

"Well then I'm not sure how much help I can be." He licked his lips as a smile crept its way onto his face. "We could always start from the beginning."

I looked up at him and found a playful smile on his face as his hand stretched out across the table, fingers tapping along the worn-out wooden top.

"You know the beginning. Things between Jade and I were fucking awesome at the beginning."

"I meant from the beginning, like when you were ten and you kissed Linda Thompson when you knew that I liked her. I think that's where everything started to go downhill for you."
I let out a laugh as I leaned back in my chair and shook my head.

"You're never going to let that go, are you? She was too young for you, and honestly, you didn't have my skills." I winked as I pretended to pop my collar, something we had done from the moment someone had said it was cool.

"Hey, I could have had her if I really wanted her. But no, you had to go and kiss her. Turn her into a lesbian." His smile was contagious, and I was thankful for the lighthearted banter.

"Don't blame that one on me!" I put my hands up in surrender. "It was one kiss, that was it! But you know, I heard that Maggie ended up kissing her after I did, and honestly, I think that was her turning point."
I smiled as I remembered such distant memories.

"Maggie could have turned anyone, she was drop-dead gorgeous."

"They both were."

We sighed at the same time and when I looked back up at him I found comfort in his eyes as he waited for me to talk about the real issue.

"Jade left me," I blurted out as I looked down and spun my spoon in a circle on the table.

"I'm sorry, man. Chase told me that she never showed up yesterday for brunch and that she sent a text instead. What happened?" He picked up his cup and took a drink, his eyes never leaving my face.

"Honestly? I have no fucking idea." I exhaled loudly and pushed the spoon to the side as I turned to face him directly.

"What did the message say?"

"Not much other than she didn't want to lead me on so she was going to leave town so we'd have a clean break."

"Ouch." He flinched subtly.

"Yeah."

"All of this just happened out of the blue after she came over to talk to you the day before?"

"She literally left my house smiling and held onto my hand for a minute as she walked out the door. We had talked about Cindy and the ultrasound, we even talked about her living with Chaz. None of that changed how we were while she was there. I don't see what could have changed after she left when we literally sat down and had a handful of tough conversations before she agreed to come over yesterday. I can't imagine her saying yes to brunch if she was upset with me."

Grant nodded his head as he followed along and sipped his coffee.

"Have you tried to talk to her since?"

"Yeah, I tried calling and texting her Saturday night to see if we were still on for Sunday but she didn't respond. So I thought maybe she was at Mia's, having dinner like they had originally planned before that storm hit. I asked Mia and she said Jade wasn't there and offered to go check on her."

"So why not ask Mia for an update?"

"That's the thing, Mia said that Jade wasn't home." I swallowed past the lump that was starting to form in my throat. "So I decided to go by Jade's apartment this morning to talk to her, and according to Chaz, he hasn't seen her since he got home Saturday night."

Grant's brow pulled together as he took the information in and I was relieved that he felt the same way I did about it.

"That's weird. Has she been at work?"

"Nope. I went by SlowMo's and Arlene said that Jade had the weekend off. She's supposed to go in at four tonight for the dinner shift."

"So are you here to officially ask me out to dinner?" A smile tugged at the corner of his lips and I felt mine follow.

"Well, it has been a while since I've been on an actual date. I guess I could lower my standards some," I joked.

"Maybe she just needs some time? It's only been a few days since you talked to her on Saturday, maybe something else came up."

"Maybe, but it just doesn't feel right. This isn't like Jade and it's driving me crazy that it's so out of the blue. She was fine on Saturday. She would have shown up on Sunday but something got in her way and I can't figure out what."
"Well, I wish I could offer you some advice on that but I feel just as

clueless as you. I would love to be able to tell you how to fix it but the only thing I've got is to give her time and space. If that's what this is then it will sort itself out."

I blew out a breath as I tapped my foot on the tiled floor, shaking my head before I turned to look at him again.

"You know I can't do that, right?"

"Yeah."

"So I'll meet you at SlowMo's at six?"

"We'll be there."

He let out a laugh as I finished my cup of coffee and headed off to work.

The day went by at an incredibly slow pace given that we were dead with everyone staying home due to the weather. I was sitting at one of the tables in the back working on some paperwork when I heard the bell chime on the front door. I looked over to see blonde hair walking up toward the bar area and got excited that Jade had given in and come by to talk to me.

Julia pointed in my direction from behind the bar and I smiled as I waited for her to turn around, completely disappointed when I saw Cindy making her way toward me. She was grinning from ear to ear as she waddled toward me and I made a mental note to ask Jade to change her hair color the next time I saw her.

"Hey Noah, how's it going?" she asked as she leaned in and tried to hug me. I watched her with a blank look on my face as my body refused to touch her. Her face fell and her smile was replaced with a frown before she pulled out the stool next to me and sat down.

I raised an eyebrow as I watched her, moving the papers that were scattered across the table out of the way.

"What do you want, Cindy?" Annoyance heavy in my tone.

"I wanted to let you know that I got in touch with the clinic back home, and they were able to send over the original ultrasounds to the doctor's office. I have another appointment on Friday. Maybe you can come with me again?" Her voice got higher as she practically squealed.

"I don't think so, sorry." I lowered my head to focus on the report I was working on before she interrupted me. Sometimes I liked to get out of my office to work on things but today it seemed like it would have been better to be cooped up inside the four walls that felt like they were closing in than to sit with Cindy.

"I can reschedule it if another day works better for you?" She reached over and gently squeezed my arm, bringing my attention back to her. I pulled my arm away from her, letting her hand fall on the table in its absence.

"Don't worry about it, just keep your appointment."

"But it's important to me that you be there, Noah."

"Look, Cindy, I have a lot of work to do and I'm not interested in going to the appointments with you anymore. We have nothing left to say, so if you don't mind, I have work to do." I gave her a pointed look before turning my attention back to the papers in front of me.

I watched as she stood up and pushed her stool in before walking behind me. I let out a loud sigh as I waited for her to leave, startled when I felt her behind me. Her hands ran down my chest and over my stomach as she leaned down behind me. I could feel the warmth from her body as her stomach pushed into me, her breasts pressed into my back.

"What do you think you're doing?" I demanded as my hands reached up and grabbed hers, holding them in place so they'd stop wondering down my body. There was no one else around but it still felt beyond inappropriate, even for me.

"You seem really stressed, I could help you with that," she whispered as her lips hovered by my ear. Her tongue ran down the side of my neck as she shifted and forced her breasts to rub along my back. I could feel her hands trying to get out from under mine as I quickly flung them around and spun myself out of her reach.

"I don't need your help with anything, I need you to stop."

"No one has to know, we can do it right here. It could be our little secret." She licked her lips as she started to bend down to climb under the table.

"Cindy, no."

"You can't tell me that you wouldn't enjoy my lips around your thick cock again. I still remember the way it stretched my mouth as I sucked it, pulling you all the way to my throat." She stepped closer as I kept my grip on her hands. "You don't have to do anything, just use my body however you want it. If you don't want to come in my mouth, you could always come on my tits. They're nice and big right now." She looked down and pulled her hand free as she ran a finger along the top of the low cut shirt that was barely containing her breasts.

I shook my head as I tried to turn away but as her fingers dipped lower into her shirt, a glimpse of her bra showed. It was a black lace bra with tiny red flowers, just like the one Jade had. I looked closer at the shirt she was wearing and noticed that it was super tight and didn't seem to fit, just like the bra that was barely containing her. The shirt was a black workout tank top that I had seen Jade wear plenty of times, including when I saw her on Saturday.

"Is that Jade's shirt and bra?" I asked as I stared dumbly at her, praying that she hadn't gone that crazy to go out and buy the same clothes as Jade.

"Of course not!" she exclaimed with a tone that sounded forced. "Why on earth would you even ask that?"

"Jade has a bra just like that. And she wears shirts like that all the time."

"Well then maybe she's been copying me?" A smug look landed on her face as she watched for my reaction.

"Yeah, maybe." I turned my attention back to the pile of stuff on the table in front of me and quickly worked to pile it up before turning and walking away from Cindy.

Thirty Four
Jade

I was sitting in the chair, bound to it once again, but this time I had the added humiliation of being topless. I had no idea what to expect next from Cindy after she lost her mind hearing Noah in my apartment this morning. There was a cold chill in the apartment and I didn't know if it was because I was completely exposed from the waist up, or if it was from being in shock still.

After Cindy cut my hair, I was in total disbelief that she would do something like that. But then I saw her wave my hair around like some sort of prize and I knew that she was completely crazy. She muttered to herself about needing to take it one step further, that's all she needed and Noah would finally start looking at her the way he looked at me.

She went to the bedroom and got ready but as she was about to walk out the door, she changed her mind and closed it softly before walking over and picking up the gun. While keeping it aimed at my head, she forced me to give her my shirt and bra, then insisted that I didn't deserve to have anything else to wear. I was mortified when I saw her change into it, wearing the clothes that I had been wearing as she struggled to fit them over her pregnant body. The workout top was stretchy but only to a point. When added with a bra that was too small for her, her cleavage was pushed up and over the top, making her look like a very pregnant, cheap prostitute.

It had been about an hour since she left according to the time on the microwave. I eyed the gun still sitting on the counter where she left it and contemplated whether I could get to it before she got back. If I could somehow find a way to hide it from her, then I could try to overpower her the next time she untied me without having to worry about her shooting me. Even though I knew it was damn near impossible to do anything while I was bound to a chair, it was the only hope that I had left.

A few minutes later I heard a key in the door and grunted in disappointment that she was back. I waited for the door to open but it didn't. Outside I could hear faint voices and tilted my head to try to hear. I could easily make out Cindy's annoying voice, but the other voice, the one she was talking to, was soft and feminine. Mia.

My heart started racing as I imagined Cindy doing something to Mia and prayed that she would just let her be. I held my breath and tried to calm myself so the pounding in my ears from my racing pulse would stop and allow me to hear what was happening.

"Hey, Mia. How's it going?"

"I'm fine, thank you." Mia's voice was further away so I had to strain to hear it.

"Are you looking for Jade?"

"Yeah, I was hoping to talk to her before she goes to work."

I waited to see what Cindy would say, knowing that Mia would know no one was home when I didn't answer the door. I had heard Chaz leave shortly after Cindy left earlier and knew he wouldn't be back until after he got off of work.

"Jade's not home, I saw her leave this morning."

"You did? Do you know where she was going?"

"She didn't say. But she looked like she had been crying and she had her suitcase. It looked pretty full."

My heart sank.

"Oh, that's right, I remember now. She did say she was going out of town for a few days to see her mother. I completely forgot. Thanks for letting me know, I'll touch base with her when she gets back."

I was thankful for Mia's quick thinking even though I knew she had no idea what was really going on. She trusted her instincts and that meant she would be safe from Cindy.
"No problem." Cindy's voice was overly cheerful and I let out a heavy sigh knowing Mia should be walking away and going home.

"Hey Mia," Cindy called out. "I would love to get together sometime, maybe have some girl time, if you're free?"

"Yeah, I'll have to check my calendar. Things have been busy with the baby and my maternity leave is almost over."

"Okay. I just wanted to see if we could sit down and talk about things with Noah and me. I feel bad about everything that's happened and he won't listen to me anymore. Even after I told him that the doctor from the other clinic sent over the original ultrasounds and lab results."

"I don't think I should be getting involved Cindy, I'm sorry. I'm sure you guys will figure it out."

"I hope so, I would hate to lose him in his baby's life over something so silly."

I cringed as I listened to their conversation and silently pleaded with

Mia to just walk and leave before it was too late.

"Well, I better get going. Rylee is going to need a nap soon."

Thank the lord. Go, Mia, walk away.

I heard the key in the door once more and waited for her to unlock the door.

"Oh hey, Cindy, do you think I can get those pictures back that you borrowed since I'm here?"

I closed my eyes and shook my head.

"I haven't made copies of them yet, can I bring them by in a few days?"

"If you show me which ones they are, I don't mind printing copies and bringing them back to you," Mia pushed as her voice got louder and I knew she was walking closer to the apartment.

"I couldn't put that extra work on you. I'll go out and get the copies made today and I'll drop them off tonight. I'm feeling a little tired so I need to get inside and rest."

I could hear the aggressive tone in Cindy's voice and prayed that Mia heard it as well and backed off.
"Okay, that's fine. I'll see you tonight."

I heard footsteps as Mia walked away and a few seconds later Cindy walked in, looking furious. She had a plastic bag on her arm as she slammed the door shut and glared at me.

"Looks like we're going to have to deal with you sooner than I thought."

She stalked over to me and my eyes went wide as I watched her lift the skillet from the stove and swing it at my head. The pain was radiating as my head whipped back and everything went quiet.

<u>Thirty Five</u>
Noah

I waited in my truck at SlowMo's for Grant and Liam to show up, feeling uneasy that Jade's car wasn't in the parking lot. A few minutes later I saw his truck pull up beside me and we all got out and went inside. It was busier than I had expected for a Monday night but we were seated right away and taken to a table in the back. As we were walking back, I let out a chuckle when I saw that Chase and Mia were sitting at the table next to where they were seating us.

"Apparently this is the place to be tonight," I joked as I bent down to hug Mia before patting Chase's shoulder.

"We decided it would be nice to get out for a bite to eat tonight," Chase said as he eyed Mia.

Grant and Liam sat down at the table as I pulled off my jacket and hung it on the back of my chair. I bent down to kiss Rylee on her head while she slept in her car seat before sitting down to join everyone.

"No, we came to check on Jade." Mia's voice was filled with tension as she leaned forward and rested her arms on the table in front of her.

Chase pulled his mouth into a thin line and turned to look at his wife.

"I thought we weren't going to say anything?" he asked her quietly even though we could all hear.

"It's fine, it's the same reason that we're here." I pointed to Grant and Liam and looked directly at Mia. Something had happened that made her concerned and I was going to find out what it was.

"Have you seen her?" I asked her directly before my eyes shifted to scan the room.

"No, and Arlene said that she hasn't shown up for her shift. She was supposed to be here at four." Mia sighed heavily and leaned back as a waitress reached across her to set the glasses of water on the table for her and Chase.

"Something's not right," I said to no one in particular.

"Maybe she's sick, there's no reason to freak out right away," Grant spoke softly as he sat a menu in front of Liam to look at.

"I doubt she's sick." I tapped my foot anxiously and looked around once again, hoping she would somehow just appear.

"I agree, she's not sick." Mia leaned back against the chair and studied me.

"How do you know?" Chase asked as he rocked the car seat to keep Rylee asleep.

"Because I went to go see her today."

"You went to see her?" Chase's eyebrows shot up as he turned in his seat to look at her.

"Yes. I was worried."

"And you didn't bother to tell me until now?"

"You would have told me not to go."

"You're damn right I would have."

I watched as they stared at each other, neither of them giving.

"So what happened when you went to see her?" I asked, needing to know everything I could.

"She wasn't home." Mia folded her hands on top of each other as she sat them on the table in front of her.

"How do you know?" My eyes searched hers as I waited.
"No one answered the door. But her car was there."

"Maybe we need to ask her landlord to let us in? Demand a welfare check? What if she's really sick?" My voice was getting higher as panic started to rush through me.

"Don't you think Chaz would know if something was wrong with her? After all, she's not living there by herself anymore." Chase spoke calmly as he looked at me.

"Chaz told me he hasn't seen her since he's been home Saturday night." I shifted in my chair and nodded no to the waitress as she approached. I didn't care how hungry anyone was, I needed to know what was going on.

"Okay, so who was the last person to see her?" Grant asked as he passed his phone to Liam to let him play a game while we talked. There were packets of crackers on the table that he slid over to him as well.

"I saw her Saturday afternoon when she came over and I haven't heard from her since." I chewed my lower lip as my feet felt like they were going to take off from tapping so quickly.

"According to Cindy, she saw her today."

"What?" I narrowed my eyes at her as she said Cindy's name. Everyone's eyes were now on Mia, waiting for an explanation.

"She told me that Jade wasn't there. That she had left earlier with a suitcase and looked like she had been crying."

I felt like my world was collapsing around me, the words trapped in my throat.

"What else did Cindy say?" Chase asked with a stern tone in his voice.

"Nothing about Jade. I pretended that Jade had told me she was leaving for a few days, that she was going to go see her mom. Then Cindy asked about hanging out and wanting to talk about things with Noah. I told her that I didn't think it was a good idea for me to get involved. She was acting weird and I couldn't put my finger on it, so I asked if I could get the pictures back that she borrowed. She didn't want to let me in the apartment, so I kept trying." Mia shrugged her shoulders and looked away from the table, avoiding the pissed off look she was getting from Chase.
"You did that when you had Rylee with you?" Chase asked, his finger reaching across and pulling Mia's face back toward his.

"She was safe, I had her wrapped around me in her sling."

"Mia! Do you have any fucking idea how much danger you put her in today? How much danger you put yourself in?!" Chase's voice boomed around us, causing the others sitting near us to turn around and look.

"We were fine, Chase, I knew what I was doing," she snapped.

"No, Mia, obviously you didn't. If you thought Jade was in trouble, you should have come to me. I would have gone to check on her. You don't go putting yourself, or our daughter, in harm's way."

"I was fine! She's my best friend, Chase, and she risked her life to save me from Damian. I owe it to her to save her from whatever the hell is happening!" Her voice broke at the end and we watched as the tears ran down her face as she pulled away when Chase tried to hold her.

"I know Mia, I'm sorry. I just, I can't stand the thought of anything happening to you or the baby." Chase reached over and pulled her into him, holding her as she wiped her eyes.

"So what do we do now?" Grant asked.

"I have no idea." I ran a hand through my hair and prayed for a sign that would tell me where she was.

"Did Jade really talk to you about leaving town for a few days?" Grant asked Mia.

"No, we hadn't talked about her leaving, and as far as I know she never had any plans to leave. She was happy to be here and finally putting some roots down. I just made that up to see how Cindy would react since she told me Jade left."

"In the message that I got from Jade on Sunday, after she stood me up, it mentioned that she was leaving town so we could have a clean break."

"Do you really think she would just up and leave?" Chase asked as he kept an arm wrapped around Mia's shoulders.

"I don't know. Maybe? She's talked about her childhood and how every time her mom ended a relationship, they would leave town. Maybe she's just doing the only thing she knows how to do."

I looked across the table at Mia and saw the sadness on her face. As much as I didn't want to believe it, I knew that I was right.

Thirty Six
Jade

I woke up to a throbbing headache and was surprised that I wasn't
bound to the chair. I looked around and saw an empty room,
knowing it was the guest bedroom in Cindy's apartment. The layout
of her apartment was opposite of mine which meant that our master
bedrooms shared a wall, and her guest bedroom was at the other end.
Given that her apartment was the last one on this floor, there were no
neighbors to share a wall with. I could scream as loud as I wanted to in
this room and no one would hear me.

I sat up and looked down, thankful that I now had a T-shirt on and was
no longer naked from the top up. It was a ratty worn-out T-shirt and
part of me prayed that it wasn't something Cindy had recently worn. I
would almost rather that she pulled it out of a dumpster than to wear
something she had worn. She was pure evil, and I didn't want anything
from her on me.

I ran a hand through my hair out of habit and felt my stomach drop
when I felt how short my hair was. When I first moved here my hair
was rather short, but this was even shorter and not by any means
straight. I cringed at the thought of how horrible my hair looked and

wondered just how uneven it was. There was a strong chemical smell that lingered on my fingers from touching my hair and I tried to figure out what it was. Then it clicked from the numerous times I had colored my hair on my own. Store-bought hair dye. I groaned as I thought about how I had no idea what she had done while I was passed out.

I heard footsteps approaching and watched as the door handle turned before the door opened and Cindy walked in.
"You're finally awake I see," she said as she walked over and brought the chair and rope in with her. I stayed quiet, not having the energy to try to figure out what to say to her. My body felt like it had been run over by a truck and I feared that I had been hit with more than just the skillet that knocked me out. She smiled as if reading my thoughts.

"I got you a few things that you'll need when you leave, but I'm still waiting for your ride to come pick you up."

"What are you talking about?" I asked, my voice barely above a whisper.

"You're leaving town, just like you've told everyone you were. And now, thanks to me, no one will recognize you as you go."

I watched as she stood there, looking me over.

"I'm not going anywhere." Why was my body so weak? I felt like every tiny bit of strength I had had been pulled out of me and stripped away.

"Of course you are. And I have a friend from back home who will be escorting you just to make sure you don't get any ideas about trying to come back."

I rolled my eyes as I looked up at her, the look on her face changing as she glared at me. A second later her fist landed on my cheek, knocking me back down to the floor. I struggled to get up, but it was impossible as her foot kicked me over and over. I laid where I was, curled up in a fetal position as I prayed it would stop.

Thirty Seven
Noah

The room was dark as I crept along the wall, staying hidden in the shadows as I tried to get to Jade. I could hear her whimpering, knowing she was in pain. Each step I took forward felt like I was further away, the sound of her cries fading in the distance. I tried to walk faster, desperate to get to her. Soon I was running, faster, until I was out of breath. I got close enough to see her, her face covered in blood. My hand reached out to grab hers, to pull her up off the floor, but when I touched her it was no longer Jade. Staring back at me was Cindy.

My eyes flew open, my breathing rapid as my heart raced out of control. I sat up in bed and pulled the covers off of me as I got up and went to the kitchen for a glass of water. The nightmares about Jade weren't unusual, but tonight's really got to me. There was something about it that felt like more than just a bad dream. It felt like it was real.

I glanced at the clock on the stove, confirming that I was up for the day. It was already five in the morning and I didn't feel like going back to sleep for another hour and having more nightmares. I started a pot of coffee before making my way to the guest room to work out before heading in to work. At this rate, I would soon be in the physical shape

I had been wanting to be in for a few months now with all of the extra lifting sessions I was adding in as a stress reliever for everything going on with Jade and Cindy.

A few hours later I was in my office working on a report when I heard voices from Chase's office. I kept my head down and tried to focus on the information in front of me but as the voices grew louder, my focus became nonexistent. I shoved the paper away as I stood up and walked out of my office to see what all of the fuss was about in his.

"I don't care what everyone says, I know better. Something is wrong, I can feel it," Mia whispered loudly as she sat on the edge of Chase's desk and faced him. I cleared my throat as I leaned against the doorway and crossed my arms across my chest. They both looked at me at the same time, a faint blush creeping up Mia's neck as she turned to look at me.

"Everything alright in here?" I asked as I looked between them.

"Yeah, everything is fine." Chase sighed heavily.

Mia's eyes locked onto mine and I could tell something was wrong. I'd known her long enough to know that look.

"What's up, Mia?"

She went to say something when I saw Chase's hand gently squeeze her knee, forcing her to turn her head back to him. I raised an eyebrow at him in response.

"Fine." He leaned back in his high back leather chair and laced his fingers behind his head. "Mia is convinced that something is wrong with Jade."

My eyes shifted to Mia as she turned back around and watched me. I gave her a quick nod for her to tell me why she thought something was wrong. I had been feeling like something was wrong myself but had been attributing it to the nightmares and stress with how everything ended.

"It's not like her to just leave, Noah. You know that. I know that." Her voice was quiet as she talked.

"I don't know what I know anymore." I ran a hand down the scruff on my face and let out a deep breath.

"She wouldn't just leave you, I know her better than that. If she was going to leave, she would have done it a long time ago. When you guys first broke up. But she didn't, Noah, she stayed. And since then, she's been there for you every step of the way. I was wrong last night when I thought that she would just up and leave because that's what she's been used to, I didn't give her credit for how far she's come in her relationship with you."

I watched as Mia turned around further, giving me her full attention as she spoke.

"She acknowledged that she was used to running from relationships the night you guys came for dinner and she broke it off again, but Noah, she wasn't ending it because she wanted to leave. She ended it so you didn't have to choose between her and the baby. She loved you enough to spare you that decision because she didn't want you to regret your decision if you chose her."

"How am I supposed to trust that she didn't just up and leave?"

"Because I went by her apartment this morning and her car is still there. How would she leave without her car? She loves that car, she wouldn't just abandon it."

"You went by her apartment again this morning?" I asked as I looked past her to see Chase's jaw clenched as he listened.

"Yes, I went by again. I talked to Chaz and he still hadn't seen her. He mentioned that Cindy went by on Sunday to get Jade's phone, she told him that Jade was with her building baby furniture for the nursery."

Her eyes locked onto mine as I felt a shiver run through my body. There was no way in hell that Jade would have gone over to help Cindy then send her to get her phone.

"Did he say what time on Sunday?" I asked as I swallowed down the bile that was threatening to make its way up.

"It was after noon."

I closed my eyes as I pinched the bridge of my nose and shook my head. How had I been so stupid?

"So what's your plan?"

"I want to go check out Cindy's apartment, see if anything looks odd. It took everything I had in me not to barge into her apartment this morning while I was there, but I didn't since I had the baby with me. I do think we need to seriously look into this though." Mia stood up and turned to face me.

"You can't just show up at her apartment, she'll know that something is up."

"No, she won't. When I talked to her yesterday, I asked her about getting the photos back that she borrowed. She was so desperate to get me away from her apartment that she promised she would go make copies and drop them off at my house last night, but she never showed up. So I can go over with the excuse of getting the photos from her." Mia rolled her eyes as she exhaled heavily. "I was so stupid not to question why she didn't want me in her apartment yesterday. I should have been thinking clearer."

"You also had our daughter with you," Chase reminded her as she shot him a look.

I let the thought roll around in my head and tried to find a flaw in it but couldn't. Mia was actually on the right path and I couldn't imagine that Cindy would be on to her.

"What about Chase? How are you going to explain why he's there? She'll think you're ganging up on her if he shows up and she'll shut you out immediately." My mouth was working faster than my mind but I hated that there was already a problem with the plan.

"Chase isn't going with me. No one is." She pulled her shoulders back as she stood taller and looked at Chase out of the corner of her eye.

My eyebrows shot up and I looked at Chase sitting there, fists clenched. There was no way in hell that he was okay with this.

"Mia, I don't think it's the best idea for you to go there by yourself. You don't know Cindy, and if we really think that she knows what happened to Jade, there's no telling what she might do."

"I appreciate the concern, I really do. But I'm not only the best option we have right now, I'm the only option. Unless you want to go in there with guns blazing, be my guest." She folded her arms over her chest and shifted her weight on her hip as she waited for me to respond. I looked at Chase, catching his attention before he could look away.

"What do you think?" I asked, already knowing what he thought.

"I hate the idea of it but I hate even more that she's right."

"Well, let's at least come up with a plan before you go running over there. I want to make sure we think through everything before we just send you into the fire."

"It's not that complicated. I'm just going to go to her apartment and ask for the photos. I'll try to get her to let me in so I don't have to stand outside in the cold. While I'm in there, I'll look for any sign of Jade and see how Cindy is acting. If I'm wrong and Jade isn't there then no harm, no foul. At least I got the photos back and I didn't make Cindy feel like we were accusing her of anything."

"And what if Jade is there? Then what do you do?" Chase asked sternly, drawing her attention back to him.

"I don't know," she whispered. "I fight until I get her out of there. I protect her the way she tried to protect me from Damian."

"So I'm supposed to tell Rylee that her mom got hurt, or worse, killed because she needed to run off on her own to go fight some crazy pregnant lunatic?"

I saw the hurt flash across her face at his words. But he was right. If Jade was there then it would be incredibly dangerous for Mia to go in by herself.

"Um, speaking of Rylee, where is she?" I asked as I looked down and noticed the car seat wasn't on the floor by Chase's desk where it usually was when she was sleeping.

"I dropped her off with my dad and Arlene after I left Jade's apartment. They've been wanting some time with her and I needed to take care of this, so it was a win-win."

"Obviously Chase and I can't both leave since we have no one to be here when we open. So, I'll go with you to Cindy's apartment, but I'll wait downstairs in my truck until I get a signal from you. That's my compromise, you don't go by yourself but you can go up to her apartment by yourself."

"Deal."

Mia leaned down and kissed Chase before grabbing her phone and jacket from his desk and following me out to my truck. I had a terrible, terrible feeling about all of this.

Thirty Eight
Jade

I came to and was still in the same room I was in when Cindy had beat me unconscious again earlier. I struggled to try to sit up but my body wouldn't allow it so I stopped trying and let myself lay where I was on the floor. I had no idea what time it was or how much time had passed since Cindy had been in here last.

The doorbell rang and I felt panic rush through me as I remembered her saying that she had a friend who was coming to take me out of town. There was a devious smile on her face when she said it and part of me wondered if I would make it to another town with this so-called friend of hers. I listened as her footsteps padded along the floor to answer the door and waited to hear a man's voice as I expected that was who would be coming.

My stomach sank when I heard Mia's voice instead. I silently pleaded with her to leave. Turn around, walk out the door, and leave. Nothing good could come about from her being here. My body laid still on the floor as I tried to lift my head enough to hear them talk.

"Hey, Mia, what are you doing here?" There was an edge to Cindy's tone and I prayed that Mia would pick up on it and just leave.

"Sorry for just stopping by, I was out running errands and thought I would swing by and grab those photos we talked about yesterday since you didn't make it by last night to drop them off."

"Oh, right. Sorry about that, I got busy and totally spaced it. Can I bring them to you later?"
"I was hoping I could just get them now since I'm already here. That way neither of us has to be out in this cold longer than necessary."

"Okay, I guess I'll get them real quick."

I could hear the sound of the door as she started to close it, followed by a loud thud.

"You don't mind if I come in while you get them, do you? It's awfully cold outside and I wouldn't want to be stuck out in this weather for too long."

"Of course not."

Cindy's tone was getting increasingly hard and I could picture her gritting her teeth as she talked. I tried to force myself up, to try to warn Mia to run and get out of there, but my body was too weak from the recent attacks.

"Thanks, you're the best," Mia said in a cheerful tone as I heard the door close.

"You can have a seat on the couch while I go look for them," Cindy offered as I heard her walk by my door on her way to the master bedroom.

"Thanks. Actually, do you mind if I use your restroom?" Mia called to her as I heard her walk away.

I didn't hear Cindy answer as I heard Mia quickly open and close the closet door before opening and closing the bathroom door. A few minutes later I heard Cindy's footsteps approaching as I watched in horror as the doorknob turned to open the door to the guest bedroom. Mia's eyes went wide in horror when she looked down and saw me on the floor, her hand flying to her mouth as she took a step closer.

"I thought you needed the bathroom?" Cindy asked as she stood behind Mia, the skillet flying up behind Mia's head and knocking her down to the floor next to me.

"Great, looks like I have two problems to deal with," Cindy said as she bent down and rolled Mia into the room next to me. I felt tears run down my face as I looked at my best friend lying unconscious on the floor next to me.

Thirty Nine
Noah

I checked my phone for the tenth time in the five minutes since I had seen Mia walk into Cindy's apartment. My body was humming with anxiety as my foot tapped against the rubber floor mat underneath me while I waited. Part of me wanted to rush up there and burst into the apartment, make sure everything was okay, but I knew that I needed to give Mia the benefit of the doubt that everything was okay and that her plan was working.

My eyes shifted over to movement across the parking lot as I saw Chaz get out of his car and take the stairs two at a time up to the apartment. I wanted to go confront him and ask him where the fuck she was but his story had been the same with everyone else as it was with me which made me believe that he really didn't know where she was.

Ten minutes turned into twenty minutes since Mia had gone inside and I had practically chewed a hole through my cheek with each second that had passed. I got a text message from Chase asking for an update and sent him one back confirming that I hadn't seen Mia but I was on my way up to check it out.

I hopped out of the truck and jogged across the parking lot, taking the stairs just as fast as Chaz had, feeling the adrenaline pump through me as I practically sprinted to the apartment. I knocked softly, waiting to see if I could hear anything inside. I didn't want to mess something up if Mia was actually okay and getting information, but it was eerily quiet inside which had me worried. I knocked harder and waited a few seconds when I heard footsteps and saw the door swing open as Cindy answered it.

"Hey, Noah. Now's not a good time," she said breathlessly as she wiped a bead of sweat from her forehead with her arm.

"I didn't ask if it was." I pushed past her and stormed into the apartment, searching for Mia.

"Where is she?" I demanded, watching her flinch at my tone.

"Where is who?" She pulled her brows in as she stepped around me and stood by the hallway that led to the bedrooms.

"Mia. Jade. I know they're here, tell me where they're at."

She continued to look at me like I was crazy, which sent my blood pressure even further through the roof.

"WHERE. THE. FUCK. ARE. THEY?!" I shouted as I took two steps toward her and got in her face.

"I wouldn't do that if I were you," she warned as she stood in front of the door to the guest bedroom. My eyes zeroed in on it and I knew they were inside it.

"Move out of the way, Cindy. Now!" My voice echoed through the apartment as the picture frames rattled on the wall behind me.

She narrowed her eyes at me as she stepped to the side and let me pass. I heard her walk past me into the kitchen as I opened the door and found Jade and Mia on the floor. My eyes shifted quickly back and forth between them, trying to figure out the extent of their injuries. I was furious with myself for ever letting Mia come here by herself, and even more so for not getting my ass up here quicker.

Mia groaned as she sat upright and looked at me. She nodded toward Jade as I made my way to her. I bent down and checked for a pulse. It was faint but it was there. Her body was covered in dried blood and bruises, cut marks on her wrists and arms. I leaned her head back and looked at her face. Her hair had been cut short and died brown, with spots of color missing. I cradled her head in my hand as I used the other to pull my cell phone out to call for help.

"I wouldn't do that," Cindy warned as she came in and stood behind me, a gun pointed at my head. "Step away from her now or I'll put a bullet in your friend's head." She quickly pointed the gun at Mia before turning back to point it at my head. As she moved, I noticed a necklace hanging on top of the sweater she was wearing. I looked closer and my stomach sank when I saw the locket Jade's sister had given her, hanging from Cindy's neck. I slowly sat my phone down on the carpet next to Jade and raised my hands in front of me as I watched her.

"What are you doing, Cindy?" I asked calmly as I studied her while keeping an eye on both girls without her noticing.

"I'm fixing what you screwed up. I'm making things right."

"Okay, and what's that?"

"We're supposed to be together, Noah. We're having a baby. Starting our family. But how can we do that if you're just going to keep chasing after her?" She pointed the gun at Jade and instinctively I stepped to the side to shield her. She stared at me as her jaw clenched.

"See what I mean?"

"Cindy, we can be together and be a family without you having to hurt anyone. Just let me get them help then it'll be just you and me. No one else, just us and our family."

"I don't believe you. If you call for help, they won't understand what's going on. They're going to blame me. And then we won't get to be together." Her hand shook nervously forcing me to keep my focus on the gun as I didn't trust her not to accidentally shoot it.

"We can leave, we'll get in the car and leave. Once we're gone, I'll call for an ambulance to come help them. Then no one will know anything, and we'll be gone."

"That's the most ridiculous, stupidest thing I've ever heard. You're just lying to me, telling me what you think I want to hear."

"Cindy, just give me the gun. You don't want to do this," I begged.

Her mouth turned up into a devious smile as she looked directly at me.

"Actually, I do." She turned quickly and pulled the trigger, my heart stopping as I watched the bullet fly through Mia's body. She clenched her stomach as she fell to the floor, blood pooling underneath her.

I lunged forward and grabbed for the gun, forcing it out of her hand as it fell to the carpet beneath us. She was quick as she tried to escape my grip on her, scratching and clawing as I tried to pin her in place. I heard a loud sound as the front door burst open and heavy footsteps rushed into the room. Cindy and I both reached for the gun at the same time as I watched muscular arms wrap around her waist and swing her out of reach. I grabbed the gun and spun around to see Chaz holding Cindy with her arms bound behind her. Her breathing was heavy as she tried pulling against him with no luck.

"You okay man?" he asked as he looked me over.

"Yeah, thanks. Get her out of here while I call 911. Don't let her out of your sight."

I grabbed my phone and waited for the dispatcher to answer while I ripped off my jacket and held it against Mia's stomach to try to stop the bleeding.

<u>Forty</u>
Noah

Everything from that point went by in a blur as the paramedics loaded Jade and Mia on stretchers and rushed them away by ambulance. I rode in the ambulance with Jade, watching as they hooked her up to countless devices, trying to keep her alive. I folded my hands together and rested my head on them as my feet tapped anxiously on the floor as the ambulance sped toward the hospital.

Our ambulance pulled up right behind Mia's and I watched as Chase came running toward it, stepping to the side as they brought Mia out and rushed her inside. He ran a hand through his hair and looked up at the gloomy sky before turning his attention to me. A few minutes later they had Jade out of the ambulance and were rushing her inside as well, leaving Chase and I outside in the cold.

"What the fuck happened?!" He demanded as he looked at me, shaking his head.

I rubbed a hand down my face, frustrated that I had been asking myself the same fucking thing.

"Chase-," I started but stopped when the lump in my throat choked the rest of the words from coming out. I looked away and shook my head, embarrassed.

"Stop. Just stop, Noah."

I knew he was pissed, and I didn't blame him. I would be too. If it wasn't for me, his wife wouldn't be in the emergency room, fighting for her life.
"I'm so sorry," I choked out as my voice broke, unable to keep the emotions out.

"Me too." He pulled me into a hug and patted me on the back as I hugged him back. We went inside and checked in with the receptionist at the front desk where we were informed that both girls had been rushed into surgery and we would need to wait in the emergency room waiting area for an update.

We sat in silence for a few minutes before I saw two uniformed cops walk in and stop at the receptionist's desk. She pointed in our direction and they nodded and walked towards us.

"Noah Wilder?" The female cop asked as they stood in front of us.

"That's me." I leaned forward in my chair as they took a seat across from us, pulling out a notepad and pen.

"I'm Officer Perry and this is Officer Daws. We would like to ask you some questions about what happened this morning."

"Okay, whatever you want to know."

The female, Officer Perry, smiled kindly at me as she waited for the other officer to get his notepad ready before she began her questioning. I gave them a quick rundown of everything that had happened leading up to the shooting in Cindy's apartment. I noticed Chase's hands balled into fists as he listened, guilt flooding me for not getting up there sooner. He trusted me to keep her safe and I let him down.

"Thank you for your statement, we'll be back later to speak with Mia and Jade when they are out of surgery." She stood up to leave and I hated the thought that filled my mind. What if they didn't make it out of surgery? I sighed and leaned back against the chair, closing my eyes while I tried to focus on anything other than wondering what was happening in the operating rooms.

"Look, Noah, about what happened," Chase leaned forward and rested his elbows on his knees as he turned his head to look at me. "It's not your fault."

"Bullshit."

"It's not. You had no idea what was going to happen. Regardless of whether we wanted her to go or not, Mia was going to go to that apartment."

"I shouldn't have waited so long to go up there. I should have been right there with her."

"Then you guys would never have been allowed inside. No one would've known that Jade was there." Chase shook his head as he looked down at the floor. "I'm not happy about what happened, not by any means. But I honestly don't think we would have found Jade any other way. Mia saved her life by forcing us to let her do this."

"And it almost cost her hers," I breathed out.

"I know."

I looked over at him and saw the worry etched into his face as he tried to be strong and be a good friend to me. His wife was lying on an operating table while we were stuck doing nothing but praying that she would make it. A few minutes later I watched as the doors to the emergency room flew open and Grant came walking towards us with concern on his face. We stood to give him a quick hug before he sat across from us and looked down the hall.

"Any word yet?" he asked cautiously.

We both shook our heads no. I looked up at him and saw the same sadness I had seen on his face when we were at this very hospital when his wife died. My heart felt like it was about to burst from the mounting pressure.

"Where's Liam?" Chase asked, breaking the silence.

"With mom. He didn't need to come back here for this."

I ran a hand over my shoulder and rubbed the muscles in my neck, trying to get some relief.

"So what happened with Cindy?" Grant leaned back against his chair but didn't fully relax.

"Last I saw Chaz was still practically sitting on her until they got her in handcuffs."

"Chaz?" Grant's eyes went wide when he heard the name.

"Yeah, he actually came in right after the gun went off and held her until the police got there," I recounted as I could hardly believe it myself.

"No shit?" Grant chuckled.

"No shit. Who knew he was actually a decent guy?" I leaned back against the chair and thought about how wrong I was about him and that Jade would have actually been safe living with him after all.

"That's some crazy shit. Chaz is a good guy and Cindy is a psycho. Who would have ever guessed?" Grant asked as he tried to fill the silence between us. I watched as Chase kept his head down while he sent a text message, likely to Mia's dad.

"You're telling me." I shook my head and tapped my foot on the tile floor, desperate for someone to give us an update.

"Did Cindy admit the baby isn't yours?" Grant shifted in his seat, keeping his eyes peeled on the door leading to the emergency room as a doctor lingered near the door, talking to a nurse. There was so much tension between the three of us that none of us could seem to sit still.

"No, she's still insisting that it's mine."

"What are you going to do?"

"Just wait it out I guess? Get the paternity test as soon as the baby is born and if it's mine, I'll fight for full custody. Either way, no child deserves a mother like that."

The doors to the emergency room slid open as the doctor made his way through, pulling off the surgical cap from his head as he walked over to where we were sitting.

"I'm guessing one of you is here for Jade Allyson?" He looked back and forth between us as he sat down. There was no one else in the waiting room.

"That's me," I raised my hand sheepishly, "Is she alright?"

"She's out of surgery and is in recovery right now, we should know more once she's awake." His smile didn't reach his eyes and I knew there was more he wasn't saying.

"Doctor, please. She's the love of my life. Just tell me." I leaned forward as my eyes pleaded with his. He let out a heavy breath and looked around as if he was making sure no one else would hear what he was about to say.

"There's no way to know for sure what her recovery will look like because we don't know how long she was unconscious. She lost a lot of blood and was pretty dehydrated, but thankfully, she didn't have any damage that wasn't repairable. However," his chest fell as sadness filled his tired eyes. "We weren't able to save the pregnancy."

My eyes shot up to his as my brows pulled together in confusion. Grant and Chase whipped their heads over in his direction as well.

"I'm sorry, I don't think I heard you correctly." I leaned closer as I waited for him to repeat himself, to correct what I thought I had heard.

"The pregnancy was no longer viable due to the extent of her injuries. I'm very sorry."

"She was pregnant?"

"It was fairly early, I would say around eight weeks. But definitely pregnant."

I covered my mouth with my hand and leaned back as I felt Chase's hand pat my knee.

"I had no idea."

"I can discuss the loss with her when she's awake. Unfortunately now we just wait for her to come to, then we can see what her recovery will look like."

He shook our hands before walking back to the emergency room, leaving me to sit in stunned silence as Chase sat beside me and Grant across from me. My head was spinning, not knowing that Jade was pregnant, only to find out that she had lost it because of me. Because someone else was so wretched and vile that they would use her to hurt me. I clenched my fists as I worked my jaw, the fury inside me starting to build.

"Let's go for a walk." Chase patted my shoulder as he stood up and led me down the hallway. We stepped outside into the cold air as I turned around and kicked a trash can, releasing some of my anger and frustration in the process. There wasn't much that I knew at that moment other than I would go to my grave making Cindy pay for what she took from me.

Forty One
Jade

The sound of faint talking around me forced me awake. My eyes felt heavy as I struggled to open them, the room overly bright with white walls and fluorescent lights hanging from the ceiling. A few nurses stood beside my bed wearing scrubs while a man in a white lab coat talked to them while looking at something on a clipboard. As I looked around I saw a handful of machines turned on, each making its own noise, which thankfully wasn't any louder than their voices.

I tried to pull myself up into a sitting position, the feel of the tape on my hand pulling against my skin as I saw the needle underneath. A nurse turned to look at me and stepped away from the others as she walked to my bed.

"Did you want to sit up some?" Her voice was soft and friendly, immediately putting me at ease. My throat was sore and felt raw from screaming so I nodded my head yes. She pushed a button on the side of the bed, and I relaxed against the pillow behind me as the bed was adjusted so I could sit up without having to actually try. The other nurse and doctor turned their attention to me, both waiting for me to get situated.

"Hello Jade, I'm Doctor Murphy." He smiled as he sat down on the stool that he pulled out from underneath the counter across from the bed. I tried to give him the best smile I could but stopped when the pain increased. His lips pulled into a thin line as he offered a sympathetic smile in return.

"I'll try to avoid asking you too many questions for now as I know you're probably still feeling a bit weak, however the police will be in shortly to talk with you now that you're awake."
I listened carefully and nodded my head in acknowledgment.

"You had quite a few severe injuries that required surgical intervention, but I'm happy to say that we were able to stop the internal bleeding and everything looks like it should heal just fine. Unfortunately, we weren't able to save the pregnancy." His eyes lowered as he said it and my head tilted to the side in confusion.

"What?" I managed to croak out, the pain worth it if it meant that he repeated what he just said. There was no way I was pregnant. I had been told years ago when I was diagnosed with Polycystic Ovary Syndrome that my chances of getting pregnant would be slim.

"You were pregnant, I would say around eight weeks, however the injuries to your abdominal area were too much for the pregnancy to overcome. I'm so very sorry."

I watched him in disbelief, unable to believe the words he was saying. How did I not know that I was pregnant? My heart dropped as I thought about how devastated Noah would be when he found out. We had never talked in depth about having a family of our own, but we had recently started thinking about it after Cindy showed up. Or at least I had.

He spent the next ten minutes talking to me about recovery and what I could and couldn't do for the next few weeks. Basically, I needed to do as little as possible for the next week while my body tried to heal. While that sounded wonderful, I knew it wasn't realistic given that I had rent to pay and other bills that required that I go to work this week. I tried to keep my anxiety from skyrocketing as he talked, and then again after he left, and I talked with the police about what had happened. I did my best to get the details out without straining my voice too much, and thankfully they were very sympathetic and didn't try to rush me. I was ready for everyone to leave so I could rest. As they were finishing up, they gave me an update on Cindy after I agreed to press charges and confirmed that she would be serving time for attempted murder.

I froze in place as they discussed the shooting and that they didn't have an update on the female victim who was in critical condition. I remembered Mia coming into the room but I blacked out shortly after that and had no idea until right now that she was lying somewhere on an operating table in this hospital, fighting for her life.

Tears slid down my face as they wrapped up their interview and quietly exited the room. A few minutes later I heard another knock on the door and silently groaned that I couldn't get one moment of rest. I watched the door open as Noah peeked his head around the door before coming in. He stepped inside and closed the door quietly behind him, lingering near the foot of the bed as if he wasn't sure whether to come near me.

My heart felt like it was breaking all over again, first for Mia, and now for myself. I hated that Cindy had pushed Noah and I so far apart that he wasn't sure if he was welcome in my hospital room. I lowered my head into my hands as the tears flooded out as I sobbed uncontrollably. I could hear his footsteps as he quickly crossed the room and made his way to my bed, sitting on the side next to me as he wrapped his arms tightly around my shoulders and pulled me into his chest. I turned slightly, afraid to accidentally disconnect one of the many wires that were hooked up to me, and too sore to try to move. He planted soft kisses along the top of my head as he held me and let me cry.

"Shhh, it's okay baby. I've got you, you're safe now," he whispered in my ear.

I felt my body crumble against his and any strength I felt I had left quickly withered away in his arms.

Forty Two
Noah

There were very few moments in my life where I had ever felt as completely helpless as I did now. Holding Jade in my arms as she cried ripped my heart out. I wanted to do whatever I could to make her feel better and yet there was nothing that I could do. She was laying in that hospital bed because of me. Her best friend was fighting for her life, because of me.

I took a break to go give Chase and Grant an update on Jade when the nurses came in to do some additional bloodwork. As I was heading back to the emergency room waiting area, I heard low voices right as I was about to turn the corner. The tone of voice stopped me in my tracks as I recognized it as the voice of Jade's doctor. I stopped to listen.

"I'm so very sorry, we did everything we could. Unfortunately, she did not make it." His voice was even as he delivered the devastating news. I heard crying as he said the words, silence filling the room. A few minutes later a door closed, and the sound of sniffling lingered behind.

I ran a hand down my face before bending over and trying to catch my breath. There was no way this was happening. Mia couldn't be dead.

They had to be wrong. There had to be more that they could do. She deserved to live, and her baby girl deserved to have her mother in her life.

I sank down against the wall and sobbed hard into my hands as my body shook with grief.

Forty Three
Jade

After the nurses collected what they needed they went on their way and finally I was left alone to rest for a bit. I wasn't sure when Noah was coming back, but I knew that he was probably busy keeping Chase from going crazy while they waited for an update on Mia. I had tried to ask the nurses if they knew how she was doing but they weren't able to give me that information.

The tv was on with some random cooking show playing as I tried to eat some cold applesauce, hoping it would soothe my throat. I watched as they moved around the kitchen, every move deliberate as they created masterpieces from basic ingredients. The more I watched, the more into the show I got, and part of me was anxious to get out of this room so I could get home and attempt to make something half as fancy as they created.

A little while later they brought a food tray for lunch and I looked at it with a judgmental eye as it was nowhere near as impressive as what I had seen on tv. I pushed the food around the plate with a spoon as I debated whether to try to eat or not. My appetite had yet to return but I knew that if I wanted to have a quicker recovery, I needed to take care of myself. I forced a spoonful of mashed potatoes and gravy into my mouth and worked to swallow and get it down, the pain from my throat making it harder.

Deciding that there was plenty of time to eat later, I pushed the tray away and pressed the button to lower my bed. I adjusted the pillow behind my head and tried to roll over as far as I could on my side, given that I was still hooked up to a handful of machines. Once comfortable I closed my eyes and felt my hand slide down to my stomach. The thought that there had been a baby inside of me tore at my heart as I pressed my hand harder where my baby had died. The tears came rolling down my face as I grieved for a life that I never knew existed until after it was already gone.

A few hours later I woke up to a loud beeping noise and rolled over to see what was happening. I felt dizzy and a little nauseous from the sudden movement and before I knew it a handful of nurses came rushing into my room. I tried to keep my eyes focused on what was happening, but the room started spinning and next thing I knew, everything was black.

Forty Four
Noah

I had been a terrible best friend by avoiding Chase for the last hour after hearing the news about Mia. Maybe I was just selfish or maybe I just couldn't handle the grief on top of the guilt of knowing that her death was my fault. I had walked outside to get some fresh air and the next thing I knew, I had walked a few miles away from the hospital. My mind was chaotic as I tried to figure out how to get past the anger so I could be the friend he needed me to be. But how could I do that when I couldn't even begin to forgive myself.

My pocket buzzed against my thigh as my cell phone vibrated. I pulled it out and saw Grant's name on the caller ID.

"Hey," I answered as I ran a hand through my hair.

"Where are you?" His tone was hard, and I knew he was mad.

"I went for a walk."

"Well get your ass back here now. Jade was just rushed back into the OR, she had a complication from surgery."

He hung up before I could ask anything more. I shoved my phone back into my pocket and took off running as fast as I could. Once I made it back to the hospital, I went flying through the doors to the emergency room, scanning the room for the receptionist who was supposed to be at the front desk. I slammed my hands on the desk in frustration before I felt a hand on my shoulder and spun around.

Grant eyed me cautiously as he took a step back and put his hands up in front of him.

"You okay?" he asked with concern.

"Where is she? Is there an update?"

"The doctor just came out and said that she had started bleeding again, but they were able to find it and stop it. She's going to be okay."

His words calmed me as I felt my heart pound in my chest. I looked into the waiting room and found Chase sitting there with his head in his hands. In my rush to get back to Jade, I had forgotten that I also needed to get back to him. I patted Grant on the shoulder as I smiled and walked over to Chase.

I sat in the chair next to him and patted his back in an attempt to comfort him.

"I'm so sorry, man. I should have been here when you got the news. I just, I couldn't handle it, and I left. And I know, it was a dick move and I'm sorry. I feel terrible and I don't expect you to ever forgive me."

He slightly turned his head and looked up at me, his eyebrows pulled together in confusion.

"What the fuck are you talking about?"

"Mia. I heard the doctor giving you the update as I was coming back from Jade's room. I'm so sorry, I don't even know where to begin. Have you told Joe and Arlene yet?" My mind started to wander as I thought about all of the people we needed to tell, the arrangements that needed to be made. There was a lot that needed to be done.

"Again, what are you talking about?" He gave me the oddest look as he pulled back and leaned against the back of the chair and watched me. Grant stood across from us, leaning against the wall, giving me the same odd look.

"I'm talking about Mia! What the fuck is wrong with you guys? She's dead and you're acting like nothing fucking happened?!" I was about to lose my mind.

"Mia's not dead," Grant said from across the room. My head turned in his direction, one eyebrow raised.

"What?" I was beyond confused, I knew what I had heard.
"Mia's not dead," Chase said and watched me. "Why would you think that she was?"

"Because I heard the doctor when I was coming back. I stopped before I came around the corner and heard him saying that they did everything they could and that they weren't able to save her," I explained as I looked back and forth between them.

"So you just assumed it was Mia?" Chase was still giving me a look like he thought I had lost my mind.

"There was no one else in the waiting room when I left, so yeah, I thought it was Mia."

"Another family came in right after you went to see Jade. A woman who had been in a rollover car accident. She died within minutes of them trying to operate. That's who you heard the doctor talking about."

I put my face in my hands and shook my head, both frustrated and embarrassed.

"Okay, so do you have an update on Mia?"

"The doctor came out a little while ago and confirmed that everything went well with her surgery. The bullet missed any organs and had a clean exit. She's in recovery and they'll let us know when she can have visitors, but she's going to be fine," Chase said with a smile.

"So then everyone is okay?" I asked, still not believing it. Grant and Chase chuckled as they watched me, the guy who always had it together was a literal hot mess.

"Yeah, everyone is going to be just fine," Grant assured me from across the room. I let out the breath I felt like I had been holding all day and sunk down lower in my chair as I waited for another update.

Forty Five
Jade

The next few days passed by relatively quickly and before I knew it, I was being released from the hospital. I packed up the few things I had with me and sat on the edge of the bed while I waited for the nurse to hand me the discharge paperwork to sign. My fingers gripped the pen harder than what was needed as I scribbled across the papers. The relief of being able to go home and not have to deal with Cindy felt so nice, almost unbelievable.

As the nurse smiled and walked out the door, I saw Noah pop in behind her, a bouquet of roses in his hand as he walked toward my bed. I smiled back at him, genuinely happy to see him.

"Beautiful roses for a beautiful lady." He held the flowers out for me to take, a tingle spreading across my skin as our hands touched. I nervously reached up to tuck my hair behind my ear when I remembered the mess Cindy had made of my hair. I tucked my head into my chest, embarrassed to have anyone see me this way.

"Thank you, but I'm far from beautiful," I mumbled as I held the bouquet close to my chest.

Noah's finger gently reached beneath my chin and slowly lifted my head as his eyes locked onto mine.

"You are gorgeous," he tried to assure me as I fought to look away.

"Jade, look at me." His voice was soft as he sat down next to me on the bed. "There's not a damn thing that you could do to yourself that would ever make me think you were any less beautiful than what you are. I love every single thing about you."

"What about the things other people do to me?" I winced when his eyes moved from my face to my hair.

"You're still the most beautiful woman I've ever seen. You could be bald, and you'd still be beautiful. Believe it or not, I'm not in love with your hair." He chewed his lip to keep from laughing.

"You seemed to love it when you had your hands wrapped up in it every time we had sex. Now what are you going to do?" I smirked, loving that we were finally getting back to our normal, playful selves.

"Well," he let out an exaggerated sigh as he shrugged his shoulders. "I guess I'll just have to find something else to hold on to. These might do," he joked as he reached across and cupped my breasts. I rolled my eyes as I playfully swatted at him.

"You ready to go?" he asked, bringing my attention back to the fact that I had been discharged yet I was still willingly hanging out in the hospital.

"Yeah, I'm definitely ready to get out of here." I stood up slowly, making sure I didn't lose my balance again before I trusted my body's strength. A lot had improved over the last few days, but I still wasn't anywhere near where I was before having two surgeries back to back.

"Do you think you could give me a ride?" I asked once I had myself situated.

"You know, I was thinking about that," he paused and studied my face. "Instead of taking you back to your apartment, why don't you come stay with me?"

"I don't know if that's such a good idea." There was a hesitation in my voice, and I hated it. Why was I still so reluctant to want to stay with him?

"Okay, I won't push. Just thought I would ask." He pulled his lips together into a tight smile as he stepped to the side and held his hand out for me to walk by.

"I'm sorry, Noah," I said as we walked out into the hallway.

"Don't be, it's fine."

Except everything about his tone and body language told me that it wasn't. It wasn't a big surprise that Noah didn't stay long after he got me back to my apartment. Once I was inside and situated, he talked with Chaz for a few minutes before making up an excuse to leave. My mind raced as I tried to replay everything that had happened over the past few months, desperate to figure out why I was pushing so hard against staying with Noah.

Then it came to me. Before, I had Cindy and the baby to blame for not wanting to get too close to Noah. It was easy when I could say that I was walking away to give Noah a chance to be the dad he wanted to be. To allow them the chance to be the family they should be. But now that Cindy and the baby weren't in the picture the way they had been, I didn't have anything else to focus on. I realized that all along I was the one who was scared to take that next step. Because it wasn't just a step. It was a leap. And fuck if I weren't about to fall.

496

Forty Six

Noah

In the blink of an eye, two weeks had passed, and we were all trying to figure out our new normal after everything that happened with Cindy. I had spent more time at my lawyer's office putting together the paperwork that would be needed once the baby was born, assuming that somehow it ended up being mine. After reaching out to the doctor's office they confirmed that they did receive records from the other clinic Cindy had been seen at, but due to privacy restrictions, they couldn't discuss those results with me.

It felt like I was in a constant state of anxiety as I waited for Cindy's due date to get closer so I could get confirmation on whether or not I was the father. The only thing that put me at ease was knowing that she was locked up and couldn't hurt anyone else. In an effort to give Jade some space, I had been trying to make myself helpful with getting Chase and Mia back on their feet but every time I saw her struggle to hold the baby or wince in pain, it broke my heart. I hated that I was the reason she had to go through all of this.

I stepped outside into the bitter cold as I walked to my truck. It was the beginning of March and while spring would officially be here in a few weeks, that didn't mean shit in Colorado. I pulled my beanie down lower to cover my ears as a chilly wind whipped past me. A few minutes later I was in my truck, free from the wind but not spared from the cold. I quickly started the engine and drove off, heading for Grant's house.

As I pulled up, I noticed Chase's truck parked in the driveway and Jade's car parked in the street. My hands started sweating as I thought about seeing Jade. I wanted things to go back to normal between us but unfortunately, they hadn't. The more time she spent with Chaz, the less time we spent together. I felt an overwhelming amount of jealousy as I watched them sitting together on the couch as I walked in, laughing at something he had said. I looked away as I walked off into the kitchen and found Grant sitting at the kitchen table across from Chase and Mia. I smiled awkwardly as I held out a wrapped gift, waiting for Grant to take it.

"Happy birthday," I said as he pulled me into a quick hug and thanked me. He sat the gift on the counter behind me with the other gifts people had brought. I looked around, quickly scanning the room after noticing Chaz sitting by himself on the couch. I felt eyes burning into my head as I looked down and caught Mia smiling at me.

"I'm pretty sure she just went to the bathroom," she said as she nodded to where Jade had been sitting.

"Who?" I asked dumbly. I was a nervous wreck and it showed. I heard her laugh quietly under her breath as she turned her attention back to Chase as he whispered something in her ear that made her giggle. I walked over to the fridge and held the door open as I looked inside at the beer options. As I was debating between the three options available, I felt someone move behind me. In an instant, I recognized the light floral scent and felt the pull in my chest as I tried to breathe. I turned around and found Jade standing behind me, her thumbs tucked loosely in the front pockets of her skinny jeans.

"Hey," she said as she smiled at me, new happiness in her eyes.

"Hey," I whispered. I took a minute to stop and look at her, to really take her in. Since the last time I saw her, she had colored her hair. It was now a dark brown with subtle highlights streaked through it. There were soft layers that framed her face and the back had been cut short again, similar to how she had worn it when she first moved here. I found myself staring when I heard her giggle and tug at my shirt sleeve.

"You okay over there?" she teased, bringing my attention back to her.

"Yeah, I was just taking in your new look."

"Do you like it?" she asked as she ran a hand up to her hair and tugged at a stray piece, pulling it back behind her ear.

"I do, it looks good on you."

"Thanks." She looked so nervous and uncertain of herself which killed me when I remembered how much confidence she had when we first met.

"Did you find time to go to a salon?" I asked, making random conversation.

"Actually, Chaz did it." Her eyes lit up when she said his name and I felt my stomach drop. It felt like someone had hit me with a bowling ball.

"Chaz?"

I had given him credit for being a good guy with the whole Cindy situation, but helping Jade cut and color her hair seemed a little over the top. Even for him.

"Yeah, it turns out that he's actually going to school for cosmetology. He offered to help, and I let him."

"That was nice of him, I'm glad you guys are getting along so well." I kept my tone even and void of any emotion as I grabbed the bottle opener and opened my beer. I took a long drink, allowing the cold fluid to attempt to cool off the anger I could feel rising from my jealousy.

"He's actually been a great roommate."

As much as I loved hearing the enthusiasm in her voice, it killed me that it was all for Chaz. I took another drink from my bottle as I tried to keep from saying anything stupid.

"That's great, I'm happy for you. I'm gonna go mingle, it was nice to see you." I pushed away from the counter and started to walk past her when I felt her hand wrap around my arm and pull me back.

"Noah," she sighed. "Can we talk? Please?"

"Honestly, Jade, I don't know what else there is to say. I've been trying to talk to you for weeks, but you haven't wanted to listen. Maybe it's best if we just stopped. You have Chaz, and from what I can tell, he's making you happy. Isn't that what really matters?"

"Chaz is gay," she blurted out and my head spun around to look at her, to wait for her to burst into laughter at the joke she just told.

"What are you talking about? He's far from gay."

"I hate to break it to you, but you're wrong." She folded her arms across her chest and leaned back against the counter where I had been standing.

I pulled my eyebrows together in confusion as I thought about what she said. There was absolutely no way he was gay when we had fought each other throughout high school on who could get with the most girls.

"I think there's been a misunderstanding, you must've heard him wrong."

"See for yourself." She nodded behind me and I turned to find Chaz lingering in the doorway, talking to Chase and Mia. As I looked down, I saw him holding someone's hand, but I couldn't see who it was because they were on the other side of the wall. A few seconds later a body turned around and my jaw dropped open when I saw Joey, the bartender from Malarkey's. He wrapped an arm around Chaz as they said their goodbyes and walked out the door.

"No fucking way," I said more to myself than anyone else. I turned back to look at Jade as her eyes danced wildly as they watched my reaction.

"Told you." She pursed her lips together and immediately I wanted to grab them and kiss them.

"Okay, so you were right. Apparently, Chaz is into men. But that still doesn't change things between us. I wanted this to work between us more than I have ever wanted anything else in my life, but this feels too complicated, Jade. Every step forward we take, we end up getting knocked back five." I looked away and shook my head in frustration.

Out of the corner of my eye I watched as Jade leaned down, getting down on one knee as she watched me. I turned and stared at her, not believing my eyes.

"Life is hard, Noah. There's no guarantee that we are meant to be together nor is there a guarantee that we'll have a happily ever after. We're going to have hard times and battles that we won't want to fight. We're going to be pushed to limits that we didn't know we had. But at the end of the day, you're the only one that I want to go through all of this with. The good times, the bad times. All of it. Together." She let out a loud sigh as she quickly glanced around the room at the handful of people who had made their way in to watch.

"I know you wanted to do this first and I'm sorry we didn't get the chance. But I couldn't wait around and hope that you might want to do it again, so I'm gonna do it myself. Noah Wilder, will you marry me?" I swallowed hard as I sat my beer bottle on the counter behind me before reaching down and helping Jade up. I held her hands in mine as I stared into her eyes, watching the anxiety build as she waited for my answer.

"Fuck yeah, I'll marry you," I growled before I pulled her into me, crushing my mouth down on top of hers. I could feel the heat from her body as it touched mine and wished that no one else was around so I could do what we really wanted to do. I could feel her giggle as the crowd erupted in cheers as I pulled her up and she wrapped her legs around my waist. I held our kiss as long as I could and soon heard the room get quiet as people walked out and joked about us getting a room.

I slowly helped her to her feet as her legs fell from my side and slid to the floor. She smiled up at me and cupped my cheek with her hand. To think that I was so ready to give up and call it quits five minutes ago and now here I was standing in front of my fiancé. While I would have loved to have been the one to propose to her, I loved that she was the one to ask me. If there was ever any doubt about how she felt about us, it was removed the second she asked me to marry her.

"You sure you wanna marry a guy like me?" I smiled as I pulled her hand into mine and brought it up to my lips to kiss it.

"You bet your ass I do. Are you sure you wanna marry a girl like me? I don't have that big, fancy job anymore. Now I wear a uniform and smell like greasy food..." She raised an eyebrow as she smirked.

"It's okay, I've been known to have some food fetishes, I think we can make it work." I winked as she playfully swatted my shoulder. I wrapped my arm around her waist and pulled her into me, bringing her closer for another kiss.

"So does this mean that you're finally going to move in with me?" I joked, hoping it wasn't too much of a sore subject.

"I guess it does." She pulled back and wrapped her arms behind my neck as she looked deep into my eyes. "But I'm still holding you to those four orgasms per day."

I let out a chuckle as I clicked my tongue against the back of my teeth.

"Well, lucky for you, the fiancé package just got upgraded to FIVE per day." I pulled her closer letting my groin line up perfectly so she could feel the bulge that was starting to form in my jeans.

"In that case, is there another upgrade once we're married?" she teased as she rocked her hips forward against me.

"You're gonna be the death of me, woman," I growled as I nipped at her neck, causing her to squeal and try to squirm away.

Epilogue

Noah
3 Months Later

I sat next to Jade on the old wooden bench seat as our hands wrapped together as we waited for the judge to come in. I looked across the small courtroom and stared at Cindy as she sat at the table next to her state-assigned lawyer. Behind them stood a guard ready to strap the handcuffs back on her if she got any ideas. She looked over her shoulder and glared at Jade and I before turning her attention back to the front of the room. Being a total dick, I lifted Jade's hand and brought it to my mouth for a kiss, making sure her diamond engagement ring was in plain sight for Cindy to see. I didn't have to wonder if she saw the ring after she turned her head around and slammed her fist down on the table, forcing the guard to step forward while keeping one hand on his gun that was holstered.

I checked my watch after getting a glance from my lawyer to get my ass up to the table before the judge came in. I kissed Jade quickly on the cheek as I slid out and walked up front to sit where I was supposed to. A few minutes later we all rose as the judge walked in and sat down. I held my breath as I waited for the news that had been tormenting me for the past few months.

As we sat down I felt a hand clasp my shoulder and looked back to see Chase smiling at me as he gave me a reassuring nod. Mia sat beside him with Grant sitting on her other side. There's never been a doubt about how many people I had in my life who would be there to support me and today they were all lined up behind me. I let go of the breath I was holding and sucked in another one as the judge began to speak. "I see here that this is a court-ordered paternity test and we're reading the official results. Is that correct?" She slid her glasses down her nose and looked back and forth between the two lawyers.

"Yes, your Honor, that is correct." My lawyer sat back down next to me as we waited for her to continue.

"Well then, let's get to it," she said quietly as she read through the report before reading it out loud. "Based on the DNA sample collected from Noah Wilder, this test confirms that you are not the father of the child in question."

I felt the air rush out of me as I leaned forward and shook my head in relief. A few hands patted my back quickly before the judge continued. I heard random chatter around me as the judge wrapped up and went on her way. I turned around and found Jade grinning ear to ear as she leaned over the half wall to hug me.

"It's finally over, baby," I whispered in her ear.

"I'm so happy, now we can finally have our happily ever after." She held onto me as if nothing else mattered. And at that moment, it didn't.

Thirty minutes later I was sliding into the seat next to Jade at SlowMo's. Everyone decided a celebratory lunch was in order after finding out that Cindy would no longer be a part of my life. Deep down I felt heartbroken for the baby, having Cindy for a mother and not knowing its father. I took comfort knowing that he was being cared for by one of the most amazing families in town until they figured out the next steps.

I looked around the table and smiled as I watched the people who had become my family sit and talk with each other. Everything felt so calm and back to normal. Jade was offered another position at the bank after Cindy was arrested. After a very long and overdue apology, Jade happily accepted the position of branch manager at a higher rate than she had been at when they fired her. She was happy to be doing the job she loved with the people she enjoyed working with.

Living together had been easy and seamless as she moved in right after we got engaged, like the very next day. Chaz agreed to continue her lease and ended up asking his boyfriend to move in with him after Jade moved out. It still blew my mind to hear that he had a boyfriend. After quite a few rounds of beer one night, he finally came clean to us and admitted that he had known since high school but was scared to tell anyone. So he made up stories of the girls he had supposedly been with, dealing with the consequences of getting a bad reputation instead of just coming clean.

I looked across the table and smiled at Mia as she held Rylee, letting her play with her necklace. Rylee looked just like Mia and my heart skipped a beat every time I thought about what could have happened if the bullet would have been a fraction of an inch over. There wouldn't be a beautiful mother to compare this sweet baby to.

Jade's laughter next to me pulled me back into the conversation as she teased Grant about making the moves on the new waitress at SlowMo's. Her eyes lit up as she watched him blush when the waitress headed towards the table. Her fingers gently slid the locket around the chain, moving it back to where it should be. By her heart. I hadn't seen Jade take the locket off once since she got it back, a constant smile on her face every time she touched it.

The waitress leaned across Grant, placing the glasses of water in front of us. She smiled down at him before turning her attention to Liam.

"Need anything else, Champ?" she asked, casting a glance back at Grant.

"Nope." His answer was short as he kept his attention focused on the ketchup bottle as he tapped his palm against it, flinging bits of ketchup across his plate.

"What's the deal?" I asked as I nodded toward the waitress after she walked off.

"Nothing." He shook his head and looked down at Liam. The waitress made her way back up to the register and smiled at Grant as she looked over at our table again.

"You sure about that?" I chuckled.

"Yeah, we're good. Summer break just started so we don't need any distractions." There was a sadness in his tone and I made a note to try to pull him aside soon to talk to him. I knew that he was more open to the idea of trying to date again, but from the looks of it, Liam wasn't ready for him to move on from Renee.

After we finished eating, we said our goodbyes and climbed into the truck. I was about to head back to our house, it felt so fucking weird to say that, but had another idea at the last minute. Jade sat quietly next to me the entire ride, holding my hand as it rested on the middle console. Her window was rolled down as she held her arm out and let the warm breeze caress it as we drove down the deserted back road.

I pulled the truck over to the side of the road, under the big old tree that I loved coming here for. We hopped out of the truck and I held out my hand to help her climb up into the bed. I quickly reached into the backseat and grabbed the blankets I kept back there for this exact reason. I quietly closed the door and jumped into the bed of the truck, helping her lay the blankets down before we got comfy.

I leaned back against the window of the cab and pulled her into me. Her body felt so soft and fragile against mine, a constant reminder for me of what she had been through. Also, a constant reminder of how strong she really was. I heard her yawn as her body sank lower, knowing she was exhausted from our late night last night.

"You want me to take you home so you can rest?" I offered as I leaned to the side to look at her.

"I'm good here. I like the fresh air and quietness."

"Me too," I whispered in her ear.

"But we can't fall asleep out here, and if we get too comfortable, we're definitely going to fall asleep," I warned.

Her head tilted to the side as she turned to look at me.

"Are you worried about having another bad dream?" Her voice was filled with concern as I felt my body get tense as she brought it up. I hadn't had a nightmare about Jade since she got out of the hospital. It felt like once Cindy was locked up and Jade asked me to marry her, everything just sort of stopped. No more bad dreams. No more doubt or insecurities about our relationship.

But hearing Jade ask about them made my body react the same way it did when I would have a bad dream and I realized that it was because those nightmares almost came true. The dreams of Cindy holding Jade hostage and trying to take her from me- that was a fucking reality. And now it would forever be a living nightmare.

I forced a smile as I looked down at her and tried to force the tension out of my voice when I spoke.

"No baby, I don't worry about bad dreams anymore. Those are gone now that I have you." I watched as her eyes lit up as she smiled back at me. "However, this is bear country and unless you want to be a snack, we shouldn't be getting too comfortable out here."

"Got it. We don't want the bears to eat me." She giggled as she pressed further against my chest.

"Exactly. That's my job." I tickled her sides as I made snarling sounds against her neck, enjoying the sound of her laughter as it floated around us.

The drive back to the house was quiet, the soft sound of Jade snoring filling the cab. I drove slowly and took my time, making sure to avoid going too fast on the rugged roads so it didn't wake her. Every time I looked over at her, her face looked so peaceful but all I could see was the woman who had laid on the floor in front of me and almost died.

My hand tightened around the steering wheel as I tried to force the thought out of my head. Even though Jade and I had come so far in our relationship over the past few months I still couldn't get past the guilt that ate away at me knowing that her life had been put on the line because of me. No matter how much I tried to force the thoughts away, they always sat right there in the front of my mind, reminding me of how much I didn't deserve her.

An hour later and I had run out of back roads to take so I decided to head home. I waited for the garage door to finish opening, the loud creaking sound waking Jade up in the process. She yawned as she looked around then smiled at me.

"Why did you let me sleep the whole way home?"

"You looked like you needed it," I said as I hopped out of the truck and walked around to her side to help her out.

"I'm not a delicate flower anymore, Noah, the doctor said I was fully recovered. Remember?"

I opened the door leading into the house and stood to the side to let her go first.

"I know but I'm a firm believer in the idea that if you're tired, you should sleep." I shrugged my shoulders and winked at her as I walked past her to go into the kitchen. The truth was that I wanted her to sleep because regardless of what the doctor had said, I knew Jade and I knew she wasn't back to herself yet. She got tired too often and too easily the past few weeks and I was damn sure going to make sure she was getting the rest she needed.

I glanced over my shoulder and smiled when I saw her curl up on the couch and cuddle into her favorite throw blanket. It was the start of summer but that didn't mean she didn't like to cuddle her blankets. She pulled it up under her chin and bent her knees up to her chest as she rested her head on them. The light filtered in through the window, casting a warm glow on her beautiful face.

"So, what do you want for dinner?" I asked as I held the refrigerator door open and looked inside. "I can grill burgers, or we have a frozen pizza that I can toss in the oven."

"Fix whatever sounds good to you, I don't know if I'll eat." Her eyes watched mine as she said it, knowing that I wouldn't be happy about her not eating.

"Why not?" I closed the door and walked over to sit next to her on the couch.

"I just don't feel like it. I'm a little nauseous."

"Hmmm, you're nauseous and tired. Maybe you're pregnant?" There was more hope in my voice than I had wanted and I instantly regretted it when I saw her eyes drop and look down at the floor.

"You know I'm not pregnant."

"You could be. It happened once, you never know, it could happen again." My voice was soft and gentle as I placed a hand on her knee.

"That was a once in a lifetime thing Noah, you know that. You were there when we talked to the doctor. The chance of me getting pregnant again is slim to none. And the chance of me being able to carry the baby to term would be even less. It would take a miracle."

Her eyes filled with tears and I felt terrible for making her talk about this again. She was right, I had been there with her at the doctor's when they had told her she was unlikely to get pregnant again. It felt as soul-crushing now as it did then. But part of me couldn't give up on the idea that we were meant to be parents. That she was meant to be the mother to my children. That feeling gnawed at me the same way the guilt did. Soon there wouldn't be anything left.

I leaned forward and pulled her into me, holding her as I heard her sniffle. Her chest fell heavily as she tried to stop the tears that I had caused.

"I'm sorry Jade, I shouldn't have said that. I didn't mean to upset you."

"It's not your fault for wanting something that I can't give you," she whispered.

I leaned to the side to make sure she could see me before I started talking. Gently I reached over and held her chin between my fingers as I turned her face to look up at me.

"Jade, you give me everything I could ever want or need. There's not a single thing that I could want that you're not giving me. Who knows what our future holds, but just because we may not get our miracle baby, that doesn't mean that we can't have our own family. We can make this into whatever we want, and as long as you're in my life, I know it will be beautiful."

I felt my heart pull deep inside my chest as she reached up and cupped my cheek before pulling my face down to kiss her. It was at that moment that I realized that the things we considered to be our imperfections weren't the things that actually defined us. The things that I thought we needed to make us happy no longer mattered. She was all that I needed to make me happy, and I finally had her.

513